CURRENTS

Currents

Eva Moraal

Translated by *Jonathan Ellis*

Lemniscaat New York

This book was published with the support of the Dutch
Foundation for Literature.

**N ederlands
  letterenfonds
dutch foundation
for literature**

First published in the United States and Canada in 2016 by
Lemniscaat USA LLC • New York
Distributed in the United States by Lemniscaat USA LLC • New York

Library of Congress Cataloging-in-Publication Data is available.
ISBN 13: 978-1-935954-38-5
Printing and binding: Lightning Source, La Vergne,, TN USA
First U.S. edition

I heard the sound of a thunder, it roared out a warnin'
I heard the roar of a wave that could drown the whole world
(...)
Who did you meet, my darling young one?
(...)
I met a young girl, she gave me a rainbow
I met one man who was wounded in love
I met another man who was wounded in hatred
And it's a hard, it's a hard, it's a hard, it's a hard
And it's a hard rain's a gonna fall.

From: *A hard rain's a gonna fall* – Bob Dylan

PART ONE

Dos alarm. A piercing sound that gets louder and louder. And you can't do anything about it except get up. I try to put it off as long as possible and bury my head under the pillow. Of course, I never manage to stay in bed.

Once my feet touch the ground, the sound stops.

It is exactly two minutes past seven on Monday morning. I walk across to my desk, where I've put my HandComputer. The first thing I see on the screen is Dad with dozens of microphones being pushed into his face. He gives a reassuring smile: *nothing the matter, people. We've got everything under control.*

I look to see whether it's live.

It's live.

So he didn't come home last night. Not that I would have heard anything, the number of sleeping pills I take. I rub my hands over my cold arms, walk to the bathroom, and get undressed. I stand under the shower and it starts as soon as the sensors detect my presence.

"Warmer."

I let the hot water stream over my face and over my long curls, which stick to my wet back. I stand still and take hold of myself. Today is the first day at the new school. After six long months.

When my skin begins to protest, I get out of the shower and reach for the towel that Maria has laid out for me. I walk back to my room and see the red lamp burning on the Digital Oracle System. I'm running late.

I quickly get dressed: jeans, T-shirt, and a sweater. With my hair still wet, I go downstairs. The house is big and empty. I look the other way when I walk past Isa's room

In the kitchen Maria, our Wet maid, is making breakfast. "Nina." Her smile is always warm, always genuine. "Good morning."

"Morning," I mumble and reach for my mug of coffee. The shower hasn't helped.

"Where's Mum?"

"Mrs. Bradshaw is still in bed."

Hadn't expected anything else.

Erik, Dad's second driver, comes in, places his hands on the kitchen table, and looks at me.

"I suppose there's no chance that I can take the bus?"

He shakes his head.

"Your father's instructions were very clear."

"OK, let's get going." I empty my mug in one gulp.

It's cold outside. It's only November, but it's been freezing for days. A deep layer of snow covers the lawn and the tops of the high fence that separates us from the rest of CC1. The pale blue tarpaulin over the swimming pool is sagging under the weight of the snow. Mum's rosebushes almost collapse under the thick white blanket.

Snow is water. Even more water. Suffocating, all-drowning water.

Next week, the weather will change. Since the Second Great Flood several decades ago, even air traffic between the Regions has been virtually disbanded. The weather has become too unreliable, especially with the impenetrable mist-banks that occur after any lengthy rainfalls and reduce visibility to zero. This is the first real winter we've had in years.

Erik goes into the garage ahead of me. Dad's sport's car is parked there. Some vintage model from the twentieth century which runs on gasoline. He takes it out for a spin now and then, but never goes far. Dad is far too worried about damaging his precious car.

The second official car, electric like most vehicles, is parked next to it and Erik opens the door for me. The windows are tinted. I can look out, but no-one can look in. I used to think that was pretty cool. Isa and I would pretend that we were on a secret Wet mission outside the two Closed Communities. Now I'm just glad that nobody can see me.

Erik drives out of the garage and up the draveway, and communicates at the gate via his HC with Frank, the porter. The first checkpoint.

We drive through our neighborhood. Here in CC1 and CC2 is where my Dry friends live with their parents, behind high fences with cameras and security everywhere. In the distance I see the new digiscope with its brightly colored glass wall and the shopping center behind it. In the park, children are playing in the sandpit.

We approach the heavily guarded entrance gate to CC1: the second checkpoint. One of the Dry Defenders comes out of his station. His red uniform contrasts sharply with his pale face. Erik lowers his window and shows his pass, which is scanned. The man nods and takes a step back as his colleague opens the gate.

We drive into the flooded world.

The school is in District One, in the center of our Region, the smallest of the five that, since the First Great Flood, make up the Five Regions. We don't have far to go and can avoid the worst districts; the outer districts near to the water, where buildings are barely habitable. Most of them have given way to high-rose grey concrete flats, built on artificial mounds.

On the street, people hurry along with hunched shoulders. Nobody wants to spend much time outside in this awful weather. The occasional cyclists glides past, a daredevil on these slippery streets. A few Dry Defenders are walking around, standing at crossings or gathered together in groups. "Blowers" (from Blow-driers) or "reds" are what the Wets call the Dry law enforcers. I feel like a peeping Tom. Yet my digipen still glides automatically over the screen, as I draw faces, shapes and poses. It calms me down.

I am not allowed to use my real name at my new school. Too risky. I'm not Nina Bradshaw, I'm Nina Baker. I keep on repeating it to myself. "Nina Baker. I'm Nina Baker." Dad is paranoid. I'm sure I'll get it wrong.

Erik stops in front of a low building that looks as if it has been built pretty recently. It looks more like a stack of building blocks rather than an actual school built to withstand storms. Groups of students stand around, talking in the quad while a few maintainence workers shovel snow aside. Some boys are throwing snowballs.

"Erik, can you stop around the corner?" I saw the kids in the quad look up and stare at the car. Erik nods and drives on a bit. Erik's okay.

"Thanks."

I get out, wait until he's turned the corner, and walk towards the entrance.

It's just a school, Nina. Just a school. Probably other Dries have been sent here as well. I can't be the only one. And yet I'm nervous. When I enter the quad, I know they're looking at me and I walk quickly towards the old-fashioned door, the kind you have to open yourself.

Inside isn't much warmer than outside. Dad has a lot of influence in the ccs. If he wants something to happen, it happens. Not here, apparently. I walk along a corridor where some teachers and other students are standing. Screens hang on the wall. DOS news flickers in the background. So they're not all that backward here after all.

Once I figure out where the office is, I report to the secretary.

"Name?" The woman in her fifties, with a pair of spectacles perched on the tip of her nose, doesn't even look up.

'Nina Baker.'

I nervously fiddle with a lock of hair while the woman takes her time to look me up in her HC.

'Good," she finally says. "Here's your schedule. You can log in on your PP with the general password and then change it to whatever you want." She hands me another HC and looks at me, her eyebrows raised.

'What?" Panic turns me hoarse.

'Next!" Her eyes shift to the person behind me and I hurry off. I'm getting just as paranoid as Dad. Of course she doesn't recognize me. Isa and I haven't been on DOS news for years, and we haven't even been outside the ccs.

I go from the general school page to my personal page and enter a new password. I look at my new timetable and am relieved that there aren't any surprises there. My first class starts in five minutes: language & ancient literature.

The first bell sounds and before I know it, the school fills with people. One of them, a girl, bumps into me and I drop my bag and HC. My things get kicked everywhere, disappearing in the sea of legs. No point trying to collect everything till they've all gone.

My hands are shaking as I pick up my bag and begin stuffing my things back in it. She did that on purpose. I heard her laugh. And I wanted to be in the class before all the others came in. I quickly brush away a tear. I don't want to cry. Not here. Not now.

'Here.'

I look up and see a boy standing in front of me. He has a large nose and watchful, brown eyes with long eyelashes. His skin is the color of coffee, like the latte Maria makes, soft and creamy. He gives me Isa's golden locket.

'Thanks.'

He nods. His left hand taps on the edge of the window sill.

'Where do you have to go?'

I look at my HC.

'L3.'

'Come on.'

He starts walking with long strides. I rush after him, not daring to say anything. When he reaches the classroom, I want to thank him but he's gone inside before I can say a word.

'Ah Max, I was rather afraid that we would have to make do without you today." The voice is that of a balding, older man. His round face has a friendly expression. His clothes are old and threadbare. So unlike the teachers at my previous school. I quickly lower my eyes, but of course he's already noticed me.

'And you are...?'

'Nina," I mumble.

Max walks to an empty table. The others stare from him to me. I hope I haven't caused him any problems.

'Nina, welcome to Delta College. Choose somewhere to sit so that we can get on with the lesson.'

MAX

The Dry comes and sits next to me.

She's not from around here. Saw that straight away. That golden locket – Li would have pocketed it in a flash. You could get a lot for that.

I try to concentrate on Collingwood. Normally I'd pay attention. The man knows how to explain things. And with the exams approaching, I know I have to be extra alert. Not being alert means at least one grade lower. And I can't have that if I want to be one of the few Wets to win a scholarship to the university.

But this Dry... this Dry distracts me.

She's drawing with a digipen on the screen as she stares outside. Sharp nose, wide mouth, freckles. Big, blue eyes and long blond curls hiding her face.

Marlie bumped into her on purpose. All those Dries at school. It was to be expected after the recent floods. Some Dry school or other that had the misfortune to get wet feet. On DOS news, I saw Bradshaw expressing his "heartfelt sympathy" for the families of the victims. Pride comes before a fall, says Ma. Out here, where we always have wet feet, we saw it coming. And now they have to come to school here. Nothing and nobody is safe from the water, not even the Dries, no matter what they tell themselves.

Under the table, I drum my legs with my fingers. Too much energy. I should have taken a run this morning, but Li hadn't come home again and Ma was in a right state.

'Max?'

Fuck.

'Yes, Mr. Collingwood?'

He looks at me expectantly, raises his grey eyebrows. Shit, what was the question?

'Zeitoun,' whispers Nina next to me.

'Huh?'

'Zeitoun,' she repeats louder. Immediately she turns deep red. The others start to laugh.

'Well, Max?" asks Collingwood.

'Uh, Zeitoun, sir.'

We're reading the book in the original. Collingwood is an old dinosaur, stubborn and determined to give lessons in dead languages. Classic English hasn't been taught in most Wet schools since the Board of Governors severed all links with foreign powers. Just keeping up appearances, says Li, who sees a conspiracy theory in everything.

'Zeitoun, yes." Collingwood looks at me and then at Nina and says slowly: "Thank you, Nina. You were very helpful to Max. This clearly isn't his day." He holds up his hand to put a stop to the snickering that's just beginning.

I don't know what's wrong with me today. Helping a Dry...

I always have to poke my fucking nose into other people's business.

As soon as the bells goes, I stuff my HC into my backpack and quickly leave the room.

I don't look round.

Math and biology, and then at last a break. My stomach's rumbling. I've only had one sandwich, and that was five hours ago. I make sure I'm at the front of the queue and then carry my tray to my usual place in the corner next to the kitchen and sit down. I eat too quickly and burn my mouth.

I'm just about to take another mouthful when Damian and two of his buddies come in. Damian moves his hands dangerously close to the ass of the hot chick in front of him. He runs his tongue over his lips and his buddies laugh at what he says; no doubt some sort of horny remark. Sometimes they really are too gross for words. I look away, concentrate on my food and on the scratches on the table in front of me.

Just as I'm about to take my last mouthful, I feel a hand on my shoulder.

'Finally made some friends, Morris?'

'Bugger off, Damian.'

He gives me a pat on the back and sits down opposite me, his two goons behind him. Damian is small and sinewy, and has an ugly, shaven head. Lars is big and heavy, and so fucking stupid that he could even teach a Dry a thing or two. Tim is the smartest of the bunch. And that says enough. I don't understand how I could ever have been friends with him. I'm so not in the mood for this.

I feel the anger coming, exactly where it always starts. A knot in my stomach that twists and shoves and pulls me as tight as a string. I can't get away.

'I get it, you pulling a move a Dry like that.' Damian pulls a sympathetic face, which, if possible, is even uglier than his normal gob.

I place my hands on my stomach. Calm down, man, calm down.

'You have to get it somewhere, eh?' he continues. Tim

and Lars laugh out loud, while Damian looks round as if he's the fucking governor himself.

I so want to punch his face.

Ignore him, Max.

I take a sip of tepid tea, so that I can't say anything. Ignore them.

'And in some way she's...well..." Damian licks his lips again and winks. "Wet.'

Before I know it, I stand up and throw a punch. The knot always wins. Damian is not quite quick enough and I hit him right on that crooked nose of his.

Satisfaction.

'Bastard!" He grabs his nose and groans.

I try to get away, but Lars sticks out his foot and I crash to the ground. I try to scramble up but end up taking a kick in the stomach from Tim. All I can do is in my arms and legs to protect myself, while I still hear Damian swearing that I've broken his nose.

A crowd of kids is standing around us now, shouting and jeering. I wonder who they're supporting.

When Lars comes at me again, I kick up and around wildly, and when I hear a scream I know I've hit him. I've just enough time to get up and throw a punch at Tim, right in his stomach.

'Hey! Hey, STOP IT!" sounds from the hall.

Fuck.

The adrenaline rushes over me in waves. I can't stop myself. I want to destroy that filthy bastard, completely destroy him. Damian, recovered from the initial shock, senses this because he's already standing there ready. His fist connects with my jaw. My head spins and I taste blood. My rage still isn't spent. That's the thing about me: When I lose it, I lose it — and I don't stop till the bitter end. I'm just about to put in the knee so that I can get at his stupid head, when somebody grabs me from behind. Two other teachers grab hold of Damian.

'STOP IT!" thunders Granville. Now I recognize his voice. Granville, the PT teacher, is made of stronger stuff than Damian and his mates, and he grabs me firmly. He twists my arm up my back. I scream from the pain.

'You're coming with me," he says. "You too," he gestures to the others.

We're pushed out of the cafeteria and I lower my head. I still feel the rage rushing through me. It surges through my body like the water at the height of a storm. I try to breathe in and out calmly. Fuck, if only I'd taken a run this morning. That bloody brother of mine.

I look up, I don't know why, and stare directly into Nina's frightened eyes. Then Granville gives me a clip round the ear and we are out of the caf.

We end up sitting opposite Principal Davenport, a small thin woman, always in a suit. This time it's bright red. A sharp face, with piercing, heavily made-up eyes. A Dry, of course. I've been in to see her often enough.

'You lot again." She sighs. Insincerely. She couldn't care less.

'Max started it," says Damian quickly. He slurs his words and I feel satisfaction.

'Silence!'

Davenport looks at Granville.

'They were fighting in the cafeteria I couldn't see who

started, but this one here" – he pulled me up straighter – "knew how to defend himself.'

Davenport shakes her head benignly. "Max Morris. You're exactly like your brother.'

Knot. Breathe slowly and deeply. You are not like Li. Let them think what they want.

She looks from me to the others.

'Because the finals are coming, I won't be suspending anyone. Just this once." I sniff. I'm one of the best pupils in this whole rotten school. I can get the class's average up all by myself. She knows that just as well as I do. "However, two weeks' detention should hopefully teach you that we will not tolerate violence at Delta College. What you do there I will leave to Mr. Granville.'

And that is that. She turns towards the window overlooking the quad. Granville grits his teeth. I can tell that he doesn't like her any more than we do. He pushes us out of the door and says, "Go and clean yourselves up, and then get back to your classes. Report to me this afternoon. At four. Precisely. If you're late, you'll be out of here.'

He rushes off.

We stand for a moment, saying nothing. Then Damian walks over, pushes his shoulder against mine, and hisses in my ear.

'You're dead meat.'

He walks off. Tim and Lars follow him.

NINA

I'm standing in line for lunch when I hear the scream.

I look up and see Max. A boy's holding onto him while another is kicking him hard in his stomach. I hold my breath.

But Max scrambles up. He lashes out fiercely and then again. He's completely lost it — he just keeps hitting the boys with a grim determination. It's scary. This sort of thing never happened on the Mainland.

'Hey, get a move on, Dry slut.'

I'm so flabbergasted, the insult barely registers. I dump food onto my plate and walk away.

Almost everybody is now watching the fight. Some cheer the guys on.

They're animals.

I start feeling sick and see Dad's face in front of me. Everything under control.

'STOP IT!'

A teacher, his neck muscled like a bull's and with the same sort of fiery look in his eyes, charges into the cafeteria. Two other teachers follow closely behind.

The fight is soon over, although Max is the last to give in. His eyes are large and red; a trickle of blood runs from the left corner of his mouth. It's hard to believe that this could be the same boy who just helped with my stuff.

The bull drags Max along with him out of the caf, and we stare at each other for a second. I'm shocked by the hard expression in his eyes and quickly look away.

One the fighters have left the caf, and everything goes back to the way it was. People sit down, talking in groups, acting as if nothing has happened. I stand there like a statue. I force my legs to move and sit down at an empty table. I eat what's on my plate without tasting it. Perhaps that's just as well.

'Hey!'

A girl sits down opposite me. She has red hair and is wearing large earrings. Gold. A locket round her neck. Gold as well. And she's wearing clothes that you can't get anywhere except where I come from. A Dry.

'You're new here, aren't you?'

I nod.

'I've been here for three months, but there are more of us." She gestures at a group of kids walking towards our table. "They always try it in the beginning.'

'What?'

'Intimidation. Those WEtTOs are capable of anything." She looks at a girl at the table opposite us, with an expression she'd probably use to inspect a bum on an enormous rubbish heap. The glance is answered with the same fury.

'You're not alone.'

I smile, feel myself relax a little.

Three boys and two girls come and sit with us.

'Benjamin, Ruben and Joey, Cynthia and Sophie," she says. Too many names and faces to remember in one go. "And I'm Nikki.'

'Nina," I say.

'Where are you from?'

I swallow and say in as normal a voice as possible: "cc1'.

'Hey, that's where I live as well!'

Nikki's short curls dance and her grey eyes light up. I like her, I think.

'And your last school?'

Now it got more difficult.

'The Mainland.'

'Oh.'

'Was that the school that six months ago...?" asks another girl — Sophie, I think. She has long brown hair, worn up in the latest fashion. She's wearing an expensive sweater, a brand I recognize from Isa's wardrobe.

'Yes," I say and look down again.

'Holy crap..." That's Benjamin; a boy with short blond hair, in a checked shirt with suspenders. He has soft eyes and an even softer, friendly face.

I smile faintly.

'And now you're here," sighs Nikki. "Just like us.'

Just like them.

If only it were that simple.

When the last bell goes, I hurry outside. "See you tomorrow?" calls Nikki after me.

I turn round and nod.

'Sure thing.'

I rush across the quad and suddenly notice them there: the boys from the fight. The Bull is giving them instructions on clearing away the snow. One of them is already off to the side, digging furiously.

Max.

I run the other way. Erik is waiting for me round the corner and I quickly get in the car. I only look out when I'm certain that the school is out of sight.

MAX

As soon as Granville lets us out, I sprint across the quad and run. Damian and his goons will never catch me.

Running is my salvation. Running is my drug. When the high takes over, I can hardly feel my legs; they seem to move all by themselves. I run. My breathing gradually calms down as I drop into my familiar tempo.

I know Damian means it, but I also know he's a coward who'll never try anything without his friends. I promise myself that this will be the very last time I ever interfere in things that don't concern me.

I've washed off the worst of the blood. Not that I'll get away with it with Ma. My jaw is swollen and feels strangely hot. My stomach aches and my left eyebrow is torn. But I can't help laughing when I see Damian's face in my mind's eye and hear him groaning about his broken nose.

Li is standing outside. Of course he sees me before I can slip into the flat's entrance.

'Hey, little brother.'

What does the prick want? But if I don't say anything, he'll find out later.

'Hey, Li.'

He's fucking hanging around as usual, with his friends, Julius and Ramon. Down the road a bit, a man in a long overcoat with an upright collar walks off towards the bus stop sprayed with WEtTO slogans. I've seen him here before. What's he want?

I shake my head.

Li walks over and places his hand on my shoulder, with a cigarette butt between his index and middle finger. He's almost two years older than me but some people can't tell us apart. Li is slightly more angular and heavier, but I'm a bit taller.

'Fight?'

He grins and his buddies laugh. He always acts tough when they're around.

'Drop it, Li.'

'What?" He touches my jaw and I jump from the pain. "They really worked you over.'

'You should see them.'

I can't stop myself bragging.

'Well done, little brother. You're not as innocent as you look." He laughs.

'Shut up, Li," I mumble, half annoyed, half satisfied. Before he can say another word, I walk quickly to the stairs.

'I heard that, Max!'

I give him the finger. If he'd been around this morning, none of this would have happened. Then I could have gone for a run, could have controlled myself. Fuck, why can't I ever control myself?

I take the stairs two at a time. The lift hasn't been working for years. Seventh floor, fourteen flights, one hundred and forty stairs— I count them. It calms me down. I push the key into the lock and hear Ma in the kitchen.

'I'm home!" I go straight to my room to change into some other clothes and scrub my blooded face.

'Max!'

Too late. My head is still sticking half out of my blood-spattered T-shirt.

'Where were you?'

She sticks her head round the door and I see her face change from curiosity to concern.

'It's nothing, Ma. Honest.'

She walks across to me and inspects first my jaw, then my eyebrow.

'Anything else?'

'My stomach.'

'Can you bend over?'

'Yes, Ma, I can bend over.'

She looks at me then gives me a slap, right across my face. On the good side, thank goodness.

'Ow!

'That's so you'll behave yourself next time. I won't have you kicked out of school, Max!'

She doesn't want me to be like Li. But she doesn't say that, of course.

'If I could've gone for a run...'

'That's no excuse and you know it.'

'They were being gross and —'

'Max, I don't need to know what they did. You just have to keep your hands to yourself! You know what those boys can be like!'

She's angry. I bite my lip until I taste blood.

'Go and wash and change. Dinner will be ready in a quarter of an hour.' She turns around and walks out of the room. I see my disheveled head reflected in the window.

Fuck. Fuck. Fuck.

NINA

I look out the window on the way home from school. Just before we turn left towards cc1, I recognize the girl that bumped into me in the corridor. She's with a few others and they're pointing at the car. The girl stands and stares a little longer than the rest, then spits on the ground with obvious distaste before turning around and being dragged off by a friend. I'm relieved she can't see me through the glass.

I settle into the back seat, take my HC out of my bag, and flip through my homework. It's an old model and you have to enter a lot more yourself. Otherwise it's not that much different from the one at my old school. Work takes my mind off things. I take my digipen and start on one of the assignments. As I do it, I doodle in the margin. Erik has turned on DOS-news.

'The food bank in District Seven today sustained heavy damage. An angry mob stormed the building because Points are no longer being accepted there. After someone threw a snowball-covered stone thrown and shattered the window, the Wet mob followed suit and decided to take matters into their own hands. It is understood that WEtTO...'

'Close.' The panel between Erik and me slides up. I don't want to hear any more. District Seven again. More riots. WEtTO again: the World Entente for terminating Terror and Oppression. At the moment, Dad's spends more time at Regional Hall than he does at home. When the neighborhoods were flooded again a year and a half ago, WEtTO support grew rapidly. Dad doesn't say much about it. I know they're also having problems in the other four Regions.

My digipen scratches across the screen.

We reach the heavily guarded gate to cc1 and undergo the same check as this morning. When they notice that I have a new hc, it is x-rayed.

I wonder where Nikki lives. It seems odd that I've never seen her. But perhaps it's not so odd. We all seem to live on our own little islands.

When we reach the end of the drive and Erik opens the garage door, I see that Dad's official car is already parked there.

So he's home.

Erik opens the door for me. Once inside, I walk past the kitchen and see Maria there. She smiles at me as she bends down to put a casserole in the oven. As usual, her thick black hair is done up in a bun and there's a brightly colored flower stuck in it. I go up the stairs before she straightens up and disappear into my room.

After a while, the dos light flashes on my screen. Maria's voice echoes through the room.

'Dinner's ready, Nina.'

I've just started on Collingwood's assignment about Zeitoun. The book is about a man who survives a flood in the south of what was then called the United States. But what happened there is not at all comparable to what happened here, and it took place so long ago! The United States don't even exist anymore. Why do we have to read about things that took place ages ago, while what's happening here and now... Irritated, I shut my hc.

I quickly go downstairs and ignore Isa's room. I know that Mum's been in there today. And yesterday. And the day before that.

In the dining room, Mum and Dad are sitting at either end of the long table. The curtains are half drawn and the cherrywood paneling makes the room dark and oppressive. As if the mood around here isn't bad enough as it is.

I sit down at the table, opposite the place where Isa always sat.

Dad says grace. I keep my eyes open and study my parents.

Mum is pale. She is clasping her fingers so tightly together that her knuckles are turning as white as chalk. Her eyelids are trembling, as if she is about to burst into tears. It wouldn't be the first time. I look like her. We both have the same honey-blond curls and wide mouth. Our cheeks are dotted with freckles and our pointed chin sticks out just a bit too much. She was pediatrician in the hospital. Until a year and a half ago.

Dad is his usual dominant self. You can see that he's no longer young – he looks slightly puffy and has got a bit of a pot belly – but there's something boyish about him. The touch of grey at his temple gives him the authority he needs as Governor of the Fifth Region. Isa had his eyes; clear blue and piercing, eyes that always drill into you.

When Dad finishes grace, he turns to look at me. "So, what was it like at school?'

Maria begins to carve the meat while Dad holds up his plate.

'Okay," I mumble.

'Erik took you right to the gate?'

'Uh huh.'

Somehow I expect — no, I hope — that he will ask something more, but he gives his undivided attention to the piece of meat Maria pushes onto his plate. The clock ticks audibly. Dad licks his lips. A trickle of red from the roast drips down his chin. I immediately see the boy at school. His blood, trickling just like that down his chin. I stare at the meat on my own plate. When Maria comes in with potatoes and vegetables, I quickly push most of it to the side.

Mum hardly eats anything; perhaps two mouthfuls of vegetables and a bite or so of her potatoes. She plays with her food and constantly looks at the vacant place opposite me.

Say something! The silence is driving me crazy.

The door to Dad's study opens and a young man in an impeccable pin-striped suit comes in. He's wearing an earpiece and carrying the newest HC, which is half integrated into his forearm. Felix Samuel Feliks: Dad's personal assistant.

He's only a few years older than me — twenty-two, twenty-three at most. I remember exactly what Isa said when she first saw him: "I've got to have that one, Nina!" Isa always got everything she set her sights on. But Felix Feliks was out of reach, even to her. Yes, he was always polite and always charming. He smiled and always paid us compliments, the Bradshaw daughters, and also Mum, who I once saw blush when he compared her to the "beautiful princess Helen," whoever that may be.

But in the end he has always maintained a distance. I admit, he's certainly not unattractive with that satin blond hair and those intelligent blue eyes. But I never completely understood Isa's infatuation. Once, I got home early from school and bumped into him as he came out of Dad's study. Our eyes met briefly and I was startled by the bitterness I read there. Of course, he apologized immediately. He placed a hand on my arm and gave me that perfect smile: the smile with which, according to Isa, "he could get you to do anything'. Perhaps Isa had been more right than she realized, I suddenly thought. It would be impossible to think of the Bradshaw household without Felix.

Now, Felix walks straight over to Dad and whispers something in his ear. His velvety voice is the only sound in the room. He points at his HC, touches the screen, and holds the image under Dad's nose.

Dad reads. He relaxes.

He wipes the jus from his chin with the napkin next to his plate. He gets up. He nods in my direction and as he walks past Mum, he gives her a pat on the shoulder. Felix follows him into the study. Once the door closes behind them, however, their voices become agitated.

I look down at my plate. I look at Mum. We stare at each other.

She looks away.

I make my excuses and escape upstairs. My dinner remains untouched on the plate.

MAX

Li hits me round the head when he comes into the kitchen. He sinks into one of the rickety chairs next to me. The thing creaks dangerously.

'Hey," I protest weakly, while I rub the back of my head.

'Tell me, little brother! Who, what, where?'

He tips the chair back. Ma turns from the stove, pan in hand. She puts it down in front of us.

'Liam! A chair's got four legs!'

'What?" He throws his hands in the air and gives me a wink. I can't suppress a grin. How often have Li and I fought each other? And how often have we helped each other out of the shit?

'Damian," I sigh. "And Lars and Tim.'

Li whistles softly through his teeth.

'That bad-ass! And Tim..." He slams his hand on the table. The lid on the saucepan trembles and Ma calls, 'HEY! Is that necessary?'

Tim and I were mates. Best friends — until he decided that Damian was cool. As if I had time to hang around and make trouble. Fuck them.

Ma dishes up and we dig in.

I look up now and then as I work my way through some potatoes and gravy. Li's in a good mood. Even Ma can't keep the smile off her face when he tells us about Julius. He got it into his stupid mind to walk up to a Red, a beer clasped in his hands, and ask him with barely disguised derision whether he knew where a glass container was. But nowadays, when Li's in a good mood, it means that shit is bound to follow. I can tell he's done something again. Has to be that. Only when Li's pulled something off does he look as if he's outdone the Governor himself. That grin of his. I know better.

Later.

First I have to run. First I have to empty my head.

I gulp down my last mouthful and quickly get up. I walk to my room the closet I share with Li. My HC is on my desk, staring accusingly at me. Homework. I ignore the thing, rummage through the mess on the ground, and fish out my running gear. I pull my shoes from under the bunk-bed, grab the keys from the cabinet by the door, and sprint down the stairs to warm up for my run. I don't feel the cold anymore when I take my normal route between the high flats, towards the dyke.

We live on the edge of the Region. Greenhouses and marshy meadows stretch out between the inhabited world and the dyke, but not as far as in the other four larger Regions. How often has this area been submerged by water? District Seven is the last place you'd want to live. Not that you have much choice as a Wet. CCs are forbidden territory for us. Or you have to sell your soul to the devil and become a Wader; a Wet who voluntarily – voluntarily, damn it! – works for Dries. Everything for that little bit more protection that Dries allow them. I spit on the ground.

As I walk past the overgrown allotments, I think about Ma and how she looked when she realized she would have to give up hers. Outside the CCs, the ground has become too salty and too boggy to grow anything. And everything grown in the greenhouses goes into the distribution system controlled by the Dries. I know that Ma would rather that I didn't walk here, certainly not after the dyke breach last month, but it's quiet here. You're not disturbed by Wets or Dries or anyone who's going to want something from you.

I'm not scared of the water. Never have been. Not even after Pa drowned. Six months ago. A long time, but a short time as well.

I run past some children playing. When the dyke looms up, it becomes really deserted.

The wind is icy and it starts to snow. But I've found my rhythm. And when you've got your rhythm, you can go on forever. I breathe deeply, in and out, in and out. Snow settles everywhere: on my clothes, my hair, my head. I don't give a damn. Running is the only thing that can stop my thoughts going round and round.

I pick up speed. I want to go even faster. My heart beats against my ribs, my legs are fucking heavy, but I don't give up. Because only when you've pushed yourself over the limit does it feel fantastic. Feels like you can do anything, really anything.

Come on!

I run past the woods, see the first sandbags, and know I've only got a little way to go. The warm sweat trickles down my spine. There's the dyke. I speed up again and use my momentum to get to the top. I have to use my hands and feet on the last bit, but then I'm at the top.

The water.

Fucking *endless.*

Endless grey, cold, bleak water. With windmills near the

coast and in the distance, the skeletons of the Submerged Territories that separate the Regions from each other. They reach out far, to the start of the Foreign Territories.

What does it feel like to drown?

I pant, put my hands on my knees, and hang my head. Icy snow glides down my neck under my clothes.

I curse loudly.

What would it be like to drown? Every time I come here, that bloody question raises its head.

I stand still too long. The stabs of pain in my hands and feet disappear and give way to a cold, dead feeling. The sweat leaves an icy trail on my back. I've got to get back, but I can't tear my eyes from the water. I straighten up too quickly and see black patches.

In the distance, a light turns the snowstorm yellow. A water board or a patrol ship. Or a cargo ship bringing provisions. Perhaps.

I turn round and leave the water behind me. Until next time.

NINA

I slowly mount the stairs and trail my hand along the wooden bannister; the same bannister Isa and I would slide down as children.

Isa's room looks the same as it did on the day she died. Her familiar scent engulfs me. I immediately see from the bed that Mum has been here today; Maria hasn't had time to straighten everything up. Otherwise... otherwise nothing has been moved or thrown away. Isa could walk in at any moment.

Isa's room is lighter than mine. That's because of the windows that reach from floor to ceiling, but also because of Isa's fascination with white. Everything had to be white. All the walls, all the cupboards, all the posts, even the frame of the DOS screen in the corner. Only the photos of family and friends which hang everything give the room some color.

I walk over to the desk — white, of course — where her HC is lying. Instinctively I touch the screen and jump when it welcomes me and asks for the password. Before I have time to think, I type it and I'm in.

Isa and I never had secrets from each other. Sisters.

The screen shows a half-finished language assignment, there is one last message from her boyfriend, Johan, who she was crazy about, and I see the photo of the two of us that's also in my locket. We're laughing and tilting our heads towards each other.

Isa looked like Dad. She was almost a head taller than me

and more sturdily built, even though she was a year younger. She had his blue eyes. Just like him, she could look at you in a certain way and then it was simply impossible to say no. Nobody wanted to disappoint Isa.

I quickly return the HC to precisely the same place and turn round guiltily. I'm alone. Of course I'm alone. I turn the thing off. I don't want Mum to notice anything. I suppress the urge to straighten the bedspread and leave the room. When the door closes, I lean against it for a moment. Closed. Like it's been closed forever.

'Isa!'
I'm on the mainland and wading through ice-cold water. I know she's there. She wasn't outside in the quad with the others. She must still be in the building.
'Isa!!'
The water rages, churns, and roars. The storm reaches its climax and the sky is pitch black.
The lights inside stutter once, twice, three times, then go out.
'Nina!' *I hear her voice in the distance. Then nothing. Deathly silence, like in the eye of the storm.*
'Isa? Isa!'
I shout and shout, but there's no answer.
The water is already up to my knees and my jeans are soaked. My legs are so cold. I hardly have the strength to put one foot in front of the other.
Can I hear it raging inside?
I look round, but see nothing. My heart beats in my throat, in my head, in my everything. It beats and chases blood through my body and suddenly gives me the shot of adrenaline I need.

Because the water's coming.
And I don't think about Isa anymore, but I get away, as quickly as possible, away, away from the water, away from Isa, away from death.
Then the water takes me.

I wake up screaming.

The light comes on automatically. Beads of perspiration run down my brow and my hair is sticking to my forehead. My back feels cold and my mouth dry.

The house is deathly quiet.

I wrap the blanket around me and walk to the cupboard that opens for me. I grab the pills. I need more. A lot more. I go to the sink and run the water. Waste. You should be ashamed of yourself, Nina. All I can do is look at the flowing water that holds so much: promise and hope, despair and treachery, life and death. I hold a glass under the tap and let it overflow, until my hand is just as painfully cold as my inside. I take two pills and swallow them.

MAX

"I said you weren't to go there anymore," says Ma as soon as I come in. She's on her own. Ma always knows where I go for my runs. I swear she's got a sixth sense.

I'm soaked through but I couldn't care less. I feel great. Fantastic. I've run out all the rage.

'You've been to the water, haven't you?" I let her sit me down at the kitchen table.

I don't say anything, just take off my shoes as if nothing's happened and shake my wet head.

'Hey! Not in here.'

She's already put water on for tea. The surrogate coffee, the only stuff you can still get these days, is gross. She sorts through one of the cupboards and throws me a towel.

'Here.'

I take off my wet jacket and dry myself. I'm glowing from the exertion.

Ma makes more noise when she's angry. The mugs in the cupboard rattle threateningly, the drawer with cutlery is opened with more force than necessary and slammed shut, the tea pot lands in front of me with a hard thud. She puts some herbs in the tea egg and fills my mug. Tea is hardly the word for the warm, flavorless water that I gulp down. At least it's hot.

She sits down opposite me and sighs.

'I suppose you're not going to promise me that you'll never go there again." It is more a statement than a question.

I purse my lips into an apologetic grin and am about to open my mouth to say something. But she beats me to it.

'I was watching DOS news. There were more food riots this morning. *Somebody* threw a stone through the food bank window.'

I blink and read in her eyes what I suspect myself.

'Fuck.'

'Max! Watch your mouth," she says, as usual. Pa would have answered: "I'll do what I bloody-well like in my own house!" Pa, who always swore like a Wet dockworker at anything Dry.

'Stupid prick!" I say louder.

'Max...'

'Yes?" My eyes burn. Ma doesn't look away.

'Leave it to me, Max.'

If I was outside, I'd have spat on the ground. Fucking idiot brother. What's he thinking? That he can solve everything by messing around?

'Max...' Ma says with a hint of a warning in her voice.

I nod, my lips pressed together, and walk from the kitchen to my room.

The knot is back.

Five hours later, the light goes on and Li stumbles in. He kicks off his shoes and shivers. Snow drips onto the concrete floor.

I'm lying in bed, under the blankets. It's ice cold. The trick is to get in while you're warm and get to sleep quickly. Once you wake up frozen through, it's usually time to get up again.

It's the middle of the night and Ma's on night shift at the clinic. Li immediately sees that I'm awake.

'Hey, little brother.'

He bends over me and breathes out. His hot breath stinks. Alcohol.

'Party?'

Li grins. Doesn't he hear that I'm angry?

'We had some celebrating to do, sure.'

I shake my head. My big brother.

'We're not stupid, you know," I say. "Me and Ma."

'What?" He hops around on one leg to pull off his jeans and almost falls against the desk. Drunken jerk.

'We know all about your bit of fun this morning.'

Ma may not want me to interfere, but today's the day for opening my big mouth. Apparently. I can't keep it shut.

Li stands still, one leg still in his jeans. It looks stupid. At the same time, there's a very un-Liam-like threat about it. He's eyes grow large and he takes a step in my direction.

'What do you know?'

I return his look without flinching. Do I have a death-wish or something? I know what Li's like when he's drunk too much.

I'm the first to lower my eyes.

'Well done, little brother.'

Knot.

Easy, Max.

'Fuck you, Li," I say and turn over towards the wall.

'Same to you, Max.' He climbs into the bed above me. I hear his teeth chattering. And in five minutes he's snoring.

I lie awake until the alarm goes.

NINA

DOS alarm.

Deep, black sleep. I can't wake up. It's like a blanket, like down, like a cloud in which I sink as soon as I resist. And why should I resist anyway?

Alarm.

I try to open my eyes. They won't open. I've felt this before. When? Everything is so slow, sluggish, dull. My arms and legs are too heavy to move.

'Nina?'

I recognize that voice. I want to turn over, but my neck is stiff.

'Ouch," I mumble. I rub my tense muscles.

'Nina?'

'Yes?" My voice sounds even duller than the rest of my body.

'Are you up?'

Maria. She must be at the door.

'Yes, I'm coming. Just a mo.'

I hear her footsteps going down the stairs.

Then I remember the pills. And the nightmare. I groan. Coffee.

I drag myself to the shower and then get dressed. I avoid the mirror. I know all too well what that dream does to me.

When I go into the kitchen, Maria has already poured my coffee. She runs a reassuring hand across my shoulder before she returns to preparing breakfast.

Erik is waiting for me in the car. During the drive to school, I scroll through the assignments that I haven't completed. I draw imaginary faces in the margin with my digipen.

Erik has the DOS news on. A reporter's voice breaks through the mumbling and crackling. 'And so you are saying that you are now certain that WEtTO is behind the attack?'

'We can, indeed, state that with almost one hundred percent certainty," my Dad's voice answers, "but I want to assure the population —'

The reporter has guts because he interrupts him: "That would mean that this is the second time in two weeks that WEtTO has struck. First the theft of those Points in District Two, and now this.'

Would others hear the way Dad snorts?

'As I already said, we can now say with great certainty who is responsible for this cowardly act, and I would like — " There is crackling again and the reporter tries to interrupt a second time, but this time my father is too quick for him. '— I want to assure the people of the Fifth Region that provisions will be restocked by the end of this week. The food distribution will not be endangered. Thank you." More disturbance and retreating footsteps.

'And now the weather with...'

The solution is so easy, according to Dad.

I walk the last bit to school. I again feel the nerves I felt yesterday, until somebody waves at me. It is Nikki. Relieved, I walk over to her. Locks of red hair stick out from under her woolen hat and the rest of her face is almost completely hidden behind a thick purple scarf.

'Hey!" she calls.

'Hey.'

Benjamin is standing next to her and one of the other girls as well. Cynthia, I think. When the bells goes, the four of us go inside. A lot better than yesterday. Cynthia is the grade below me, but I have a number of classes with Benjamin and Nikki. Nikki helps me to find my way and I no longer have to sit by myself. During the lessons, she sends me amusing digi-messages with all sorts of questions, and although I'm not really in the mood for it, I can't resist her cheerfulness. It's nice to feel like things are getting normal again.

In the break, we meet the other Dries. A small group compared to the rest, although there are a few new faces again. They talk about the latest digifilms, about the lessons and how things are different here, yet really just the same. Benjamin shows Ruben his new TonePlayer, while Cynthia and Sophie discuss what to wear to the party Sophie is throwing next week.

First I join in, but I can't really concentrate. It feels as if I've been out of things for a long time and it takes to much effort to keep up with the conversation.

Nikki is the only one who notices my silence.

'Hey, something wrong?'

'No, nothing. Just slept badly." I smile faintly.

She nods as if she understands and she goes back to talking to one of the other new kids.

I slowly chew the cafeteria food, but I'm not really hungry. I allow my eyes to sweep across the faces. Wets. Carefully, without allowing my gaze to stay on one person too long. They're looking at us too. And talking about us. I hear the remarks. Sometimes whispered as they pass, sometimes intentionally out loud. Elbows that poke somebody, followed by loud laughter. There's something about them, but I can't put my finger on it. It's just like some stupid quiz on DOS. The answer is on the tip of your tongue, but it just won't come to you.

Then I get it.

Color — or lack of it. They're so grey. There's no color. None in their clothes, not even in their eyes.

I swallow a bite of food and don't realize that I've been staring at somebody for slightly too long.

'Something wrong with me, Dry?'

A girl — the same girl who bumped into me yesterday? — is staring with open hostility at me. I quickly look away and my gaze lands on him.

He's sitting in the corner, at the same table as before. His nose is buried in an old-fashioned paper book; they're still used a lot here. He's bashing on his taped-up HC. He can't sit still. His fingers drum on his legs, on the table and on the HC. His head moves as if he's listening to music, but I can't see a TonePlayer. His chin is a blue bruise and stands out sharply against his light-brown skin. Color.

Suddenly he looks up. I quickly drop my gaze before our eyes can meet.

MAX

What does that Dry want?

My head's still throbbing. I ran this morning, but the lack of sleep is beginning to get to me. Bloody Liam. He was still lying there snoring when I got up. Li'll sleep most of the day since Ma isn't home.

In the caf, I scroll through the assignments I haven't finished. I sigh, lean back, and look at the table where she's sitting. My hands tap out the rhythm in my head. Now she's talking to some other bitch, the one with bright red hair and a purple scarf. Dries think they're so special.

I struggle to keep my eyes open. Damian and his mates are laying low, but I know it won't be long. I have to keep awake. When the bell goes, I quickly get my things and leave the hall. I'm going to be on time for a change.

I don't hear the others come in as I sit there reading on my HC. When I look up, she's sitting next to me. I'd forgotten that we had this class together. And that this was the last empty seat. She stares straight ahead, says nothing, and then starts drawing. Fine. I can ignore people too. I don't know what the hell got into me yesterday.

Collingwood starts his lecture and I concentrate on taking notes, listening carefully. I want to know this. I want to know everything. When the bell goes, I get up and am about to leave the class when Collingwood calls me over.

'Max? Can you stay a moment? Nina? You too.'

What?

I just manage to keep my mouth shut. Collingwood looks at us, half leaning, half sitting on the table.

'You didn't hand in your assignments yesterday," he says.

'Sir, I... Something came up," I said quickly.

'I'm sorry, but I..." echoes Nina.

Collingwood holds up his hand.

'Nina, you're new so you have some catching up to do. Since you both helped each other so well yesterday, I thought you it would be a good idea for the two of you to finish the assignment together.'

We're both too astonished to say anything. Then we both start talking at once. Collingwood holds up his hand again.

'Max, Nina." He looks from me to Nina, who lowers her eyes. "You'll do the assignment together and hand it in to me by Friday next week.'

I shrug my shoulders. Nina raises her pointed chin and nods.

'Right. That'ss all. You can go.'

He turns and walks over to his desk, sits down, and acts as if we're not there.

Working with a Dry! What's Collingwood thinking?

I dash out of the classroom. Nina follows a few seconds later. In the hall, I whirl around to face her but it's like she doesn't dare to look at me. Dries are such cowards when they're on their own.

I look down at her. Man, she's really small. Her hand moves uncertainly to her bag, an expensive one it seems, real leather. Does she think I want to steal it or something? The sunlight reflects from her locket and I again think of the Points that thing's worth.

'Well?'

She looks up warily.

'How are we going to do it?" I ask impatiently.

She shrugs her shoulders.

'How about if we split it? You do one bit, I do one bit."

She hesitates for a moment. 'Have you looked at it?'

'No..." I sigh and open my HC.

'There's a discussion in it. We can't just split it up.'

'Fine," I say, exasperated. That bloody Collingwood. "Let's meet next week. Tuesday. During afternoon study period. After lunch-break. I know a quiet spot.'

She doesn't answer straight away. A curl falls in front of her eyes. That must be irritating. She doesn't do anything about it, however, and my hands itch to push it away. Instead, I drum on the windowsill with my left hand.

'Okay," she says finally.

'Okay," I answer.

Crap.

NINA

When he turns the corner, I take a deep breath. That boy gets on my nerves with his incessant drumming. And the way he looks at me... I bite my lip.

What is Collingwood trying to prove? Being held after class has completely unnerved me. For a moment there, I was terrified he'd figured out who I was, and he wanted to test me. But how can a Wet teacher at an even Wetter school know anything about me?

Thanks to him, I'm late for my next class and get in trouble again. After just two days, this former model pupil of the Mainland has earned the reputation of a slacker.

I don't know what's gotten into me, but when the teacher tells me to pay attention, I start laughing.

'What is so funny, Nina Baker? Would you like to share it with us?'

The rest of the class breaks out into giggling and jeering.

Thiss teacher is a classic Dries hater. I can see it in her piercing eyes, on her pursed lips. So I take things one step further and say: "No, I do not want to share it with you," and walk out of the room.

Of course the sourpuss follows me out and sends me to the principal, who gives me a detention.

I phone Mum to tell her I'll be late, and I can see on the screen that she is studying my face.

'What's wrong?' Tense, anxious, worried.

'Nothing, Mum. I just have to stay late, uh, to finish something. Something I can only do here," I lie. I hope the school don't send her some sort of notification about the real reason.

'Erik can still pick you up?'

'Yes, Mum. I've already sent him a message.'

'Do you want me to ask Maria to keep something warm for you?'

'Yes, please.'

'Be careful, darling.'

'Yes, Mum." I disconnect.

During second break, I'm a hero for the Dries. Nikki tells at length what happened. She makes it seem like a much bigger deal and I almost want to drop through the floor.

'That Wet was going on about *nothing*, and you know she always picks on us. Nina was so cool! She just stood up, as calm as can be, and walked out of the classroom.'

'You've got a nerve," says Ruben, a boy with long brown hair and a ring through his eyebrow. Benjamin laughs, while Cynthia and Sophie stare at me, wide-eyed.

I try to play it down. "I just wasn't in the mood."

Nikki still hasn't finished. Apparently most of the action took place after I was sent out. A Wet and a Dry got into a fight because the first guy said something about me which, according to Nikki, couldn't be repeated. The sourpuss had to fetch Mr. Beursma from across the hall to separate them.

To my surprise, when I arrive in detention, Max is already sitting there too. He stares at me and I know that we're both thinking the same thing: Not again!

As the room starts to fill up, I quickly choose a table as

far away from him as possible. I sigh when I see that Collingwood is supervising the detention. Of course. A perfect end to a perfect day.

Mrs. Sourpuss has given me a special assignement to complete during detention: Copy out a passage from a book that's loaded onto my HC. I open the file and pick up my digipen, ready to start.

My pen hovers over the screen.

This isn't just any random book. That's perfectly clear once the title page appears. It's a history of the First Great Flood, and not the history I know either.

This book doesn't begin with those familiar words that every Dry and every Wet hears on his or her first day at school. No "I believe in the Five Regions." No "I believe in the struggle against the water." No "I believe we shall ultimately defeat the water." And certainly no "I believe that in the end we shall all end on dry land." In this book there is no dry land.

Everybody and everything is drowned.

Eyes, hundreds of eyes, stare at me from just as many photos. I drown in them and they drown in the water. There are hideous photos of people in mortal peril, knowing that they are not going to make it, that the water is coming, and that it will carry them off into the depths, where a nameless grave is awaiting them. There are photos of buildings about to collapse, with people jumping out of them from great heights. But it doesn't make any difference. There is no salvation because below the water is waiting, the hungry water that swallows them without a second thought. There are photos of ships unable to ride the towering waves, whose crew may well have understood how senseless their desperate attempts were much sooner than the people in the so-called safety of their cities, behind the dunes, the dykes, and the locks. The capsizing ships are tossed around like toy boats in a much-too-large bathtub. The water is angry and grows stronger as I turn the pages.

These are not the beautifully drawn illustrations I know from The Book of the Regions. It is not the history every child hears, of the famous General Zandt who leads the people to the new promised land and builds the dykes and the walls behind which they will be eternally safe from the water. It is not the story of persistence, unity, and single-mindedness with which the people, against all expectations, built up a new Dry existence. It is not the story of the victory that ensured the Low Countries could continue to exist in the Five Regions, their pride intact.

Quite the opposite, in fact. It is not the story of the victory of man over water, but of water over man, and of men over other men. For when the water withdraws...

I forced myself to move my digipen to the screen. Word for word. I don't want to read more than one word at a time. I don't want the sentences to lodge in my mind the way the pictures have done. For I know them. I know them all too well. They are the same pictures as those in my dream.

I write on, stoically. I don't want to think. I really don't want to think about it.

The tension in the room is unbearable, almost like home. I rush through the assignment and send it to Collingwood. I hope he doesn't check it too carefully.

Max's digipen taps. I hear the deep breathing of the boy behind me.

Collingwood picks up his HC when it beeps. He reads the

file I sent him, the expression on his face betraying nothing.

'You can go, Nina.'

He doesn't have to say it twice. I quickly stuff my things in my bag and leave the room. The tapping of digipen follows me in my mind, right up until I hear the door of the car closing beside me.

MAX

She doesn't look the type to get detention.

Ms. Reiger has given her the book. The book containing the truth about the First Great Flood. About how one group was able to set themselves up high and dry and leave the rest to their Wet fate. She's tried it with other Dries too. See how they react when confronted with the dirty Wet reality. Collingwood knows full well that it's forbidden, but he doesn't do anything about it. He's not always as nice as he looks.

I see her looking. Dries know nothing of the real world. They don't need to know anything, thinking they're safe behind their thick walls. But there's something in Nina's expression that I can't place. She keeps looking round as if somebody's breathing down her neck.

Not much later, I hear Collingwood say she can go. I just catch a glimpse of those perfect blond curls as she disappears into the hallway.

Don't interfere, Max.

Damian whistles softly through his teeth.

He and his mates are keeping their eyes on me and I know I'll have to make a run for it when Collingwood lets us out. Not that he's hurrying. How long? My legs are itching.

When we finally get the sign, I'm off before Damian has even stood up.

Li is at home. He's sitting on the settee with Ramon and Julius.

DOS news is on and Bradshaw is talking. About WEtTO and retribution, about order and authority. The usual bullshit. As I take off my shoes, I glance sidewise at my brother. He can hardly contain himself.

Hate fills his dark eyes, staring at the screen as if hypnotized. Hate fills his hands, grabbing a can of beer. Hate fills his whole body, tense as a bunch of Blowers at the entrance of a C.

He holds Bradshaw responsible for Pa's death. Li says that Bradshaw intentionally waited too long before giving the order for total evacuation; until the last Dry was rescued by Wet relief workers from that damned school. By then was too late for Pa and his crew: the dyke was breached. They were doing maintenance work. Fucking *maintenance* work.

I study the Governor of the Fifth Region. A man the same age as Pa, but totally different. He has everything that Pa never had and never will have: Dry versus Wet.

Is Li right?

Bradshaw has charisma. You have to give the man that. But his face is just a bit too bloated and you can see he doesn't feel at ease. WEtTO has struck again. Yesterday evening they got into CC1 and set fire to a couple of cars. No dead or wounded; a warning. Bradshaw has "everything under control" and "will ensure that those responsible are caught and punished as quickly as possible." Does he actually think anyone believes him?

I look at Li. How deep in the shit is he? He turns off DOS and spits in the ashtray. He's shaking.

Ramon takes a long drag on his cigarette while Julius finishes his can of beer. They're an odd couple: one with chocolate-brown skin, the chest of a bodybuilder, and dreadlocks;

the other a beanpole, thin as a skeleton and as pale as death. They don't realize Li is about to explode. And I really don't want to be around when that happens.

I go to our room and change clothes. My legs still feel heavy, but I can't sit around indoors.

I don't go far this time, just far enough to make me feel better. When I get back, I see them from a distance.

Boxing.

As I approach, I see that Li's eyes are those of a mad man. Beads of sweat run off his bushy eyebrows down his face and he keeps brushing them off with his gloved hand in irritation. Liam boxes, just like Pa did. For me, I run. I think my release valve is healthier.

'Feel like taking a few jabs?'

'I've got better things to do, Li.'

'Come on!' He feints and punches the air.

Ramon, his sparring partner, laughs. "I think your little brother's scared he can't take you on," he says.

'Piss off, Ramon." I want to run off, but Liam stops me.

'Come on! Just one round."

I find myself hesitating. Is it the challenging look in his eyes? His confidence that he can beat me just like that? Li knows exactly how to play me because I'm going to give in. Fuck, how does he manage it?

'Okay, fine. One round.'

Li's eyes glisten.

'Just because you need to be taught how to lose once in a while, Li.'

'Only one of us can be the best, little brother.'

Ramon takes off his gloves and throws them to me. I'm crazy. Fighting with Li when he's so worked up. As I jog to warm up, more people come and stand around us. An audience. That's all I need. From the corner of my eye I see Kara, my girlfriend before Pa died. Kara loved watching me fight, and complained that running made me too boring. Looks as if she's got herself a new guy.

'Ready for a good pounding?'

I turn to face Liam who's grinning like a maniac. The Morris brothers are giving another free show. We're so fucking good at it.

'Are you?" I counter.

The fight begins. My second in two days.

Li has the weight, I have the speed. I know I'm finished if he gets hold of me. We are urged on from all sides. Julius is shouting the loudest for Li; Kara seems to have forgotten her new guy and is shouting one profanity after the other.

We know each other too well.

When Li tries a feint so that he can hit me with his left, I duck, low, so that his blows don't connect. Li guesses my next action just as easily. He catches me with a hard punch to the shoulder and I almost end up on my ass. That sets me off. I let my brother have it with a hard right in his arrogant face.

The spectators roar with appreciation.

Li stands still. He spits on the ground and wipes the blood from his gleaming lips with the back of his hand. "You'll regret that," he slurs.

Then the fight really gets going.

And, dammit, I'm enjoying myself. The adrenaline that rushes through your veins when you fight is different than when you run. Better if you win. More dangerous if you lose. And I usually lose against Li.

We only see her when she's under our noses.

Ma. Heavy bags in both hands. The spectators slip away, like scared dogs, tails between their legs.

She looks at Liam. She looks at me. I swallow. She only looks. But I still turn my face away. And I know Li can't face her either. She says nothing, nothing at all, and at the same time she says everything. She turns away, walks to the entrance way and leaves us standing there, our faces red with shame and our jaws bruised.

'Fuck,' says Li.

'Fuck,' I echo.

A dog yaps, its bark echoing between the concrete flats. One of the neighbor kids rides by on a broken-down bike. The cat belonging to the people across the street pisses in the sandbox.

Li is the first to say anything.

'Good right jab, little brother.'

A second trickle of blood flows down the corner of his mouth onto the pavement.

'I didn't see your one coming either." I rub my back.

We look at each other. We both shake our bloodied heads. And we grin.

NINA

A week has gone by and life at the new school is almost becoming normal.

I'm sitting next to Nikki in the cafeteria. She chatters without a break and, to be honest, she's starting to get on my nerves. She's talking about a new digifilm starring some hot new actor or other and constantly fiddling with her hair. I can tell that she's trying to impress Benjamin, but she's blind to that fact that his attention is fixed on somebody else. On Ruben, would you believe, who's looking at Nikki with those big puppy-dog eyes. So *that's* happening.

Yesterday evening, I tried to work on the assignment for Collingwood. I didn't get very far. My thoughts kept wandering. To Max. To the pictures in that book. To Isa. To the water.

Nikki has stopped talking and is staring at me, all mad about something.

'What?" I say.

'Hello! I'm talking to you and you're just not listening!'

'Sorry.'

She rolls her eyes.

'I forgive you. Just this once." She laughs as I smile apologetically at her.

I don't want to upset her. She can't do anything about it.

We have chemistry and then history. I have trouble keeping my eyes open. Lack of sleep. Nikki sits next to me and I copy her notes. When the bell goes for lunch break, I leave the classroom and go to the cafeteria, because I expect Max'll be sitting there at his usual table.

'Hey.'

He's leaning with one leg against the wall and tapping his fingers on the rough stones. His chin is still sporting its multi-colored bruise and I see that one of his eyebrows is torn. A pale scar is beginning to show on his brown skin.

'Hey." My voice still sounds as if I've only just got up.

'Before you ask how I knew you'd be here: all schedules are on Delta-DOS.'

'Okay.'

I hadn't got that far. My surprise hadn't go much further than being surprised to see him standing there in the first place.

'Come on.' He says it with an authoritative tone that would make Collingwood jealous. I almost feel like staying where I am. But when I think how Mum and Dad would react to DOS mail from school, telling them I'm behind in my assignments, I decide to follow him.

Just like that first time, he walks quickly and I have trouble keeping up with him. The school's bigger than I thought. Corridor after corridor, classroom after classroom. We walk past showcases with stuffed animals ande turn the corner just past the chemistry lab. Through a window, I can see the street where Erik always lets me out and picks me up, so I figure we must be somewhere in the back of the school. We go through a corridor with cracked tiles and an unevenly paved floor. The damp walls are covered with so many different shades of mildew that they are almost beautiful, except for the awful smell.

I turn up my nose.

'A bit nasty?" He laughs as he walks towards a door.

I don't say anything. Is he trying to get to me? He opens the door and says in a tone that drips with sarcasm: "After you!'

I ignore it and go in.

It's an old classroom that's apparently being used now as a sort of storage place; it's filled with forgotten things that were once used in the school. Tables and chairs, old-fashioned blackboards, cupboards and showcases. Rows of pictures stand against the wall. The smell of rot immediately greets me.

'Where are we?" I run my finger over an old, dusty desk.

'No need to be scared. Nobody ever comes here. It's been officially declared redundant.'

'I'm not scared.'

'No?' He doesn't believe me.

'Shall we get started then?" I stick out my chin. It's so annoying that he's a head taller than me. Intimidation works better if you're bigger than the other guy.

'Fine.'

He pulls a half rotten chair from the rubble for me, wipes the desk clean, and gets out his HC. He turns it on and scrolls to the assignment. I do the same.

Max sits on the desk. He swings his legs as he hammers angrily on his HC. The thing won't work.

'Here," I say. "I've got it." I've put the latest DOS-version on my "new" old model; now at least the thing can handle the endless flow of information.

We have to discuss the influence of the literature of the late twentieth and early twenty-first century on the climate debate taking place at the time. *To what extent did these writers have any influence? How would you describe their contribution to the developments that followed?*

I hold up my HC for him. He shrugs his shoulders as if he couldn't care less, but takes my HC just a fraction too quickly.

'Man," he gasps. "Have you got DOS-5? How did you pull that off?'

'Umm...'

I can hardly tell him where I got it. Dad wouldn't appreciate my knowing his password.

'Forget it. I don't need to know.'

We start on the assignment. One of us has to defend the proposition that the influence of the authors was marginal. The other has to present arguments that demonstrate that their books incited public debate. I find it difficult to concentrate. Quite honestly, I don't really care. I really can't think of much to defend the first proposition. My gaze keeps slipping away, and that rotten smell is clogging up my nose.

I'm startled when Max suddenly stands up and punches a wooden board with his fist.

'Fuck. Doesn't it interest you a bit? Doesn't it matter to you how we all ended up in this fucking mess?'

Instinctively I flinch. Suddenly I notice how hard his muscles are under his T-shirt. His dark eyes light up like two specks of flame.

'I...'

He doesn't let me finish.

'Drop it, will you? I'll do it myself. What else can you expect from a Dry?" He turns around and grabs his bag, ready to leave the room.

Something is triggered in me. It's as if an old-fashioned

light switch has been thrown, and for the first time in ages I feel something other than the oppressive emptiness and the constant absence. It takes maybe a second before I get it. Whatever, I go with it.

It's rage.

'Hey!' I shout.

He turns round. His whole body is shaking. Even his nostrils are shaking.

'How dare you assume anything about me!' I jump up from my chair and storm over to him. I may not have forgotten my fear, but at least I've hidden it away.

'I don't presume. I simply observe.' His voice is cold. I feel the distaste, perhaps even something worse than that.

'Well, keep your stupid observations to yourself,' I snap back.

I take another step closer. His scent fills my nose. A scent that suddenly takes me back to that last summer evening, when, after all those days of heat, the rain had finally come.

The anger leaves me as quickly as it came. The fear remains where it was all that time.

Am I going crazy?

He stares at me. His breath comes in short, heavy jolts. A vein beats on his forehead, a bead of seat slides down his big nose. He moves his arm, lifting it slowly.

Is he going to hit me?

I don't know how long we stare at each other. I don't even know what I see. I'm the first to look away. I don't have the nerve to look at him anymore. Only when I hear his angry footsteps echoing in the deserted corridor do I finally look up.

MAX

Knot.

I want to hit something. I've got to hit something. Now.

Before I know it, I've smashed my fist into the half-rotten cupboard door. Splinters fly everywhere; one of them buries itself deep in the flesh between my thumb and forefinger.

Fuck.

Get out of here, Max.

I walk faster and faster. Faster and faster, until I'm not walking, until I'm running. They won't notice anyway. Nobody ever comes here. But...

You wanted to hit her, man!

A girl! A Dry.

She should have kept her mouth shut.

Still... I couldn't hit her. But I wanted to, man. I really wanted to. The thing is once I lose it, I lose it completely. And I can't control myself. Never.

I begin to walk slower as I reach the part of the building that's not deserted. Now I'll have to finish that stupid assignment by myself. I'm not dumb enough to leave it to a Dry. I saw how she looked. No, how she looked away. None of them want to know. Just look away. Just fucking look away.

Just like when they buried Pa.

Suddenly I see Ma's face when that Blower brought the news. We'd stayed up the whole bloody night. Ma had bags under her eyes; she'd just worked five night shifts. She stood there and said nothing. She didn't cry, took the message, turned around, and disappeared into her bedroom. We heard a stifled scream and a couple of vases hit the ground.

That was the only time. After that, I never heard her fry or react. She arranged everything, did everything. We didn't have enough Points for a headstone. Pa was buried with the rest of them. Some semi-official occasion or other, with a few of those highfalutin Dry officials who didn't even take the trouble to disguise the fact that it couldn't be over soon enough for them. One had a voice as silky as an eel, eyes like hard blue beads, and a smile that looked as if it had been painted on. His words were sweet and smooth. I knew better.

Ma still visits the grave every Tuesday.

The Dries who died were given full attention on DOS. Photos of happy families suddenly torn apart, and all sorts of interview with the few Dries who had lost anyone. I couldn't watch. Dries are all the same. Fuck them. Fifty men in Pa's shift didn't make it.

Suddenly I understand why Li threw that stone through the window. If I want, I can let his rage be my rage. It'd so damned easy.

I wish I could run. I play with the idea of bunking off. Get outside. Away from this suffocating place.

Suddenly I stand still.

I shake my head.

I really can't have any more detentions. I don't want to disappoint Ma. Sure, I want to get out of here but not like that. The first exams are in a month's time and I'm certain I can improve my average a bit. I don't want to screw up. Fuck, not now. I've almost got my feet on dry land. I want it to be true, that it can happen.

But Pa. Pa also thought like that. Drowned in that bloody water.

NINA

At school, I can easily avoid him in the days that follow. In my head, he follows me everywhere. In the scratches I make on my digiscreen. In the accusing words that echo in my head. In the ticking of the sleet on the window. But most of it, in what he has set lose in me. Isa, the Mainland, Dad's words, Mum's silence. It's as if I'm feeling it all for the first time. And I'm scared stiff.

Friday morning, I have to drag myself out of my bed. Today I've got a meeting with Collingwood. With Max.

Nikki immediately notices that something's the matter with me. In the first break, we sit talking together as usual.

'What are you looking at?'

'Hm?'

Only when she mentions it do I realize that I'm sitting there looking at him.

'Oh, nothing," I say quickly.

She looks at me as if to say "you're not fooling me'. I sigh. *Perhaps I should just tell her. Somebody who doesn't have anything to do with it all.* I turn to her and say: "That boy there. Collingwood wants me to do an assignment with him.'

Nikki turns round.

'That Wet? A bit dark, skinny with a big nose?'

For some reason or other, her description irritates me.

'Max. His name is Max." It's out before I realize it. And immediately the feeling returns, the fear that grabs my throat.

'Hey." Nikki places a hand on my arm.

I don't know what to say.

'I'd be fed up too if I was lumbered with a Wet." I open my mouth, but quickly shut it again. "Come on, it's only a Wet.'

I swallow. I force myself to answer Nikki.

'Yes, you're right. It's only a Wet.'

But it doesn't matter, whatever I tell myself. Once the bell goes and I walk to Collingwood's class, my nerves are jangling. I make sure I'm the last to enter the classroom. I slip into the seat next to Max without looking at him.

Collingwood begins his lecture and I try to keep up. But my thoughts keep wandering. My hand moves involuntarily over the screen, drawing things that calm me down: the swing in the garden, the bench under the pergola, our old dog Sasha. And as I do it, I let Collingwood's song-like voice wash over me. He knows how to tell a story. He's even enjoying it. *Everything'll be all right, Nina.* I repeat it to myself, again and again. *Everything'll be all right.* I stare stoically straight ahead and ignore the rhythm of Max's fingers on his keyboard.

Finally the bell goes. Relieved, I start to gather my things. Collingwood tries to say something above the noise of the scraping chairs about an assignment. I only half listen. I want to get out of here. It'll be on Delta-DOS.

'And it's a joint assignment, boys and girls! Remember, I want to see real team work.'

I look at Max and he looks at me. I'm startled by his rage. He kicks his chair away and walks over to Collingwood. The classroom is as good as empty.

'Sir, I'd like to do this one on my own." He twiddles his thumbs. His backpack falls to the ground with a bump.

Collingwood stays calm. He gathers his things before he says anything.

'I was very happy with your work.'

'Yes, but I..." Max tries. He looks accusingly at me. I know what he wants to say. He did most of the work. "You two complement each other.'

I don't say anything. I'm a coward, as always.

'If both of you can find a different partner, that's fine with me," says Collingwood drily. He knows that'll never happen. I'm the only Dry in the class, and Max always sits on his own. Collingwood's attentive look goes from Max to me.

'Listen, in school as in life, sometimes you have to suck it up and do things that you don't particularly like to do.'

Max opens his mouth to say something. Bright red patches spread over his cheeks and neck. Collingwood holds up his hand.

'You will just have to make the best of the situation, Max. Collingwood sighs and rubs his neck. He likes Max, I realize. Why does he make things so difficult for him? Max says nothing and shakes his head. He picks up his backpack and storms out of the classroom. The silence hangs around us like a heavy cloud. Once again I have the feeling that Collingwood can see inside me, as if he knows who I am.

'Nina?'

'Yes sir?" I blink my eyes.

'You really did good work together.'

I try to smile. "Thank you.'

He is silent, sighs slightly, and leans against his rickety desk. 'Max is a smart boy. Just a bit impetuous.'

I'm not quite sure why he's telling me this. I nod.

'May I go sir?'

He sighs again. 'Yes, you may go.'
And as quickly as possible, I do.

MAX

I can't believe that Collingwood. He's got some nerve. Complement each other? Make the best of things? I'm not like Li, but my brother's right about one thing. Wet is Wet and Dry is Dry. *If you hadn't stuck your nose into things that didn't concern you, you wouldn't be in the shit, Max.*

I walk through the deserted corridors without knowing where I'm going, until I stop in front of the classroom where Nina and I tried to work on the assignment. *My* spot. I go inside, climb onto one of the desks, and take a few deep breaths.

Rot.

I massage my temples with the tips of my fingers. The past few days... the past few days have been shit. Li was off somewhere and Ma had a bad temper because she had to work overtime at the clinic. I had to finish Collingwood's bloody assignment on my own, in addition to all my other homework, just to hear that we "complement each other well." If I hadn't run off...

I look around. Most people wouldn't dare come here. Officially unsafe. Since Pa's death, I often sit here. Tim was fed up with what he called my "going on about a dead man', and when I ended it with Kara, I had nobody to sit with.

I couldn't care less. I prefer being alone.

I jump from the desk and go to the window. Ice crystals are forming the most beautiful patterns. I breathe on the glass and the crystals start to melt. If you blow hard enough, their perfect shapes disappear in less than a second. No more than a drop of water. My eyes wander across the straggling bushes and the tall briar, bare and covered with a thick layer of snow. Not much of a view.

I think of the time Pa wanted to teach us to swim.

Ma was against it. Only later did I realize that she was scared we'd end up like her own pa and ma, drowned when she was just a little girl. Ma wants nothing to do with the water. A Wet. As if that's possible. Pa insisted that we learn to swim. He took us to a stretch of still water behind the dyke, which was connected via a lock to the Submerged Territories. In the summer, there were always swimmers there, even though it looked more like a swamp than a swimming-pool. Pa had endless patience with us.

'Yes, keep your head up, Max!'

'Breathe in through your nose and out through your mouth.'

'Well done, son! You're getting the hang of it.'

And every time: "Liam, leave your brother alone!'

Li always wanted to climb the dyke, to get to the water on the other side, and he constantly dared me to go with him. And of course I did it that time. Pa knew nothing about it, otherwise he'd have freaked out on us.

I slid down the dyke on my backside until my feet touched the surface of the water. Salty spray splashed up. It was still cold, early in spring. I forced myself to take step after step until I felt the tide, fell forward, and swam.

'Better start getting your Points together, Li!" I shouted to my brother. "You'll have to pay up!'

He couldn't have that. A few seconds later, he grabbed me by my legs.

We swam a long way along the dyke. Then we floated on

our backs for awhile. Goosebump covered my body but I didn't want to be the one to get out of the water first.

'Hey, Max," said Li suddenly.

'What?'

'What do you think's out there?'

'Out where?'

He pointed to the west.

'Water.'

'Duh." He ducked me under.

I came up spluttering. "Hey!'

'Seriously, man. What do you think's out there? Could we reach it?'

'Not without a waterboard, a million Points, and a valid ID card.'

He sniffed.

'You think you'll never get away from here?'

I wanted to shrug my shoulders, but that didn't have much effect in the water. I shivered with cold.

'I don't know what I want. Or, well, I just want...'

'Just want what?'

'I don't know, Li.'

He didn't say anything. We floated a little further. The sky grew overcast. My teeth began to chatter.

'I know what I want," he said suddenly. But before I could ask him what, he swam with powerful strokes to the dyke and heaved himself onto the bank.

I look at the ice drops that follow the cracks in the window. Water. Does Li still know what he wants? Do I know what I want? I kick an old sofa. The sound seems dull in the musty room.

I pick up my bag and leave the classroom.

NINA

'Hey, Nina! Over here!'

Nikki waves. Benjamin gives me a broad grin and Cynthia moves her chair to make room.

'You should hear what happened to Benjamin yesterday," says Nikki as soon as I sit down. Her words don't really get through to me, but I laugh or smile at the right moments and say "Really?" or "Cool!" when called for.

But it's the words of Max and Collingwood that keep popping up in my mind.

'Doesn't it matter to you how we all ended up in this fucking mess?'

'You two complement each other.'

'What else can you expect from a Dry?'

'Max is a smart boy. Just a bit impetuous.'

'What else can you expect from a Dry?'

What else can you expect...?

Nikki gives me a nudge.

'Is that the Wet who...?'

I look up and see Max sitting down at his table. He does his best to ignore me, to ignore everyone. I nod.

'If I were you, I'd stay away from him.'

I look at her.

'He's got a bit of a reputation, you know?'

'What do you mean?" My voice sounds hoarse.

Nikki moves closer and whispers in my ear. I feel her excitement. For her, this is some game or other.

'He's got a brother who got kicked out of school. And do you see how he lost it last week?" I don't say anything. But Nikki doesn't need any encouragement. "He and those other guys have gone at each other before, they say. They have to report to Davenport almost every week.'

Nikki lets her gaze wander over the Wets, until she gets to three boys who are making a heck of a noise. One of them, Damian I think, is balancing a can on his forehead and the others are trying to knock it off.

'Hey, don't worry about it. We'll be out of here before long." Nikki's big grey eyes are so friendly. She reminds me of Isa.

I smile.

'Why don't you come out with us this weekend? We're going see the new digifilm about General Zandt.'

Benjamin turns round and joins in the conversation. He really is a Mainland boy, with his perfect, neat haircut. He reminds me of Johan, Isa's boyfriend.

'You've really got to see it! Right, Cynthia?'

'Eh? What?" She takes her headphones off and scrolls rapidly over the screen of her TonePlayer.

'I don't know whether..." I start to say.

Nikki interrupts me. "Oh come on! I don't think you've been out for ages.'

I smile again and shake my head.

'We don't bite," says Benjamin. Cynthia is about to chime in too, so I quickly nod.

'Okay then.'

Nikki claps her hands.

'Perfect! We can discuss time and place and so on via DOS, okay? And I think I'll have to convince my father. Since the attacks, it's like he wants to keep me on a leash!" She rolls her eyes and the others laugh. Cynthia nods vigorously and says her mother's been exactly the same way. Then they start in on some discussion about the relative hotness of all the actors in the film.

Again my mind wanders. Those thoughts again. And I again, the voice I hear most is his.

What else can you expect...

MAX

I stare at myself in the mirror.

Yellow mouth, crooked nose and a new scar right through my eyebrow. My hair is now so long that I have to tie it back in a ponytail.

'Admiring yourself, little brother?'

Li comes in, buck naked, and takes a towel from the cabinet below the sink. I wish he'd stop calling me "little brother'. It's beginning to get on my nerves.

I turn on the tap and hold my head under the water.

It's Sunday and Ma is on the weekend shift. Li and I are on our own at home. I have no idea how late he got in last night. I fell asleep over my HC and only woke up when I heard him snoring, one leg out of bed.

'Yo! Don't you dare turn on the hot water!" shouts Li from behind the shower curtain.

As I leave the bathroom, I turn it on, full blast.

I pay for that, because Li swears and runs after me. It's good that we live on the seventh floor, otherwise everybody would be admiring a Wet willie. Not that there's much to admire, of course.

I flop down on the settee with a sandwich and drink some tea. DOS is on as usual. Li sits down next to me, towel around his waist, his head even Wetter than normal.

'A couple of the guys will be dropping in this afternoon," he says casually.

I shrug.

'Ma won't be back until late.'

I turn to face him.

'And?'

'And you've something better to do than lay around on the settee all day.'

'Have I?'

'You have today.'

He looks at me. It's dead quiet. Then I raise my hands and say: "Fine. I'll get out of your way, Li.'

He grins and pats me on the back.

'Thanks, Max.'

I try not to be astonished at the fact that he not only thanks me, but actually calls me by my name.

We watch some Dry film or other while we chew at our sandwiches. It's a poor imitation of what you can see in the digiscopes. The Wet villain is too ridiculous to be believable and the Dry again saves the world. It feels the same as when Pa was alive. Ma was driven crazy by the remarks we threw at the actors.

'How long do you think he's been Dry?" I ask, as the Dry hero tries to pick up an ever Drier girl.

'Just as long as it takes a Dry to become Wet." Li's eyes glisten. "Years and years.'

We both laugh out loud.

'Time to Wet your whistle..." says Li as the Dry hero drinks some beer.

'... Here's a brother of the Wet persuasion!" I add, and we toast each other with our tea mugs.

When, after an hour and half, the Dry hero finally realizes which WEtTO has cheated him, we shout in chorus: "He's been hung out to Dry!"

As soon as the film's over, the Morris brotherly love comes to an end. Li disappears into the bathroom to get dressed and when he returns, he doesn't need to say anything. His raised eyebrow says enough.

'I'm going, I'm going." I want to go for a run, but one look outside changes my mind. I grab my jacket from the coat rack and let the door close behind me.

It's bleak outside. The wind pulls impatiently at my clothes and the drizzle turns into a shower. I pass the playground with its broken slide and see-saws. I walk quickly, avoiding the big puddles. I only see her when she's right under my nose.

'Hi, Max.'

Kara is standing under a shelter, smoking. She's stamping up and down to keep warm. I remember how her Ma doesn't want her smoking inside.

'Hi Kara." I go to walk on, but she stops me.

'You really got the better of your brother last week."

I stop. I know what she's thinking. When I was still going with Kara, I was always on about Li. How I really wanted to get the better of him.

'Here." She holds out a cigarette. I hesitate.

What the fuck, Max.

Our faces are close together as she lights my cigarette from hers. I smell the familiar scent: smoke mixed with cheap soap. Her short blond hair tickles my neck. She keeps her face next to mine for just a beat too long.

'Thanks." I inhale deeply.

'So, how are you? Still planning to be the new Governor?" She's playing with me, like she always did.

'Ha ha, Kara."

She laughs and shakes her head.

'Always a short fuse, those Morris brothers."

She takes a step closer. I feel the inviting warmth of her soft body. I inhale and slowly blow out the smoke.

'Hey, Max..." She places the hand holding the cigarette on my shoulder. "If you like, we can go upstairs..." She nods towards the hallway.

I see it all before me again. Kara's house, Kara's room, Kara's bed.

Not much needed to get movement down there.

She kisses me. I kiss her back. I grab her ass and pull her to me.

Nina.

I pull away from Kara.

'What? What's the matter?"

She tries to grab my hand. I take a step backwards. "If you think Bart'll be angry..."

I shake my head. Who the fuck is Bart?

Nina. Why did I see Nina?

'I broke up with him, Max. I..."

'Kara, sorry, I've got to be going."

'But..."

I take another step backwards.

'Thanks for the smoke." I hold up the cigarette.

'But Max!" she calls.

'Sorry!"

I start to run. I take one more drag and then throw the butt away. I blow out the smoke. I blow and blow until there's no breath left in me. But Nina still doesn't disappear from my head.

NINA

On Saturday I go to the digifilm with Benjamin, Nikki, and Cynthia. It is easy to lose myself in the simple all's-well-that-ends-well story. After the film, I talk about the story and actors with almost as much enthusiasm as my new friends do. I spend all Sunday enjoying that strange, light feeling that tells me that everything can be the way it used to be. Until I have to go to school on Monday.

Max seems to be doing his best to ignore me even more than he did last week. During class, he intentionally pushes his chair to one side, and then sits with his back towards me. When our hands accidentally touch, he pulls back, as if I'm contagious.

What else can you expect...?

At the end of the week, Collingwood reminds the class that the joint assignment has to be finished in two weeks. Perhaps it's my imagination, but as he talks, it seems as if he's looking straight at me.

'In two weeks!" he says again, and then nods. He knows more. That thought hits me again.

I spend my breaks with the other Dries. We talk about homework, who does what with whom, and other empty gossip. Nikki can't stop talking about the party she's throwing on the weekend. I'm invited, but I say I can't go. During my classes, I generally fill the endless hours by drawing on my HC or staring out of the window. And at home, I shut myself up in my room, just like Mum, just like Dad

When I wake up on Saturday morning, I can hardly believe another week has gone by. At school, time passes so slowly. Minutes last hours, hours seem like days. It's the routine, that feeling of uselessness, the endless repetition of the same thing. I thought everything would be better when I went to school again; the feeling, or rather the non-feeling of the past six months. My DOS box is full of messages and photos of happy, dancing, drunk people. Nikki's party. There's also a message from Cynthia about the Mainland. They're planning to build the school on a new site. I can't look at it for long.

Instead of doing my homework like a good little girl, I pick up my digipen and HC and go outside. It's quiet. Snow has again covered the grass, and the trees are bending under their heavy white burden. The cold gets into everything. In a strange way, it feels good, that feeling that says: you can't avoid me.

I draw the ice crystals that are like mosaics against the windows.

I draw Maria behind the kitchen window, her hands covered in dough.

I draw a robin, an almost perfect round ball that hops from twig to twig.

When I am so cold that my fingers can't do what I ask of them, I go back inside and continue drawing.

The fruit bowl on the kitchen table.

The upstairs hallway with closed doors.

A dim room filled with old things, where a watery sun shines.

I stop and stare at my last drawing.

I'm sitting in what was once our old playroom. Everything is neatly stored away in boxes and cupboards. Only Isa's big teddy bear is sitting alone on the swing near the window. In a corner of my drawing, I recognize what I was planning to draw. But what I'm holding in my hands isn't this place. It's the room where Max took me to do the assignment.

I trace the drawing with my finger: the piled up furniture, the old chairs and desks, the cobwebs in the corners of the ceiling, the mildew in the window frames, the dusty skeleton. The odor of decay suddenly wells up in me, just as bad now as it was then.

I erase the drawing.

I feel myself blush. As if I've seen something I shouldn't have. The empty screen looks accusingly at me. I pick up my digipen from the cupboard and want to break through the emptiness. Something stops me. And I suddenly ask myself whether I really know what that is.

MAX

Monday.

The bells goes for the end of the last lesson. I slowly pick up my bag and drop my HC for the umpteenth time.

I can't get her out of my head. A Dry! Are you mad? If Li knew that I had a thing for a Dry, he'd beat the hell out of me. And he'd be right as well. Kara has tried to phone me. I've ignored her. The bitter aftertaste of the cigarette stayed with me for the rest of Sunday.

My brain must be so fucking dried out that I don't look where I'm going.

'Morris.'

Damian. Lars and Tim are standing behind him.

'I've no time for your bullshit right now, Damian," I say as calmly as possible. I quickly look round. Nobody. I'm alone.

'You broke the rules," he says, unperturbed. "And what do we do with somebody who breaks the rules?"

Tim grins.

'We punish them."

Just look at him being all tough, the filthy prick.

Knot.

'I told you I hadn't finished with you." It isn't difficult to guess what Damian is imagining. His fist against my head. I think of Ma. Angry again. Concerned again.

Knot.

Then I hear footsteps. Squeaky shoes and a soft voice.

'Everything all right, boys?"

Collingwood.

I sigh with relief. I'm not scared of the bastards, but I can really do without any extra problems. Damian's disappointment clearly shows. I'm not much of an actor, but he's not one at all.

'Yes sir, everything's fine," I say quickly.

Collingwood stops and looks at us for a moment. He says nothing. Just looks.

'Sir?"

'Yes, Max?"

'I have to be going."

'Okay, Max. Off you go."

He doesn't have to say it twice. I sprint off. I know I haven't got much time. I run, pushing people aside, trying to get outside as quickly as possible. I only see her when it's too late to stop.

'Ouch! Can't you watch where..."

'Nina!"

'Max?"

'Sorry, sorry, I..."

'What?"

'I've got to go. Damian..."

'The guy who looks as if he slaughters rabbits in his spare time?"

Despite the tension, I have to laugh.

'Yes, him... He..." My breath won't calm down.

'What? Is he after you?"

I nod.

She thinks for half a second. Then she pulls me with her. "Quick," she hisses.

We push through the crowd, ignoring the insults shouted at us as we band into people, and run out to the back of the school building. Outside it's fucking icy and Nina almost goes head first, but I grab her arm and pull her up.

'There!"

I'm stupid enough to look round and see a furious Damian, followed closely by his goons.

We're never going to make it.

Suddenly Nina pulls me to the right. We disappear among the bushes and a second later, we've left the school ground. She knows exactly where she's going.

'Just a bit further," she pants. "It's not far."

She turns the corner, behind the school building. In the distance I see a car with tinted glass.

Blowers have cars, flashes through my mind. Dries have cars.

I turn round again. I can't see Damian and the others, but I can hear their voices. Damian's sweating and panting, Lars's hyena laugh, and Tim's heavy footsteps.

Nina begins to gesture. I can't see anybody, just the car.

Suddenly the car starts moving. Drives towards us.

My legs refuse to move. I shake my head, back and forth, back and forth, from the car to Damian, who has just turned the corner, and back again.

'Come on, Max!" shouts Nina.

I don't know what to do. I don't know.

'Do you really want to be beaten up again?"

I want to say that I can take on those three, but then I see Ma in front of me. Ma looking at me with my umpteenth black eye and shaking her head. And I run after Nina.

Somebody opens the door from the inside. Nina jumps

into the car and pulls me in after her — were we holding hands all that time? I tumble into the back seat, hear a click, and realize I can't get out. The car starts without a sound and before I know it, we're driving off along the street, leaving Damian, Lars, and Tim behin, cursing.

Fuck.

I've never been in a car. It's warm in here, and smells of expensive leather and detergents. I hardly dare place my Wet hands on the seat.

'Are you okay?"

Nina touches me. I flinch away.

'I'm okay," I answer brusquely.

Through the Plexiglas window, I see the driver in front. A driver! Is she brought to school and picked up every day? *Easy, Max.*

'Erik can drive you home, if you want."

Erik. That Erik's a Wader. Always on the lookout so that the water doesn't surprise him and give him wet feet.

She keeps on brushing a lock of hair behind her ear. With her other hand she fiddles with the golden locket. Home... Damian, Nina, a car, a driver. Too many images, too many thoughts. *Keep calm, man!*

'Yes, that would be great," I say slowly.

She looks at me expectantly.

'Where do you live?"

'Oh, uh, yes... District Seven, block c, number 589."

'Erik?"

Man, she gives orders as if she's the Governor! I'm covered in sweat.

'Understood," comes through the intercom.

I don't know what to say. I don't know if I should say anything.

I stare outside, making sure my hands don't touch anything. There's a damp patch where my thumb touched the leather. We drive through District Four, Five, Six, ever farther from the center of the Region, away from the safe walls of the Closed Communities. Some low buildings are still standing here and there. Their foundations have had to be strengthened because they are under constant attack from corrosion. In the distance, I see the tall flats looming up.

I look to the side. She's staring outside, just like me. What is she seeing? What is she thinking? Why do I want to know what she's thinking?

The closer we get to my home, the worse the roads become. Cars only come here if there's something wrong. That's often the case, but then it's always the reds on the warpath, never Dry girls with personal drivers coming to drop off a Wet classmate.

Please don't let Li be at home.

'Let me off here.'

'What? Why? It really isn't any bother...'' protests Nina.

'I prefer to walk the last bit," I cut her off.

Nina falls silent. She presses a button and my door swings open. "See you tomorrow?"

What should I say to her?

'I guess.''

I get out. The door closes automatically behind me. The car starts moving then accelerates rapidly. I can't see her through the tinted glass. I turn round and run the last bit home.

NINA

He runs like a wild animal, with big strides, natural and graceful. My hands itch to draw him. The moving figure gets smaller and smaller, until I can't pick him out anymore in the shadowy neighborhood.

Adrenaline is still racing through my body, a mix of fear and excitement.

I think of how I dragged him along, his hand in mine. About how we nearly fell and how he looked when he saw the car. I think of what could have happened if I hadn't been there, precisely at that moment.

I look outside.

Half-collapsed and waterlogged buildings stand alongside hastily constructed emergency dwellings. Tree roots break up the tiles on the pavement, like snakes creeping out of their holes. People walk quickly, zigzagging, hands in pockets and shoulders hunched against the biting wind. The road too is uneven and full of holes, so that the single courageous cyclist fighting the elements finds it hard to ride in a straight line. Only the streetcar lane is in reasonable repair. And above all this tower the flats of District Six and Seven. Big grey concrete blocks, with strange patterns of peeling paint on the walls. Row upon row, the small windows neatly in line. Not a single flat has a balcony. One of them is where Max lives.

Didn't he want me to see where he lives? For the first time, I feel uncomfortable that nobody knows who I really am.

That he doesn't know. Yes, a Dry, but not just any Dry.

'Home?"

Erik has turned to face me.

'Nina?"

I nod quickly.

'Yes, home. And Erik..."

'Hmm?"

'Thanks."

Before Erik can reply, he's interrupted by a panicky voice. For a second I think there's someone inside, but then I realize that DOS is always on in Dad's cars. On the small screen, I see a confused woman talking to a reporter, while a large black cloud looms in the background. She gestures towards the cloud and tries to explain something, but is drowned out by the sound of sirens. An attack has taken place on CC2.

First the food bank, and now this. They robbed a shopping center and then burnt it to the ground.

They. WEtTO. Wets.

There were no deaths, but the porter was slightly injured when he tried to reach the disconnected fire-fighting system. Apparently it was just after closing time. They show more images. Before and after. I start when I recognize the place. Isa and I used to go there a lot, sometimes with other friends, generally together. We would hang out in one of the cafés or parade along the shops in hopes of being noticed. Isa met Johan there. Now a fire is blazing eagerly in the sky.

Erik turns off the sound.

I welcome the silence like an old friend. I turn my head away and wait until we drive through the gates to CC1.

MAX

Whenever I run, I promise myself I won't ever fight again. Running gives you a kick that's ten times, no, a hundred times better than fighting. Different than fighting. And it does what fighting never does: I finally shut up inside.

It was as if I voluntarily entered the lions' den. Jeez, she was so easy with that Wader. As if it were the most normal thing in the world. Perhaps I should have let her take me home.

When I get to our flat, I don't see Li. His mates are also noticeable by their absence. Odd. Generally they hang around here at this time; when they've finally dragged their lazy butts out of bed or have gotten back from wherever. Li's really impossible to be around then — he thinks he's oh-so-important.

I run up the stairs, counting the one hundred and forty steps. I put my key in the lock, open the door, and walk into the cold, bare hall. I see Ma's silhouette in the doorway to the living room. She's just standing there. All those thoughts from a moment ago are suddenly unimportant.

'Ma?"

I run over to her and take hold of her. She clamps onto me and stares at me with red eyes. Has she been crying? I can't imagine it.

'Li," she says.

'What? What's the matter with Li?"

Knot.

What has the prick done this time?

I hear a familiar voice. Bradshaw. DOS. I go past Ma into the living-room and look at the old screen, with the picture that always flickers. I look at Ma, then at the screen and then at Ma again.

'There's been an attack in CC2,' she says. She fiddles with the hem of her blouse. "They robbed a shopping center and then set it on fire. People have been arrested.'

They? WEtTO? Li?

Bradshaw is speaking. "We have been able to apprehend a number of the perpetrators. Two are still on the loose, but we have strong indications as to their identity." I'm startled when I see Ramon's face, followed by a few guys I don't know.

I sigh with relief. Not Li. Not my retard prick of a brother. But as the relief begins to subside, the knot comes back again.

"Where is he?"

"I don't know, son." Ma shrugs her shoulders, drops them again. I have never seen her so lost. Not even after Pa's death.

"Can't we do anything...?"

"No. Nothing. If we start asking questions, they'll only get suspicious of him."

Ma's right. If he's picked up, they'll let us know.

I stare at Bradshaw and hear his threatening words, see the faces of Ramon and the others appear again and again. WEtTO has robbed a shopping center. *Then it'll be busy on the black market in a few days*; the thought flashes through my mind. Everybody will want their share of the loot.

Ma explodes without any warning.

"Why can't that boy just keep his head down?" She wants

to hit something, I see it in her eyes, in the way she's standing. I not her son for nothing.

"Ma, don't do it."

"Max ...!"

I take her hand. She's shaking. Pa may have let his fists fly, but when Ma is angry...

"Mama, please!"

"Max," she says again, softer. I drop her arm. "Liam," she murmurs. "Oh my stupid boy." And then she really cries.

I don't know what to do. Ma never cries. She never bloody cries!

I carefully reach out my hand and place it on Ma's head. "Come on." I take her to her room and help her into bed. She lets it all happen. When I want to leave, she grabs my hand.

"Stay." Her eyes bore into mine. "You'll stay with me, won't you, Max?"

Her long nails cut into my skin, she's holding me so tight.

"I'm here, Ma. I'm staying with you."

A shadow of a smile appears on her tear-stained face.

"You're a good boy," she murmurs. "A good boy."

She doesn't let me go. Only when her breathing is calmer and the sobbing has stopped, when she's asleep, only then can I free myself from her iron grip.

I creep to my own room, scared that she'll wake up. Li's mess welcomes me. A pair of trousers on the ground, sneakers you always fall over, dirty sock on and under the desk.

Prick. Bastard. Bloody brother. I hate you.

I creep into bed with my clothes stilll on and pull the blankets over me. My eyes prickle and I push the balls of my hands against my eyes until I see dots.

It takes hours before I fall asleep.

***

Somebody turns on the light. I wake with a start. It's still dark outside. Li is trying to climb into his bed.

"Liam!"

I grab him.

"Hey! What's the matter? Let go of me, man!"

I let go. Relief gives way to anger.

"Where were you, prick?"

"Out."

"Ma knows, Li."

"Ma knows what?" His eyes grow large and he curses.

"Do you really think you can hide something like this from her?"

"What did you say to her?" He wants to grab me, but I'm faster and jump out of bed. I glare at him defiantly.

"I haven't said anything and you know that. Ma isn't stupid. We thought they'd got you and him both!"

"What? Who?"

He acts surprised. As if he doesn't know what I'm talking about. "Ramon."

"What about Ramon?"

I look round and see Li's HC on the desk. DOS-news is still dominated by the attack. I push the screen under his nose.

"Shit." He scrolls down to the latest news about the attack. Stares at Ramon's photo. "Shit," he says again.

"Liam?"

Ma.

She's in the doorway. She's only half awake.

"Ma, I..." Liam begins.

She walks to Liam, grabs him and hugs him, lets go of

94

him again and looks past him. She's going to hit Li, I thought. Just like she hit me. But no, she does nothing, her hands hang down her side. A tear dribbles over her cheek. She quickly wipes it away.

"Were you involved?"

"No, Ma, I swear. Ramon..." Li shakes his head, as if swallowing his words. "But I wasn't Ma. I swear it."

Ma doesn't move, she's so strangely quiet.

"So if they come here, you don't know anything."

"No, I don't know anything."

She stares at him.

"I mean it, Liam. You know nothing if they come here. I don't want you bringing that into my house."

He casts down his eyes. Is he ashamed? Or doesn't he want Ma to look into him.

"I don't know anything."

"Then it's fine."

She looks one final time from me to Liam and back again. Without saying a word, she leaves the room.

NINA

Maria is sitting with Mum in the kitchen when I come home.

"Hey."

Mum looks up and smiles. Maria comes over to me and gives me a hug.

I don't need to ask where Dad is. I see him gesturing wildly on the screen in the corner. His face is red and he's clearly worked up. His eyes glisten. As always, Felix is standing five feet behind him, his handsome face inscrutable.

"So he won't be home for dinner?"

Mum knows immediately what I mean. "They've picked up a few but the rest are still on the run." She sounds worried. "Your father went to the Regional Hall immediately once Felix gave him the news.

"Oh."

I walk to the stove and sneak a taste of the pasta sauce Maria is making.

"Watch it, Miss!"

She puts her hands on her hips and I smile.

"It's delicious, Maria."

Maria shakes her head, laughing, and drains the spaghetti. Mum gets up and sets the table. We always eat in the kitchen when there's just the two of us. The DOS screen is showing blurry photos of two young men. One is dark and has long dreadlocks, the other is short, with fair, crew-cut hair. They're so young. They can't be much older than me. I hear

Dad ask the viewers to contact the Dry Defenders Switchboard immediately in District Seven if they recognize any of these "cowardly perpetrators."

Maria dishes up.

"Is school working out all right?" asks Mum after a few mouthfuls. She plays with her food

She means: are you being bullied and are you doing your homework? "There are some other Dries," I say.

The relief can be seen on her face.

"Also from the...?"

She can't say it and I nod quickly. "And from the other CC."

I tell her about Nikki, Benjamin, and Cynthia, about a few teachers, and about the school that is like a maze. Lighthearted things. I see that Mum's attention quickly wanes; she stares at her cold spaghetti as if it's a nest of worms.

"Mum?"

"What, darling?" Her soft voice still sounds the same but her eyes look right through me.

"Nothing." I force a smile. "Never mind, Mum."

She gets up. "I'm going to lie down."

"Okay, Mum."

"Wake me up for tea?"

"I will."

And she disappears from the kitchen.

Maria picks up my plate and puts it in the dishwasher. I get up and help her clear the rest of the table.

"And the boy?" she says.

"Hm?"

"The boy you took with you?"

I take a step backwards. Maria always knows everything.

"How…?"

She produces a HC that only just manages to stay in one piece.

The sides are wrapped in black tape. Max's HC.

"This isn't yours I take it?" Maria smiles mysteriously.

"No, but how do you know it belongs to a boy?"

She turns the thing over and I see his name on the bottom. Of course, every HC is registered.

"Oh yes." I smile sheepishly.

"He's not from here." She means that he's a Wet, just like her.

I don't know what to say. I reach out my hand and Maria does the same. Before she gives me the HC, she takes my hand, holds it for a moment, and looks at me.

"I won't say anything, Nina. But please be careful." I'm not angry. I love Maria. She has always been there. I know she won't say anything.

"I am being careful."

She nods, lets go of my hand, and we fill the dishwasher without exchanging another word.

Upstairs I look at Max's HC. The thing must have fallen out of his bag when we tumbled into the car. And Maria checks the car every day to make sure everything inside is in order. Dad is very particular where his cars are concerned. I turn on the HC, and of course get no further than the start page. Do I want to get any further? I turn it off and set it aside.

I take my own HC, scroll to the Delta College page and search for Max Morris. His personal page is virtually empty; I'm not used to that. On the Mainland, a good page meant everything. Isa and I spent hours on it at the start of each term. After all, everybody can view it. Max looks bored in his mandatory photo. He's only filled in fields that are absolutely required.

I close the page and stare straight ahead. My fingers reached for my digipen, and before I know it, I'm drawing. A coffee-colored face. Drumming fingers. A boy who cannot sit still, who is constantly moving. I draw Max.

MAX

I wake up with a pounding headache. I rub the back of my head and look in amazement at my jeans and sweater.

Everything comes back all at once.

"Li?"

No answer. I throw off the blanket, get out of bed, look up. He's not there.

My eye falls on the window that looks out over the bare square in front of the flat. The playground is deserted. A few miserable trees, planted after the Second Great Flood, creak dangerously in the wind. I push the curtain to one side and see my brother with Julius standing next to him. And someone else. That man in the long overcoat.

Li is gesturing wildly and is walking back and forth like a real Morris: back and forth, back and forth, much to the annoyance of the man. Suddenly he grabs Li and shakes him like a doll. Li, my big brother and the terror of the neighborhood. He's too surprised — too scared? — to do anything about it.

I force myself to keep watching. The man calms Li down and speaks to him. He seems to be explaining something. I see my brother nod while Julius nervously looks around. The man says something else and gives Li a thin packet before he walks away, as cool as can be.

I let the curtain fall back into place. Behind me I hear the shuffling of slippers.

"Ma?" I turn round. "Did you see...?"

"Yes."

She hugs herself, her eyes still red. She just stands there, while Li is throwing away his life and putting us in danger. What's she thinking? Why the fuck doesn't she do something?

I think back to the time when Li finally got kicked out of school. Ma was furious. Li had been in a fight and broken somebody's arm. Pa wanted to go to Davenport. He thought it was ridiculous.

"Always that damned Dry prejudice!" Pa had shouted.

"He brought it on himself, Rob," answered Ma.

"Brought it on himself? Brought it on himself? Damn it, Yvonne! He's just a boy! Boys fight." Pa paced back and forth in our small kitchen. A kitchen cabinet was thrown shut with a crash. Li and I sat together on the settee in the living-room.

"Liam should have kept his hands to himself. You know that." Li and I looked at each other.

"Shit," whispered Li.

"Fuck," I replied.

Pa cleared his throat, the way he always did when he was angry, and Ma tapped the counter nervously. We were all waiting for the explosion. When it came, it was still unexpected.

"You know what that is, Yvonne?" said Pa softly. "Well?"

Silence.

"Well?"

Scraping, a chair pushed aside and a sigh from ma.

"Well, Robert?" Ma never called Pa by his full name, never ever.

"That's betraying your own." Pa tapped his chest. "Your own!"

And then came the blow. A slap against his cheek. We saw that when he came home, deep in the night. For Pa had stormed out, snorting with rage. He had thrown the door shut behind him with such force that one of the windows broke.

I turn away from the window overlooking the park towards Ma.

"Are you just going to keep letting Li do what he wants?" I say the words softly. I can't hide my disappointment, nor my anger.

"Max, calm down."

"I am calm." Knot.

Ma comes over to me and places a hand on my shaking arm. "Li wants... Li does it, because..." She stares outside. What does she see? She's like she was when Pa died. A Wet wrung out to the very bone.

"Li does it because...?" I repeat, impatiently.

"He does it because he thinks he can make a difference. Change the world."

"He does it because he's fucking angry and wants revenge," I throw back at her.

"Perhaps you can't separate the one from the other."

Ma walks over to the window. Is she looking at Liam, the lost son?

Or does she see something else? I simply don't get why she's not angry with him anymore. Why she's so damned weak.

"It's Liam's choice, Max. I want to do everything to stop him, to keep him at home, but it's still his choice." Her rough working fingers rub over her light pink dressing gown. She's still hugging herself. "I don't want this, just like you, Max, not in this way. But he's still my son. So if they pay us a visit, he must be strong. And so must we."

She turns round.

"Right?"

I say the only thing I can say.

"Right."

NINA

He's not in the quad when I arrive.

"*See you tomorrow?*" *I'd asked.*

"*Yes, tomorrow,*" *he'd replied.*

Tomorrow is today. Where is he? Should I have...?

Nikki walks over to me and I can see from her the look in her eyes that I won't be able to avoid a chat. She takes me to the lockers, where she sits me down on a bench.

"And?"

She's standing in front of me. She's put up her red hair in multi-colored ribbons. Her red lipstick contrasts with her pale skin.

"And what?"

"That Wet! Everybody's talking about it!"

"About what?"

I'm so distracted looking for Max, I barely register what she's asking me. Nikki rolls her eyes.

"That you just ran out of school with a Wet, while being chased by a bunch of morons!"

"Oh, that."

"Yes, that."

I decide that a half-truth is the best strategy.

"Okay." I take a deep breath. "I have to do this assignment with him. And, and... then these boys appeared out of nowhere and I lost it. I knew that Erik was waiting round the corner for me and when Max said that the boys wanted to beat him up... Well, I don't think that anybody, not even a Wet, deserves to be beaten up for nothing." I exhale. Does she believe me?

Nikki tilts her head to one side and purses her lips.

"Okay... I, well, I wouldn't have had the guts for that."

I laugh.

"Guts had nothing to do with it. It was just self-preservation."

"You're a strange one, Nina Baker."

I shrug my shoulders.

"If I were you, I'd watch it."

I open my mouth, then think better of it.

She stares at me for a moment. Then she turns round and walks away.

***

I get to the classroom early, even Collingwood hasn't arrived yet. I put Max's HC on his desk. I hope he doesn't think I've broken in. If he comes. The rest of the class starts to trickle in, and now and then I look to see whether he's among them.

He's not. Did they get him after all?

Collingwood starts the lesson. I only half follow what he's saying, and look out over the grey school quad. Most of the snow has since disappeared. Each time I see someone crossing it, I think it's Max.

He must be ill.

I haven't got him into trouble, have I?

I turn round and see Damian and Tim sitting at their desks. Damian immediately notices that I'm looking and slowly licks his lips with his tongue. You don't have to explain what that means, even to me. I quickly lower my eyes and hear them snigger.

"Something funny, Mr. Baak?"

Collingwood sees everything.

"No sir."

"Otherwise I would like to hear it." Collingwood raises his eyebrows.

"Yes sir."

When the bells goes, I slowly pack my bag. The HC is still on the table next to me. This is the only lesson Max and I have together. What should I do?

"Nina?"

Collingwood is standing next to me. He looks normal. Not like a teacher. But what do I know of Wet teachers?

"Yes sir?"

"Is that Max's HC?"

I nod. "We were working on your assignment together and... and then Max forgot to take it with him." I'm getting better at thinking up half truths.

"Hm."

"Do you know where he is?" It's out before I realize it.

"Max?" He looks genuinely surprised. "At home, I assume. He reported in sick this morning."

I can't suppress a sigh of relief. Sick. Only sick. He didn't stay at home because of me.

"Something wrong, Nina?"

"No, nothing sir."

"Shall I look after Max's HC for him?"

I glance at the screen that's still on the table. It's the easiest solution. It's not my responsibility.

"I'll drop it off for him," I hear myself say.

Collingwood smiles. His light blue eyes shine and he suddenly looks years younger. "That would be great, Nina. You know where he lives?"

I nod.

"Good."

He walks back to the front of the class as I slip Max's HC into my bag.

MAX

They arrive two hours later, when it's too late to go to school. I report in sick. A dark-grey car drives along the bumpy road between blocks B and C, tinted windows, snow chains still around the tires.

Li stares at the car. His mouth is pursed into a straight dash. Ma is sitting on the settee, her eyes closed and a mug of tea in her hands. When the bell goes, I open the door as if we'd agreed to do it this way.

Two Dry men in suits are standing at the door. Not Blowers. *Why aren't they Blowers?* One of them, small and almost completely bald, has an earpiece in and is rounding up a conversation, while the other, not much older than Li and me, looks past me down the hall.

"Is this the house of Liam Morris?" A soft voice, so sweet it makes you gag.

I nod.

His eyebrows are light, almost invisible. It makes his face look naked. His blond curls were each so perfectly in place that he must have treated them one by one with gel. His clothing is expensive and Dry. I have a vague idea I've seen him somewhere. And his voice...

"We want to ask him a few questions."

I'm just about to ask the man for identification when I hear a voice behind me: "I'm Liam Morris."

The man smiles and nods. He takes a step inside and I move aside, almost as a matter of course. The other follows close behind. "Come in," says Li. He throws me a glance and I know what he wants to say: leave this to me. I've got everything under control.

Of course, Li.

The blond man disappears into the kitchen after Li and the other Dry takes up his position near the door. Our kitchen is suddenly off limits and if this wasn't so fucking serious, I would've laughed.

Ma is still sitting on the settee. She doesn't say anything, stares straight ahead, fiddles with a lock of hair. She is nervous.

First I sit next to Ma, my elbows on my knees, my head in my hands. I nearly go crazy from the near silence. From her irregular breathing, from the tears behind it, from the uncertainty. From the voices that sound through the flimsy walls but which you can never quite understand. It lasts for hours. Or does it only seem like that?

I get up and pace back and forth. I go to the window and stare outside. At the ponderous sky, from which wet snow is falling, at the hail clattering on the concrete ground. The sand in the sandpit explodes in puffs. I tap the window with my fingers and trace the drops running down the outside. I hum something that comes into my head.

Suddenly Li is in the room. His pupils are large and his left hand is trembling. But at the same time he has a look about him I've never seen before. As if only now he really knows what he wants and how to get it. I only realize he's saying something when he places his hand on my shoulder.

"Max?"

I look at my brother.

"They want to ask you some questions."

I look past my brother, see the blond one standing behind him. When the man notices me looking, he smiles. A smile that knocks me right off balance, more effectively than any Dry word you can think of. Again, I could swear I've seen him somewhere before. I get up.

"Okay."

I rub my hands over my jeans. Li pats me on the back and Ma nods at me.

The blond Dry walks off into the kitchen as if he's been visiting us for years. But I've been here on earth long enough to know from his careful tread and the effort he makes not to touch anything just what he really thinks of us.

"Sit down, Max."

He pushes back a chair for me. I stare at it and sit down. He wipes his hands on a handkerchief which he then neatly folds up and returns to his trouser pocket. He sits down opposite me and immediately cuts to the chase.

"Where was your brother on Wednesday night?"

Ma has drilled us well and I answer immediately.

"At home."

"At home," he repeats. He looks at me with his piercing light blue eyes. Something's going on. Of course something's going on.

I nod.

He smiles again, pulls his chair closer to the kitchen table, and holds out his hands, palms up, towards me.

"Max," he begins, "I'm not after you or your brother."

He licks his Dry lips.

"But some serious things have happened, Max. Boundaries have been breached, ones that shouldn't have been breached." Again he stops.

"Do you understand that, Max?"

He waits until I do something, say something. I'm damned if I'm going to give this guy anything, even though my brother's a prick.

"I know that you understand, Max," he finally says himself. "And I know that you also understand that it is my responsibility to ensure that these boundaries are not breached again."

He carefully folds his hands. Light is reflected from a gold signet ring on his little finger.

"I want you to think very carefully before you answer, Max."

I stare at him. Take in his clean, Dry hands, his Dry head, and his Dry quirks. What's he thinking? That I'm so wet that I can't keep things straight in my mind? That I'm going to sing just for him?

"Li was at home."

He leans back and stretches his arms as if he's just got out of bed. He sighs. His glance catches mine.

I start.

I fucking start from what I read on his oh so calm eyes. Not just the normal repulsion for Wet things, the contempt the Dries always feel because they were accidentally born behind a sixteen-foot high wall, supposedly protected from the water. There's all of that. There's all of that, but there is also something I can't quite place.

Suddenly I see the neighbors' bloody cat, the one that always shits in the sandpit. The time it caught a bird and brought it upstairs. The cat would release the bird time and again, and then, with a quick tap with his paw, would drag it back again. Until all at once it had had enough of the game and bit off the bird's head in one bite.

He's the one in charge here. And I know that he's intentionally showing me that it isn't a mistake or a matter of allowing me to slip out of his control.

I don't have any control.

My legs tremble as if they might walk off all by themselves and I don't where to put my hands. Drops of perspiration run down my spine into my underwear. I can hardly contain myself.

Finally he looks away.

"Thank you, Max," he says and gets up. "That was very enlightening." He smiles. "We'll see ourselves out."

I'm too gob-smacked to say anything back.

When the door slams behind them, Liam swears loudly. I hear his footsteps before I see his angry face. He strides over to me and grabs me by both shoulders.

"What did you say, Max?"

I struggle like a fish on dry ground.

"Well?"

"Nothing, man! Nothing!" I say and shove him off me. "Nothing at all."

He stands there and stares at me. Fuck! Doesn't he believe me or something? I looked past him and see Ma standing in the doorway, her arms crossed.

"Liam, leave him alone."

Li turns round and their glances cross. She doesn't look away. How long has she been standinging there, staring? Then Li shakes his head and walks out of the kitchen. A few minutes later, I hear the door slam shut a second time.

NINA

As I walk out of school after the final lesson of the day, I admit to myself that I'm finally losing my mind.

You're a strange one, Nina Baker. Nikki got very close to the truth... even my name is a lie.

Max's HC is burning a hole in my bag. I know I can't get out of it. But is it can't or won't? It sends a thrill of tension through me, so different from the suffocating emptiness of the last few months. I place a hand on Erik's shoulder as soon as I get into the car.

"Erik?"

I look at him. Erik has been Dad's personal driver since I was little. He has thin, gingery hair, and you can see his patchy skull. He is broad and muscular. How old is Erik? Forty? Fifty? I don't know.

"What's the matter, Nina?"

"Can I ask you another favor?"

He purses his lips.

"I promise you I won't get you into any problems. And strictly speaking I'm not breaking any rules.'

He shifts his mouth as if tasting something and taps on the steering wheel with his index finger. He's got freckles, I suddenly notice. A lot of freckles. On his nose, under his light grey eyes and on his high forehead.

He gives in. "Just this once then. Where do you want to go?"

"District Seven, block c, number 589," I say quickly, before he has time to change his mind. "And... thanks, Erik."

He smiles.

"District Seven, block c, number 589," he repeats. "That boy?"

"Max. He forgot his HC. Yesterday. Left it in the car." I smile apologetically. "He's ill."

"And you're returning his HC."

"Exactly."

"Uh huh."

I don't dare look at him. Fortunately he lets it drop and starts the car.

I stare straight ahead as we drive through the various districts, my eyes fixed on the high, concrete flats in the distance. This time I'll get to see where he lives. Right at the edge of the Region, where I have never been. Because the dyke is behind District Seven. And behind the dyke is the water. I bite my lip.

We pass the spot where Max got out yesterday and drive into District Seven. People stare at us. Children jeer, and some run alongside of the car trying to look inside. The road gets worse and worse. The streetcar lines from the city center stopped a way back, and even cyclists dismount because there are too many holes in the road. Most people don't pay attention to whether they walk on the pavement or in the road. When we drive past the first block, I start taking note of the addresses. Letters are on the sides of the buildings, although they are hardly legible after years of rain and wind.

A...

B ...

C.

Here it is. This has to be the one.

"Erik. Can you let me out here?"

"Are you sure?"

I see the concern on his face, just as it was on Maria's yesterday. I suddenly feel ashamed. That I've never asked him anything about his life. Not really.

"Yes, I'm sure." I smile. "I'll be right back."

"I'll leave the DOS on."

Erik opens the door for me.

It's blowing hard outside. High blocks, flat land, and not a single tree or any other protection. I see a sandpit, where a cat is doing its business. A woman walks past holding the hand of a small child. Is she coming from the deserted playground up ahead? She quickly looks away and roughly drags her inquisitive child with her.

I tighten my scarf, pull my fur-trimmed hood over my head, and start walking. I stay close to the flat, counting the numbers above the double doors into the hallways. His number doesn't appear until the fourth entrance, the last one. I have to open the door myself, just like at Delta College. When I get inside, I automatically head for the elevator.

"You'll have to walk up, sweetie."

I turn round and look straight into Max's eyes. But it isn't Max.

"Sorry?" I stammer.

"The elevator hasn't worked for years. If it ever worked at all."

"Oh."

"There." He points to a corridor.

I look at it and then back to him. A young man, with Max's eyes and Max's hair. No, his is longer and he's wearing it in a tail. And his nose, his nose is different. Is this Max's brother? His cousin? Or am I imagining things?

"Well?"

"Sorry?"

"Aren't you going upstairs?"

"Yes... upstairs."

"Well, go on then."

He takes a step forward and again we stare at each other. I suddenly ask myself how it was possible that I could have thought that this was Max. I quickly set off along the corridor, his laughter following me.

There seems to be no end to the stairs, and I'm panting when I get to the top. Number 589 is on the seventh floor and I can see swampy meadows and gleaming glasshouses from the window in the stairwell. Behind them is the dyke, and behind that the water. You can even see the windmill farms from here. I have to stop and take it all in for a moment. I've never seen the water like this. So real and so immense.

There's no bell on the door, just a nailed board with the number 589. I knock.

At first, I don't hear anything, then a woman's voice calling something incomprehensible, followed by shuffling footsteps. A key is pushed into the lock. The door opens. I take a deep breath.

MAX

"Nina?"

"Hi Max," she says and looks straight down at her shoes.

I had assumed that I was about to get rid of the umpteenth inquisitive neighbor when I answered the knock at the door. Ma has had enough of them. But this time, it isn't a neighbor.

I look down at her. A flurry of thoughts crowd my mind at once.

Did Li see her? What did he say? And what's she doing here, dammit?

I keep my mouth shut and say nothing.

She fiddles in her bright yellow, shiny bag. Bet it's waterproof. Her long curls tumble down over her shoulders and across her... I force myself to look away.

"Here, you left this."

She's holding out my HC. I stare at the thing. My HC? How did she get that? The only thing I've done since last night and this morning is lie on my bed and curse my brother. I didn't even realize I'd lost it.

"In the car," she adds.

I simply nod and take the thing from her. I don't know what to say. I'm still far too flabbergasted to see a Dry, a Dry *girl*, standing at my Wet door.

"Are you feeling better?"

What on earth is she talking about? I stare at her just a bit too long. "You were ill, weren't you?"

Ill... Oh yes. I'm ill. I nod and shrug my shoulders. "Nothing too bad."

"Max?" comes from the passage behind me. Ma. Fuck. Of course now she has to know exactly who's at the door.

"Oh, hello."

I can hear in Ma's voice that she's immediately on her guard, she takes on a sort of defensive posture when she's afraid of being screwed.

Nina blinks. I'll bet she starts studying her shoes again.

But no. She smiles and holds out her hand. Her hand! Even for Ma, that's a first.

"Hello, I'm Nina. Max and I know each other from the Delta College."

Ma looks at me, at Nina and at her outstretched hand. "I've come to return his HC. He left it behind."

Ma is just as bewildered as I am, but she can hide that sort of thing so much better. She nods politely at Nina, ignores her outstretched hand, and turns to me. "Is that right, Max?"

Nina lets her hand fall to her side

"Apparently." *Ma, leave me alone,* I say with a glance. I'm not in the mood for trouble. I've already been interrogated enough today. Not now.

Her eyes become slits in her face and she shakes her head oh so subtly. But then, thank goodness, she turns around and walks off. "You can tell me the story later," she says over her shoulder when she's almost in the living-room. *The cross-examination will take place later* is what she means. I sigh. It's far from over.

"Well, I'll be going then," says Nina. She bites her lip, looks around her.

Suddenly the sun breaks through. For a second, I see

nothing, but as my eyes grow accustomed to the bright light, I see her, Nina. The way she's standing there, against the background I know so well: the grey sky, the graffiti-covered concrete and the rusty railing. It's as if I only now realize that things can be different. I see how the light shines through her, as if she's the fucking light herself. I see how a girl is standing there. A girl! Man, you can't be imagining this. It's real. Look at her. *Look, Max.* I don't want her to leave. I don't want to have to think about Blowers, about Li or about Pa. I want something else. Something better. And I want it now.

"Stay," I say.

"What?"

The sun is reflected in the door's window and shines in her blue, blue eyes. She blinks again

"Perhaps you'd like to stay for a bit?"

"Now?"

I shrug my shoulders, drum on the doorpost with my fingers.

"Um... yeah."

"I..." She chews her lip. "Erik is waiting downstairs."

"Oh."

"But I can tell him that I'm staying a little longer," she adds quickly. "My parents won't notice if I get home a bit later." She types something and then closes her HC.

We stare at each other. She smiles. I smile back. I hold the door open for her.

NINA

I'm inside before I know it.

It's so small. The hall is suffocatingly narrow and low. Max can just about stand up straight, but he has to duck to miss the lamp. There is nothing much hanging on the walls. Here and there, you can even see the bare concrete under the old wallpaper. On the right there's an old wardrobe without doors, with coats hanging in it and shoes sticking out at the bottom. There's the smell of soap, wet laundry and cigarettes. Sounds are coming from a room at the end of the hall.

"That's just Ma. In the living-room," says Max. "You hear everything here."

I quickly nod.

She had his eyes. Or rather, he has her eyes. She was like an open book before her gaze became so suspicious. I was shocked by it. Do they all look at us like that?

Max takes my coat and stuffs it into the cupboard. Only on the third attempt does it stay put.

"Here." He opens the first door on the left.

I walk in ahead of him. A bunk-bed dominates the small room; my room must be easily five times as big as this. Posters and pamphlets about people and things I have never seen are on the walls. Old photos, perhaps of the family, alternate with Wet celebrities and Wet buildings. Under the window, between the bed and a wardrobe, stands a small brown desk. On it, there's a device I don't recognize. Below there are stacks of thin, square plastic cases. Against the other wall there is an old-fashioned brown bookcase, overflowing with paper books.

"Are these all yours?"

Max closes the door behind us. We are on our own in the small room.

"No, not all of them." He shakes his head and looks to one side. "I share this room with my brother."

So the boy downstairs was his brother. And he shares this hole with... "Haven't you got a Reader?" I ask as I trail my finger along the top shelf of books.

Max doesn't answer.

I bite my lip. Of course he hasn't got a Reader. It would cost him far too many Points. But he doesn't say anything.

"The books belonged to my pa. He got them from his pa." He's trying to change the subject.

"Oh." I clam up. Hasn't he got a father? Are his parents divorced? I don't dare to ask because I'm afraid I'll also have to give answers that I can't give.

"Would you like to sit down?" He pushes the battered office chair, the only chair in the room, towards me.

"Okay."

I sit down on the chair and he crawls onto the bottom mattress. He has to keep his head down to keep from bashing it against the top bed. It doesn't look very comfortable. Max doesn't seem to mind.

We fall silent. The longer we remain silent, the less I know what to say. The sun that was shining at first now goes behind a cloud, and I suspect it's starting to get dark outside.

"Would you like a drink?" he suddenly asks.

"Yes, please," I answer quickly.

"I'll go and get something. Tea?"

"Good."

He's left the room before I can follow him.

Why am I getting so worked up? I feel my HC vibrate and I get it out. "Everything okay?" I read. Erik. I know that he's only concerned, but exactly because things aren't okay, I feel irritated. I quickly type that everything is fine and turn the thing off.

Nothing's the matter. Nothing's wrong. You're visiting a boy. In his room. That's all.

I get up, take the only two steps possible in the small room, and look at the books. The stimulating scent of paper is so strange and yet so familiar. Dad has a library with old books, but he never reads any of them. I went in there once as a child. It had a perfect hiding-place behind one of the tall cupboards. But I have never seen a bookcase with books that have actually been read. Books with dog-eared pages and broken spines. With notes scribbled in them and torn dust-covers. I recognize a lot of the titles, but many are unfamiliar. Some are in other languages, ones I don't understand. It's strange to see the books that I read as a child not on the smooth screen of a Reader.

I turn towards the desk, bend down, and examine the small, square plastic cases. I pick up one. It's flat with a black-and-white photograph on the top. A man with a trumpet. His white teeth glow in his dark face. He's on a big stage, holding his trumpet as carefully as a dancer holds his partner: loosely, gently and with an assuredness some people have by nature.

This must be music.

And this...? I stare at the device on the desk and touch it.

I study the case in my hand. I fiddle and pull and finally manage to separate the two thin halves.

A CD. He's got CDs. Then that thing on his desk must be a CD player. Mum told me about them. That she used to have one.

"Would you like to listen to something?"

Startled, I almost drop the case.

"Max! I..."

He takes the two steps to the desk, places mugs with steaming tea on it, and takes the CD case from my hand.

"I didn't know what it was."

Max takes out the silver disc, places it in the device, and presses a couple of buttons. Music sounds from all corners of the room. It completely fills the room.

"No Reader, no TonePlayer, no DOS music." He smiles and shrugs his shoulders. His fingers tap to the rhythm of the music. "CDs last a long time. Some of these belonged to my pa's pa."

"They're as old as that?"

He nods.

"But I bought most of them myself."

"I didn't know you could still buy CDs."

"You can out here."

I look down in shame. I keep on saying the wrong things. I know nothing about this boy, about his life, about what happens outside the cs. And he knows nothing about me. Not even my real name.

"What's wrong?" he asks. He looks serious, concerned. I have to suppress the urge not to stare at him.

"Sorry, I..."

"What?"

"Perhaps I should go." I sigh.

"Why?"

"Because..."

"Because I'm Wet and you're Dry? We already know that, don't we?" Wet and Dry. It's out in the open.

He sounds as if he's angry. Not at me. At something, somebody else, perhaps just at everything around us.

"Yes, we already know that," I say softly.

"You know what? I don't fucking feel like it anymore!"

When he sees my startled reaction, he quickly adds: "No, I don't mean it like that." His hand hovers indecisively above my arm. "I want you to stay. I mean... you know... enjoy this." He waves his arms around and moves around the room. He misses a pile of CDs on his desk by a whisker. "Don't you listen to music? What damned difference does it make where it comes from? I'm fed up having to tiptoe around on my Wet toes and constantly worry about taking a false step. I don't want to bother about fucking Dry or Wet. Not now. Not fucking now."

I have never heard him talk as long as that in one go. I stare at him in amazement.

"How about you?" he asks. Like he's challenging me.

I didn't know a Wet could have so much fire in him. "No. And the moment I say it, I know I mean it. "No, I don't want that anymore either."

MAX

I hand Nina the mug of tea.

"Thanks."

She smiles and looks at me. Really looks at me. Now I'm the one who can't look up.

Man, pull yourself together.

We sip the scalding tea. I've used two bags and know that Ma'll be on my case. But she was the one who taught me to take care of guests.

When I've finished my tea, I get up and flick through the pile of CDs. Nina watches over my shoulder.

"Where do you get them all?"

"I know a place that sells them pretty cheap."

"What are you playing now?"

"Jimi Hendrix."

"Who?"

I laugh. Dries don't now this sort of music.

"A singer from the sixties. Twentieth century."

"That's ages ago!"

"Sure. Cool, don't you think?"

"You could say that."

I find what I'm looking for, take Jimi out of the CD player, and put on The Beatles.

"This is even older."

She takes the CD box from me and flips through it. She smiles. "Look at the monkey suits those guys are wearing. And that hair!"

"Who knows what they'll say about us in a few years' time?"

She puts the CD down.

"Yes, who knows."

I show her more, play them for her. Other old musicians, CDs given by my pa's Pa to my pa and then passed on to me.

She likes Bob Dylan and asks me to leave the CD on.

"He was a protest singer," I say.

"Oh."

"I like his lyrics."

"Do you understand them?"

"A little. Pa told me what he was singing. And I looked up the rest in a dictionary."

She nods.

"I like his voice. It's so raw, real. He knows what he's singing about."

"Hm."

We fall silent and listen. This time, the silence isn't oppressive.

The song is the last number on the CD and I get up to play it again.

"Max?"

I turn round.

"Yes?"

"I think about it too. About how we got ourselves into this mess," she says quickly, almost spitting out the words. Then she again starts studying the tips of her shoes.

She also thinks about how we got ourselves into this mess.

My finger hovers for a moment above the button on the CD player. After tonight, my head isn't all that quick.

"I may be Dry, but... but that doesn't tell the whole story."
She looks up.

Man, her eyes are so blue.

"I'm sorry." I sigh.

"What?"

"Sorry I was such a prick when we did that assignment."

"Oh, well..."

"I was a prick," I continue. "Ma always says that the Morris men have an extremely short fuse." I grimace.

Nina throws me a questioning look. "A Wet with a short fuse..." she repeats. Her eyes light up when she gets the joke and shakes her head.

"She also says we have a sense of humor. And that's what keeps her from running away from us screaming." I look at her, really look at her. I want her to laugh. *Laugh, Nina.*

And Nina does laugh. Out loud this time.

"You're a strange one, Max Morris," she says. She pushes a curl back into her pony-tail. When she looks up, it flops out again. I go back and sit on the bed and put my hands under my thighs.

"May I draw you, Max?"

Again she knows how to take me by surprise.

"Draw?"

"It's nothing special," she says quickly. "But my hands want... I... I always draw and I just saw you with your CDs around you and then I saw exactly how I should draw you."

I tap my fingers against the edge of the bed. What should I say? With Kara, I just had to go along with everything that seemed to happen automatically. I shrug. "Okay."

She immediately begins sorting through her bag, and gets out her HC and a digipen.

"Do I have to do anything?"

"No, nothing. We can just talk."

I nod.

She starts. Her hand flies across the screen. Now and then she looks up. It's almost as if she sees me but doesn't see me. It makes me pretty fucking nervous.

"Tell me some more about your music. What else do you like? And where do you get those things?"

When I start talking, I grow calmer. Whenever I stop, she asks another question. Before I know it, I'm talking enthusiastically about white records and black markets, and I take special CDs from my collection to show her. Nina nods and laughs and admires, but at the same time, her hand never stops.

"Finished."

"Already?"

"It's only a sketch."

"Show me."

She passes me the HC.

I don't know how she did it, but it's me. She has intentionally left the CDs and the desk vague, although the outline of the room is clearly recognizable. I have never seen myself in this way. There are some photos, but they are from a long time ago. We've not had enough Points for new ones for years. I study myself. I didn't know I move so much. I look like a spider with all those arms and legs that never stay still. And my head is black and blue. I laugh.

"What? What's the matter?"

"Nothing. I just had to laugh at myself. I look so strange."

"You don't look strange at all," she says, offended.

"No?" I point at my chin, which by now has started to turn yellow, and the tear in my eyebrow.

"That'll get better."

I give her back her HC.

"Since you're here, shall we do some work on the Collingwood assignment?"

Her glance turns to the screen. She seems shocked.

"Oh no! Sorry Max, I... I have to go. I didn't realize how late it is..."

"Your parents?"

She nods.

She quickly types a message into the HC and presses Send.

She packs her bag. I walk her to the door. Ma is in the kitchen doorway.

"Bye, Mrs. Morris," says Nina shyly. I think we're both nervous about how Ma will respond.

But Ma smiles and says: "Bye, Nina."

I walk her down the stairs, I don't want her to walk on the street here on her own. Fortunately, Li isn't around and the car is parked in front of the entrance to the flat. Nina looks at me from the passenger seat.

"Well... see you tomorrow?"

"Yes. Tomorrow."

I watch her until she disappears into the distance.

NINA

"Sorry, Erik."

He looks at me.

"Do you know what you're doing, Nina?"

"I have to do an assignment with him. For school. We lost track of time," I say. "And I don't think Dad would have approved if I had taken Max home with me. He sees a Wet wolf hiding everywhere."

Erik laughs. "Yes, your father has a lot to put up with at the moment."

It's dark when we drive home and the streets are as good as empty. It is even quiet in cc1. When Erik drives into the garage, I notice that the light is still on in the dining-room. My hands feel damp and I wipe them on my jeans as I enter the dining-room. Mum and Dad are both sitting at one end of the table. They look up. They are not alone.

"Nina!" Mum pushes back her chair, walks over to me, and gives me a hug. "Where were you?"

Felix smiles at me from Isa's former place. I stare at him a fraction too long and feel my heart sink.

"Nowhere. At a friend's. We lost track of time," I say awkwardly. I bite my lip.

Dad clears his throat. He places his napkin to one side.

"You know the rules, Nina."

"Yes, Dad." Is this really necessary? With Felix here? So embarassing.

"Well?"

Felix picks up his napkin and dabs his lips. His pallid look slides almost unnoticed from me to Dad. He's amused, I realize.

Amused at our little family drama. Doesn't Dad realize he's making a fool of us both? I turn to face him.

"Sorry, Dad. But we were working on an assignment and..."

"The rules?" Dad interrupts.

I wish the ground would open up and swallow me. The rules. I know exactly what the rules are.

"Reginald." Mum's voice quivers. "Is this really necessary?"

"Eline." Dad doesn't brook any contradiction.

He turns to me and waits for me to begin.

I bite harder on my lip and force myself to raise my eyes. If I say it, it'll be over.

I don't look away as I recite the rules. "Always state a time. Always say where I am. Always leave my HC on."

Dad nods briefly and picks up his knife and fork. For him, that's the end of the matter.

I go to sit down, but Mum still has her arms clasped round me. "We were only concerned, darling. We love you so very much," she whispers into my hair.

Concerned.

My mouth is shut tight. I wait until Mum lets me go and I can sit down. I look up.

Felix is staring straight at me, his eyes bright blue. He smiles. A smile that curls his thin lips but doesn't make his eyes any warmer. Humiliated, I look away and quickly go to my place. For the rest of the meal, all I see is the food on my plate.

After supper, I can't get upstairs quickly enough.

I want to see him. I electronically lock the door and fall onto my bed. I whip out my HC and look at my drawing. Not one of my best, but it's him. Max.

I hope he didn't mind me wanting to draw him. I have never asked anybody before. Except Isa. I flip through my files and suddenly see the last drawing I made of her. Spring. Outside on the lawn. We were sunbathing. She was sporting a wide straw hat and smiling mysteriously.

I throw the screen away. It falls to the ground with a loud bump. Perhaps I'll be needing tape as well. I feel broken. Like Max's HC.

I didn't feel that this afternoon. I think back to his room.

"Bob Dylan," I say. It takes some time for DOS to find him. As if the system has to dig back in time. Then there's the same voice I heard in Max's room. The same, but at the same time different. It doesn't sound right here.

"Off."

Silence.

I crawl to the edge of my bed and pick up my HC and digipen. I place my pillows against the wall and lean back on them.

First I draw Max. Then his mother and his brother. The hall with the cupboard without doors, the overflowing book-case, and the tiny bunk bed. I draw the view across the land, in the direction of the dyke, the far too narrow dyke, with the water glistening behind it. I draw the flat, the concrete and the flaking plaster, the cat in the sandpit and the woman who dragged away that inquisitive child and quickly walked off.

I look at my drawings. I look at them until the DOS alarm indicates that it's time for bed.

MAX

When I get upstairs, Ma's standing in the doorway.

"One day you come home with a bruised jaw and a torn eyebrow, the next you invite in some Dry or other. Should I be worried, Max?"

"She came to return my HC. We have to do an assignment together. And her name is Nina."

"Nina."

Ma arches her eyebrows. I walk inside and close the door behind me.

"She's just someone from school. Nothing more."

"No?"

I follow Ma into the kitchen and sit down at the table. She's put out the loaf of bread. No hot food today. So much for Governor Bradshaw's promises.

"You like her," she says as she sits down opposite me and starts slicing the loaf.

I really don't feel like lying anymore. Not to myself. Not to Ma. There have been enough lies. "Yes, I like her."

"Okay."

"Okay?"

"Yes, Max, okay. I'm sure you'll make the right choice."

I stare at Ma, hardly daring to believe it, and I think back to yesterday. "How do you know I'll make the right choice?"

She stops slicing. "I trust you, Max." Then she laughs just a bit too quickly. "Oh, you're both hot heads, you and Liam.

Don't you think I know that?" She points her knife at me. "Just promise me you'll be careful."

I nod.

"Good."

We eat while Bob Dylan continues protesting in my room. Afterwards, I start my homework with a sigh. As I finally send the last assignment, Li walks in. "New girlfriend?"

I turn around with a start. Did he see Nina?

"What did you do?" It sounds fiercer than I meant and I curse silently inside.

"Nothing, little brother. Absolutely nothing. Just told her she had to walk up the stairs to get here."

He throws his bag on the ground and takes a book from the shelf, leafing through it nonchalantly. He hasn't finished.

"Pretty girl, for a Dry," he says, while pretending to read. "She looked familiar."

"She's from school, Li. I have to do some assignments with her."

"Oh, assignments. Smooth, Max."

I feel his grin.

"You know, Li, if you pulled your head out of your ass, you might realize not everybody is out to screw you."

He turns round sharply and snaps the book shut. "No? Then why's my little brother going round with a Dry?"

"Fuck you, Li," I throw at him and try to slip past him out of the room. But Li is faster and stops me.

"Tell me that it's nothing more than that."

He looks at me, fury in his dark eyes, my eyes, Ma's eyes. Fury everywhere in his tense body. I can't answer him. I don't know what to say.

For Li, my silence is a confirmation of his Wet suspicions.

"Pa would have skinned you alive," he spits at me. Then he lets me go and storms out of the room.

I can't sleep. Li doesn't come back and his last words keep racing through my head. Not much later, I hear him go out. His footsteps sound hollow in the empty stairwell.

I look up to him, my big brother. When Pa was around, we were the three men of the house. We drove Ma crazy. If there was a water alarm outside, we'd play football in the living-room. Ma didn't mind because it was a distraction for us. Pa agreed. I don't think she had a vase left in the end.

We were always outside: playing football, chilling, getting up to mischief. Pestering Blowers by throwing stones or paint at their cars. Always together, the Morris brothers.

With Pa, we'd go to the dyke. To fish.

"Yes, boys, it's that time of the year again!"

I can still hear him, the old man, early in the morning when it was still dark.

Li and I would run on ahead, leaving Pa to struggle with all the stuff. See who got to the dyke first. At least I always won that competition. "So boys, now it's time for..."

"Pa-ah!"

He pretended not to know what on earth we meant.

"Boys! Surely you don't begrudge your old Pa wetting his whistle?"

He had put the drinks in the refrigerator the night before and put them in his bag early this morning. Ma knew, but when we went fishing, she turned a blind eye.

Li could never sit still and generally went off exploring. But Pa, he looked and looked. Sometimes I wondered: What's he really looking at?

Once, a few weeks before his death, we were sitting to-gether. Li didn't go with us anymore. The fish weren't show-ing much interest and when Pa's line suddenly tightened, it took me a while to notice it.

"Pa! Strike, Pa! Before it gets away!"

Pa kept staring straight ahead. His eyes were locked down. What was he thinking about then? He only looked up when I grabbed the rod from his hands.

"You almost let it get away!"

"What, son?" His right hand automatically went to where his rod had been.

"That damned fish!"

Together, we fought to land the fattest herring ever. The beast obviously had no intention of giving up its life without a struggle. We were drenched by the time we finally got it onto dry land. We returned home in triumph.

Sometimes I think that Pa already knew that the water would take him.

NINA

"Hey."

I'm standing at his table. I have never been so aware of who I am and what I am doing.

He smiles. "Hey."

I know that everybody's looking, but I couldn't care less. "We still have to finish that assignment."

He nods.

"But not here. Later."

"Okay," he says.

We eat our lunch in silence. I push most of my meal onto his plate. He stares at me for a second, his glance inscrutable. He eats it all.

Noise and half-whispered remarks swirl around us, but nothing is clear enough to be understandable. *Do you know what you've got yourself into, Nina?*

I think back to yesterday. I smell my mother's sweet perfume and hear Dad telling me to recite the three golden rules. Strictly speaking, I'm not breaking them... I look at the Wet boy in front of me, devouring that inedible mess as if he hasn't eaten in days. His cheek is now more yellow than blue now, and the wound in his eyebrow has finally closed. His T-shirt is too thin, and his jeans are old and worn. When he sees me looking at him, he grins without any shame, which makes him, if that's possible, look Wetter than ever.

I grin back.

I realize that I haven't felt so good in ages.

During the study period, Max takes me to the deserted section of the school, where we work together on Collingwood's assignment.

"No, no, fucking no!" He waves his arms around, and I have to dodge to one side to avoid being hit. "That is so ex-act-ly not what he means! Look. Just look." And he makes me re-read the passage before we can go on.

Collingwood has his favorite subjects, I notice. Once again, it's about the years before the First Great Flood. Again we read about all the warnings that were given. Max believes that people could have, no, *should* have prevented the disaster. I'm more cynical and suggest that those who claimed to foresee the disaster were alarmists, crying in the wilderness. Nobody appreciated the true nature of the danger threatening us.

In the end, Max and I cannot agree. He thinks I'm being a stubborn Dry, but if one of us is fanatical, it's Max.

If he knew who my father was...

I immediately shake off the thought.

On Thursday, I have class first thing. Max isn't at school yet. When I go into the class, Nikki ignores me. And when I put my bag down next to her, she gets up and and makes a point of walking to another table. She would rather sit on her own than next to me. It hurts more than I thought.

I force myself to sit there, stay cool. I take my HC from my bag and look stoically at the screen until the teacher comes in and starts the lesson. I only notice that I have a message when the bell goes for the end of the lesson. Could it...? I open the flashing envelope and stare at the screen.

"We'll get your Wet friend. Get the picture, Nina?"

No sender and the message is encrypted. I erase it before my imagination runs away with me.

In the break, I show Max my drawings. When we get to a drawing of his Ma, he looks at me with open admiration. "How do you do it?"

"What?"

"It's her. Ma. Always present. And her eyes..."

"You both have the same eyes."

"You think?"

"So does your brother."

He stiffens.

"My brother? When did you see Li?"

I'm shocked at the undercurrent of rage in his voice.

"He was downstairs. When I came to return your HC."

"Did he say anything to you?"

"That the lift wasn't working. And he pointed me towards the stairs. He wasn't super friendly, but I wouldn't expect him to be." I shrug, pretending to be nonchalant.

"Nothing else?"

"Nothing else."

He sighs and shakes his head. He taps his fingers on the desk.

"Sorry. Sorry... I..." He looks away.

"Is there... is something the matter with your brother?"

"No," he says quickly. Too quickly. "No, there's nothing wrong with Liam. It's just that recently we've had... different interests."

I hear in his voice that he doesn't want me to go any further and so I scroll on.

I only remember the message at the end of the day. "I got a DOS mail during chemistry," I say as we pack our bags.

"Mail? What about?"

"I deleted it. I won't be intimidated."

"What did it say, Nina?" he persists, his dark eyes getting wider. I tell him.

He swears.

"Damian."

"How do you know?"

"I've known that prick all my life." He clenches his fists and walks up and down.

"Oh." I don't really know what to say. Then I place my hand on his arm. "Hey, relax. He wouldn't dare do anything here at school."

He shakes my hand away. I start and he notices it. "Sorry," he says at once. "Sorry."

"You don't need to apologize."

"Yes, I do."

We say goodbye. There's something in the way he walks away that makes me regret my openness.

On Friday morning, he's waiting for me at the entrance to the school. There is a thin layer of snow on his cap and on the tip of his nose. I resist the urge to brush it off. How long has he been waiting here?

"Hey," I say to him.

"Hey."

He kicks the snow with his right foot. "So, the assignment for Collingwood is finished," he says.

"Yeah..."

"And he hasn't given us a new one."

"Not yet."

He hesitates. "I don't know if it's such a good idea to..."

"To what?" It comes out fiercer than I intended.

"... to be..."

"Max."

He says nothing but looks at me with his piercing eyes. What does he see? What is he thinking about? Doesn't he want to see me anymore? And before I know what I'm doing, the words have slipped out. "Come visit me."

He starts. "What?"

"At my house."

And at that moment I know that's what I want. That I have doubts about everything, except about this boy.

I smile. "Come for a visit. Sunday evening," I say. "Mum and Dad are going out to dinner."

"But ... how?" is all Max can say when he understands that I really mean it. After all, Wets can't just go into the CCS if they don't work for Dries.

I let my glance glide over his worn jeans and T-shirt. "Perhaps you'll have to wear different clothes. I'm sure Erik and Maria will help."

Max taps his fingers on the frozen back of the seat next to him.

"Maria?"

"Maria works for us. I trust her."

He places a hand on his neck and shakes his head.

"I don't know whether..."

"I've been to your place, now I'm inviting you to mine. Refusing an invitation from a girl is very impolite."

He remains silent for a moment.

"Okay."

Only when I walk across the quad at the end of the day do I realize exactly what I've done: I've invited a Wet to the house of the Governor. Mum and Dad must never find out about this.

MAX

I'm crazy to have said yes. Mental.

My head and my body don't do what I tell them anymore. If they ever did.

This week... Man, this was the best week I've had in ages.

I was startled when she talked about Li. And then she told me about that mail, probably from from Damian. Then on Friday, once I'd finally gotten my head together, I was about to tell her that we should take things slower. Then she goes and asks me this...

My thoughts turn to that afternoon in the kitchen. That Dry with his questions and Li storming out in a rage. It's not safe for her to come to my place. Is it safer if I go to hers? She doesn't know the effect she has on people. And she hasn't the faintest idea what effect she has on my Wet head. I'm going crazy.

Since Tuesday, Li has only come home once and that was just to check on the mess he's left behind. Ma is worried, even though she acts as if nothing's the matter. The Dries haven't been back. That means nothing and we both know it.

When I wake up on Sunday, he's still isn't there. Where is that prick?

I feel the knot in my stomach and hear Ma in my head: "It's Liam's choice." The choice of an egocentric bastard who's never used his brains, that's for sure.

I look in the mirror. My tired, unshaven yellow cheeks stare back at me. My hair is far too long and is starting to get on my nerves.

"Is something wrong, Max?"

Ma comes into the bathroom in her pinafore and slippers.

"Can you cut my hair?"

Ma arches her eyebrows.

"Any special reason?"

"No, you know, it's irritating."

Ma used to be a hairdresser before going into nursing. She sometimes still does it for friends.

"If you really want me to..."

I nod.

She leaves the bathroom and goes to the kitchen. She waves at a kitchen chair.

"How much?"

"All of it."

"All of it?"

"Yes."

"You're sure?"

"Yes."

I feel different. I want to look different.

"Okay," says Ma and starts cutting. When she's got rid of most of it, she gets out the clippers. "Finished."

I rub my hand over my head. All she's left is a soft downy layer. I get up and go to the broken mirror in the bathroom. I inspect the new me.

My torn eyebrow is more noticeable, just like my angular jaw and my big, crooked nose. I look tougher. Older. Is this me?

"Isn't it okay?" asks Ma. She's leaning against the doorpost. "Don't worry. It'll grow back again. Good thing is, it'll save on towels." Ma's always practical.

I smile and see the boy in the mirror smiling back. Yes, I decide. I like him.

The day's really dragging. After I finish my homework, I play around with my HC for a while, and when I'm tired of that, I organize my CDs. At least it gives me something to do.

I simply can't imagine that I'll be going into a CC.

As kids, we always talked about it. What it would look like and you could get there. When Ron Richards didn't turn up for school one day, the rumor went round that he had broken in and got caught. It turned out that he had mumps, but that only emerged after a few imaginative stories had found their way into the world. Li and I sucked them up and told them to Ma and Pa.

Nina says that she can get hold of some other clothes. That I shouldn't worry about it. Dry clothes. I'm glad Li can't see me.

"Ma?"

It is five o'clock and almost dark. A small light is burning in the kitchen. Latest ordinance. Ma raises an eyebrow.

"I'm going out."

"At this time?"

"I've got to. I'm going crazy sitting around inside."

I don't say where I'm going. I don't want to worry her even more.

"Okay, son. Go on. What time will you be back?" She's put on her pinafore over her old jeans and is holding a cup of tea tightly in her hands. Man, she looks awful. Her forehead has deep lines and her dark eyes have sunk so far into her face that you can hardly see them in the dim light.

"Not too late. I'll let you know via DOS."

She nods. She feels there's more to it She says nothing.

"Ma?" I say as I pull on my coat.

"Hm?"

"He'll be home tonight."

"Let's hope so."

"He can't be as stupid as all that."

"No?" She laughs — short and hard. "Be careful what you say, Max."

NINA

Will Max be there?

Erik looked doubtful when I told him my plan. But Maria was able to convince him. Maria. I don't know what I'd do without her. Until now I've only bent the rules; now I'm going to break the law.

As soon as Mum and Dad left, I cleared away everything that could point to Bradshaw. All the photos, all Dad's golfing trophies, all Mum's medical diplomas and her paintings. If we go in through the garage, he won't see anything relating to the Bradshaws. I want to show Max my house, my home. But what do I actually want to show him?

Then I see Max in my mind. Max who's helping my pick up my things. Max in front of his bookcase. Max passionately talking about his music and his future. The boy I like. I tell myself there'll be enough time later to show him who I am. Not now. Not yet.

When I walked past Isa's room this morning, I found myself smiling, without even realizing it.

"A boy, Nina!"

I saw us sitting around, talking, comparing, assessing. I felt an overwhelming urge to barge into her room and pour out my heart to her.

This afternoon, I bought some clothes for him. I didn't have the slightest idea of his size and had to explain to the salesgirl what my "brother" looked like. My hands were shaking, so it was a relief that the woman chattered away non-stop, without really expecting me to say anything back.

I'm holding the pile of clothes in my lap. I can't really imagine what Max will look like in a pair of pale blue jeans and a green sweater. Dry clothes. Nice clothes. I want to give them to him.

"Is he here?" asks Erik.

"He said he'd come down."

I hear a knock.

"Erik."

Erik opens the door and Max stumbles in onto the rear seat.

"You're here." I turn round.

"I'm here."

He pulls the hood from his head.

"You haven't got any hair!"

He grimaces.

"And?"

I study his unexpectedly open face. His jaw is more prominent than before and his big nose stands out more. His large dark eyes with those long eyelashes are suddenly striking, and only now do I notice how small his ears are. He looks older. No longer a boy, more a man.

"It suits you."

He shrugs. "I felt like something new."

I smile, take the clothes from the bag, and give them to him. "I hope it's the right size."

"Do you want me to change now?"

"Yes, I think that would be the best idea."

He holds the clothes as if they contain something nasty. I feel a tiny stab in my stomach.

"Really?" he says uncertainly.

"Yes, for the guards," I reply. "You can take them off when we get home." I can hardly hide my disappointment. I thought he would be pleased with the new clothes.

"All right." He sighs and and then a moment later, throws me a pointed look. It takes me couple of seconds before I catch his meaning..

"Right! Sorry, I'll turn around!"

I keep my eyes fixed ahead as Max pulls off his old clothes and puts on the new ones. I see a smile on Erik's lips as Max swears at the buttons on the jeans. I can't stop myself from stealing a glance at his thin but muscular torso in the rearview mirror. I quickly look straight ahead again.

"Okay. I've put them on."

"Give me your old clothes. I've got a bag."

I quickly put them away and look at him.

He has almost changed from a Wet into a Dry. Almost. Only his face, with that half eyebrow and the pale yellow jaw, seems a bit strange. For the rest... The clothes fit perfectly. Something tells me to keep my mouth shut.

"What?"

A surly look is in his eyes.

"Nothing."

I quickly turn away and Erik starts the car.

MAX

I tap on the smooth fabric of my new jeans. The pullover itches like mad against my skin. I should have bloody well kept my T-shirt on. Why can I never do even the simplest things right?

I don't know what to say. Not that Nina's doing much talking. She's not sitting next to me, like the first time, but in the front, with Erik. Her *driver*.

Ahead of us is Mrs. Collins with her dog. It never shits on the grass but always in the street. She used to babysit us when Pa and Ma were at work. She takes care of a lot of the children around here. As we drive past, that mongrel of hers starts barking at the car. She turns and looks straight at me. A Wet looking at a Dry.

No.

The windows are tinted, like almost all the cars in the CCs.

I feel better when we leave District Seven and I see the tram driving alongside us. Light. People talking, laughing, gesturing. A boy tugs at his mother's coat. We pass our school. Closed and dark, the tall gate locked. Nina sees it too, and her hand goes to her locket. For the first time, I wonder whose photo she's got in it. She always touches it when she's nervous. That trinket would get us enough Points to last six months.

Stop. You're thinking like Li.

But I immediately see Ma in my mind, sitting at the

kitchen table. How she's always mending our clothes, her feet in worn slippers, her eyes too close to what she's doing.

"We're almost at the gate," says Nina.

A dark shadow that seems to stretch away forever looms up. The wall of CC1.

"What should I do?" My hands are shaking. I hide them under my legs.

"Nothing. Erik will do the talking."

Nina turns round to me. She tries to reassure me with her glance. She's just as nervous as I am. "You're one of my friends, just over from the Fourth Region and you haven't got your official ID card yet." She winks her eyes.

"Okay."

Erik slows down and stops. He presses a button and his window goes down. Outside it's started snowing again, some of it blows inside. Erik leans out of the car. I can't hear exactly what he says because of the wind. A bright light shines in my eyes and I back away. But the light goes out as quickly as it came on.

"Fourth Region?" I hear.

"Yes, we've just picked him up from Dock 2," says Erik. Hell, that Wader can really lie.

The Blower shines the light inside again, but this time I'm ready. Two Blowers look at me inquisitively. I nod at them. As long as they don't ask anything. As long as they don't ask anything. As long as they don't ask anything. But they only have eyes for Nina, who looks on with a friendly smile as one of the two scans her ID. The other takes off his Blower's cap and leans inside Erik's window.

Knot. *Easy, Max. He'll bugger off soon. Nothing'll happen.* I can't hear what he says to Nina. The fierce wind blows snow into my face. The knot grows and grows. Doesn't she see what a crawler he is? I force myself to look the other way before I explode. Finally one of them says: "Okay. Carry on."

The gate swings open. We drive into cc1. We drive into a *fucking* cc. I have to pull my fingers free of the seat. Nina turns round a smiles.

"We did it!"

I try to smile but I'm feeling even more agitated than ever. A cc. The lion's den. Doesn't Bradshaw live in cc1? I have never really believed Li's wild stories. Suddenly I see his fat gob on the dos screen offering his condolences while the Blower is telling Ma that Pa has drowned.

I try to concentrate on what I see outside.

All I can do is stare. Houses as big as half our school tower above us, surrounded by enormous gardens and high fences. We pass a floodlit building on stilts, as big as our flat. No, bigger even. Is it... Yes, fuck, the thing's made of glass! Of glass. Hundreds of people are bustling on the dozens of floors. Bright lights flash and I hear music. A shopping center? A digiscope? Or both? I have never seen anything like it in all my Wet life. And it's all so damned clean here. We are driving along a straight road, one without holes or bumps. The snow has been swept away; a salt truck drives ahead of us. Trees are flagged with posts and there are special paths for cyclists and pedestrians. Man, there are even people walking around outside. I see a man and woman with a baby stroller and a dog on a leash. As we drive past the park, I realize that they're heading there. The park, dammit. In District Seven you only go to the park to get a shot or get away from life. It's busy here, even in the dark, and everything looks bright and shiny. I don't believe it. My mouth literally hangs open in amazement. I quickly shut it when I notice that Nina is looking at me.

"We're nearly there. Just one more gate. They already know somebody's coming."

I nod. I wouldn't know what to say.

When the gates to Nina's house, estate or whatever you want to call it swing open, I can almost swear that Erik whispered "Open Sesame" into his HC. High trees line the drive and light up as if they are lamps. At first, you can't see the house in the shadow of the dark hill. Then Erik turns right and it appears.

Nina's house.

It's fucking huge. Huge. Much bigger than I could ever have imagined. Two enormous stairways lead to a double door, and there's a balcony above it. A balcony where you simply want to stand and shout as loud as you can. Two wings, each with several stories, rise high on either side. It only now dawns on me that she actually lives here.

Nina's gaze burns.

Right at the end of the drive, a door opens. A bright light shines over the gravel in front of it. A garage. A double garage. The car screeches inside and the doors automatically close behind us. The car stops. Erik gets out, and so does Nina.

I stay where I am. My Wet ass is glued to the seat.

"Max?"

Nina's head appears in the door opening.

"Yes?"

"Are you okay?"

Are you okay? Are you okay? So much is racing through my head. Mrs. Collins and her dog, the sleazy Blower and his red head, the people bustling around behind glass and this, here, Nina's house. Nina's house.

I look into her eyes. Her blue, blue eyes. And I get out.

NINA

"That looks like somebody who could do with something."

We both look up at the same time. Maria is in the doorway, her hands on her hips. Black curls dance around her round face, her apron, as always, is covered with stains.

"You must be Max."

He nods. He's lost for words.

"Food's been ready for some time, lad. No time to mess around!" Maria disappears down the corridor to the kitchen.

"Come on. Nobody keeps Maria waiting," I say, happy to have an excuse to take his hand and pull him inside.

I saw him staring. Saw how his dismay increased with every turn, every street. *Is this a good idea, Nina?* I shake off the doubt. He'll just have to get used to it. Just as I had to get used to his home.

"Sit down, lad," says Maria as we enter the kitchen.

Max stops, allows his gaze to take in the room. What does he see? The big kitchen table, littered with Maria's pots and pans and other kitchen appliances. A vase of flowers is standing in the middle. Maria always picks fresh ones. This week they're white lilies, Mum's favorites. Maria has cleared two places on one side, and the smell of pasta greets us.

"Dig in," she says.

I offer Max one of the chairs and sit down opposite him. I see him hesitate.

"Shall I...?" I point to the pasta.

His stomach groans loudly and clearly. He immediately blushes. "Sorry, I... uh..."

"I told you there was somebody who could do with something," says Maria, rescuing the situation.

I smile quickly and Max looks apologetic. I pick up the spoon and pile pasta on his plate, then some on mine. Max is eating before I've had a chance to take a single bite. The boy eats so quickly! I'm only halfway through my plate, and he's already scraping up the remains of his second helping. It takes a moment before I realize he's staring at my plate.

"What's wrong?"

"You've left your meat."

I look at the edge of my plate, where I've neatly pushed all the meat balls. "Yes... I don't really like it." I shrug my shoulders. "Would you...?" I push my plate over to him.

Again he hesitates.

"Otherwise Maria will throw it away."

Wide eyes.

"Okay, then."

He eats it all. I bet he'd lick his plate if he was on his own.

Once we've eaten dessert, I get up and walk towards the hallway. Max stays where he is.

"Max?"

"Yes?"

"Coming?"

"But... shouldn't we help with dishes?"

"Maria will put them in the dishwasher."

"Oh."

He pushes back his chair, slowly gets up, and looks at Maria. I can't see her face. She nods at him. He nods back and finally leaves the kitchen with me.

I'm impatient. I want him to myself. I want him to relax and enjoy the evening.

Again I take his hand. A real boy's hand, big and rough but with long, slender fingers, longer than I had expected. He feels warm. I drag him along the corridor into the hall and up the stairs. Not yet. First I want to show him something. Or rather, let him hear something. I don't give him any time to look around, to admire Dad's collection of antique china or to notice the glass roof through which the full moon is shining. The doors to the conservatory, furnished as a sitting-room, are open. I stop and he bumps into me. His body is even warmer than his hands.

"Sorry," he says quickly.

"No problem." I smile nervously. "Sit down."

I point to a sofa directly opposite the sliding doors. Outside, the frozen lawn stretches into the distance, the stars shining above. He keeps his restless hands clenched in his pockets. He hesitates for a moment, then walks to the sofa and sits down. I sit down next to him and turn to the DOS installation, ingeniously integrated into the cabinet behind us.

"Bob Dylan," I say. "*A hard rain's a gonna fall.*" I hope I pronounce the old English properly. I hope...

Music fills the perfect acoustics in the room. I breathe out and turn towards Max.

MAX

"What's wrong?" She tries to catch my gaze, her eyes wide and uncertain. She wants to place her hand on my arm, but before she can, I jump up.

"Sorry, Nina... I..."

Easy, Max.

"Shoud I turn off the music?"

I nod.

"Off."

Knot. That bloody knot again. She's so fucking Dry when she talks. Man, this house. That Wet woman, Maria... And she didn't even eat her meat.

"I thought I could give you something in return."

I look up.

"I've got so much."

I bite my lip to keep my Wet words inside. Yes, she has a lot. I take a couple of deep breaths, stare past her at the ridiculously large garden.

"I can't do this." My voice echoes in the high room.

"Do what?"

"This." I gesture at everything around me.

She gets up, walks to the window, and stares outside. She hugs herself, her arms around her slender waist.

"Sorry, Max." Her reflection in the glass looks at me. "I didn't mean it like that." She turns round. "You know, the stupid thing is that I don't feel good here either. I hate this house. I even hate my own room."

I say nothing.

She clenches her hands into fists and walks to a cupboard hidden behind a curtain. She must have touched something, because suddenly the doors to the garden slide open. Fresh air floods in. More than fresh — cold. Nina takes a step outside and looks back at me.

I follow her.

We walk over the grass that crackles under our feet. We go farther, in the direction of what I gradually recognize as the edge of a wood. Nina shivers and I automatically put my arm around her slim shoulders. I shiver as well. We still don't say anything. A shape begins to appear in the shadow of the trees. I only see what it is when we get close. A summer house. Nina reaches into the pocket of her jeans and pulls out a key, which she uses to open the door.

A light goes on. It's small inside. Cozy. I see an old settee in the corner. Garden things are piled up, waiting for the summer. Cobwebs hang from the ceiling. It smells a bit musty, but not unpleasant or anything.

'We ... I always came here when I didn't want to be found," says Nina.

She sounds different here. I sound different when I open my mouth.

"A hideaway."

She smiles.

"Yes. A hideaway."

I take a step inside and run my hand over a garden chair. Brown dust clings to my fingers.

"Something happened... with you too?"

Nina nods.

"A while ago."

She sighs, walks over to the settee, and sits down. Her hands in her hair, her elbows on her knees. She chews her lip.

Nina.

I want to tell her. Her, Nina. I want to tell her about Pa, about Li, and all the shit of the last few months.

I sit down next to her.

"Nina?"

"Hm?"

She turns to face me. Moonlight shines on her pale cheeks. I can almost count the freckles. Man, I've never been this close to her. My whole body tingles.

"What?"

"My Pa is dead. He drowned six months ago."

NINA

"Oh no..." I swallow. Six months. The flood. *Isa.*

"It was an accident, they said." He stares outside, across the lawn. "Li thinks Bradshaw was behind it. I don't know."

"Bradshaw?" I manage to stutter. It is as if a hand is clasping my throat. I force myself to keep breathing calmly. Max turns to face me.

"Li says that Bradshaw left Pa and the other forty-nine people in the school. That they could have been saved. He's obsessed about it. He's furious. He's..."

He shrugs his shoulders, pushes himself up from the sofa and starts pacing up and down.

"They came to tell us that evening. We'd been waiting a day and a night. We didn't know anything. Didn't know who had survived, who hadn't."

He stops and clenches his fists. I bite my lip.

"Ma... Ma said nothing. She listened to what they said and when the Blowers had gone, she locked herself in her room. Li and I tried to follow her, but she'd locked the door, and, and... Man, I've never heard Ma scream so loud."

He drums his fingers on one of the windows.

"They put them all together, all the Wets who worked at the school. Erected some stupid stone or other, held a speech, and then filled everything in. Ma goes there every Tuesday. Keeps it tidy."

His voice breaks at that last sentence. He's standing with

his back to me. I want to see him. No, I don't want to see him. What is he seeing? What's going on inside? What would he think if he knew who he is looking at?

Bradshaw's house.

Bradshaw's home.

Bradshaw's *daughter*.

It's as if somebody has plunged a knife into my stomach and given it a twist.

I didn't know. I really didn't know. Is it true what he said about Dad? Of course he wouldn't lie about his father.

My memories of that day are all a blur. And I want to keep it that way. It all happened so quickly. The dyke breaking, the water pouring through, destroying everything in its path, the second dyke breaking and collapsing, cutting Isa off from us. But perhaps stranding others too...

Maybe I've got it wrong. Who says that this was the same flood or the same place? DOS news couldn't even keep up with where the water went. Houses were destroyed, three schools and two shopping centers. But I never heard anything about so many Wets being drowned on the Mainland.

Suddenly I realize that just because I hadn't heard about it, doesn't mean it didn't happen.

"It is better if you don't know some things," said Dad the day after Isa was buried. I had never seen him so grey and so subdued. What was he talking about? What... what did he do?

"Nina?"

I force myself to look up. Concerned. He looks concerned.

Liar. You're a liar, Nina.

What should I do? A tear trickles down my cheek. I don't dare say anything.

"Hey, you can't do anything about it." He takes a step towards me. A second tear falls into the dust on the ground.

"Don't cry, Nina, please."

He sits down next to me, hesitates briefly, and then carefully puts his arm around me.

"Hey," he whispers into my hair.

He holds me tight and I let him. I hate myself, but I let him. I bury my lying face in his Dry sweater. A third tear disappears into the soft, smooth fabric.

"Oh fuck, Nina..."

I look up. His face is so close. I breathe his breath. He breathes my breath.

Then it's only a tiny step.

His lips feel surprisingly soft when they touch mine. He breathes out and I taste his excitement, which so easily dissolves into my excitement. His tongue opens my lips and slips inside. He pulls me to him and I feel him, feel him.

I have never felt anything like this.

He knows what he's doing, this boy I hardly know. One hand slides down my spine to that area of skin just above my buttocks, while the other moves under my sweater towards my breast. My hand also starts exploring. I stroke his short, fluffy hair, his soft, round shoulders, and his burning chest. I can't control myself.

Nina Bradshaw!

I pull myself away from him. He looks at me, shock filling his dark eyes.

"What? What's the matter? Am I going to fast? "Oh fuck, Nina. Sorry. Sorry! I'm such a prick. But, but... you were so close and you..."

"Max."

He thinks it's him. He falls silent. He looks so lost. He's still excited and has trouble hiding... it. I have to do something. I have to explain it to him. He trusted me, didn't he? But where to start. I'm so scared. He doesn't know who I am, but perhaps I can explain. Surely Max will understand?

"I want to show you something." Is that me? Are those my words? Do I know what I'm doing?

He looks questioningly at me. I try to smile. "Not here. In the house." It helps to say the words.

"In the house," repeats Max.

"Yes."

"Okay."

I take the key from the shelf next to the door and go outside. I can't bear to look. I'm going to tell him.

Max follows me, and when we reach the grass his hand searches for mine. I let him. Without his grip, I'm not sure I can stand. Not sure of the direction. Not sure we can keep walking.

I look up, up at the skies, at the stars that witness everything, and think back to the night after Isa's death, when it was just like this, just as beautiful. I was angry, furious, I wanted to pull the stars out of the sky and stamp them out because they were shining so brightly above the chaos on the Mainland. I walk faster. I feel Max's tension, which is also excitement. He doesn't know anything. *Go on, Nina.*

We go back inside, walk to the big hall.

I stop.

Come on, Nina, lost your nerve?

I want to show him Isa's room. I want to show him that I have lost somebody as well. That Dad, Governor Bradshaw, lost his daughter. That we're the same. That the water has hit us all.

Is that really true? I don't know any more. I only know that I can't *not* tell him. *Isa. The wave. The emptiness.* I take a deep breath.

I take him up the stairs.

We stand in front of Isa's room. Hand in hand.

I move my hand to the sensor to open the door.

MAX

"Nina!"

We look behind us, startled. Nina pulls back her hand. The door to the room remains closed.

It's Maria. She's out of breath. Nina rushes to her and takes hold of her.

"Maria, what's the matter?"

"Your father..."

"What's the matter with my father?"

Maria stares at me. Warmth and sympathy in her gleaming eyes. Fuck.

"There's been another attack. Here in CC1. The digiscope... Your father has gone there."

The digiscope? Oh fuck. Li hasn't...

"And Mum?

Again she glances in my direction.

"She's almost home."

Everything starts racing through my mind.

Li, oh fuck, please don't let them get him! But... what has Nina's pa got to do with the attacks? Is he an important Blower or something? Or does he work for the Council? Oh man, if only Li hasn't screwed everything up for himself. Have they already caught somebody? Her mother. She said something about her mother... How do I get out of the house? How can I get home before her mother sees me?

The storm won't calm down.

But Nina, Nina is keeping her head cool.

"Maria," she says. "Get Erik. Erik has to take Max. Now. At once!"

Maria nods and rushes down the stairs.

"Come on," says Nina to me. She pulls me with her down the stairs and pushes me into a space. "There's a door in the corner. It leads to the garage." She points.

We hear the sound of a car and voices.

They're already here.

"Mum'll come in through the kitchen, Dad's driver will go round the back," says Nina with certainty. She blinks her eyes. A second later she's gone, back into the hallway.

I'm alone.

My eyes gradually grow used to the dark. A tiny gleam of light comes through a small window in the corner. Feeling my way, I walk in the direction Nina pointed out to me. I curse as I almost fall over and my hand touches something with a sharp edge.

My heart is beating like crazy. Did they hear me?

Nothing happens.

I can still hear voices, farther away. Nina and her mother? I walk on until I reach a door. I put my ear against it. I can hear nothing. My hand moves to the handle. I push gently.

"Come on!"

My stomach takes a dive.

"Here. Hurry up, lad!"

I see Erik standing next to his car. The Wader. Of course. He points to the open trunk. I look at it and at the man in front of me. He's waiting for me to decide. But I don't have a choice.

I nod at him and climb into the car. I fold my legs and

pull my head down between my arms. It's already hurting.

Erik looks down.

"Okay?"

"Okay."

And he slams the trunk.

NINA

"Mum. What's happened?"

I hold her while Maria puts on some water. I just hope she's her zombie self and doesn't notice the sound of a car starting.

The last look that Max gave me is etched in my memory.

He trusted me.

He opened up completely.

And you didn't tell him anything.

I never swear, but now I want to curse, scream, lash out. I clamp my teeth together and keep looking at Mum.

"The digiscope..." Her eyes stare past me. I don't know what she sees. "All those people!"

"What happened, Mum?" I repeated, softly. "Mum? Look at me, Mum. Please."

Maria puts done a cup of tea for her. I let go and place Mum's fingers around the hot mug.

"Mummy, it's okay. You're home now. Nothing can happen to you."

Suddenly she looks at me. Really looks at me. I'm startled. It's strange to see Mum again.

"That's exactly the problem, Nina," she says. "Nothing can happen to me. But what about all those other people? People inside, people outside. It can't go on like this, and Reginald..." She stops, stares at her tea and sighs.

I don't understand what she's talking about. People outside and inside? Does she mean Wets and Dries? And Dad?

"What's the matter with Dad?"

Mum looks as me, as if she's wondering what she can tell me. She shakes her head. Her eyes once again fill with that familiar, glazed look.

"Nothing, Nina, nothing. Your father's just doing his job."

Maria takes Mum upstairs and helps her take off her tight red dress, the one she bought last year for "special occasions". I walk on and pass Isa's room. My eyes linger on the door. I can still feel Max's hand in mine. Quickly I open my own door and flee inside.

I send Max a DOS message. If only they don't get caught.

No, don't think about it. I mustn't think about it. Erik knows what to do. Everything'll be all right. Everything.

Out of habit, I look at the DOS screen in the corner.

A fire is raging in my room and gives everything a strange orange glow The heat of the flames seems to fly off the screen, where glass bursts into thousands of pieces and the metal melts into strange, unrecognizable shapes. The steel structure of the most beautiful building in CC1 looks like a skeleton against the starry sky.

The same stars as then.

A reporter talks quickly and pictures appear of rescue workers trying to pull people from under the rubble. They've put some dramatic music under the pictures so that the viewers do not have to listen to the groans and screams of the wounded.

The picture changes again to a scene of the digiscope before the explosion, filmed on someone's HC camera. We hear laughter in the background and see some party-goers heading toward the building. The camera concentrates on a happy face and then on the digiscope or its surroundings, and on groups of people apparently on their way inside. Then suddenly there is a rumbling noise that grows louder and louder and ends in a massive crash. The camera pans: the beautiful starlit sky, the digiscope with fiery flames springing from it, panicking people in colorful party gear, and finally the hard, stone ground. The camera remains on the ground, motionless, like it's in the eye of a storm. Then its owner picks it up and continues to record the burning digiscope.

Small puppet-like figures spring from the higher storeys, jumping to escape the flames. I can't believe they're people. The voices of the party-goers around the camera mix together and with every new explosion, the group holds its breath and then lets out screams of disbelief.

I turn off the screen. I think I'm going to be sick.

I get up and walk to the bathroom. I undress and stand under a hot shower. The water calms me. My thoughts return to what was real just an hour ago.

You kissed him, Nina.

So different to the boys I've kissed before. This is a Wet. A wet kiss. I giggle at the stupid joke and touch my tingling lips.

When I get out of the shower and go into my room in my pajamas, I see the bag with Max's Wet clothing, left behind in all the commotion; Maria must have put it in my room. I pick up the bag and open it. I take out his old clothes and at the bottom find an old-fashioned book. I hold it in my hands and stare at the title without reading it.

I know where I want to be.

I stuff his clothes back in the bag, push his backpack under my bed, and walk from my room to the library.

The spines of hundreds of unread books stare at me from behind glass doors in the wooden cupboards. Leather arm-chairs, each with its own footstool, are meant to give the room a luxurious and relaxed feel. One of the cupboards is not a bookcase, but a liquor cabinet. Dad's special place.

My eyes glide over the titles, looking for a book that I know my dad must own. Dad collects everything, even things that aren't supposed to be collected.

I find it. The glass cabinet is locked, but I know Dad well enough to guess the combination: Isa's date of birth.

The History of the Great Flood. It is the book I had to copy from during detention. A first edition, by the look of it. I hadn't expected anything else of my father. I turn the page and begin to read. This time for real.

MAX

Finally the trunk opens. Bright light — a lamp-post? — blinds me for an instant. Wait a moment, Max. Wait a moment. I carefully stretch my arm and swear as I hear a crack. I kick my feet to get some life back in them; it's as if somebody is sticking pins in my skin, but not quite getting through.

I was fucking scared.

I thought they had me when Erik was stopped and some Blower or other asked for his ID card. Nothing happened. They waved him through when he said he was on some business for his boss. Waders. Bloody paddlers.

"Need any help?"

Erik stands there watching me struggle, but his look shows that he has no intention whatsoever of actually lifting so much as a bloody finger.

"No, I'm fine," I answer brusquely.

I climb out of the trunk, legs first, sit on the edge for a moment, and then jump off. I'm shivering. This Dry clothing may be nice, but it doesn't keep you warm.

Erik looks at me. His ginger hair, or what is left of it, is blowing around. He's really sturdy. Built like a house, broad and heavy.

"Do you know what you're doing, lad?"

What? The question is unexpected. I'm not used to hearing this guy talk if nobody has asked him anything. But I'm

Wet, just like him. And in his eyes I'm just a brat.

"What I'm doing?" I say, looking him straight in the eye.

"I know they paid your brother a visit."

How does he know that?

"My brother has nothing to do with anything," I say, just as calmly as him. "And I have nothing to do with my brother." I spit on the ground.

"Are you sure?"

"Yes, I'm sure."

Does he believe me? My head is racing. How could a Wader like him know that they've paid a visit to my brother? Who does he work for? I force myself not to look away. I have nothing to hide.

"Nina's house is troubled, Max."

I had expected a lot, but not this. He continues to stare at me. He's no longer a Wader, or the driver. He's talking to me, man to man.

"Troubled?" I hear myself say.

"A lot has happened."

I immediately see Nina before me. In the summer house. How she looked at me, her eyes wide and unfathomably deep. I want to ask him, but Erik is quicker.

"It's not for me to tell you more than that."

He turns round, gets in, and drives away.

When I get home, the first thing I do is kick off those damned Dry clothes. I stuff them under my bed. I put on my old pyjamas and walk to the living-room. Ma's sitting there on the settee.

She's awake. Of course she's awake. She's watching the images of the collapsing digiscope in a trance. They are repeated over and over again.

"Ma?"

"Max!"

She turns round, obviously relieved.

"Have they already...?"

She knows what I mean. She shakes her head.

I sit down next to her on our old settee.

I feel a strange mixture of satisfaction, revulsion, and doubt as the images flicker across the screen. I've seen the building with my own eyes now. I've seen the people who, only a few hours later, were burned alive. Not swallowed by water, but by fire. *Dries are pretty flammable, little brother.* His grin. *They should have kept a Wet around.* I can practically hear him saying it.

Has he really gone and done it?

How can so much happen in so short a time? The different voices in my head are driving me crazy: Pa, Li, Ma, Nina.

Nina.

Man.

I let myself be ruled by my prick. I like her. My body likes her. I think back to how she tastes, light and sweet as those vanilla wafers Pa sometimes brought home for us. I think of her small, incredibly sexy body. Fuck, I want more. I take a cushion and place it on my lap.

She stopped. Something was wrong. She wanted to show me something. Was it to do with what Erik said? I think of her last look. I saw something in her eyes. But I don't know what. I could think about it until my brain explodes, but I still won't know.

I sigh. Tomorrow.

On the DOS screen, the Dries are still jumping from the burning building. Suddenly it hits me how tired I am.

"Ma, I'm off to bed."

She turns to face me.

"Okay, son."

I take her hand and squeeze it gently. "Go to bed. There's nothing you can do."

I already know her answer.

"Let me be, son. You go to bed."

I nod, kiss her, and leave the room.

My room, our room, feels small after Nina's house. I look at the pile of old CDs, hear Bob Dylan in that ridiculous room. Those fantastic acoustics. I feel a pang of jealousy. I shake my head and start sorting through the pile until I find something I like. I send Nina a short message that I'm home, lie down on the bed, and listen. I click off the light with my bare foot.

I've almost fallen off when I hear the front door, followed immediately by Ma's voice.

"Liam! Finally!"

Li storms through the hall, pulls open our door, turns on the light, and starts grabbing clothes from the wardrobe. He puts everything into a big bag.

"Hey, little brother," he says without looking around.

I push the blanket off me and get up.

"What the fuck are you doing?"

"Nothing to do with you, Wader."

"*What* did you say?"

Li stops what he's doing and pushes his rolled up socks against my chest. I go to grab his hand. He's quicker.

"Your Dry girlfriend. What's her name?"

"Oh, you want to know her name? So that you can take care of her, just like you took care of those other Dries?"

Li laughs and I get angrier.

"Hey." He holds up his hands. "I only asked, man. I've got other things on my mind than those dead Dries. And it's Baker, isn't it?" He says it with that so-called innocent look of his and suddenly I can't take it. I can't take it! It's the final fucking *last straw*.

I lash out at his arrogant ugly mug.

Li doesn't see it in time and blood splashes round in a perfect arc. He curses — I learned that right hook from him. I stand there looking at him in amazement and don't see his knee until it's too late. I double up and groan with pain. Li grabs me and spits in my ear.

"That's the first and last time you pull that shit on me, Max. And shall I tell you something? I've got proof. I've got proof that Bradshaw set up Pa and all the others. Some Dry bitch or other was trapped in the school. That's why he left them all there. For a Dry, Max. One single Dry."

I try to squirm free and kick his shins. He lets me go and I smash my fist into his face.

"Max! Liam! No!"

Ma.

She tries to grab me and Li at the same time. I immediately let go. Ma's voice is enough to bring me to my senses, but Li completely loses it. He throws a punch with his left hand and hits Ma full in the face. I hear a nasty crack and blood pours from her nose as she falls to the ground.

Silence.

Icy silence.

Li looks at me. I look at him. We look at Ma on the ground.

I hear her groaning softly. I kneel down next to Ma, take

her in my arms. Li stands there motionless. Only his eyes are moving, seeing things I can't see.

"Piss off," I say softly.

Li stares at me. His eyes narrow.

"Get out!" I say louder. Ma groans.

He looks from Ma to me and back again. I get up and push him outside, into the hall. He doesn't protest. I pick up his bag of things and walk past him through the hall. I open the front door and throw them outside.

He just stands there, staring at Ma on the ground.

"Fuck off, Liam. Just go and leave us in peace!"

I want to go back to Ma but Li is still standing there in the doorway. "You've got such important work to do? Well, get going."

"But Ma..."

"You've already done enough for her."

He hesitates for a second. Then he pushes past me, nudging me with his shoulder, and picks up his bag of things. He turns round and looks me straight in the eye. My fucking big brother. "Tell Ma I'm sorry, but I've got no choice, Max." He doesn't wait for an answer and runs down the stairs, taking them two at a time.

I watch him go, slam the door, and walk back to my room. Ma is sitting on my bed, a handkerchief against her bloody nose.

I hold her. I hold her tight and feel the anger pour off me in waves.

NINA

I read until my head is so full that I can't take in any more. I read how the once promised land is nothing like what came into being in the Five Regions. I read that nobody actually knows what is happening in the Foreign Territories, or even if the Foreign Territories actually exist. I read that our victory over the water has not been a victory at all. For the water is still rising and it does not look as if it will ever subside.

When DOS shows three o'clock, I close the book. The house is quiet. I return the book to its shelf and close the doors. As I leave the library, I hear the garage door opening.

Dad is back.

I want to go to my room, but change my mind. I walk softly downstairs and slip into the place where I pushed Max. Voices sound from the garage.

"In any case, we've caught one of them, Excellency."

"That's not enough, Felix. Not enough."

I hear Dad sigh. Then footsteps, going towards the kitchen. They carry on talking, but I can't understand anything more. I know where they're going. And I know where to go if I want to hear what they're saying.

Our old playroom is next to Dad's study. I've not been in there since Isa's death. All our old toys are still there. Our dress-up wardrobe, our dolls, the big game computer with its DOS screen. And the corner, where we used to listen to Dad when he was working.

"... do everything we can, Excellency," says Felix as he enters the room. His soft, melodious voice contrasts with Dad's deep tones.

"Here! In cci! What am I going to say to the Council of Governors? That WEtTO rules here? That they can even get into our own backyard? I want results, Felix. Now!"

I have never heard Dad so angry and I'm shocked by the pent-up rage in his voice. What is he going to do? What does he want to do? He snorts as he paces up and down in his study. His breathing is heavy and labored.

Felix clears his throat. "We could send them a warning, Excellency."

What?

"What?" Dad's question echoes my thoughts.

Felix remains silent.

"What sort of warning, Felix?"

Dad stops and in the fraction of a second before Felix speaks, I see them before me. Dad behind his desk, his hands spread out on the top, forehead bathed in perspiration, his teeth biting his lower lip. And Felix opposite him: calm, controlled, and impeccable.

"We could declare martial law. Then normal legislation and law would no longer apply." Felix waits for a moment to add emphasis to what he says next. "Martial law will gives us the space we need to do what we have to do. Without concessions. And WEtTO knows it as well."

I hold my breath. The government last declared martial law when the First Great Flood swept over the provinces. I think of the images of the WEtTOs on the dos screen. Just boys.

It's quiet.

Dad gets up and I hear clinking, the pop of a bottle being

opened and the sound of liquor being poured into a glass. At least, that's what I assume. He takes a gulp and sighs deeply.

I bite my lip.

"Okay," says Dad at last. "We'll broadcast an announcement on all DOS channels, so that we're sure those damned terrorists hear us. Make it clear, and I mean *very* clear, that we will not allow ourselves to be ruled by WEtTO."

Oh *Dad*.

There's a pause. What next?

"Do you have something to add, Felix?"

"There is something else, Excellency...?"

"What, Felix?"

"You could set an example."

"An example?"

Another silence. I can hardly believe what I hear. I see the logic even before my father understands him. The logic of the Five Regions. The logic of Dry versus Wet.

I hear the leather of Dad's chair creak. A second sigh in the chilled silence of the room. Felix has also sat down.

"An example, yes," he says, so softly that I can hardly understand him.

Dad breathes in and slowly lets it out again. He takes another sip. I hear the ice clinking in the glass.

"To give extra force to your threat..." begins Felix. Again he allows a silence to fall.

"Yes, Felix?" says Dad, waiting.

"To give extra force to your threat, you could announce that Ramon Campion will be executed within forty-eight hours unless WEtTO givse up those responsible for the attack," said Felix, completing his sentence.

Again there is silence.

I close my eyes and think back to the Dad of the past, before he was Governor and worked at the Regional Hall. When he came home in the evening after work, just like Mum. When there were four of us. I see us all sitting at the kitchen table in our old house. No dining-room. Maria was there and helped with the cooking, and sometimes ate with us. I see Dad laughing out loud at Isa pulling faces. When did that man disappear from our life? I don't know. I really don't know.

"Each of his crimes carries a sentence of at least twenty years, Excellency," says Felix, interrupting my thoughts, carrying the logic to its inevitable conclusion. "And the death penalty..." He takes a sip of his own drink, as if wanting to increase the tension, "... can, of course, be reintroduced under martial law."

The death penalty.

The Dad of now is quiet. He moves his glass, the ice cubes sloshing in the expensive liquid. His breathing is heavy. I've closed my eyes and my hands are in my lap.

Don't do it, Dad.

Dad takes another sip and puts down the glass. "Felix," he says. He coughs. I have difficulty hearing him.

"Excellency?"

Again the leather creaks; Dad is fidgeting as if he is sitting on a bed of nails rather than on a comfortable leather chair. "That is perhaps... not a bad idea, Felix," says Dad.

The death penalty?

"We have to act now, Excellency," insists Felix. Dad sighs.

Don't do it. Don't do it. Don't do it. Because of I repeat it often enough, it will come true.

"Felix..."

For a moment I think Dad's going to say that Felix has now gone too far. I really think so.

But then my father says: "You're right."

I feel a lump in my throat.

"We must act now," says Dad, with a new note of certainty in his voice. I can hardly breathe.

"We have no other options."

"No, Excellency," Felix agrees. "We can't do anything else."

"WEtTO demands 'firm action.' Well, they'll get it!" says Dad.

I feel tears welling up. I have to struggle to keep my breathing under control. Dad — acting like a murderer? Was Max perhaps right...

What happened with Isa back then? I know that Dad did something, tried to do something to save Isa. To get her out of the building. What happened back then?

No, Dad is still Dad. He is not an evil man. He doesn't make decisions without thinking about them. Not then and not now. How many people are there under the rubble of the digiscope? How many people have WEtTO killed with their senseless actions? He is not an evil man. He is not an evil man.

I can't convince myself anymore.

I run out of the playroom and up the stairs. I don't want to hear it, know it, see it. The images of the past, the present, and the time to come run like a vivid digifilm in my mind.

In my bathroom, I quickly look for the pills, the pills that let me escape for a while. I finally find them. My hands are shaking as I swallow one, two, three at once. I lie on the bed and wait for black sleep to save me.

MAX

Ma won't hear about going to the hospital.

"They'll ask questions, Max. And certainly now."

"Ma, you're in pain and you're bleeding everywhere. Your nose is crooked and you passed out."

She grimaces and finally agrees.

I hate Li. I hope they catch him. He deserves it, the prick. The Morris men have always had a short fuse and it's not the first time that we've got into a fight, but you don't involve Ma. That's the rule. You never involve Ma.

I can't bear her still being worried about Li, but I know she is because when we're on the streetcar, I see her eyes constantly wander to the DOS screen.

Yet I'm startled when I see Ramon's face as large as life on the screen. Two Blowers are pushing him into a bus, his arms fastened behind his back. Something about martial law flickers at the bottom of the picture, while a reporter interviews the head of the Blowers.

Ma swallows. I put an arm round her.

We have to wait for hours in the hospital. The hospitals in the two CCs are crowded, so less urgent cases are being sent here. The waiting room is bare and stinks like all these building stink, from some disinfectant or other. My eyes wander over to the Dries waiting around us. I bet most of them have never seen a place like this. A place were damp patches cause green mould on the walls, where the floor is crooked and where the staff walk around in dirty uniforms because they can't get the stains out of their white hospital clothing.

After four hours, they call us in. Ma has to shake me awake.

The doctor is a Wet. He examines Ma's crooked nose. "How long have you been sitting there?"

I tell him.

He sighs.

"The last Dry I treated had a small cut in his finger."

I say nothing, let him do his job. Ma's in pain, certainly when the doctor feels her nose.

"I can't take any x-rays. We're too backed up. It's certainly broken, though."

Ma nods carefully.

"Pass out?"

"Yes," I say. "About a minute."

The doctor gets up, looks at the DOS screen in the corner. "Five o'clock," he mutters. "Have you been up all night, Mrs. Morris?"

"Yes."

"No other complaints?"

"No."

"Then I'm afraid I can't do anything more for you."

"What?" I jump up. Ma's nose is all crooked and he can't do anything about it?

"Calm down, Max," says Ma. She immediately grimaces again.

The doctor places his hand on my arm. I want to push him away, but the man is stronger than he looks.

"I can't do anything without anesthetics. The hospital is overfull. You wouldn't want me to straighten your mother's nose like that? And she's been up the whole night, so there's probably nothing wrong with her head."

The knot pulls and twists. I know the man thinks it's just as shitty as I do. That he wants to do more, but can't. "Can we come back later?" asks Ma.

"I really don't know when that will be possible, Mrs. Morris." He walks to his desk, picks up his HC and types in something.

"I'm sending a prescription for painkillers to your local health service. Do you have any Points?"

Ma is about to say no, but I beat her to it. I'll sell something. I'll get the Points.

"Yes, we still have some."

"Good."

I help Ma up and we shake the doctor's hand.

"I'm really sorry, Mrs. Morris," he says when we reach the door. He looks tired, has bags under his eyes.

"You can't do anything about it," says Ma. "You're doing your job as well as you can."

The man nods and shows us out.

We walk through the crowded corridor and leave the building. It is still dark. The night seems to last forever.

The first tram will leave in less than half an hour and I get Ma to sit on the bench while I walk around. She says nothing about the Points, just stares straight ahead. My body is bouncing with adrenaline. I tap my fingers on the glass of the tram shelter.

Suddenly I hear Li's words in my mind. What he said about Pa, about Bradshaw.

And shall I tell you something? I've got proof. I've got proof that Bradshaw set up Pa and all the others. Some Dry bitch or other was trapped in the school. That's why he left them all there. For a Dry, Max. One single Dry.

Could that be true?

But then something else forces itself into my mind. How he lost it and did something that even Pa in all his anger never did.

He hit Ma. And you never involve Ma. Never.

That's the rule.

NINA

Isa! No!!

I wake with a start. The sounds are still echoing in my ears, the sound of buildings collapsing and people screaming in terror.

I open my eyes and take a deep breath.

Max.

Yesterday. The attack. Dad. The ultimatum.

Everything floods back all at once and I break out in a sweat. I push off the blanket and in my hurry to get to my HC, I stumble over the clothes on the floor.

"Got home safely. See you at school. Max."

I breathe out and quickly send a reply.

You've got to tell him, Nina.

In the kitchen, Maria's watching the news. The rescue activities are still underway and when I enter, I see a ten-year-old boy being rescued. He's been buried for nearly twelve hours. Cheers sound from the crowd watching behind the barriers. Some of them are carrying signs with threatening slogans. There are photos of well-known WEtTOs with their throats cut, a rope round their necks, or a large red cross through their faces. Armed Dry Defenders are standing at a distance and keeping an eye on the crowd. At the bottom of the screen is the news I already know: at 4 am, Governor Bradshaw imposed martial law.

"Coffee, Nina?" asks Maria.

"Thanks."

We say nothing about the weekend. What is there to say?

"Where's Mum?" I ask.

"In bed."

"Did she get any sleep?"

"Yes, with a little help."

I nod and sip the coffee.

My eyes follow the images on the screen. The burning digiscope gives way to scenes of Dad flying to the First Region in a helicopter, where he's met by Governor Klarenbeek. He has been summoned for an emergency meeting of the Council of Governors. Together the two men disappear into the Regional Hall.

I cannot suppress a shiver when I imagining Dad getting into his car this morning on the way to the airport, followed closely by Felix.

The following item is about the rise of WEtTO and the recent wave of violence after the last floods. I turn away. I can't watch.

You've got to tell him.

In the car, I ask Erik to turn off DOS. He does what I ask without saying anything. Does Erik have children? A wife? I look at him as if seeing him for the first time.

I want to tell him. I'm going to tell him.

Dry Defenders are now posted at the corners of various streets in CC1. At the shopping center, everybody wanting to go in is scanned. Outside the CC, you hardly notice any difference. People are still hurrying to work, groups of children are walking to school, and the odd cyclist is trying to negotiate the uneven roads. I've never noticed before how many Dry Defenders are always on the streets outside.

Erik lets me out where he always lets me out and drives off. I take a deep breath and start walking towards school. I hope Max is there.

"Hey, Dry bitch!"

I stop and look round. Three boys are approaching. Do I know them?

"Looking for your Wet boyfriend?" says the second.

I know that voice. It's Damian. Oh no.

"Are you going to hold his hand?" teases the third.

They laugh.

Run, Nina.

My fingers tighten around the strap on my bag. I look behind me and in front of me. There's nobody. I'm all alone. *Now!*

But before I can do anything, they're already on me. Three boys. Three men. And I'll never be take them on all on my own.

Damian's nose is still yellow, just like Max's jaw. On him, the effect is completely different. It's so... Wet. He smirks and his teeth — even yellower than his nose — appear. Smoker's teeth. Wet teeth. The other two boys are behind him: one big and heavy, the other tall and skinny. Lars, I recall, and Tim. They know exactly what they want, what they're going to do.

Damian takes a step closer, supposedly inspecting me. I can't do anything but stare back at him. He takes another step, his hand touches mine. I shiver. I smell his sour sweat, the smoke in his Wet clothes, and I feel his hot breath on my skin. My skin. His mouth is suddenly next to my ear. "You're rather tasty, aren't you?" He whispers, but loud enough for the others to hear him. "Not really as Dry as you look."

Tim and Lars laugh. Damian half turns as if to accept the

applause. He grabs my arm and pulls me roughly against him. "If you want a real Wet, you should try me, bitch."

And I feel him. I think I'm going to be sick. Breathe, Nina. Breathe. He shifts one hand to my crotch and grabs my head with the other. I close my eyes, but it doesn't make any difference because his scent is everywhere, his hands are everywhere, and his tongue is forcing itself into my mouth. I do the only thing I can think of. I bite.

Damian immediately releases me and swears loudly.

"Dwy whowe. That whowe pit my pongue!

I try to run, but Lars is quicker. He grabs me and pulls at my coat. "If Damian can't handle you, I'll go first," he says and smirks. Damian swears again and pushes Lars aside. Blood is dribbling from the corner mouth and his eyes are like red beads. Only one thought can be read there. He grabs me and hits me hard in the face. I feel the punch reverberate in the back of my head. I groan softly, watching as the boy pulls down my jeans.

"Please!"

"D'ya hear that? She wants it so bad she's begging for it!"

Again they laugh. I close my eyes. Snow falls on my hair, on my naked stomach and naked legs. The rancid smell gets closer and closer. My arms are held tightly. I can't do anything. Can't do anything at all.

Then I hear footsteps.

MAX

I wanted to wait for her, to tell her that perhaps it would be better for us not to see each other. I don't want to put Nina in danger. Now that Li's left and martial law has been declared, the Dries will certainly be back looking for him.

I knew where Erik would let her out. Thank God I knew.

I force my legs to move faster, faster than ever. The knot completely takes hold of me, turns my guts inside out.

I fly at Damian.

We roll over the thin layer of snow, and I punch him in his filthy, foul mug, once, twice, three times, until somebody grabs me from behind and gives me a kick in the stomach. I've gone crazy, lost it, I've never been so furious. Everything I learned from Pa and Li comes back to me. I know exactly how to twist out of their grasp, duck their punches, and I know where to hit those fifthly bastards where it hurts most.

Lars throws his weight into the fight. I duck and trip him up with an outstretched foot, at the same time avoiding Tim's fist and smashing a punch into his head. Damian is laying on the road, groaning. I want to hit him harder, I want to kick in his Wet brains, I want to destroy him. I nearly fall over my own legs trying to get to the bastard and, from the corner of my eye I see Nina hurriedly pulling up her clothes. A molten rush of shame flows through me and I surf that rush, using it to fly at her filthy attacker.

I don't hear anything, I don't feel anything other than intense hatred as I kick the boy on the ground again and again. I kick and kick and punch with my fist, but I can't wipe that picture of Damian, Damian holding her, Damian pulling down her jeans, Damian trying to take her, from my mind. I don't realize that Tim and Lars have taken off. I don't realize that Nina is now the one who's trying to pull me off him, begging me to stop.

Only when Granville grabs me roughly by the arm and almost dislocates my shoulder, do I come to. Only then do I see her standing there, wide-eyed with shock, snow and earth and brown leaves in her hair. His left cheek is streaked with blood. Whose? Hers? Damian's? Mine?

"Calm down, boy. Calm down."

Teachers and pupils come running. Granville holds me tightly. I can't go anywhere. I don't want to do anywhere. It's all gone. It's all gone. There's nothing left in me.

Tim and Lars are talking to Collingwood. They point at me and at Damian who is still lying on the ground, his arms and legs pulled up. He's not moving.

"We were just standing there talking, honest, nothing else, and he suddenly stormed at him and started hitting him like a lunatic."

"We couldn't stop him, sir.'

'He even hit *her* when she tried to stop him."

All eyes turn to Nina.

'Nina?'

She stares at Collingwood. She says nothing. Her gaze is empty, so terribly empty.

Damian groans when Reiger kneels next to him and carefully raises his blooded head. He feels his pulse.

"Damian, can you hear me?"

He groans again. He raises his beaten head and our gazes cross. He screams.

"Get him away from me! Get him away from me!"

He's scared stiff. Of me. Of *me*. I can't take my eyes off of him until Granville gives me a clip around the head – "Come with me, Morris" – and drags me away through the crowd.

I hear them talking. I hear them whispering. And see them, no, feel them pointing.

"That's Max. Max Morris."

"His brother was kicked out of school last year."

"Isn't that the kid who was in trouble last week...?"

"He's always on his own."

I look at the ground, at my footsteps in the soft snow. I see Nina before me. How she looked at me with those empty eyes.

Oh fuck, have I really messed it up?

"This is the last time you do something like this, you little ruffian," he hisses in my ear as we walk across the quad.

I don't say anything, try to keep my footing as he drags me into the building. When he reaches Davenport's room, he barges in without even knocking.

The skinny woman is sitting at her desk and looks up, irritably. "Max Morris. What is it this time?"

I'm just a fly for that Dry. An irritating insect that keeps landing on her hand and each time she has to brush it off. Granville fills her in.

When he's finished, Davenport stands up. She sighs and walks from behind her desk. The click of high heels echoes through the nearly empty room. Davenport pushes me onto the chair in front of the desk so that I have to look up at that woman.

"Have you anything to say?" Penetrating voice.

What if I tell the truth? Will they believe me? Will it make any difference? They'll kick me out of school anyway. Everything is over, no matter what. Everything is over.

"Damian..." I say.

"What about Damian?"

"He..." I can hardly get it out, I see it all before me again. The words are pure venom. "He, she... He was raping her." I say it as quickly as I can.

Davenport looks at Granville.

"The girl hasn't said anything, ma'am."

"And the others?"

"They said he attacked them for no reason. He pushed the girl out of the way."

She sighs deeply, walks to the window, and stares outside. Granville waits patiently; his heavy butcher's hands keep me in my place. Finally Davenport turns round. She looks at me as if I'm a mongrel running under her feet.

"What on earth is wrong with you Wets!"

I feel Granville's hand stiffen. His fingers drill into my collarbone and I bite my lip to keep myself from screaming.

"Don't bother coming back, Morris. You're suspended. Immediately. I'll be reporting the incident and you can expect a visit from the Dry Defenders." Her eyes go down to her HC and then raise again. "Ask the others to come in, Granville. I've just heard that the third one can walk again. Bring the girl as well."

Granville nods. His hands relax. Just slightly. "You can go."

She says it without looking up. I suspect that the force with which Granville drags me from the chair is his way of getting rid of his Wet frustration. He pushes me in front of him into the corridor.

I see them coming. Tim and Lars in the front, followed by Damian with Reiger holding him up. His head is cleaned up, if you could ever call that filthy head clean, but his left eye is almost completely closed and he can only breathe through his mouth. He's limping. Nina and Collingwood follow. He's holding her shoulder and speaking softly to her.

I want to stop. Granville's not having that.

"Keep moving."

Nina looks up.

Look at me.

She sees me.

Nina.

She looks away.

Why does she look away?

Granville drags me roughly to the door and throws me out.

NINA

"What happened, Nina?"

Ms Davenport looks abut the same age as Dad. She wears her hair pulled back in a severe ponytail, which only makes her thin face look even sharper. I've never seen anyone as thin as her. She tries to be friendly, but it is perfectly obvious that she's only here because she has to be. A Dry working in a Wet school; there must be a story to that.

I see Max.

I only see Max. How he kicks Damian, kicks him over and over again. I thought he would never stop. I tried to stop him. Didn't I?

I wanted him to kick Damian. Wanted him to punch him. But then he just lost it and no matter what I shouted, he wouldn't stop. Lars and Tim ran away. I could have done something. I didn't. I was scared. Was I scared of him?

"Nina?"

I look at Davenport.

"I asked you what happened."

The woman doesn't know who I am. Nobody here knows who I am. If I say what happened, if I tell them I was attacked by Wets, I'll never leave CC1 again, and, knowing Dad, I probably wouldn't even be let out of the house. Then I'd never see him again.

Yet without Max's intervention... I don't want to go there. He's already been kicked out of school. The way he beat up that boy...

How can everything suddenly go so terribly wrong? I don't say anything. I don't know what to say. I don't know anymore. The woman in front of me sighs. "You've nothing to say?" I blink and shake my head. I don't want to have to decide. All I want is to get out of here. Out of this place. And away from the boys waiting outside.

"Any other injuries?"

She points at the graze on cheek which I got when Damian threw me on the ground.

I shake my head again.

"Do you want to do home?"

I nod.

"Is there somebody who can come and pick you up?"

I nod again.

"Good."

She bends over me and smiles at me. Her purple make-up makes her eyes hard. I can suddenly imagine why she has been assigned to a Wet school.

"Go home, Nina. You've been through a lot." I nod again, get up, and leave the sterile room as quickly as I can.

I tell Erik I fell down. Somebody from school is sure to phone. Since nobody must know who I am, it'll go through Dad's secretary; it'll take at least a day before Mum and Dad hear about it. Particularly now that Dad's not at home.

"Fell over?" asks Erik, studying my inured face in the rear-view mirror. We drive out of the street.

"A Wet tripped me up. In the snow." A half-truth is better than a lie, I decide, against my better judgment.

Does he believe me? I don't know. I'm a bit ashamed when I see his concerned look. But I don't want to tell him what happened. I wouldn't know how.

"Did that boy do something to you?"

"No, Max didn't do anything!" I say aghast. Or perhaps everything, I immediately think. "He helped me."

Erik nods and turns into the main road.

"Can we go straight home? Please?" I hope he won't ask any more questions. I know Erik is only concerned. I know Erik is only taking care of me. But I can't answer his questions at the moment. His look is insistent, but I keep looking straight ahead.

"Home. Okay, we'll go home."

I smile and hope he understands.

When we get home, I run upstairs, take off my dirty clothes, and go into shower.

All the clichés are true.

The hot water warms my body, but I remain cold inside. Now I'm alone, I feel Damian's hand where nobody should put it, smell his rancid odor, his hot excitement forces itself over me, and I taste his bitter, smoker's tongue.

I close my eyes. I want to forget it.

Max.

Where will Max be?

And I suddenly remember that I still haven't told him. That he still doesn't know who I am. Who I really am. My silent tears mix with the hot water. The water that will never be able to wash me clean again. The water I hate, but which I need more than ever.

MAX

Outside I do the only thing I can do. I run.

A thicker layer of snow covers the silent streets and cools my hot head. Where can I go? I can't go home. Not yet. Ma's at home. Today she's on the night shift and won't be leaving until around four o'clock. And I can't see her yet. I can't handle her disappointment on top of everything else.

The last Morris has also messed up everything,

I'm confident you'll make the right choice. Her words. Not mine. I've never trusted myself.

Maybe I should have gone for hel instead of rushing in like an idiot. But then I would have been too late and Nina would have...

I have to stop and take deep breaths to get the rage under control. My hands grip the crumbling wall next to me, just to get a hold on something. In a flash I see myself beating the daylights out of that piece of filth. And in my mind there's nobody to stop me. This time I go on until I'm sure he'll never open his filthy mouth again. It feels so fucking good.

No. No. *She couldn't even bring herself to look at you.*

I want to bang my head against the wall and almost do it. Like when I was a small kid. Li did it as well. Too much energy. Always too much energy. You can still see the dents in the wall above my pillow.

I yell in frustration. My scream sounds so pathetically

soft. Wind and snow catch it and throw it back in my Wet face. I swear silently, but my legs are moving again. I only realize where they're taking me when I'm almost there.

The cemetery.

In this weather it's almost deserted. I open the wrought-iron gate that must date back to the twentieth century if the rust is anything to go by. A few centuries worth of dead people are here; some of them have even been here since before the First Great Flood. It's the only place where everyone is equal, Dry or Wet. Although. My eyes are caught by the artificial mound where the Dries are buried. Even a dead Dry doesn't want to get wet feet.

I walk along the gravel path down the middle. Everything in front of me is white, the cemetery is untouched. It feels like the day of the first snowfall of the season, and you're the first person outside, and your footsteps are the first in that white world.

It is so quiet here. I'm not used to it, this quiet. There are usually people everywhere. It's always so busy. And when they aren't any people, there are DOS screens to remind you that you are never alone and there's never enough room for you. That's it. Not enough room.

Snow crackles under my sneakers. I walk slowly, to make the feeling last longer. I look at the old gravestones, covered with moss and clothed in a thin layer of snow. The names of people from the distant past go by. Not Dries or Wets, just people.

One date catches my eye. A certain Charles Green died the day before the First Great Flood. Before all the shit began. One day. That Charles was lucky. I shake my head and walk on.

I know where I'm going. At the back, in the neglected corner. That's where they put us Wets. That's where my future lies. Pa is buried there in a communal grave. *Thrown*, says Li. None of the workers had enough Points for their own grave or funeral. Everything was paid for by the Region.

I stop in front of a simple stone bearing the names of the fifty drowned workers. I brush off the snow with my bare hands. A short text is engraved above the names. Something about God and how they will be better with Him. Bullshit. Pa didn't believe in God. And Ma certainly doesn't. How can you believe in a good God if you're a Wet?

Let us pray.

I relive that day. I'm standing next to Ma and holding her hand. Li is standing on the other side and staring straight ahead. Everywhere there are familiar faces. There's Jack, the boy I used to play football with. He's not only lost his Pa, but also his two brothers. Mrs. Goddard is sitting on a chair next to him. Her husband was one of Pa's best laborers.

"Let us pray for those who have been taken from us."

The Dry who is holding the funeral service puts his hands together. I keep my eyes wide open, so does Li, just like most of the Wets. Our silent protest. As his polished words sound in my hand, I suddenly realize something.

It was the same Dry who came to interrogate Li. That voice, that sickly sweet voice, that false laugh and those hard, bright blue, beady eyes. That's why he seemed so familiar to me. Could Li be right? Was the man sent by Bradshaw himself? It can't be a coincidence...

Man, don't be so paranoid.

I shake my head and look at the grave. If I don't watch out, I'll become just as crazy as Li.

"Pa," I say out loud. I come here for Pa, after all.

My fingers trace the grooves of the letters, until I reach the Ms. The M of March, Mad, Malleable. The M of Morris.

Morris, Robert. There he is. My Pa.

"Hello, Pa."

I kneel down and stroke his name with my half-frozen fingers. I lower my head, my cheek touches the cold stone. I take a deep breath.

"I've screwed up, Pa."

I breathe out, rub my stinging eyes with the balls of my palm.

"Sorry, Pa. I'm so sorry."

I get up and walk away.

It's half past four when I put the key in the lock. That has to be a safe space of time.

The door isn't locked.

Is Ma still at home? No, she can't be. They'd give her the sack. A burglar? Come on, who'd want to break in here? Who is it, then? I hear footsteps. Familiar footsteps.

The door opens for me.

"Hey, little brother."

Liam. The last person I expected after what he did. "And you just shut your mouth, if you know what's good for you."

Knot.

"Li." I'm shocked by the threat in my own voice. Not that Li pays much attention.

"Come in."

He holds the door open for me and grins.

Something's the matter. I can see it. He knows something.

And he's so damned pleased that I don't know what it is. He can't wait to tell me.

I walk past him without lowering my gaze. He closes the door and walks with me. I want to go to my room but he takes my arm and pushes me towards the kitchen. I don't know why I let him.

I'm not even surprised when I see who's sitting there, together with Julius and another woman I don't know.

The man in the long overcoat.

His hat is on Ma's kitchen table. Next to a cup of tea. Ma will be furious about the tea.

"Max, isn't it? I'm Harry."

The man gets up and puts out his hand. Harry. No surname. I wonder whether it's his real name. His voice is surprisingly low.

I look at the outstretched hand in a leather glove. I nod.

Harry has hung his overcoat over the kitchen chair and is wearing a grey suit. A Dry suit, but he isn't a Dry. You can see that at once. His light-brown hair is too unkempt and no Dry would wear a beard and a pair of spectacles. I've no idea how old he is.

"We have information about somebody which you might find interesting, Max."

Harry looks at me. His green eyes flash.

What?

I avoid his commanding gaze, look at Li. Li, who is pushing an HC into my hands.

"Look, Max. Look!" He can hardly contain himself. Harry nods encouragingly.

I hesitate.

I don't want to know anything about Li's new life. About

WEtTO. *Yes, about WEtTO.* I don't want to know anything about people who murder other people and think that that will get them what they want. My brother, the fucking terrorist.

But I'm also curious.

I know that it's something big that Li wants to show me. I know him well enough to get it. I know my brother long enough to know that he knows I want to know.

My hand takes the HC while my head screams at me not to. My eyes look while my mind says: *Don't do it. Run. Protect yourself.*

Then my hands connect with my head, my eyes with my mind and I finally realize what Li so desperately wants to show me.

That Nina Baker is Nina Bradshaw, the Governor's daughter.

***

"Bet your Dry girlfriend didn't tell you that, did she?"

I hear Li but at the same time I don't hear him.

I think about the girl who I helped gather together her things. I think about the girl that said she also thought about how we've got ourselves into this mess. And I think of the girl I got kicked out of school for because I had to poke my Wet nose into Dry business.

I look at the screen. I scroll through the photos of the house where I was one night ago — one lousy night ago. The photos were taken with a telescopic lens. They are grainy and the backgrounds are fuzzy. But what they show is clear enough. Bradshaw getting out of his car and being met by his wife — man, she really looks like her mother. Bradshaw walking up the steps to the house with the woman. Bradshaw putting out a hand to his daughter who is waiting at the top of the steps for him.

His daughter.

The Governor has kept his family out of the publicity for years. I can vaguely remember once seeing pictures of him and his wife. I can't remember children.

But here she is.

Nina Bradshaw. Nina *fucking* Bradshaw.

I look up. Li is leaning against the worktop and studying me, while Harry is waiting with folded hands until I get my head together again.

"What do you want?" I finally ask. I place the HC on the kitchen table. I don't recognize my own voice — it sounds empty and clipped.

"We now know for sure that Bradshaw was behind the decision that caused the death of your father and his colleagues," says Harry. His too-friendly eyes look inquisitively at me.

Knot. Stabbing, threadbare, tightening knot.

"There were Dries trapped in the school where your father was doing maintenance."

Dries? Li had spoken of one Dry.

Harry continues unperturbed.

"Your father and his men were helping with the evacuation. Or rather, they were forced to get the pupils out before the building collapsed from the force of the rising water."

Harry falls silent, unfolds his hands, and places them on the kitchen table.

He looks straight at me.

"Max... Bradshaw abandoned those men. He left them behind when the dyke gave way and the building collapsed."

I don't get what he's trying to say. I shake my head.

"He let your father and those forty-nine others drown because a Dry was trapped in another part of the school. He directed the rescue workers there. That's why he engineered the extra dyke breach which led to your father drowning. So that the water could be diverted." He held his breath for a second. "But he was too late."

For the first time, I heard a hint of satisfaction in his controlled voice. He doesn't care that that Dry drowned. For him, that's justice.

"You see Max? Do you believe me now?" Li can't contain himself any longer. He throws his hands in the air and his dark eyes flash like fire. "Harry can show you the order, Max. We have proof that Bradshaw murdered him!"

"And that's why we have to act now, Max," says Harry.

"Now!" echoes Li.

"What do you want?" I ask. *What do I want?* My eyes go back and forth between Harry and Li.

"What do we want?" Harry gets up and walks to the window. He pushes the lace curtain to one side with his left hand. He looks outside. The woman taps him on the shoulder and shows him something on her HC. He nods.

He turns round. His grass-green eyes bore into me. I want to look away, but I can't. Something in his look holds my gaze and when he begins to talk, I can't do anything but listen to his deceptively simple words.

"We want what is our right, Max. We want to be treated as people. We want to live."

All the rest is pushed into the background and I feel myself being swept along. By his words and his look, by what I've just seen and heard. And by the knot in my stomach that stabs and pulls. By the rage I can no longer contain.

Nina.

How could I think that a Wet like me could get what she had? That I could get her? I've been such an idiot. A stupid bastard who's ruled by his dick and a pretty face. Who even allowed himself to be lured into the house of his pa's murderer.

My pa's *murderer.*

He's my pa's murderer. And she's his daughter. It all suddenly sinks in.

The knot grows.

It grows.

And grows.

Until it not only strangles my guts, makes me clench my fists and tightens my throat, but also devours my weeping heart and my pounding head. Until everything in me is burning with rage, *burning,* yes, and I can hardly breathe because the knot persists and insists and eats me up until all I am is that.

Rage.

I look straight at Harry.

"I want to live too." My voice quivers. I don't have any control over my fists, which nervously begin to punch my legs.

"Who doesn't?" answers Harry quietly. Li sniffs in agreement. "I don't know what you're planning, but, but... count me in. You can't keep me out of this."

Li places a hand on my shoulder. I roughly shrug it off. Each touch is one too many. I've never been so worked up. I'm on fire, I'm so fucking hot.

Nina... Why?

My nails push into the flesh of my palms. I only notice when a trickle of blood dribbles along my finger.

"Take it easy, little brother. We'll get our revenge. Harry here's got a fantastic plan."

Harry smiles. I don't flinch. I can't flinch any more.

"What are you planning?"

It's not Harry who replies. It's the young woman who turns from her place at the window and says in an icy voice: "We're going to kidnap the Governor's daughter."

NINA

I keep on looking at my HC. I still haven't heard anything from Max. Surely he's home by now. It's nearly five o'clock and even if he went running, he should have been home by lunchtime.

I want to send him a message. I want to tell him. I'm just about to, my finger hovers over the Send button, but I don't do it. I can't. I have to tell him in person. And now, on top of it all, he's been kicked out of school. Because of me.

I ask Collingwood whether it is true. He looks at me with his soft eyes and nods. "Terrible shame," he murmurs. "Terrible shame."

I've ruined Max's future.

"Nina?"

I jump.

"Mum?"

I thought she was sleeping. After the attack on the digiscope, she's hardly got out of her bed.

"May I come in?"

"Yes, of course."

The door opens softly. She's wearing her old nightie, the white one with pink roses. Isa gave it to her last year for Mother's Day. She leans against my desk. I know what she sees.

"Maria told me you fell over."

"Yes. Slipped. Somebody accidentally bumped into me."

I'm getting better at lying. Does she believe me?

"Darling..."

I wait.

"If anything's..." She licks her dry lips. "If there's anything, you can always tell me."

What's she thinking? Does she know something? Has Erik or Maria said anything? "I know it's not easy for you and you would preferred to go to a normal school, but... but if they're bullying you —"

I hold up my hand. That's what she's thinking.

"Nobody's bullying me, Mum. It was an accident."

She falls silent.

"Really. I really like it."

She looks at me, a shadow of a smile on her fine face. Her hands search for a grip but there are too many things on my desk. She turns round and pushes a few of my special colored digipens to one side. She looks for just a bit longer than necessary.

"Who's this?"

She turns round and holds up my HC.

Oh no. What was I using for my wallpaper? Max. A drawing of Max.

"A boy," I stammer.

"I can see that," smiles Mum. She throws me a questioning look. Before I know it, I tell her. Not everything, but enough. I want to tell her.

"He's a boy from school. I've done some assignments with him for history."

Am I blushing?

"He looks..." Mum studies my drawing carefully. It's Max in profile. I've only sketched his face and shoulders, and fortunately I've left the rest vague. "He's good looking," she decides.

"Good looking?"

"Handsome." Mum laughs and so do I.

"Yes, he's not hard to look at, is he?" I blush.

"Where does he live?"

"CC2." Lying has become second nature to me. "Not lived there long. He joined Delta College three weeks ago. He's crazy about old music."

"Oh?"

"Really old. Twentieth century old. He's got an antique CD player and plays his CDs on it. You know, those silver discs in plastic boxes?"

Mum looks doubtful.

"He's loaded most of them onto his HC," I add quickly. "He played me a whole lot of things. Bob Dylan, Jimi Hendrix, Mott the Hoople, Miles Davis and a band with four stupid guys in neat suits and long hair, uh... The Beatles."

Mum nods enthusiastically.

"Yes... The Beatles. I think I've heard of them. The CDs... haven't they got some in the Regional Museum?" We fall silent.

We look at each other carefully. I can't remember the last time we talked like this.

"And he stood up for me," I say softly.

Another half-truth, but I want Mum to know that Max is okay.

"He stood up for you?"

"There's only a few of us, Mum."

"Oh."

"But you really don't have to worry yourself."

Another lie.

Mum nods. "You should ask him over sometime, Nina."

I press my lips together. The irony is unbearable. "Sure, Mum. I'll ask him."

Mum gets up. For the first time I notice she's even smaller than I am. Her blond curls have grey streaks I've never seen before, and deep wrinkles give her light eyes an expression of fatigue. She walks to the door, but turns around at the last moment. "It's good to see you a little happier, Nina."

She means it. She's pleased. I smile. I don't know what to say in answer. The door closes softly. A little later, I hear her go into Isa's room.

Mum has left the HC on my bed. I pick the thing up and stare at Max. If only it were as simple as Mum thinks.

The HC vibrates. I almost drop it.

Message from Max? Hardly daring to look, I scroll to the envelope and click on it before I can change my mind.

"Can you come over? I want to see you. M."

That's all.

He wants to see me. He wants to see me! I quickly type a reply and click on Send. Erik will take me. Erik understands.

I'm finally going to tell him. No more lies.

I quickly get my bag, stuff my HC into it, look for my shoes, and pull a sweater from the wardrobe. My coat is still in the car. In the bathroom, I check myself in the mirror. Two large blue eyes stare back at me, framed by a shock of curls and a freckled face. My left cheek is turning blue from the punch Damian gave me. It'll have to do. I don't look back as the door closes behind me and I run down the stairs.

MAX

The message has been sent. The white envelope is replaced by a cheerful V-sign on the flickering screen. Li looks at me, his dark eyes gleaming, his hands clenched in trembling fists. He nods at me.

The blond woman, Tanja, has walked over to me and is looking at me suspiciously. Her hands are on her slim hips, while she examines me from top to toe with her silent grey eyes.

"Bring her back here. We've got everything ready." She walks to the kitchen window and stares outside again.

"Once we have Bradshaw's daughter, we can negotiate," says Harry.

I know exactly what he was thinking. Finally. We'll have finally driven them into a corner.

It's what I want too.

For Pa, for Ma, for Li and for myself. For my thrown away, no, my *stolen* future, and for my damned, Wet existence.

It's what I want too.

They want me to open the door and take Nina directly to the kitchen where Li will be waiting with a hypodermic needle containing a tranquilizer. Tanja communicates with people outside. It has to happen tonight, before Ma gets back from work. Before the forty-eight hours have elapsed and Ramon, the first WEtTO, is executed. The ultimatum. I'd forgotten about it again. I only have one thought in my messed-up my head.

It won't be long before Nina sends a message that she's on her way.

I have to say it now.

I look up. At Julius, who's playing some violent game on his HC, at Tanja, at my brother who is sipping tea, and finally at Harry. He's the one calling the shots.

"I want to go with you."

Harry's eyes narrow and Li bangs his fist on the table. "You can't leave Ma by herself!"

I laugh bitterly.

"Look who's talking, Li."

He growls but keeps his mouth shut.

"Anyway." I shrug. "They'll come here straight away. They can link me to her."

Li pushes his hand through his long hair.

"The driver," I say. "He's already threatened me once and will certainly spill the beans if Nina..."

Li says nothing.

Fuck.

"You've thought of that already." It was a statement, not a question. I swallow.

"We don't do things by halves. We can't afford to," says Tanja.

"What are you going to do with him?"

Stupid question. I think of the man who said nothing when Nina pulled me, a Wet, into his car. Who hid me as the digiscope went up in flames. No. I've made my choice. The man's a Wader. A defector. Almost automatically, spit forms in my mouth. Every war has its victims. It's what I want too.

"As I said, we've thought of everything." Tanja smiles. It's quiet.

"Good," says Harry. He gets up. "Max, you can come too."
I nod and walk out of the kitchen, leaving a muttering Liam behind.

In my room, I fetch Pa's old backpack, the one he always took with him when he went fishing. I stuff in a thick pullover, a few T-shirts, my other pair of jeans, socks, and underpants. Just as if I'm going on holiday. Holiday. As if a Wet ever goes on holiday. I slip my HC into my back pocket. I hope the thing holds out. Anything else? I pull open a few drawers and find an unopened packet of biscuits. Li must have hid it here for when he got hungry. My gaze falls on the pile of CDs under the desk. The case of one of them is open, next to Pa's portable CD player. I grab the thing from the ground without looking at it and stuff it in with the rest of my things.

I heave the heavy backpack onto my back and walk to the door. I turn around. My room is empty, even though almost everything is in its place.

The last Morris. *Sorry, Ma.*

I close the door behind me.

"Mum knows about it," I say to Erik as we drive through the gate. How many lies will be needed?

"What does she know about?"

You don't easily fool Erik.

"That I'm going to visit a friend."

"Outside the gate?"

"You know very well I can't say that."

"I was only asking."

"You've seen him. Max is okay. Max isn't just any Wet." Erik looks to one side. He has been a driver for so long that he drives with his whole body. It all looks very easy.

"I know what a Wet is, Nina."

My cheeks immediately turn a bright red. Of course. Erik is Wet, just as Wet as Max. He lives outside, not safely inside a cc, even though that's where he spends most of his time.

"I only want you to be careful. His brother..." Erik begins.

"I've seen his brother," I interrupt. "And Max is nothing like him."

"Are you sure?"

"Yes, I'm sure."

Erik's interrogation begins to irritate me.

Why's this Wet interfering? I think. Then I'm immediately ashamed of myself.

I'm glad Erik can't hear my thoughts. He's only worried about me. And he's more than just a Wet, more than just

Dad's driver. What would have happened, or perhaps wouldn't have happened, without Erik... I don't want to think about it.

"Mum felt much better today," I say.

"Yes?"

"When I told her about Max. At least part of it."

Erik laughs. A deep rolling laugh.

"That's good to hear, Nina."

I know he means it. Erik never says anything he doesn't mean.

We fall silent. I see the concrete blocks looming up in the distance under the clear starry sky. Max's house. Max's home. Something in my tensed up stomach slowly makes its way up and lodges like a cuckoo's egg in my throat. It is too big and forces everything else to one side, until it is the only thing I feel. You're going to tell him. I push my hands under my legs so that Erik can't see how they're shaking. I wiggle my fingers and try to concentrate on that.

"Erik..."

"Hm."

"Where do you live?"

A short silence then: "District Two."

"Is that for..."

"Waders? Yes."

"So it's better than... the rest?"

He nods.

"Do you live alone?"

Again the surprise.

"I was only curious..."

"No, that's all right. I'm married. No children. My wife works in CC1 as well."

217

"Oh."

He clears his throat. "I think you two would get on well together."

"Yes?"

"Evelien paints in her spare time."

Erik is a man of few words, but he knows how to say a lot.

"She, Evelien, paints?"

"Yes. Portraits mainly." He is proud of his wife. He voice sounds different; as if it contains more of Erik the man than Erik the driver.

"What I do is nothing special, really." I lower my gaze.

"No?"

"Just some scribbles, some doodling on my HC."

We fall silent again as we drive into District Seven. The snow-covered roads have not been salted or sanded, and Erik has to drive slowly. We creep forwards. My fingers have long since stopped wiggling. I try to swallow, but whatever is stuck there doesn't move.

"And what do you do?" I ask. I have to distract myself.

"What do you mean?"

"When you're not being a driver?"

A deep rolling laugh.

"Yes, I'm more than just a driver." He laughs again, then suddenly falls silent. He sounds different yet again when he says: "I play the trumpet." Now it's my turn to be surprised.

"Really?"

"Would I lie about that?"

"No, of course not." Erik never lies about stuff like that. Leave that to others. "That's great."

Erik shrugs his shoulders. His hands don't leave the wheel.

"The instrument belonged to my father. He taught me."

Just like Max's CD player belonged to his father. And my golden locket belonged to Isa, and before Isa to our grandmother, Mum's mother.

The car stops.

"We're here," says Erik.

I look at the HC in my lap. My numb hands pick up the thing. My drawing of Max. It feels good that he isn't a complete secret. That Mum knows about him, just like Erik and Maria. Perhaps things will turn out all right after all. Mum seemed happier today. And that was because of me. Because of Max.

All that's left is to tell him.

"Bye for now, Erik."

I get out. My legs move automatically, while in my mind I'm already in Max's house and my lips are forming the words. I am Nina Bradshaw. I push my body against the door to the entrance hall. The click of the lock as it closes echoes in the bare area. Nobody is there. I quickly walk past the broken elevator towards the stairwell.

One hundred and forty steps. Max says there are one hundred and forty steps and I count them, just as he always counts them. On the fortieth step, I meet someone. I hold my breath.

The woman stares at me and I immediately see suspicion, fear, and surprise in her eyes. She's holding a small dog that pants as it looks at me. When I make no move to move closer, the creature barks and licks his mistress's hand with his small, pink tongue. The shrill sound resounds through the empty stairwell, until it vanishes outside through the gaps and cracks.

"Shh, be quiet Coco."

The woman's voice is caressing, quite unlike the rest of her body that shows distaste in every movement. We walk past each other without saying anything.

I'm there.

This is his door, isn't it? The bare one with traces of paint in the corner. Number 589.

Max. I see Max. Not on the screen of my HC, but when I close my eyes. I see him running, so effortlessly, so completely himself.

I also want to be myself. *I am Nina Bradshaw.* I knock.

MAX

"They're here."

Tanja turns round. She types something on her HC. Her fingers are like lightning. I want to walk to the window, see Nina get out, but Li stops me.

"Stay calm, little brother."

"Let go of me, Li."

"Boys!" Harry growls.

Li curses, laughs, and lets go. "You're in the right mood, Max. Excellent."

Julius is outside. Before he left the house, he pulled the ski-mask over his head. Only his grey eyes could be seen. It is just like one of Pa's old films. But this is real.

"She's walking to the entrance hall," says Tanja.

Harry nods and produces the hypodermic. He fills the long needle with a transparent substance that he sucks up from a thin vial. He passes the needle to Li.

"In her arm," he instructs.

Li nods. His eyes shift from left to right and it wouldn't surprise me if he started jogging like he does before a boxing match. He's worked up. I get why he's worked up. The adrenaline is rushing through my body as well; it's totally consumed me and it rushes through me like a westerly storm slamming the water against the dyke.

"She's half way," says Tania.

Harry turns to face me.

"Max."

I say nothing. I nod and walk from the kitchen into the passage. Half way. She's half way.

My eye notices the single light-bulb hanging from the ceiling. It's been hanging there for years without a shade, after Li and I broke the thing during a game of indoor football.

I can see us playing.

I see Li shouting that he's going to get me.

I see myself scoring. I see the lamp shatter on the wooden floor.

More than half way. She must be more than half way. I wipe away the sweat with my arm. It keeps dripping into my eyes. I am so fucking hot. Hot.

I walk along the middle of the passage and stretch out my arms. I am tall enough to touch the bare walls on either side and, with my arms outstretched, I walk towards the door. Pa's coat is hanging next to the door. We wore out his shoes long ago. I run my fingers over the cracked leather, feel the familiar folds, and inhale Pa's tobacco odor.

He murdered him.

Bradshaw murdered my pa.

It's all true. Everything Li said is true.

And Nina said nothing. She kept her mouth shut, even when I told her about Pa.

She's his daughter.

"For you, Pa," I whisper and I reach out my shaking hand. Can I hear footsteps?

One hundred and forty steps.

She's almost there. Almost there. Almost here. The footsteps come nearer and nearer. And stop in front of my door.

She knocks.

NINA

Max's hands are shaking. He clenches his hands into fists that he quickly pushes into his trouser pockets. He avoids my look and stares past me into the empty stairway.

Something's the matter.

"Hi," I say.

"Hi," he answers.

I go to take off my coat but he pulls me towards himself. I come closer and smell him: sweat and boy. Beads of sweat are on his forehead. When I touch him with the back of my hand, I feel how he's burning.

What's the matter?

"Come into the kitchen. I've got tea there," he says. He walks a few steps ahead of me. Like always, I have difficulty keeping up with him.

If he wants to go to the kitchen, we'll go to the kitchen. Then I'll tell him there.

He opens the door to the small kitchen and takes a step inside. I follow him and my gaze goes to the kitchen table, to a grey hat placed there.

A hat.

A man's hat.

I look up in astonishment.

A bead of sweat runs slowly down Max's forehead over the bridge of his nose, touches the yellow of his jaw and fall on the kitchen floor. A neighbor is vacuuming and I hear my father's voice on a DOS screen somewhere in the flat.

"What..." I begin. I point at the strange hat. Our eyes meet each other.

My mouth shuts. The sounds die out.

A sharp pain in my right arm. My hand goes to the place where the pain is. I half turn, feel that I am not in complete balance and reach to the kitchen table for support with my other hand. I look into a pair of different eyes, or are they the same? Whose? Max's? I recognize the grin, but my brain has no time to process the signals. I feel myself glide away, literally and figuratively, hear laughter and another man's voice and the last thing I see is Max, who takes a step forward, his arms outstretched. But can't catch me. For I fall quickly. And deeply.

MAX

She's still staring at me. Shock in her wild pupils. No. I bend down quickly and close her eyelids.

The knot has dissolved. All my fury disappears. Flushed away. I feel empty.

"Perfect, little brother!"

Li bends over Nina and taps her face. Nothing. No movement, no sound. It's as if she's dead.

"Harry, this stuff is fantastic!" Li grins and sticks up his thumb.

She's lying in a pile on the kitchen floor. Her head is hanging downwards like a broken flower. Li wants to pick her up. I push him away.

"Let me."

As I pick her up, he grabs the golden locket from Nina's neck. The lock breaks with a pop. He holds it up, assessing its value, and whistles.

"That'll fetch quite a bit, little brother."

Exactly as I'd imagined it. I want to grab it back, then change my mind. I shrug. "Go ahead, Li." He holds up the locket one more time, grins, and stuffs it into his trouser pocket.

I take Nina to the living room and place her on the settee. Harry and Li follow me.

"How long does that stuff work?" I ask.

"Six hours or so. Enough to get a long way away from here," answers Harry.

"And the driver?"

"Julius'll send a message when the coast's clear."

"Where are we going?"

"You'll see."

I sit down next to Nina. Her mouth is half open, as if she's still surprised. I try to close it, but each time I push her jaw together, it falls open again. Her breath is sweet and warm. It distracts me. I get up and pace back and forth, back and forth, between the settee and the DOS screen. I hear Harry, Li, and Tanja talking. It doesn't mean much to me until I hear Li say "past the dyke". Are we going past the dyke? Past the end of the Region? Into the marshes and the Submerged Areas? Nobody goes there.

Tanja turns round. Her eyes scan a message that comes in.

"Harry, Liam. It's clear."

I know what that means.

Li throws me rope and tape, while Harry begins to re-move all traces of our presence. "Tie her up. Tightly."

I look at Nina's slender hands and tiny feet. Her mouth has fallen open again. I take the rope and start doing my job. I pull hard at the knot I make around her wrists. I'm aston-ished how easy it is. It feels better, it feels good. I also tie her feet together, tear a piece of tape, and stick it over her mouth. Finally closed.

"Ready?"

Harry looks at me and I nod.

"You're sure?"

"I can't turn back now."

He laughs.

"You learn fast."

Li places a hand on my shoulder.

"Come on."

I look at the girl lying in front of me.

A Dry. A traitor. I pick her up as Li turns off the lights and we leave the house, our house, in darkness.

Below I see Julius sitting in Erik's car. There is no trace of the Wader.

The road is silent. The curtains are most probably closed on purpose, people walking their dogs take a longer route, and the kids are hanging out somewhere else.

It has started to snow again.

Harry signals us to follow him. I catch sight of an old black van, cleverly hidden under the awning of one of the old garages. Tanja walks to the door on the driver's side, Harry gets in next to her. Li walks in front of me and opens the doors at the back.

"Here."

Together we put Nina on the floor of the van. I get in first, hold Nina by her shoulders, and try to worm my way between a pile of crates and a dark sack, tied with string. I curse and kick at the sack, but hold my breath. The sack gives way.

"Is that...?"

"Yes."

"What are you going to do with it?"

"Do with it?"

Li says nothing. I hear his rapid breathing, but I can only see half his face in the darkness of the van.

"We'll dump him. In the water, where nobody can find him," he says at last and jumps in. We drive off before he's closed the doors.

I try to sit as far away from the sack as possible. The roads in District Seven are bad, but where we're driving now, they're completely useless. We're thrown in all directions. With every turn, Nina's head hits the wall of the van. I haven't the faintest idea where we are.

"Scared, little brother?"

Li's voice startles me out of my thoughts.

"I'm not scared."

"No?"

He doesn't believe me. I'm about to open my mouth. But he's quicker.

"The first time, I was scared shitless, Max. You're doing okay." His voice is softer and friendlier than I've heard it for ages. "I nearly pissed myself with fear." He grins. He wants to reassure me. "We'll dump him as soon as we can." He closes his eyes and crosses his arms. Is he going to sleep? How can he sleep now, here?

My eyes are drawn to the sack in front of me, which moves closer with every bump in the road.

Scared?

Yes, I'm fucking scared.

We brake suddenly. Nina's head crashes against the edge of a crate. She groans but doesn't wake up. Blood trickles along her thin face and drops onto my jeans. So bright, so red. So real.

"Max, help your brother, will you?"

Harry has turned round. The question is so ridiculously innocent and the man posing it seems so terribly nice. I nod like the good little boy Ma always wanted. Who would suspect what's really going on?

Li opens the doors. Moonlight shines in and Nina's blond curls light up. Her skin looks an odd silver grey. I think again of Pa's old films, about vampires who bite beautiful girls when the moon is full. That's how she looks. Exactly like a vampire. I have to force myself out of the van to stop myself staring at Nina.

Erik is big and heavy. Even with the two of us, it needs all our strength to get the body out of the van and carry it onto the dyke.

Li walks back and gets some stuff to make sure it doesn't float to the surface. We tie the weights to his legs, his arms and round his waist. I feel strangely light in my head. We roll the sack towards the water and pant and puff like two old dock-workers. It's bloody hard work.

Li nudges me. "Just a bit farther, little brother."

We push again. Until the sacks tears open, exactly next to Erik's dead head. Glassy eyes stare at me.

I swallow. Again.

I can't stop myself throwing up. I throw up over his face, over his dead head with that perfectly round hole in the forehead.

Li drops his end, walks over to me, and places a hand on my back. I shake it off. I put my trembling hands on my knees and hang my head.

"Almost done, little brother. Almost done," he says to calm me down.

I breathe deeply, in and out, wiping my filthy face on my sleeve.

"Okay," I say.

Li nods.

"I'll count to three."

We both grab an end.

"One, two, three!"

We push and the body splashes into the water, which greedily sucks it under. Circles show where Erik's body hit the water, but the surface is soon still again and there is nothing to see. As if nothing has happened.

For the first time in my life, I sit still.

I've pulled up my legs and hold them tightly. I no longer look at my brother, nor at Harry or Tanja, not even at Nina. I look without seeing anything.

When the van stops and the others get out, I automatically follow. Li says that the road ends here. That we will go on with a waterboard. Together we lift Nina from the van and over the dyke. There's a jetty below, sticking out into the water. A duck flies past and quacks indignantly as we walk along the jetty.

The waterboard is hidden among the reed. I've only seen those things on DOS. Pa says they look like normal boats but are designed to sail in the Submerged Territories, where anything could be hiding under the water. No Wet area.

I hold Nina tightly as I walk to the ship. I've never been on the water before. Li comes after me and springs with the greatest ease from the plank onto the boat. It is icy and it is still snowing.

Harry steers while Tanja and Julius disappear into the hold below. Julius is already on board; he must have dumped Erik's car and then come here. I follow them downstairs and lay Nina on a bench. I am about to sit down when Li drags me back onto the deck.

"You've got to see this," he says and points in the direction we are sailing. The wind is wet in our face.

I look.

At the flooded city that half sticks out above the water. At islands almost filled with derelict buildings. At a hill with a collapsed monument, a man on a horse riding the waves. At the water birds that scream, warning intruders away from their territory. The submerged land reaches into the endless distance.

I look until I cannot look any longer. And I still don't understand what I see.

PART TWO

NINA

Voices.[1]
I hear voices.
Where are they coming from? Maria? It's so cold. Where
is my blanket? Has Isa taken my blanket?
Isa!
Wet. It's wet as well. Wet and cold and I can still hear
voices.
My mouth feels like sandpaper. So dry. *Dry.*
Water.
No, not water again!

My breath comes in shudders, my heart beats madly, and I
see images I only normally see at night. Never when I'm
awake. Never when I can hide them away so deep.
"ISA! NO!"
I wave my arms, but something stops me. My legs. My legs
are trapped. Has something fallen on me? The water. The
water's coming and I can't do anything. I try to close my
eyes, but I can't. It's as if they are propped wide open with
matchsticks, and I'm forced to look at something that has
taken place countless times in my imagination.
How the water keeps pulling her under, how the water
plays so indifferently with her,
how the water finally picks her up and carries her away,
as if she's not worth anything more than the broken chair,

the crumpled lace curtaining,
the broken blackboard,
which the water carries along with her outside.
    She's leaving me behind. Alone. She.
    Isa.
    The water.

When I open my eyes, I'm at home. I'm lying in my bed and Maria is knocking on the door to tell me I have to go to school.
    It's the pills. Did I take too many last night?

    Dear Mum.
    She holds me tight, my mother. She holds me tight, because I've fallen off the see-saw and grazed both my knees. She has carefully washed away the dirt and put on two bandages. Bandages with summer suns on them.
    Two knees with suns.
    After rain comes sunshine.
    She holds me tight and softly rocks me back and forth. Back and forth.
    Back and forth.
    Back. And forth.

MAX

Li offers me a cigarette and I take it.

We're on the semi-circular balcony, right at the top of the building. The air is heavy and grey and so full that it almost overflows. A snow flake lands on the tip of my nose.

"I thought you were so against it."

I shrug. "I can't run here."

Ten staircases of nine steps made ninety. Up to here and no further. That is freedom. We wait until they wake up. Li laughs.

"Cooled off, you stubborn bastard?"

I ignore his remark.

The balcony railing is rusted through in most places and to my left completely swept away. I lean over the edge. How many feet is the drop? A hundred? A hundred and fifty? I take a long drag on my cigarette.

Cooled down.

My head feels as if somebody has been punching it. And somebody has been punching it. When the waterboard arrived here, Li picked up Nina.

I flipped.

It took Julius and Harry to hold me down. I was able to kick Julius in the balls, but Harry was smarter. A soldier. Who knows what to do with out-of-control kids. He took me inside, his iron hand clasping my upper arm. He almost stopped the circulation. He rushed ahead and dragged me with him into a large room with settees, beds, a DOS screen in the corner and a small kitchen. He threw me onto one of the settees and towered over me.

"You'll do what you're told here, okay?" Eyes green as poison. I nodded.

"It's your first night. A lot has happened and we know you're angry. We're all angry. But you'll do what you're told. Otherwise you'll be kicked out."

I nod again.

Then he punched me in the face, so hard that I swore from the pain.

"And I mean it," he said, before he left me behind, flabbergasted.

I know that Li knows what Harry did. I have a suspicion that Harry makes it very clear to all newcomers how they should behave. *Violence feeds violence.* Ma's words. I shrug them off me. It's my own fault. I should have controlled myself. I know why I'm here.

I exhale the smoke in one go.

I stand up straight again. More snow falls. The wind get stronger, pulls at me, at Li, at the rickety building we're standing on. It howls through the holes. The waterboard and the moored scooter bob around on the high waves below us like ducks in a bath.

"This is only the start, Max."

I turn round and look at my brother.

"The start of what?"

"Of the revolution." Re-vo-lu-tion, he says.

I know he's not finished yet. He's taken his hands out of his pocket and is leaning with his arms on the railing, which is creaking dangerously. Not that Li notices. His eyes glisten like two dark diamonds, hard and perfectly polished. He straightens up and gives me a hard slap on the back.

"We really are going to be better off, Max! And Ma. Just think of what we'll be able to give her! Just imagine it, little brother!"

Li throws his arm around me. I have to suppress the urge to lay my stupid, tired head on his shoulder. Do something, man. You're no longer a scared little boy. Not after today. I ask the first question that comes to mind.

"How far does this go?" I stretch my arm with the cigarette and draw a trail of smoke in the air.

"Far. But not endless."

"What's beyond the Submerged Territories?"

"Islands, according to Harry, and miles of dunes. Behind them more water, sea, and the Foreign Territories."

We fall silent.

I inhale deeply and blow out the smoke in circles, a trick Pa taught me. I stare at them. They dissolve quickly in the cold air.

"Not much longer, Max. It won't last much longer."

I nod. Not much longer. For the revolution has begun.

NINA

I'm awake.

I twist my tongue around to produce some saliva and try to move. My right leg has gone to sleep; I've laid on it too long. I want to massage my calves. But my arms... They're tied behind my back.

I blink my eyes and a drop of water trickles along my cheek to the corner of my mouth. Water! Something is blocking my tongue. *Tape.* The drop trickles on regardless and mixes with the pool on the ground.

The outlines of my cell gradually reveal themselves. I'm laying with my back against a cold wall. Moisture is dripping along the bricks and forces itself in on all sides. My clothing feels damp and really filthy. It even smells wet. Rotten and wet. The room isn't large, the door opposite me is perhaps two meters away. I'm lying between a few wooden crates and some sacks. No, partly on a sack filled with something that prickles. Straw? A light bulb is hanging high above me. There must be a switch somewhere.

What time is it? I have no idea of time.

I try to remember what happened, but every time I think I've got something, it escapes again. It is as if there are black holes in my head into which all knowledge of the past few hours have disappeared.

"Do you think she's awake?"

I stiffen.

A man's voice. A young man's voice. It comes closer, and so do the footsteps of... how many people? Wets or Dries? Somebody fiddles with the lock. The door opens. I feel warm moisture between my legs. For the first time in my life, I really pray. "She's awake."

A Wet men is standing in the doorway. Bright light shines in and I lower my gaze. It hurts. I groan and kick with my legs. When I open my eyes, a head is hanging over me. Only the eyes are visible. They are not unfriendly eyes, green as dark, wet grass.

The man places a gloved hand on my shoulder. "If you cooperate, we won't hurt you." A low, fatherly voice with an unmistakable authority.

I stare at him and nod quickly.

"Julius, give me some water. It's the drugs."

What...? Drugs?

The man turns to me and lifts me into an upright position. A muffled scream of pain escapes through my taped-up mouth when he pulls my arms.

"If you promise to keep your mouth shut, I'll remove the tape and you'll get something to drink."

Drink. Water. I'm so thirsty. My head goes up and down.

The man's hand goes to my mouth and he pulls off the tape in a single tug. Tears spring into my eyes and I clamp my teeth together so as not to cry out in pain again. The thirst is worse. When the man holds a cup of water in front of me and lets me drink, I'm so greedy that I spill half of it.

"Take it easy, child. Easy," soothes the man. He holds me just a bit too tightly to mean what he says.

"Is the Dry finally awake?"

A husky woman's voice without any pretense of friendliness. Where am I? Who are these Wets?

"Yes, she's awake." The man with the green eyes still holds me tight. I can smell him. Bitter, old leather and cigarettes. "Good, then we can get to work on the DOS message." I flinch. Get to work? What message?

"Later, Tanja, later."

The man gets up and lets go of me.

"Julius. Get her something to eat."

"I'll take care of it," says somebody with a catch in his voice.

Max.

All at once, everything comes back.

MAX

"Are you sure, little brother?"

Li stops me, places a hand on my arm. I shake it off.

"She deceived me, Li."

I want to see her. I want to know why she lied to me. I want...

"Max..."

Our eyes meet each other. When the knot tightens, I can't hide anything.

"Leave him alone, Liam. He knows what he's got to do," Harry intervenes.

"Make sure you don't mess it up, Max." He pulls in his chin, presses his lips together, and pushes past me, back into the corridor. Harry turns back to me.

"You know that, don't you?"

"I know it."

"That's good, lad."

He gives me the keys and goes after Li. Tanja and Julius follow him.

I'm going to do it.

I'm fucking going to do it.

In the kitchen I rummage through the cabinets looking for a cup. There's a piece of bread on a shelf, and I find some instant soup which I dissolve in hot water. I see the DOS screen from the corner of my eye. A life-size Nina. An old photo, but not so old that I don't recognize her. She isn't laughing, just looking straight into the camera. Her parents are standing behind her. Bradshaw is smiling, has his arm around his daughter's shoulder. *Bradshaw*. I feel the safe rage warm me up inside.

I'm going to do it.

I leave the room, walking back down the long, wide corridor. There's water everywhere. If you are quiet, you can hear it trickling between the walls. And the wind. The wind never stops. *Never*. Two flights down stairs and the odor of rotting and salt and wetness comes to meet me. "You have to put a Dry in to soak." Li's words. I stop by the door and listen.

I hear Nina breathing. Heavy breathing, with deep sobs. Is she crying? I hope she's crying. I want her to cry. I hear scraping. Is she sliding across the floor? I stare at the tape in my hand. "If she gets difficult," said Harry.

Do it, man.

I breathe in and open the door. She's lying with her back to the door and tries to turn round. She's scared. Scared stiff. An acrid smell. Fuck. Has she pissed herself?

"Nina."

I didn't want to say anything, but it's out before I notice.

She flinches and tries to crawl away from me like a scared mouse from a cat. I walk over to her and grab her roughly. She groans. Her hair is all messed up and full of tangles and dirt. A clod of blood is forming on her right temple, probably where she hit it last night. It looks phony, so ridiculously red. Harry warned me that the stuff they used to knock her out could keep working for a bit. That she can't see properly, or thinks she's seeing things that aren't there. But I suddenly know for certain that what's she scared of really exists.

"Please, it hurts..."

I don't know what I feel when she begs. Good. Satisfied. Confused. Uneasy. I don't want to feel uneasy. I don't bloody need to feel uneasy.

Come on!

"I've got food for you. If you do what they say, nothing will happen."

I take the bread and break off a piece. I try to put it in her mouth, but she spits it out. Blood drips from her torn lip and turns the grey bread red.

"Not good enough for you?"

Wide eyes, which she immediately lowers. Man, she's so dirty.

"My mouth is so dry. My lips..."

I throw the bread on the ground and take the soup. It's cold. She's not as greedy as she was with Harry, but moisture still drips down her chin and onto my hands in her lap. I use a bit of my pullover to wipe Nina's mouth. I think of the last time that we... No. Don't think. I take the bread and start feeding it to Nina. Like the ducks on the dyke.

Look, Max. Look at the traitor. Look. I feel myself calming down.

You see, it's fine.

It starts with a cough.

The cough gets worse. It gets worse and worse, until she's coughing so hard that I'm afraid they'll hear it above. Spit and pieces of bloody bread fly out of Nina's mouth and her eyes look as if they're exploding from her head. And she can hardly keep upright.

"Max... help!"

Eyes begging. Really begging. They're not even blinking.

She tries to draw a breath, but she can't and her face screws up and contorts as if her muscles are made of elastic. I see myself move as if somebody else is doing it. I grab Nina and push as hard as I can against her midriff.

The piece of bread doesn't fly out like it does in those stupid Dry comedies, but drops to the ground, a filthy piece of half eaten food. She pants and gasps. In through her nose, out through her mouth. She squeaks and rattles and cries. Tears drip over her cheeks and mix with the foul water and her own piss. I flinch. My hands are glowing where I grabbed her.

I get out of there.

NINA

He's not coming back.

Blood and spit and pieces of bread are sticking to my chin, my neck, even to my hair. My throat feels sour, as if I'm bleeding inside. The urine forms a yellowish stain on my light pants and the smell, together with that of the foul water, forces itself on me. I can't stop crying. I feel so dirty. I'm soaked through. He knows who I am. I shiver. Of course he knows who I am.

And he hates me.

It gets lighter. Weak sunlight shines in from somewhere high above me. Patches of old plaster stand out against the dark brick wall. In a corner there is a pile of parts of what must have been a computer, one of those enormous things I've seen in history books. Cord protrude from it like tentacles and for a moment I think they're moving all by themselves, but it's only the wind. The steel desk on three legs standing next to it also moves; the wind gets in everywhere.

I don't know what they injected me with, but my head is only now beginning to feel like mine again.

I was going to Max. Yes, I was on my way to visit Max. He'd sent me a message after... after he got expelled from school. Suddenly I feel Damian's rough hands around my waist, smell his acid odor again. That was *yesterday*. Only yesterday.

I was just too late.

They were waiting for me. That's why Max has been acting so strange. He sent the message, but it was from WEtTO. That brother of his, Liam, he works for them. *He* knew who I was. Max couldn't know. Could he?

No. If Max had known, he wouldn't have gone with me, wouldn't have told me anything, and he certainly wouldn't have kissed... I go to clasp my hand to my mouth but feel a vicious stab in my wrist where the rope is cutting into my flesh.

What are they going to do with me? I'm Governor Bradshaw's daughter. I'm the enemy. A Dry. What were they talking about? Something about a DOS message.

The ultimatum. Felix's words: "You could set an example." I groan.

They want to use me. They're already using me. Perhaps they want to exchange me for the WEtTO prisoners. And if Dad doesn't cooperate, then... I hardly dare to admit it to myself. I'm bait.

But they didn't say anything about Erik. Erik. And I think: they've murdered him. Thoughts follow each other in quick succession. I see him in the car, talking about his wife. I see his smile and his laughing eyes. How he talked about his trumpet, and his amazement at my sudden interest. I see his concerned look and realize: he didn't have any children of his own...

Too late.

Rage slowly creeps over me, rage such as I've never known, not even when I saw Isa's dead body lying in its coffin. Rage about Erik, about myself, about Max, about my own stupidity and helplessness and idiotic naivety.

I scream.

MAX

The rest of the day, I don't know what to do with my restless mind. I keep on seeing her in front of me, whether I'm playing some stupid Dry DOS game with Julius or helping Tanja unload the supplies they brought with them. The spit, the blood, her purple face screaming at me and I feel her slim waist and my arms under her sweater... Fuck. *No.*

I know what she is.

Li notices how worked up I am. He's setting up the camera for the DOS message.

"Take it easy, Max. Nobody's going to find us here. There's not a Dry who'd dare come here. Wet feet and all that," he says and laughs loudly. Julius joins in from one of the filthy old settees.

He thinks I'm worried about that? Fine. I shrug my shoulders and tap on the lens cap.

"Hey, stop that, you prick."

I ignore him.

"I didn't know you were so good with your hands," I say.

Li winks. "There's a lot you don't know about me, little brother."

He grins. He's in his element. Just like at a good boxing match or when we went fishing with Pa. I watch him working. Tanja has placed a chair against the concrete wall in the corner of the room. That's where Nina will have to sit. And read out what Harry is writing at the table opposite. My head can't take it all in since we rolled Erik from the dyke.

Li knows what he's doing.

He sets up the camera at exactly the right distance. He wants Tanja to play Nina for him. She walks with an exaggerated limp and pouts when he asks her to look in the camera. Is there something going on between them? I look away.

He spends a lot of time with the lens. Julius and Tanja go outside to smoke a fag, and Harry disappears below. I look at my brother.

"How long, Li?"

I didn't even know I was going to ask him anything.

"What do you mean, how long?" He doesn't look up.

"Here." A gesture all around. "This. With Harry and WEtTO."

He shrugs. "A while."

He doesn't want to talk about it. But I persist. "Before Pa drowned?"

Li fiddles with his HC that is connected to the camera. Did he hear me?

"Yes, before that," he says after a long time. I wait for Li to continue. "But not long."

He turns round. His hands slip from the camera. "Max."

Whenever Li is being serious, he calls me by my name. "What?"

My fingers tap the lens, but Li says nothing about it. He looks at me, his dark eyes less hard than I'm used to.

"Pa..."

"What about Pa?"

He hesitates. His fingers fiddle with the cords and wires that are jumbled together.

"What about Pa, Li?"

"Max, Pa —" he begins, but before he can finish his sentence, Harry calls out from the other side of the room: "It's time, guys." We turn around together.

"Get Bradshaw's daughter and clean her up a bit. We have something to tell the world." He grins.

"I'll do it," says Li and he pats my back as if we've just had a friendly bout of boxing. He rolls up the cord and puts the camera on standby. Without another word, he leaves the room.

Pa, I think. What about Pa?

"Well?" says Harry.

"Well,what?"

Harry arches his eyebrows. How can anything have just fluorescent green eyes?

Then I get it

"I'm going, I'm going." I sprint after my brother.

Pa.

NINA

Is it already getting dark?

I don't know. The sun has long disappeared, but it's impossible to say whether it has gone behind clouds or dropped below the horizon. I've been able to push myself up against the wall and am now sitting on the only dry piece of floor in my cell. Not that it makes much difference. I'm so cold. I'm completely frozen.

I'm scared and angry and confused.

I force myself to keep moving my fingers and toes. Can I still feel them? Yes, I can still feel them. *Stay awake, Nina. Stay awake.* It is too easy to close my eyes and go far away from here, away from all these suffocating emotions.

Am I in shock?

Another week and Christmas holidays will begin. Not that I'm looking forward to it this year. Not like I used to, when Mum and Maria would spend days preparing for Christmas dinner. The smell of Christmas was the smell of pine trees, hot aniseed milk, and Mum's special turkey. Dad was responsible for setting up the Christmas tree in the hall and which we would then decorate together. Dad did the lights. The best moment was when he called Isa and me and we were allowed to turn them on. A magical glow spread over the dark winter garden, a promise of enchantment. A promise that was fulfilled every year and without fail.

Move, Nina. Stay awake.

Somebody is turning the key in the lock and my head shoots upright. Wide awake. All my muscles tense, ready for whatever is about to happen.

The door creaks open. A light shines in. Footsteps follow, a familiar voice speaks.

"Awake, Dry?" says Liam.

I look away. He purposely shines his flashlight into my eyes.

"We're going to make a movie. For your Pa." He laughs. He takes two steps to reach me. His rough hands grab my upper arms and he jerks me to my feet.

We stand eye to eye.

I spit straight into his Wet face.

It drips from his nose, over his full lips and angular chin. He looks surprised, even as he lifts his hand, reaches for his face – soft and creamy, café latte, just like Max – and wipes away the spittle. Then I watch as his eyes change in a split second from surprise to indignation to rage. What have I done? His arm goes up and his grin twists into something halfway between a laugh and a sneer. I flinch away, he lifts him arm even higher and I know there's nowhere for me to go.

"Dry slag!"

Slap.

"Li!"

The palm of his hand hits my cheek and for a second I feel nothing, then the pain flows through me. If Liam hadn't been grasping me with his other hand, I would have hit the wall. Who said that? Max? I blink my eyes but see nothing except a ray of light dancing in front of me and two bodies that cannot be distinguished from each other.

"The Dry slag! The Dry slag!" screams Li and every time he says it, I flinch back farther, as if I can disappear into the wall. Are they fighting? I hear a groan and a thump and I don't dare look.

"Li! Stop it! Harry said to clean her up, not beat the daylights out of her!"

"Dry slag!"

Again a hard crash and a groan. I flinch instinctively.

It's quiet. Too quiet, too long.

"Nina?" asks Max.

I carefully open them. His eyes are wide, blood is dripping from a wound in his eyebrow onto the ground. The same eyebrow as before.

"Let me see your face."

His fingers are warm, hot even, when they touch my cheek. He holds the torch on me, but doesn't shine it into my eyes.

"Max," I say.

Liam groans. At once Max springs up. He looks away and turns the torch onto the speckled face of his brother. "Cooled down, Li?"

"That Dry slag," mumbles Liam. "Stupid bitch."

"Harry's waiting for us, Li."

Liam shakes his head. "Dry slag," he says one more time. He clears his throat and spits out a bloody load of saliva in a perfect arch. It lands at my tied up feet.

"Don't ever do that again, Dry," he snarls at me.

He stands up, throws me over his shoulder as if I weigh no more than a light summer coat, and carries me out of the room.

MAX

"What happened in there, man?"

Li walks quickly ahead of me. Nina's head and hands are hanging down and at every corner she sways against the walls.

Pa. He was going to tell me something about Pa.

"She's a Dry slut, that's what."

I want to ask him. Man, I want to know!

I can guess what just happened. Nina said something to him or did something and Li got angry. It's not difficult to make Li angry. Lucky for me: when he's angry he can't fight.

"This Dry slag spat on me. Spat on me!" shouted Li, almost beside himself.

So that was it. I wonder whether Nina knew what she did. A Dry spitting on a Wet: nothing could show more contempt than that.

"We have to clean her up, Li. Harry won't like it if she's got another bruise." I'm distracted by Nina's swaying hair. It's so long that it almost drags along the ground.

Li kicks open the door to the washroom.

It is just as bare and cold as the rest of the building. No showers, just washbasins that don't work anymore. There's a large tank filled with recycled water that's pumped up here. You have to fill a washbasin with a hose. It's ice cold and stinks like ditch water.

Li dumps Nina onto the ground.

"What now?" He holds up his hands and lowers them again.

I stare at Nina. She keeps quiet. She's learned her lesson. Man, she's so dirty.

"Wash her," I say.

"I'm not going to wash that Dry!"

"Li ... "

"She's your girlfriend, little brother."

Knot. Below the belt, yes.

Take it easy, Max.

"Okay," I say. I hear Nina take a sharp breath. "Then we'll do it my way."

The quicker this is over, the quicker I can ask Li.

I begin pumping water into one of the washbasins. Li leans against the door and watches. I hear him light up a cigarette. I work faster. When the basin's full, I pick up a flannel and dip it in. Fuck, it's damned cold! I pick up the soap with my other hand and turn round. This is it. Smoke travels through the room and gets up my nose.

"Can't you do that somewhere else?"

Li laughs.

"Never seen a girl before, little brother?"

Nina groans. Li is himself again. But fuck. I don't know what's wrong with me. She's a Dry. She's a traitor. She's Bradshaw's daughter. *Come on!*

I walk across to Nina and turn her round. She looks at me. For the first time, she doesn't look away. She doesn't look away.

Grab her head, man. Do it.

My hands move to her hair. There's too much to fit into my grasp. I stroke her forehead with my fingers, *she's burn-*

ing, man, burning, and rub her face with the flannel. Nina groans.

"I believe you still have to learn how to do it, little brother. Your girlfriend isn't enjoying it."

"Shut up, Li."

I take the soap and wash the rest of Nina's face, her neck, her arms and hands. Her gaze follows me, everywhere. But she keeps her mouth shut, she says nothing, even though she must be bloody cold. I get up.

"Finished?" asks Li.

"Mostly."

I tap my fingers on the washbasin. The soap slips into the brown, stinking water. Li looks from me to Nina. He takes in the sight of her soiled pants.

And he laughs. My damned brother laughs. That prick who knows everything about Pa and hasn't told me anything.

"Want me to finish up for you? Got cold feet?"

"No, we're done," I say hastily.

"I don't mind doing it. Honest. Like to see whether Dry girls are really so dry."

Nina moans.

"You see? She thinks it's a good idea."

Knot.

He takes two steps and grabs Nina. His hands grope, *grope,* and Nina tries to crawl away, but Li laughs and pulls her back effortlessly. I watch how my brother takes hold of Nina and pulls at her pants. I stand there like a little sissy and don't know what I should do. What I *want* to do.

"Aren't you two finished yet?"

Tanja storms into the room. She takes us in in one glance.

She's holding a bundle of cloths. "For the Dry." She throws them on the floor.

Li lets go of Nina. She pulls herself away, hunches up her knees, a possessed look in her large, blue eyes.

Tanja looks from me to Li to Nina. "Need any help?"

"Yes," I say.

"No," says Li.

A momentary pause. Then she says: "Get out. Clear off, both of you. I'll do the rest."

Li opens his mouth to protest. I can't suppress a sigh of relief.

"Well?"

"I'll wait outside," says Li and stamps out of the washroom. I throw Nina a glance before I follow him. Outside, I immediately turn to face him.

"If you ever try that again, Li!"

"What?"

"You know damned well what!"

"Gee, I was only teasing, man." He grins. "As if I could get it up with my little brother standing next to me."

My hand clenches into a fist and I want to hit him again. I want to beat his fucking brains out. And I don't even know why. Because he's such a prick? Because he always winds me up? Or because he's so bloody arrogant?

"Little brother." Li holds out his hand. His way of making peace. I stare out his outstretched hand, slowly shake my head. "Max," he says.

I look up.

Li's eye have softened and seem distant, as if he can something I can't.

"Pa said I should take it easy on you when the time came." He smiles. "Of course he was right."

"What? What was Pa right about?"

"Don't you get it? Smart Max." He said it the way Pa always said it. "Clever, clever Max."

"What, Li?" I scream. My voice breaks as if I'm a kid of thirteen.

"Pa asked me, Max. Pa. Our pa."

I gape at him. If I didn't have my hands against the wall, I'd fall down. Pa?

"Wh-what did Pa ask you?"

I already knew the answer.

"Do I have to spell it out for you, little brother?"

I stare at him, suddenly not wanting to hear another word.

"It was Pa who asked me to join WEtTO."

NINA

Once she's untied my hands and feet, the woman, Tanja I think, helps me undress and wash. She says nothing. I try not to think. It is so humiliating and I'm still dizzy from whatever they injected me with. The water is cold and Tanja is not particularly gentle. Although thank God she's washing me and not Li.

The clothes she then helps me put on are anything but comfortable, but at least they're clean. Are they Wet clothes? They must be. I catch a glimpse of myself in one of the mirrors above the row of washbasins. I hardly recognize myself. My face is turning purple where Liam hit me. Max washed away the blood, but neither he nor Tanja has been able to do anything about the empty look in my eyes. Pieces of straw stick out in clumps from my hair. Mum always sighed about our curls. It was a daily chore to tame my unkempt hair into something resembling a hair style.

Tanja doesn't give me much time. She looks at me with half a smile and says: "We'll have to make do with this." She ties me up again, hands and feet. Liam is waiting outside; there's no sign of Max. The woman nods and Liam picks me up.

We go through a long, dark corridor where the icy winter wind has free hand. Cracks disfigure the bare walls and each gust of wind makes the building creak like an old woman. Liam stamps through puddles and the water splashes up. As we mount a few flights of stairs, the scene gradually changes.

The corridors are wider, and steel cupboards and large, cumbersome equipment stand against the walls. It starts to look like a place where people once lived. It must have been an office I realize when I look into the rooms we pass and see desks with more dilapidated computers on them.

They take me to a room at the end of a long corridor. The room is large, the ceiling high. The tall windows that once provided a view, are now roughly boarded over; feeble protection from the wind and the rain that single-mindedly try to erase all traces of human life. The room is sparsely furnished. There are a couple of old sofas that probably also serve as beds. There is a small kitchen, a pine table with chairs around it. And in one corner there is a DOS screen, where I see myself, as large as life, with Dad behind me. I can't see any more, because I'm taken to the corner of the room and pushed down onto a chair. My body groans as I touch the hard, wooden seat.

"On my signal, you're going read this," says a voice above me.

The voice belongs to the man with the green eyes. Harry. Where is Max? The woman stands a little way off, next to the boy who must be Julius. They talk and point at the DOS screen that I can't see from here. The screen is a window to the world and questions involuntarily force their way into my mind. What is Dad doing? Has he any idea where I am? How's Mum? And Maria? Will she tell them everything now? Has Max said anything about Maria? That she knows who he is? As long as she...

"You — look at this."

My head is roughly pointed in the direction of another, smaller screen showing a text.

"If you deviate from this..." Harry opens his coat and I see a gun.

I nod quickly, feel the sweat break out all over my body.

Behind the camera, Liam gives the thumbs up. "Action!"

A white text appears on the black screen next to the camera, difficult to read from where I sit. I blink and swallow.

"Dad," begins the text. Dad. As if I have written the text myself. I swallow again when I see how Harry's right hand moves towards the pocket inside his jacket.

"Dad," I repeat, louder this time. "WEtTO has kidnapped me."

Kidnapped.

I've been kidnapped.

How odd that what has been my reality for more than twenty-four hours only now seems real, at the moment I say it out loud. WEtTO has kidnapped me. More than the gun that Harry is hiding so carefully, more than Liam's rage or Max's painful indifference, it's this sentence that makes me realize everything all at once. And so does the next one.

"If you do as they say, then... then I'll stay alive." These people mean it.

I've never been so scared in all my life.

I gasp for breath but my throat is blocked. I splutter, I cough, I spit. Spittle mixed with blood drips down my chin and despite my fear, I feel ashamed. As if the whole world is a witness to this grotesque drama, in which I, Nina Bradshaw, am the star.

I can't breathe anymore.

"Stop! Stop the tape, Liam!" Harry rushes over. He grabs me, places both hands on my arms, and shakes me roughly.

"Calm down. Calm down! Nothing will happen if you do what we say!"

I don't calm down. For I suddenly see not only how Max looked at me when Liam, it was Liam, gave me that injection, I also see Dad and hear his words: "WEtTO demands firm action. Well, they'll get it!"

What is the difference? Who can tell me that? I don't know. There is only one thing I am certain of: I'm in the middle of it. Trapped. Caught.

The tears continue, my throat fills up and I cough and spit and cry as Harry shakes me, harder and harder, his hands clenching my arms firmer and firmer. "Shut up! Dammit! Shut up, bitch!" he swears and I cry harder still, I scream until there's no air left in my lungs, not for Max, not for Dad, not even for Mum or Isa, but for myself.

"Harry! Dammit!"

Tanja intervenes. She pulls Harry off me and he lets go as soon as she grabs him, like a toy doll whose battery suddenly dies.

"Is there anybody here who can keep a clear head?" she shouts.

Harry says nothing. He puts his hands on his knees, his head drops. Liam looks straight at me. Julius sniggers. Where is Max?

Harry straightens.

"I'll say this one more time: you will read this." He pulls himself upright. "Without hesitation, without leaving out anything." He licks his lips, places a hand on the arm of the chair to keep upright.

And I read it, without hesitation, without interruption. I read out all the demands WEtTo has, all their wishes and curses, all their hope, and all their desperation. This is my role, whether I like it or not. I feel at the same time powerful and powerless.

And then I think of the book about the Great Flood. The other history. Those other people, not yet Wet, not yet Dry, but all victims of the devastating water, or perhaps of themselves and each other.

Revenge.

He wants revenge. Max wants revenge, just like his brother. And the question that has always been there but which I have never let surface, now forces itself on me: what happened on the Mainland? What happened there that Dad has never wanted to tell me? What did he do?

I don't realize that they've turned off the camera. I don't realize that my voice has long stopped speaking. I only feel something again when somebody — that indifferent Julius — grabs me and lifts me up.

"We're done," says Liam.

Harry nods.

"Make sure it's on DOS within the hour. Let's see if they think we're a serious negotiating partner."

Julius picks me up and throws me over his shoulder.

Suddenly I see Max.

He's standing in the doorway, his fingers tapping the door post. His eyes are large and bright. They follow me as Julius walks past him into the corridor. They still follow me as Julius locks the cell door behind me.

MAX

It doesn't change anything. It doesn't fucking change anything.

She's still a traitor. The daughter of a traitor. But Pa? With WEtTO?

And yet...

I couldn't keep my eyes off Nina. Man, she almost suffocated. Again. My damned hands. I think I've clenched my arms until they just about turn blue. Behind me, Harry is talking to Tanja. Harry lost his head. I didn't think Harry could ever lose his head.

Let go, man. Let go. Yes, like that. That's better. Much better. Better not to feel. That only makes a mess of everything.

I push myself away from the door post and stroll off. I don't see where I walking. Almost automatically my legs take me to the stairway, where the wind howls, where birds are startled and fly away and snowflakes make the steps treacherously slippery.

Of course I run. Upwards, back to the balcony. My body is hot from the exertion, my muscles are taut. At the top, I hang my arms and head over the railing and look at the buildings that are gradually turning whiter, all their filth and past covered in fresh snow.

But Pa? With WEtTO?

Li's lying. Pa was a simple mechanic. Pa was forced to work in the ccs when the floods started a year and a half ago. No Dry left to fix up his own mess. Better to use a Wet;

they're already used to it. Pa was angry, yes. Pa wanted things to be different. Ma wanted that too. But he would never have put himself, let alone us, in danger. His own flesh and blood always came first.

I can't believe Li. I don't want to believe him.

Better not to feel anything? As if I can bloody well do that! "Fuck, Li!"

My voice disappears oh so easily in the rushing wind. As if it wanted to say: what do you want to tell me, Wet?

"You called?"

I turn round. Li is leaning against the wall, or what is left of it.

"Leave me alone, man."

I turn my back on him. Not that that makes any difference to Li. He places a hand on my shoulder.

"I'm not lying, Max."

I say nothing.

"Pa told me. That he thought the time was ripe for change. He sometimes went into CCS. For his work. He saw things there and he thought he had to do something about them, could do something about them."

Li takes a step forward and stands next to me. He hand slips from my shoulder and he fiddles in his trouser pocket. He pulls out a cigarette and lighter. He lights the end, inhales deeply, and slowly exhales. The smoke wafts past my nose and makes me desperate for a drag, just one. Man. Have I lost my own will in just two days?

"Pa had to work in that school. The Mainland. I didn't want to tell you before." He looks aside, I feel his gaze on me. "I had to be certain that you'd understand, Max. The business... The importance..."

"What? Is there something else you're not telling me?" I am becoming impatient.

"Pa didn't want you to... Pa thought..."

"What didn't he want? What did he think of me?"

My hands have grasped the rusty pipes on the balcony and squeeze hard. I hardly register the pain. Li knows something from Pa. Liam knows something from Pa about me. And he's kept his mouth shut all this time.

"He thought you'd be like Ma," he finally said.

"And what is "like Ma"?" I can't hide my sarcasm. Why didn't Pa ever ask me that himself? Why didn't he take me into his confidence? Why did he tell Li and not me?

"That you let your heart to rule your head."

Let my heart rule my head? Did he think I couldn't control myself? Did he think I couldn't handle it, that I couldn't keep my feelings under control? Fuck! Isn't rage a feeling? Rage about injustice, Pa's rage, Li's rage? Or wanting to take revenge? Did Pa think I'd be too weak? That I wouldn't dare?

What's better? To follow your heart or your head?

I'm confident you'll make the right choice.

Ma's words. Not mine. Not Pa's, who apparently didn't have enough confidence in me. Not Li's, who only trusts me now that I've helped kidnap the Governor's daughter and dumped a body into the water.

What does my heart say?

What does my head say?

"Pa had a plan."

Li's voice seems to come from a distance and I have to struggle to follow his words.

"He found out something at that school, Max. Something WEtTO can make good use of in the struggle. He contacted Harry."

"Harry?"

Li nods.

"They'd known each other in the past. Both were in the Water Service in the Second Region. And you keep your mouth shut about this because Harry is always very particular about what he tells which people. And you've still got to earn your stripes. But Harry's cell is just one of many, Max. WEtTO is much, much bigger than this. In other Regions..." He doesn't finish his sentence, but gazes at the buildings in the water, or past them. A smile plays round his lips and his eyes have that same sparkle they had when he talked about the revolution. He really believes it.

"Pa?" I insist.

"Pa found out that Bradshaw's daughters were on the Mainland."

"D-daughters?"

"Harry would kill me if he knew I was telling you this, Max."

"*I'll* kill you if you *don't* tell me!"

Nina... Nina has... had a sister?

NO!

Fuck no...

I'm back in Nina's house, on that evening. It's only two days ago, but it seems like years. I kissed her, she pushed me away. "I want to show you something." Her hand moved to a door, Maria called us. And I hear Erik's voice again: "Nina's house is sick, Max."

Everything hidden away under that suffocating rage.

Li fiddles in his trouser pocket. He pulls out Nina's golden locket, clicks it open in one go and gives it to me.

I look at the photo it contains.

Nina and another girl. Younger. With blond hair. Sturdier than her older sister. She looks like Bradshaw, has the same ice-blue eyes. They are cheek to cheek in the photo and although you can't see it, you know they've got their arms around each other. They laugh. Happy and carefree. Dry. I stare at the photo while Li continues.

"Pa had already thought up the plan to kidnap one of the daughters. He'd prepared everything. Down to the last detail."

I want to hear it and not hear it. My legs tell me to run, but something prevents me. My hand closes round the locket and I hold that thing tight, so tight that I feel the edges digging into my skin.

"It was supposed to take place that day. Then the dyke broke and the water flooded into the school. He must already have taken her because she drowned, just like Pa."

Li's eyes glisten. He is angry. Of course he's angry.

"That Dry bastard Bradshaw didn't do a thing to help them, Max! And why? Because he thought he could save his daughter by diverting the water! She was the Dry who was trapped. That Dry prick thought she was in a different part of the building. Fifty men are worth less than one single Dry bitch, Max. Fifty."

"And Nina?"

I have to ask.

"Nina?" Li shrugs. "What about Nina?"

"Was she there too? On the Mainland, when the water came?"

"I don't know."

"Does Harry know?"

"He might."

"I want to know."

"You keep your mouth shut about it, Max. Otherwise it's my head on the block!"

I open my mouth, but shut it again. "Okay."

"Okay, little brother." Li gives me a sidelong glance. "Now you know. Now you're..."

"Initiated?"

"Yes, that's it, initiated." Then he stretches out his hand and I take it. He pulls me towards him and gives me a hug. Mates.

"We're going to be fine, little brother. I'm certain of that. It's going to be a mess, but once it's all cleaned up... Then even Ma will see it was all worthwhile. Really. Believe me.'

I nod. He lets me take a drag on his cigarette and I inhale deeply. "Harry didn't want me to tell you. About Pa and the Dry's sister. He's not sure about you, little brother. But I know I can trust you.'

Trust.

I nod again and exhale the smoke. It is immediately caught by the wind and carried away, like a fish on a hook.

"I noticed, Max. That you'd changed. When you found out who she was."

Changed. I can't go back. I've made my choice. Li trusts me now. Just like Ma trusts me.

And Nina.

But then, who said a Wet could ever be trusted?

NINA

The twilight turns into the darkest night ever. If I put my hands up in front of my eyes, it's an effort to distinguish them from the rest of the cell. Cold creeps through me. First in the tip of my nose, then the tips of my fingers.

Quickly the cold fills my whole body.

Are they just going to leave me here?

Have they already put my message on DOS? I try to imagine Dad's reaction but all I can think of is how he looked when the news came about Isa. And Isa was his favorite. What is he thinking now? Does he regret his ultimatum? And Mum. I feel tears welling up. Oh Mum, I'm so sorry.

I hear the odd noise. Footsteps approaching and then departing. A heavy engine is started. Splashing water.

Panic bubbles up.

Are they really going to leave me here on my own? Are they going to leave me here to, to...? I can't think about it. But not everybody has left because not much later I hear voices.

I close my eyes in the hope of falling asleep. Images keep surfacing and I feel myself sink further with each image. Max kissing me, Damian grabbing me by my waist and pulling down my pants, Harry shaking me over and over again, Mum leaning against my desk and smiling as she looks at my drawing. Dad's hard words and my idea of his triumphant look when Felix makes a proposal. I know it's a dream when that proposal is for Max's execution, and I wake with a start.

"Shhh."

My eyes snap open. I want to scream but I can't. A hand is placed over my mouth.

"Please. Don't scream. If they know I'm here, I'm done for."

It's Max.

I see nothing. It's still pitch dark. What's the time? "I won't hurt you. I swear it on my Pa's grave."

Something in his voice makes me nod carefully. Then I realize he won't be able to see it. "Okay," I mumble against his warm, sticky hand. My voice croaks.

His hand disappears and I hear shuffling. He walks around me.

"Give me your hands. I'll loosen the knot a bit."

I stretch out my arms. Unintentionally, my cold finger tips touch his chest, which feels like it's on fire. The smell of sweat forces its way into my nose. What has he done? Why is he here? I don't dare say anything. His big fingers have difficulty with the tight knot and he swears. When he's finally untied the knot and tied it again, he sighs. He gets up and I hear him sit down awkwardly on one of the crates.

My thoughts rush in all directions. What is he doing here? Why doesn't he say anything? What's the matter? And why are we sitting here in the dark? I hear his breathing. Panting, as if he has just exerted himself. He clears his throat and spits. I automatically flinch, but don't feel anything. Not on me. He didn't spit on me.

He's staring at me, even though he can't see me. I'm sure of it. I feel his dark eyes under those black eyebrows, in-quiring, asking, doubting. What am I feeling? I don't know what I'm feeling. Am I scared of him? Do I feel uncomfortable?

"I know about your sister."

His voice, rough and hoarse, sounds muted in the bare room. Of course he can't sit still. His fingers tap his legs, then the wall.

"Isa..." I see her before me. Her last smile. She said somebody wanted to talk to her, winked, and ran away in the opposite direction.

How can he know about Isa?

I feel his warm hands and then something hard, metal, that he pushes into my hands.

My locket!

I can't see it in the dark, but my fingers feel for the lock and automatically open it. I stroke my numb fingers over the photo. Isa.

His hands have grabbed my arms before I can do anything about it. I feel my heart beating and my head fills with alarm signals.

"Were you there too?"

His voice sounds as if he is begging, but he's hurting me and I can't say anything.

"Tell me, Nina. I want to know!"

"You're hurting me, Max!" I shout, almost in panic.

Abruptly he lets go, but I know he's still standing in front of me because the smell of sweat again fills my nostrils. "Please, tell me."

What can my answer mean? There's something going on. I take a deep breath.

"Yes, I was there as well," I say.

A groan and a thump. What is he doing? Cursing and a

smothered scream. If I didn't know better, I'd say he was bashing his head against the concrete wall.

"Max?"

"You were going to tell me, right?"

It hurts, physical pain, to hear his broken voice. My throat is burning.

"You wanted to show me her room. At your..." He hesitates. "At your house, when we..."

"Yes," I say quickly as I close my fingers around the locket and push it into my pants" pocket. Safe and sound.

"Oh fuck. Oh fuck! What have I done?"

"Max?" Something makes me reach out my hands and the first thing I feel is his short, stubbly hair. I softly stroke it.

He says nothing and I continue stroking his soft stubbly hair. It calms me down. My hands slowly move downwards. They feel his ears, the mobile cartilage, the lobes. They move to his jaw which feels strangely rough, until I realize that he hasn't shaved for days. Not a boy, but a man. My fingers feel his lips, the scabs on his wounds and the moisture; drops that trickle down his cheeks and I taste it when I shift my fingers to my mouth. Salt. He's crying.

He's crying. So silently. But he's crying.

MAX

When was the last time I cried?

Not when Pa died. I was only angry. And I ran. I ran every day until the knot disappeared and I was no longer screaming inside.

"Crying is for babies," Li used to say when I cried. I didn't want to be a baby. Men don't cry. Even Ma couldn't take it if I had to cry. A bandage on the wound and then get out, outside, into the street. You'll soon learn to stop crying out there.

But now I can't stop sobbing and I'm ashamed of myself. I'm more ashamed of myself than I've ever been in my life.

"Hey, come on," whispers Nina.

That only makes it bloody worse. I want to push away her hands and at the same time I don't want her ever to stop. I want to freeze time.

No, I want to turn back time.

"Erik is dead."

Her hand is gone.

"They killed him. Bullet through his brain."

She holds her breath.

I don't know why I'm so blunt. Perhaps it's because what they did is so blunt.

We.

Be honest, you prick.

"Li and I..." I hesitate. I push out the words. "Li and I dumped his body. Over the dyke. Into the water."

She says nothing. Nothing at all.

Is she scared of me? I'm scared of myself. Trust. Can't be trusted. I damn well deserve it. She wanted to tell you, man!

The words tumble from my tongue. "I didn't know, Nina! I swear it. I didn't know you were on the Mainland when the dyke gave way. I was fucking mad because Bradshaw had killed Pa and that you, that you... I wanted to get back at him, let him feel what it's like to have someone close taken from you. Li, that bloody brother of mine, didn't say that you were on the Mainland as well when the water came and that Pa... that Pa..."

You've got to tell her, Max. You've got to. Clear all the skeletons from the closet. The worst has already happened.

"That Pa belonged to WEtTO and was going to kidnap Isa."

It's out. My family is made up of psychopaths, me included. Ma is the only one who hasn't lost her mind. Yet.

"Kidnap?"

Nina's soft voice sounds unsure.

"Yes. Kidnap. Pa and Harry were going to kidnap her. The day that..."

"The day that.."

"Yes."

She falls silent again. I listen to her breathing. In. Out. In. Out.

Our breathing is in tandem. Man, I want to see her, I want to know what she's thinking when she looks at me. I want to see her, know for certain that I've ruined everything, that she never wants to see me again. But I don't dare put on the light, scared that one of the others will notice and throw me out, and then Nina...

"She said she was meeting someone. I thought she meant Johan. That day... that day they'd been together for six months. Johan always found an excuse. Oh no...no..."

Her voice breaks.

I jump up and grab both her hands. She starts, but doesn't pull away. Man, she's so cold.

"Dad killed her himself."

What?

"Dad knew that Isa was trapped on the Mainland. I was so cold, Max! It was the water, you know? They pulled me out. Wets. I know they were Wets. I could tell from their clothing. Why didn't I remember that, Max?"

I go to answer her, but she rushes on.

"I was cold. So cold, Max. And sat there shivering and Dad kept looking at me and asking, "Where is she? Where is she, Nina? Tell me!" He said the building was on the verge of collapse and it wouldn't be long before the water rose higher. And then I remembered what Isa had said. That she had a date."

Again Nina gasps in and out.

"She must have lied. She often kept me in the dark. Isa always made her own plans. There were so many people helping. They helped me too, Max, the Wets. I'm certain now they were Wets. I was so cold. Ice cold. Dad... Dad sent the rescue workers to the place where he thought Isa was. He couldn't have known... *I* couldn't have known..."

She gasps for breath.

"He must have forced the second dyke breach because he thought they would then be able to reach her. By diverting the water. But she wasn't there, because your father... I heard Dad shouting and he hit somebody. Wets, Max, there were

Wets! But you've got to understand, I thought I would never get warm again. And Isa... Isa was inside... Honest, I couldn't do anything!"

I want to tell Nina I understand, that she couldn't do anything, but she carries on talking, so softly I can hardly hear what she's saying.

"Dad didn't want to say. Didn't want to say where they found her. He must have realized it himself. What he had done by diverting the water. And he didn't tell us either."

She breathes out, a long, stuttering breath.

I wait for her to breathe in again, but don't hear anything. I wait and wait, panic pounding in my body like a bomb and I'm about to shake her when Nina's finally breaths in. Long. And deep.

I take her hands and start untying the knot.

NINA

I'm hardly aware of what he's doing until I can suddenly move my hands freely again. Max turns to the knots around my feet.

"What...?"

"We're leaving," he says brusquely. He swears under his breath; his fingers are too big for the tiny knot.

"What?" I say again. I don't get any of it. Erik, Isa, Dad, Max's father ... Suddenly everybody is connected together in the most horrible way and I can't take it all it any longer.

"Help me."

My fingers obey him, but my wounded body groans and creaks. Again he places his hand over my mouth. "Shhh."

I'm scared. I'm petrified and excited all at the same time.

Perhaps he's lying, says a voice in my head. Is it a trick to get you to go with him? He's lied to you before. But do I have any other choice? My hand remembers the touch his short, stubbly hair and I feel a brief moment of calmness, one moment in the endless rush of time. I taste his tears on my tongue.

My fingers work faster on the tight knot.

"Harry and Tanja have gone off with the waterboard, but they've left one of the scooters behind. It's our only chance," whispers Max in my ear as I manage to untie the last knot and carefully move my painful feet.

"Julius is as drunk as a skunk. But Li..." He pauses. "We'll have to avoid Li."

I'm suddenly certain that Max will do everything to get us out of here.

"Let me go fetch my backpack. I'll be right back."

He's gone before I can say anything.

I get up carefully and feel my bones creak. How long have I been tied up? More than a day. At least. I rub my icy legs but it doesn't make much difference, for my hands are — if that's possible — even colder than my legs and feet. It's night. I'm sure of that. But I haven't the faintest idea whether it's midnight or just after sunset. Harry and Tanja are out, Max said. Where have they gone? To Dad? Has he responded to their demands? My thoughts rush in all directions, except to what I'm going to do next. I hear footsteps. I hold my breath and quickly lie down.

It's Max who softly opens the door, closes it behind him, and gives me something.

"Here. Put them on. You're dry?"

I don't say anything.

Max draws a sharp breath.

"Sorry."

"No, there's no need to say sorry." I don't say anything for a moment. "Only my trouser legs are wet." I quickly put on the sweater he gives me. The thing is old. It stinks and itches. Real wool. Nobody wears real wool any more. You sink like a stone if wear it in the water.

"I've got a coat for you as well." I take it from him. The thing is much too big and I have to turn up the sleeves. "Sorry, but I couldn't find any other shoes."

"I'll make do with these."

He is quiet. I feel his hesitation.

"What?"

"I think... I think I should tie you up again. Act as if you want to go to the toilet or something. Julius may be as drunk, but if you're walking normally, even he will notice that something's up. And we have to get past him first."

I hear the doubt in his voice. He's afraid I don't trust him. Perhaps he doesn't trust himself. But everything in me tells me I have to get away from here. And quickly, too.

"I trust you." Before I lose my nerve, I stretch out my hands to Max.

He is quick and doesn't tie the knots anywhere near as tightly as before. His face is close to mine and with each breath, his boyish odor penetrates deeper inside me. His sweat, his excitement, his fear.

Again he hesitates.

"What?"

"The tape..."

"Do it."

His hands tremble as his sticks the tape over my mouth. His fingers linger just a beat too long against my cheek. A feather-like caress. He picks me up and opens the door. What is he planning to do?

MAX

She's so light.

I don't want to hurt her anymore. I won't hurt her anymore. I swear. I truly swear.

If only this works.

"Hey, Max."

Julius is looking at his HC. He's flopped in an old armchair in the middle of the corridor.

"The Dry needs a piss."

Will he fall for it? We've hidden my bag under Nina's coat. Li would suspect something from miles away.

Julius looks at me and laughs. Why is the prick laughing? His nicotine stained teeth appear a yellowish brown in the light of the bare bulb dangling above his thin head. He's totally drunk. I thing of him sitting on our sofa, next to Li and Ramon, always with a can of beer in his hand. I know his ma and pa. His little brother is in the grad below mine. Do they know what he's doing?

"Well?" I say.

"Patience, man, patience. Let me finish my beer. Or can't your cock wait any longer?"

What? The filthy, bloody...

He picks up the can standing on the floor next to him and lifts it to his lips. He laughs again, gives Nina a horny wink, and swallows the last dregs. It takes all my will-power not to smash his ugly face in. I breathe in and out. Deeply.

"Piss off, Julius."

He holds up his hands, fending me off.

"Cool, man. Cool. I'm not stopping you. Just make sure she's back before Harry and Tanja return. Julius wouldn't want to come between a guy and his girl."

Another laugh and a wink, but he finally gets up, so fucking slowly.

Walk, Max. Keep walking.

We have almost got past him and a sigh of relief escapes me when Julius slowly hisses: "Hey, Max, man?"

I stop.

"What?"

Nina's heart is racing next to mine.

"Was she wearing that coat when she came here?"

I turn slowly and look him straight in the eye.

"A guy has a right to make things easier for himself, Julius." I hold his watery eyes with my gaze. At the same time, I allow my left hand to glide over Nina's breast and stomach and I grab her narrow hips real tight. She jumps under my touch and lets out a muffled sound through her taped up mouth. Julius grins and waves his hand, to show he understands. I quickly move on.

Oh fuck.

This time, it's not only my head that's racing. *Keep calm, man!*

"Sorry, Nina, sorry," I keep whispering to her. Once I turn the corner, I run. Don't think man. No, don't feel. Don't feel. Nina can't say anything, but I feel her wriggling and twisting her body. Her hair tickles my arms and her hands grab me round my waist.

Tight. She's only holding me.

I breathe in and out. It's okay, Max. Is that what she wants to say?

We've gone up one storey. This is where Li is. He must be here, because he's not in the communal area and not with Julius. What did he say just now? *Think, Max, think.* He went to cool his head. That was it. The washroom.

And the washroom has a door.

If he stays in there while Nina... Yes. That could work. Dammit, it must work!

I carefully put down Nina and start untying her hands and feet. I hardly dare look at her, afraid that she'll see at once what I'm thinking. *Think, man, think.* She avoids my gaze. As I continue, I explain the plan to her.

"Li is in the washroom. I'll distract him and you go to the water-scooter. Do you know how to drive one of those things?"

Nina nods. She wrestles with the tape.

"Want me to help?"

She shakes her head and pulls it off in one go. Fuck. That had to hurt. As she looks up, a thick red drop of blood appears on her left cheek.

"Where is it?"

My hand hangs in the air, right next to her grazed cheek.

"The jetty, I mean," she adds.

"Down the corridor, third door on the left. Follow the sound of the water, and you'll find it. Don't go until you hear me slam the door."

She nods with determination.

I hesitate a moment, then grab her and give her a quick kiss. I wipe away the drop of blood with the back of my hand. I'll never hurt her again. I swear. Honest.

"Take care," I say.
My lips tingle.
"Take care," answers Nina.

NINA

He said sorry.

He didn't have to say sorry. How can your body react so conflictingly under such circumstances? I still feel the shadow of his mouth on my cheek, his stubble against the burning wound and I taste blood. A fresh drip that he can't wipe away anymore. I listen to his footsteps getting softer and softer. I clasp his backpack to me.

I wait to hear the door close.

The footsteps stop. I hear voices, just too far away to understand. Somebody's talking. Liam or Max? It is difficult to distinguish their voices.

I hear the door close.

My legs won't obey me anymore. Come on, Nina, come on! I stand stock still and don't dare move. When I finally set my legs in motion, my wet shoes squeak horribly, and with every step my heart misses a beat. The voices of the two brothers feed their way through the cracks and holes in the drafty building. If I move closer, I can understand them.

"... will they be back?"

Splashing water, somebody shakes his head.

"Always curious, little brother. Always curious. Why do you want to know?"

Liam. I see his glowing dark eyes before me and his clownish grin. Not like Max. Completely unlike Max. I shiver. "No reason. Just curious."

Footsteps coming closer. I stop immediately. The door remains closed.

"Can't you sleep?" asks Liam. His voice sounds different, softer, like I've never heard him before. He sounds concerned.

"No."

Max's voice shakes from nerves. Liam sees it differently. "If you like, we can go out for a smoke."

"I think I'm going to cut back again," says Max.

Liam laughs. "Pa swore by a good cigarette. You know that."

"Yes, I know."

Calm down, Max, calm down. I'm almost there. Nearly at the door. "I thought you'd changed your mind."

I hold my breath.

"But maybe not."

Max!

I force myself to walk on, not to listen.

Liam laughs and I hear him give his brother a slap on the shoulder. Max laughs too. Their laugh is just the same. Brothers.

One of them turns on the tap and takes a few deep gulps. I walk farther, faster, because the sound of the water is drowning my footsteps. I've almost reached the corner when I hear Liam's voice.

"Let's go and take a look at the Dry. Make sure Julius hasn't nodded off."

My legs refuse to move when I hear Max's hesitant voice.

"Liam!" His voices catches.

"What? Don't you want to see the traitor?"

Liam sounds suspicious.

"No, no, it's not that..."

"What then?"

"I... Perhaps that cigarette is a good idea after all."

"Why don't you want to see her, Max?"

Max. No little brother this time.

"I..."

"What have you done, Max?"

"Nothing Liam. I've not done fucking anything! I just don't want to see her!"

Max is panicking. Liam is quiet, but I hear footsteps moving towards the door.

"I don't believe you."

"You said you trusted me!"

Run, Nina, run! He can see you here! But I can't move. I'm frozen with fear.

"Can I trust you, Max?"

Liam's voice is soft. He sounds... wounded.

Max hesitates.

Not too long.

"Yes, of course you can..."

Liam has opened the door to the hallway and is looking directly at me.

"Fucking HELL!"

Only then do my legs start moving.

MAX

I hear Nina running away and sprint to the door where I just manage to grab the edge of Li's jacket.

"Run, Nina, run! I'm coming!" I scream, as I try to hold my brother back.

Li is furious. He curses and swears and yells: "I'm going to kill you, Max. I'm going to kill you!" I have never seen him in such a rage. He's completely lost it.

That's my advantage.

I slip past him into the corridor, land a punch in his stomach, and rush off after Nina.

"Julius!" he screams as he sprints after me. Oh fuck. Oh fuck! Oh FUCK!

I turn round and see his hand go to his trouser pocket. What's he got there? I can't keep looking, but suddenly Erik with that perfectly round hole in his head flashes through my mind. I run faster.

That's one up for me.

I hear the spluttering engine before I see the scooter. The wind's blowing hard, harder than it was. Black waves dance across the endless expanse. Snow falls in thick flakes and disappears into the water. The night is white. I slam the door behind me, but there's no lock. That's not going to stop Li for long.

Nina is sitting on the water scooter, trying to keep the engine going.

"It's a newer model. Something's different. I..."

She abruptly stops talking and looks past me. Her eyes get bigger and bigger. When she breathes out, a soft squeak escapes from her mouth. I turn round and see my brother standing there.

He's pointing the gun at Nina.

"You're staying here." He can hardly keep his voice under control.

He makes a screeching sound with each inward breath and pants as if he's been boxing for an hour. He cocks the pistol and points it at Nina's head.

I jump between them.

"No! Max!" screams Nina, and she makes a move to gets off the scooter.

"Stay where you are, Nina. Try to get that thing going." The words are automatic, so is the action.

"Max! Get out of the way."

Liam's hands tremble. His finger is on the trigger.

"If you want to get her, you'll have to shoot me first, Li." I feel myself calm down, more certain of myself. I take a step towards him. "Are you going to shoot your own brother, Li? Is the revolution worth that to you?"

Drops of sweat roll down his forehead and he blinks his eyes.

"Max, damn you, I'll say it one more time. Get. Out. Of. The. Way!"

In the distance, in the emptiness of the building, I hear footsteps. Julius. We haven't got much more time. I take another step. Li starts to squeeze the trigger.

The engine sputters, then roars to life.

And then it sputters again.

"Ma'd never forgive you, Li."

Just a moment, just another moment. Come on!

"Leave Ma out of this, Max!"

I see his eyes shift between me and the door, "Liam..."

I'm standing right in front of him. Almost...

"Max..."

"Yes! It's working!" screams Nina and in the fraction of a second that Li's distracted, I leap down the steps and kick the pistol from his hands. It lands on the edge of the improvised quay; a semi-balcony to which the scooter is tied. We wrestle as Nina unties the scooter and starts maneuvering it. Li throws a right to my jaw and I almost fall into the water. He dives on top of me, but I kick him in the balls and he doubles up in pain. I grab the pistol and chuck it far into the white of the snowy night, and then I jump on behind Nina. Julius storms outside and his drunken mind only half understands what's happening. He fiddles around in his pocket for his gun.

"Quick, we've gotta get out of here!" I hiss.

Nina hits the gas and finally the scooter starts moving.

"Julius, shoot! Shoot, dammit!" shouts Li, as he scrambles onto his knees. When Julius hesitates, Li grabs his gun and fires.

The bullet hits the water a few feet behind us.

Li shoots again, and then again, he keeps firing until there are no bullets left. I hear him curse and scream and I see him kick Julius. Snow is falling on the quay, on Julius who's groaning in pain, and on my furious, ranting and raving brother.

I look at Li until I can't see him any longer. Until he is nothing than a black dot against an ever whiter background.

My big brother.

NINA

Every shot is an attack on my nerves.

I push down the gas pedal until I realize that the resistance I feel is actually pain because the pedal is as far down as possible. I looked back once. Just once. I can hardly make out the building where Liam and Julius are standing. A white curtain, a curtain that's becoming thicker and thicker, separates them from us. I don't know how long it takes until it finally dawns on me that we've really escaped. That they're not coming after us.

Max watches longer, much longer. Even when there's nothing more to see.

His own brother tried to shoot him. He's holding me too tightly, but I don't want to say anything.

I feel blind in this strange, white night.

I wasn't lying when I said I could drive the scooter. But using one on a lake is a lot different from travelling across the Submerged Territories in the middle of the night.

Once the initial panic has died down, I realize that it's a miracle that we haven't hit something in our crazy flight or been dragged under by something. It takes a while for me to understand that the noise the scooter makes depends on where we are. The thing pretty much drives itself – at least, it can detect if we get too close to the shore or if there's something under the surface.

I notice immediately when Max finally turns round. His

weight moves slightly forward and his hot breath warms my frozen neck.

"We might be better off hiding somewhere and waiting for daylight. Until we can see what we're doing," he says, his voice flat and curt.

"Okay."

Those are the only words we exchange for a long while.

I haven't the slightest idea how long we've been going. In the night, everything looks the same and there is no moon, no stars to light the dark water. Each time the skeleton of a building looms up next to us or in front of us, fear rises in my throat and everything in me shouts: "Get away, now, quickly!" It wouldn't surprise me if we were going round in circles and are sailing back into the eager hands of Liam and Julius.

The wind increases and I have difficulty staying upright. It pulls and tugs and pushes, as if it has decided that it might as well be against us too, now that the rest of the world is. And again I'm cold, so terribly cold. Snowflakes blind me and build up on my arms, on my shoulders and in my neck. They seep through my clothes. I wonder whether I will ever be warm again.

My eyes are constantly searching for a place where we can hide, but the snow makes it difficult to see anything. It is as if we're travelling through a strange, white nothingness. It is silent, except for the wind, the slapping sound of water, and the occasional surprised water bird. This is the end of the world.

But isn't that...?

I take my foot off the gas pedal. Within a few second we come to a halt and bob gently on the waves.

Yes. My eyes haven't deceived me. Trees! And among them, something that looks like a roof.

An island.

"There," I cry.

"What?"

"An island." I point.

Max gazes past me.

"I think that's a house," I say. "Perhaps we can hide there."

I give a bit of gas, gently, so that we don't pass the island. When we are close enough, my suspicions are confirmed.

An island in the middle of endless water. A refuge.

It must at one time have been a dyke with a neat row of trees. The few that are still standing have been blown crooked by the incessant wind, and below them is a derelict house, half collapsed. When the engine stops and Max jumps onto the island, I'm startled by a storm of birds that suddenly fly up.

Dark, black birds. Crows.

I didn't know they came out this far from the Regions. Or perhaps we're closer to our Region than we think. Quickly I shake off the thought.

The crows protest violently at our arrival. They fly above our heads, screeching, until they finally settle in the tops of the trees and watch our actions distrustfully.

Together we pull the scooter on land, so that it cannot float away. The thing weighs a ton, but even the effort doesn't do much for the cold that has penetrated so deeply into me that it seems to have become part of my DNA.

"I'll go and look at the house." Max walks off before I can say anything. The dim glow of his HC disappears behind the curtain of falling snow, into the dark night.

I want to go after him, but change my mind. Max said that nobody is following us, but we haven't the faintest idea where we are and perhaps the waterboard with Harry and Tanja may pass by. I begin to break off twigs from the bushes and cover the scooter with them, so that the thing isn't visible from the water. Each time I go farther than the circle of light, I stumble over a stone or branch or something else I'd rather not think about. When I think, or hope, that the scooter is sufficiently hidden, I sit down against it to shelter me from the wind. I have never been in such a lonely place.

Where's Max got to?

I know I'm going to start imagining things if I think too much

My stomach rumbles. I've hardly eaten anything in the past twenty-four hours. I get up — is that Max? — and suddenly see a lock under the scooter's seat. I pull at it, but of course I need a digicard to unlock it. Perhaps I can use the same one that starts the scooter. I'm in luck. When Max returns, I have an emergency blanket, a couple of bottles of water, instant tea, some packets of dried food and a first-aid kit in my hands.

Max's eyes widen.

"Where did you get all that?"

I point.

"Let me have a look."

He bends down and pulls out some more food, a tube with a gas bottle and a flashlight. When he gets up, he accidentally shines the light in my face. I blink and turn away.

"Sorry."

"Doesn't matter."

An uneasy silence falls. Max is the first to recover.

"We should get some sleep, I think."

"Okay."

I follow him.

MAX

I walk ahead.

The whole way here, my head was there. Thinking of my brother. Of what I'd done. What I'd fucking done. Nina says nothing, to my relief.

But I can't get Li's face out of my mind, how he looked when he realized what was happening. And it's not the anger of the Morrises that haunts me. I'm used to that by now. Pa, Ma, Liam. I even see it in the few photos Ma has of the family. Pa's Pa always looked angry. As if he was always near boiling point and about to wreck everything around him.

Li... Li was angry, yes. He's never been as angry as this before. But before the anger glazed his eyes and made him clench his jaw, there was something else. I can't delude myself, I know what it was.

Pain. Sadness. Disappointment.

At that moment, I knew it was over. No longer the Morris brothers against the Dries, against the whole rotten world.

Over and out.

A crow sweeps down dangerously close and screeches in my ear. I swing my fist at it and it screeches louder, as if it wants to say: "Piss off, you don't belong here. This is our place."

Perhaps he's right. Perhaps I should think about where I belong.

I pick up my pace, feel a cramp in my leg from sitting so

long. If I could, I would run, but Nina can hardly keep up with me as it is and I force myself to walk slower.

I look at the house.

It once stood on a dyke. That's why it as survived the floods. No, there's more to it. It's too well maintained, as if somebody lived there after the rest had long since disappeared into the water. A hermit. Suddenly I see it my mind. Somebody who decides that the world doesn't matter anymore and turns his back on everything and everyone. Not a Wet. Not a Dry. Just a person. How long did he last? There was complete chaos when the world flooded. No, he came later. Of course he came later. He'd had enough. Just like me. He'd so had enough. And here there was nobody to bother him.

"Max, wait."

Damn. I'm walking too quickly again. I force my legs to stop and turn round.

There she is. Nina. And immediately I know that I could never be like that hermit. She's panting from the effort and there are red patches on her pale cheeks. Where they are still pale, that is. Suddenly I feel a stab of shame. She only realizes I've stopped when she almost bumps into me. She just manages to stay upright and places her hand on my arm to keep her balance. I feel her hand.

"Sorry," she says. She looks up at me.

Her eyes are large in the fierce light of the torch. Blue, I've always thought. But they are not just any blue. Silver grey specks melt into the blue. Grey-blue, silver-blue, blue-blue.

"Come on," I say and take her hand.

We have to struggle through some bushes to reach the door. She shines the torch while I flatten them with my feet.

The door is jammed and I barge into it with my shoulder, once, twice, three times, and then it crashes open and I tumble inside, into the dark room. I feel Nina behind me, her one hand low on my back, the torch in her other hand, shining around the room.

It's as if the door is an entrance to a different dimension.

Yes, the roof is full of holes on one side. Most probably those damned crows had pulled out the thatch to make their nests. Yes, there are gaps in the small windows and the walls are cracked in some places. Yes, there's a mess of dust and leaves and damp and rat shit.

But it's not empty. In the farthest corner, next to a window where bushes are trying to gain entry, there is a table that still has all four legs, with two narrow chairs under it. My gaze moves further, and I see what must have been the kitchen. A stone work surface and some cabinets, a sink with a real tap. There is a vase on the table, empty, but the green deposit shows it was once used. On the other side is a sofa, a small loveseat of old brown leather, with a wooden coffee table in front of it. An orange lamp hangs low and my hand automatically reaches for the light switch that must be next to the door. There are paintings on the wall. Of dykes and meadows and cows. Windmills. Some have water damage; sails that have run into bumpy circles, cows sinking into the mud and green grass mixing with the blue of the sky. In the middle of the room, a stairway goes up through the ceiling.

It's as if somebody left in a hurry not that long ago. My hermit.

I grin. "Look at this."

Nina comes and stands next to me. "It's as if..."

"... somebody still lives here."

She nods slowly.

"But there's nobody. There really isn't anybody," I say quickly.

She smiles. "I know. I'm not scared."

And something that's stuck inside is released. *She's not scared.*

NINA

He turns his face to me.

It is suddenly so open. No, not open. Naked. The stubble on his chin suddenly seems out of place, as if a small boy has painted his chin in an attempt to look older. Before I can do anything, ask him anything, or say anything, he walks further into the house. I follow him.

It looks as if somebody has packed his things and left in a hurry. A round vase is standing on the kitchen table, and when I get closer I can see a newspaper, with a date not so very long ago. Somebody lived here. Even after the world was flooded.

What was it like to live in the middle of the water?

I suddenly realize that this person has done exactly the opposite of what we're doing. He or she — a she, I decide when I notice the colorful planters on the windowsill — didn't take refuge somewhere high and dry where the water couldn't reach. No, she came back. Perhaps she never left. She made her home in the water, between the water, on the water. Water everywhere.

Wasn't she scared?

The floor creaks. Several floor boards are mouldy and I smell the gentle odor of wet wood. Carefully I walk round the rotten floor boards to the sofa with a table in front of it. Circles on the wood, I notice. Where is the glass? And sure enough, a glass is on the floor, completely undamaged. I bend down and pick it up. A perfect, round glass. Somebody sat on this sofa and drank from this glass. Perhaps curled up with a book on their lap — a real paper book of course — and a cat next to them. Not scared at all.

"Nina!"

I turn round, expecting to see him in the room. I'm alone. Where is he?

"Max?"

He calls again and I follow the sound of his voice. It's coming from above. I walk to the stairs, shine the flashlight upwards, and light up Max's grinning face.

"It'll take your weight."

I blink and dubiously study the wooden stairway that groans dangerously when I push against it.

"Are you sure?"

"I'm sure."

He reaches out his hand. I hesitate for a moment, then I quickly climb the stairs. Max helps me over the last bit, where a stair is missing.

I'm standing in an even smaller room. Sloping walls turn the attic into a soft cocoon. Patches of white, snowflakes that have blown in through the holes in the roof, are dotted over the gently dim room, like ripples of sunlight through the leaves of a tree. Strangely enough, it seems warm and I slowly feel the cold being driven out of me.

Max doesn't give me any time to take in the surroundings.

"I saw something there," he says and gestures at a dark corner with the weak light from his HC screen.

His hand on my arm.

Warmer.

"What?"

"Give me the torch."

I hand the thing to him.

He takes my hand and carefully leads me to the corner, where there is a pile of all sorts of things. I see a cast-iron coat-stand, not hung with coats but with fishing tackle. Tent canvas, that old-fashioned thick stuff, is folded up in piles, and below it a wooden crate with old gardening tools, a broken tennis racket and the front wheel of a bicycle, bent and rusty brown when the water has got to the metal.

"Give me a hand," says Max, clamping the torch between his teeth. He's clearing things out of the way.

I squirm in beside him, between the hat-stand and a heavy cupboard, with iron fittings. Together we push the heavy thing to one side. When I look up, I see what the torch is showing. A wall. But not just a wall. It's a built-in cupboard with two green painted doors, although most of the paint has peeled off. There is a heart-shaped opening in each door, and Max slips a finger through one of them. He pulls the doors open.

A bed. A made-up bed.

We stand looking at it. We are both silent. Close together, my leg touching his leg, his arm touching my arm.

I hear his breathing. Deeper and deeper. His breathing in time with mine.

I turn to face him. Half of his face is in the shadow, half in the light of the lamp that he nonchalantly dangles down his side.

It happens all by itself.

My hand taking his hand. My fingers feeling his fingers, one by one. Max turning towards me, the question unmistakable in his dark eyes. My almost imperceptible nod of yes.

I pull him towards me and on tip toe kiss him. It happens all by itself.

And I feel how I leave everything, really everything behind me.

MAX

She's standing next to me and she wants me.

I can hardly contain myself. Her tongue is soft, almost shy, but when I throw the lamp on the bed and pull her firmly against me, she becomes fiercer. She hardly gives me any time to breath.

Li bragged about his conquests. He had always had girls and I regularly had to clear out. Pa smiled when yet another girl sat at the breakfast table. Ma looked at each of them as if they were dirt.

Now I've got a girl.

And she's not dry.

I hold Nina tight. I'll never let her go. I'm glowing inside and out. I'm sweating, even though it's fucking snowing outside. I pick her up. I pull back the old blankets and place her on the bed.

I creep next to her.

My girl.

I look at her. I want her so badly.

"You're not cold?"

She shakes her head.

"You're keeping me warm. You're like a heater."

She smiles.

She's nervous. Just like me. Oh fuck, I'm so nervous and I want it so badly.

I vaguely smell the mildewed odor of the musty blankets,

but I press my nose into her soft curls and I sniff the sweet, intoxicating girl smell which, if possible, gets me even more worked up.

I start as I feel a hand near my crotch, round my prick. Her hand trembles, moves softly, exploring. I can hardly hang on. I start to kiss her again and she kisses me back, softly saying my name. I have never felt anything like this. I forget Li, I forget Pa. I forget everything. Gone.

My hand moves down, to her slacks, but I can't get those damned things open. The buttons are too tight.

"Let me," she says softly.

When she opens her slacks and pulls them down a little, I see her light hair. I want to ask her, but she takes my hand and leads it downward. Downwards and inwards.

She's wet.

She opens my trousers and I'm so hard it almost hurts. I move carefully, don't want to hurt her, but I don't feel it very well. Nina lies down and I push against her. My hand moves to her waist, under her sweater, under her shirt to her tits. I feel her hard nipples and the soft flesh. Fluid oozes from my prick, and I almost come, dammit!

"What's wrong?"

Did I swear out loud?

"I... I can't find it."

She bites her lower lip and grimaces. She carefully takes hold and helps me inside. I slip in.

Nina jerks and a small gasp escapes from her open mouth. "Are you okay?" I ask quickly. Oh man, I'm going to come.

She nods and I let go. I move exactly four times and then I come.

She holds my ass tightly as I shudder.

"Are you... are you finished?"

I nod.

I'm still in her.

"Shouldn't you pull out?"

I nod again and slip out of her. Man, it's suddenly so cold! I quickly pull up my trousers and fall down beside her. The bed creaks in protest.

After a while, Nina turns to face me.

"Max?"

"Yes?"

"Will you...?"

She takes my hand and guides it downwards. She moves it slowly, oh so slowly, and then lets go. She doesn't need to say anything more.

"Yes, like that..."

She sighs and closes her eyes. She is really wet.

"Kiss me."

I kiss her.

It doesn't take long before she starts to shake. She grabs me with a strength I'd never have expected from a girl and shudders so violently that it almost scares me. She shouts and kicks one last time.

Is this how girls have an orgasm? Man.

She lays there. Goosebumps on her belly. Carefully I place my hand on it. So soft. She jerks again.

"Hold me."

I hold her.

She shivers. I turn us over so that we're lying against each other and I pull the blankets round us. A tear trickles down her sweaty cheek. I wipe it away.

She is so soft. My girl is so soft.

She curls her legs around mine. I pull her even closer against me, I'll never let her go. Never.

Man, I'm so tired.

"Nina..."

I doze off. So deep. "Max ... "

I fall asleep.

NINA

Max falls asleep as the day dawns.

I look at his face from under the blankets. Dark stubble covers his angular chin and jaw. From close up I see that his big nose is covered with dozens of small dents. His eyes are still the eyes of a boy. He has long eyelashes that rest softly on his light-brown cheeks. Café latte. I smile. His eyelids are darker than the rest and so fragile. The bridge between his bushy black eyebrows is relaxed for the first time since I've known him. I've never seen him so still.

Max is sleeping.

It burns a bit down there. I didn't even realize that he'd come until I felt the moisture between my legs. I really wanted to. I know I wanted to, but I didn't expect it to hurt. I try to clean myself up a bit with things from the first-aid kit, which I'd luckily brought up here with me. It's sticky and it's getting cold. I throw the wet things next to us and pull on my clothes. I curl up, against Max. I smell of him.

Max holds me tight in his sleep.

I begin to doze off when I see her before me.

Mum.

I think back to the last time we spoke in my room. She was really interested, she was happy for me. I smile. It was almost as if she was back. Even if it was only for a moment. Mum.

I want to say hello to her. I want her to know that I'm all

right. Above all else, I want her to know what really happened on the Mainland.

I reach into Max's backpack and reach around until I find my HC. He's kept it all this time. I type in my password and the screen lights up. The drawing of Max appears. The drawing I showed her. I stroke my finger over the Max on the screen, with my other hand I caress the Max next to me. Goose pimples on his skin and a deep sigh. He's snoring softly.

I owe it to Mum.

I go to DOS-mail and open my mail box. A flood of messages appears, from Mum, Maria, Dad, even from Felix Feliks. That must have been before WEtTO announced the kidnapping. I quickly click them away and create a new message.

What can I say? I must be careful.

"Mum. Don't worry. I love you. Nina."

That's not enough. I delete the message and start again.

"Mum, I'm safe with Max. He helped me escape. Don't worry about me. Ask Dad what happened on the Mainland. With Isa and the others. I love you, Nina."

Yes, like that. That'll do. For now.

My finger hovers over the Send button. I look at the boy next to me, at his light-brown skin, his long eyelashes, and his short, stubbly hair. His hand searches for something, crawls over my side and stays there, pulls me to him. He sighs, his fine eyelids quiver. He's dreaming.

I press Send.

MAX

Sun.

Bright sun shines in my eyes and forces me to open them. Green wood. A bed. Light in a heart. Where am I?

Then I feel her arm around my waist. She sighs and turns over towards me. She throws her other arm around me. My body remembers sooner than my head does.

Fuck, Max. Even in this bloody freezing weather?

I'm ashamed of myself. Even more when she turns over and the sun shines on the purple bruise on her chin that Li gave her. I've got to get out of here.

I lift up her arm as carefully as I can, tuck her in again and climb out of the bed cupboard. Little piles of snow lie untouched on the chest, on the tent canvas, on the three pegs of the hat-stand and on the wooden floor. The wind has died down, but the cold is still in the air. I climb down the stairs, run through the room, and rush outside through the half derelict door.

Everything is white.

A thin layer of snow covers the island. The bare branches on the trees stand out against the blue morning sky. The birds have decided that I pose no threat and hop around on the grass between the trunks. They take a bored look at me and then go back to digging around in the snow and the ground under it. I only now realize that my head is pounding. I place my hands on my head and push hard. I miss my long hair. It was quite a bit warmer. "It suits you." That's what she said. I don't think I'd like to see myself in a mirror. I don't think the mirror would survive.

I walk away from the house. The island isn't large, just a few hundred meters I'd guess, with the house on one side, close to the water. The row of trees stops as abruptly as it begins and then there is the water again. There are more bushes under the last few trees and I run toward them.

As I draw closer, I see what's growing there.

Brambles. Ma always asked me to pick blackberries in the autumn. She'd make jam with them. I hated it. Now my mouth waters. Any other season would have been better for leaving.

I think about the book that belonged to Pa's pa. About some baron or other who pulled himself out of a swamp by his hair and more of that bullshit. That guy thought he could do anything. He could do everything. I thought it was fantastic. Li laughed about it, and about me. Pa joined in, but Ma said: "Leave him be. He'll learn soon enough what the world's really like." Nina and I will have to be like that baron if we want to get out of this shit. I know that. Nobody needs tell me.

"Hey."

I jump.

"Sorry, I..." she begins. I turn round and hold up my hand. "Doesn't matter. I think I was somewhere else in my mind."

"I know the feeling."

She smiles. Her face is so fucking sexy when she smiles.

I smile back, trying not to stare at the stupid big bruise on her cheek.

"Get some sleep?"

She shrugs her shoulders. She's thrown her arms around herself. The coat hangs around her. It's much too big. "What are you doing?"

Now it's my turn to shrug.

"Not the faintest idea."

She takes a step closer and her scent fills my nose. Soft and sweet and... Nina.

"The island's smaller than I thought," she says, staring out across the water.

I follow her gaze.

In the distance I see the submerged city we came from. A long way to the right, something sticks out of the water. It must have once been a church tower, but now it's nothing more than a skeleton. Here and there, small groups of trees rise from the water, as if they don't need any soil. The water must be freezing, but, strangely enough, the sun makes it glisten warmly. I think about some party or other I once went to, where they had an old disco globe revolving and it glittered in just the same way. It's actually rather pretty.

"The sun's so bright," says Nina. "I almost can't look at the water."

"No."

I want to throw my arm around her shoulder but I don't dare.

"I'm really incredibly hungry, Max."

As proof, her stomach rumbles. Loudly.

I laugh and she laughs too. I'm not the only one who doesn't know how to act.

"Well, luckily we can do something about that," I say and force myself to smile.

She smiles back uncertainly.

NINA

I made him jump. What was he looking at? Where was he with his thoughts? I'm not sorry, if that's what he's thinking.

I follow him back to the house. He runs ahead, his jacket blowing in the wind. The sun catches his downy head, with here and there a pearl of dew. Is he running away? From me?

I finally fell asleep when the light had forced its way through the cracks.

Last night the nightmare was different. It wasn't just Isa I heard calling. Fifty voices, fifty screams, fifty faces bloated by the water called to me for help. And I couldn't do anything. And then there was Dad, just screaming and screaming, "You said she'd gone there. You said she'd be there!" His red, agitated face contorted with rage and he grabbed me and shook me, until I didn't see anything but his flesh-colored lips spitting out accusations everywhere. I screamed back and I hit him. I hit him hard and called him a murderer and Mum was there too, crying like a river. Erik looked at us from a distance while blood gushed from his forehead. Then Dad changed into Felix Feliks before my eyes and laughed. He scoffed at me.

Is Dad a murderer? Didn't he do it for Isa, those things he did? What decision would I have made if I'd been in his position?

I bite my lip. I haven't the courage to answer that question. But then I hear his voice again: "WEtTO demands firm action. Well, they'll get it!" I see that Wet boy — like Max, a boy like Max — who they'd picked up, and I think: if he wasn't then, he is now.

Dad lied and he's still lying.

I speed up and join Max in the house. My nose follows something warm, something with herbs. He's squatted next to a pan on a portable gas ring and stirring with a plastic spoon. He turns towards me.

"Soup," he says apologetically.

"I'd eat anything put in front me."

"I thought we could have some of those biscuits with it."

"You're the cook."

He smiles like he did before. Awkward. Uneasy. Embarrassed.

We eat in silence.

In my greed, I burn my mouth on the hot instant soup.

Max eats slower. He chews deliberating on the dry crackers as he slurps his soup. At home, I was never allowed to slurp, but it's a pleasant, friendly sound. As if we're camping. The food is finished far too quickly and I've not had anywhere near enough.

"We had better ration it." He stares at my hand, which was moving towards the supply of biscuits. I nod.

"Yes, you're right."

My stomach protests.

"Sorry." My neck and cheeks turn red and I start to blush.

"Hey, you're not used to this," he says and shrugs.

For some reason or other, his remark irritates me. "I can take it."

"Really?"

He looks at me and for a moment, a brief moment, I see something of the Max who was furious at me, the Wet who hates all Dries, and I involuntarily flinch. Max notices my reaction, swears loudly, and springs up. He kicks a kitchen chair, which falls over with a crash, and runs outside. I stare after him, not daring to move. But when I hear him scream, my legs are quicker than my head.

"Max!"

He's kicking the bushes and the branches that spring back just as easily. Crows fly up in indignation and croak at his screams. I run over to him, grab him and even though he's white hot with rage, I don't let go. "Max, calm down, Max, Max, please. I'm not scared. Honest."

I don't say "scared of you", although we both know that's what I mean. "Max..."

He is quiet. His rage disappears as quickly as it came. They are fits, I realize. They happen and then take over. Only now do I fully understand why he runs. Why he can never sit still. I don't let go.

"Nina..."

He doesn't dare look at me.

"Yes?"

"I'm so sorry." He whispers the words.

"I know."

I get it.

"It's all my fucking fault!" He throws his arms into the air. "If I hadn't, if... if I hadn't helped them, if I'd used my fucking brains" — he smashes his flat palm against his head — "for once in my life, I would have known that you... and then Erik was..."

"Max," I say firmly.

"What?"

"If you'd said no, they would have forced you."

He pulls himself free and stares at me as if the words haven't got through.

"Do you think they would have let the chance go by?" He slowly shakes his head.

"Erik would have been done for anyway."

I feel a stab of pain when I think of Erik. If anyone's hands are dirty, they're mine. I shouldn't have gotten him involved. But I say nothing to Max. Max is staring at me, his eyes wide and gleaming.

"Can you forgive me, Nina?"

"There's nothing to forgive."

He shakes his head, laughs briefly.

"Are you really so Dry that you've got a screw loose?"

"Are you so Wet that you can't get it into your head that I don't care?"

"No?" he asks in disbelief.

"No." And at that moment I know for certain.

"But you were scared and..."

"When you explode like that, it's almost impossible not to be scared. I bet your mother has sat there with her head in her hands on many occasions. And then there were two of you as well."

"But..."

"Max." I search for the right words. "You are... When it comes down to it, you're... not like..."

"Like Liam, you mean?"

He sounds dejected.

"Yes, or... Liam is angry, blinded by his rage. Because of what happened. Because of your father and my father. Perhaps if it had turned out differently..." Do I believe my own words? Or am I just saying them to reassure Max? It is not difficult to imagine Liam's grimace, the fierce hatred in his flaming eyes. I bite my lip.

"Come on, Nina. Don't turn me into a saint! And certainly don't do it with my bloody brother!"

"I'm not! But don't turn me into a victim," I hit back.

"Not a victim? Nina... we kidnapped you!"

I shake my head.

"It's still my father who let his own daughter and fifty others drown, no matter what plans your father had with Isa, Max! Yes, Dad did it for her, but he didn't give a second's thought to those other people. And I didn't tell you who I was. I wanted to tell you, really, then, that evening..." I gasp for breath, force myself to say it. "And the worst is perhaps that I'm really just like... just like the rest. Like Isa was."

She... she would have wet herself. You bet.

"No."

He sounds touchy.

"What no?"

"You're not like the others."

"No?" I laugh bitterly. "Did you know, that last evening, Erik told me that he was married and played the trumpet?"

Max carefully shakes his head.

"I asked him. For the first time. Even though I've known him all my life."

"That's..."

"... what I should be ashamed about."

Max says nothing. He doesn't contradict me.

We stare at the water. I have to squeeze my eyes half shut in order to look at the dazzling water. The crows have decided that the island is safe again, although I imagine hearing in their cries that they would still prefer us to clear off.

We stand there, close to each other.

"Max?"

"Yes?"

"Do you... have any regrets?"

"About what?"

"About yesterday."

He grabs me and turns me to face him, takes my hands and closes his rough fingers around mine. Warm. His hand are always warm.

"I've no regrets! What do you think, Nina? Is that what you think of me, that I've got regrets about...?"

I can hardly look at him.

"If I'm honest..." he says.

He falls silent.

Say something, Max. Please.

He grins. His dark eyes light up.

"I'd like to do it again."

"You know," says Nina. She's fiddling with the locket around her neck.

"Hm?"

"Isa never did it."

"What?"

"You know, this. What we just did."

"And?"

"I mean that Isa never did this."

"She didn't fuck anybody in her life?" I grin as Nina's eyes widen.

"Jesus, Max! I'm trying to tell you something!"

I purse my lips. Nina tries to kick me in the stomach, and I manage to avoid it.

"What are you trying to say?"

She turns on her side and raises herself, her head in her hand.

"I always thought Isa was more daring than me. She was a year and a month younger, but she almost always did things earlier or quicker. She learned to ride a bike first. She was the first to climb the oak in our garden, and at school all the boys hung around her."

"Hm."

"Now I know that it wasn't like that. That she wasn't more daring than me. And... I'm going to do things she'll never do. Because she's dead. She isn't here anymore."

I look at Nina.

"Perhaps I'm crazy..." She takes a deep breath. "But she's still there for me. I... I talk to her and see her standing before me when I do things."

"Just now as well?" She surely can't mean it.

She's silent for just a beat then her whole face breaks into the most beautiful smile that any girl could ever have. Sparks of amusement twinkle in her eyes.

"No, not just now."

I shake my head.

"I think I know what you mean."

"Oh."

"My Pa..." She waits until I continue. "My pa is often there as well. In my head. Although now he can piss off."

"Because he was in WEtTo?"

"That... but mainly because he told me nothing. He took Li into his confidence and told me to be a good little boy. You see how that's turned out." I sound bitter. I sound like Ma.

"Aren't you angry?" I ask her.

"At who?" She looks at me as if she hasn't the faintest idea about what I'm saying.

"At my Pa. He wanted to kidnap your sister. It was because of him that she was in the wrong building."

"Yes..." She chews her lip.

"He's just as guilty of her death as your father is of the death of my Pa."

She thinks about it for a while, then firmly says: "No.

"What no?"

"I'm not angry at your father."

"How can you not be angry at him?"

Again she thinks for a while.

"Because I can't think anything of someone I don't know and never will know. Because it won't let me get Isa back. But... but I am angry at my dad." She looks away. "He lied to me. And to Mum. Even after Isa was drowned. Fifty men."

One of them was my Pa.

"Fifty men," she says again.

Nina lets go of her locket. It swings to and fro, to and fro; the sunlight is reflected in it like gold.

"Hey," I say. Why hadn't I thought of that before?

"What?"

"I've got Bob with me." I grimace.

"Bob?"

"Wait here."

I climb over Nina, push open one of the doors and stumble outside. My backpack. Where did I leave the bloody thing? Cold air brushes over my naked chest and gives me goosebumps. There. There it is. I fumble around, find what I'm looking for, and hurry back between the warm blankets.

I hold up the player.

"Umm... what's that?" asks Nina.

"A portable CD-player."

"No!" She beams.

"Yes." My grin almost splits my face.

I sort out the mess of cords as Nina caresses me with her soft, warm body. Her two fingers walk up my arm to my chest, draw circles around the tattoo on my left bicep and play with my navel. It tickles like mad.

"Hey! Do you want to listen or not?"

She blinks her eyes and gives me her sexiest smile.

"Well?"

She keeps looking at me as her fingers move upwards, higher, even higher, along my neck, behind my ear, until it is in my neck and she pulls me to her. She kisses me on the tip of my nose and then turns to my ear lobe.

"Let me hear it, this Bob," she says.

We lay close to each other and listen. "A hard rain's a gonna fall". I look. I look at my girl. At Nina. At her long, thin eyelashes resting on her soft cheeks, at the freckles that look like an explosion of stars, turning her face into the heavens. At her so sexy body that I want to possess again. I sigh, close my eyes, and listen. While Bob is singing, the moment seems like eternity.

Until the old battery suddenly gives up in the middle of the last song and we hear nothing more than our own breathing, our hearts beating as one, and outside the screeching crows, the wind, and the water.

Always that damned water.

NINA

When Dylan falls silent, I suddenly feel cold again. Max shivers too. I let my hand glide over his soft chest, ruffling the curly hairs, and follow the lines of the tattoo on his arm. My finger follows the line, moving further and further to the middle, until it disappears into nothing. A whirlpool.

I've got a boyfriend with a tattoo, Isa.

No!

Honest!

I don't believe you.

Max. His name's Max.

Ni-na!

"Hey, what are you doing?"

Max leans over me. His fingers are fiddling in the bag that had held the CD player. Of course. He's looking for batteries. After a while, he gives up.

"No more Bob?" I ask.

"No more Bob," confirms Max and he sighs.

We eat in the living room. It's still light, but it won't be long until it's dark again. Max tends the welts around my ankles and wrists. He doesn't say anything while he's doing it. Carefully, so carefully. It's not difficult to see how guilty he's feeling.

When he's finished with my wrists, he turns to my ankles, and I place the back of my hand against his cheek. He's burning. Doesn't this boy ever get tired? Where does he get his energy? He looks at me and I can't stop my hand reaching round behind his neck and pulling him to me for a kiss. He seems surprised, but that doesn't last long.

I wish time would stand still.

For what are we going to do? We can't stay here. We're not used to living rough and we only have what we have on. The water surrounds us. I feel the fear take hold of me again, feel his joy about what I tell him. It's too easy to give in.

Max immediately notices that my thoughts have wandered. Involuntarily his lips pull away from mine.

"What's wrong?"

I shrug my shoulders, try to pull him back close to me. He stops me.

"Nina," he says.

I sigh, bite my lip.

"What are we going to do, Max? Where are we going?"

Max is not upset. He's not scared or worried. He's determined, almost calm, although you can never really say that about him.

"We're leaving," he says.

"Leaving?"

"Yes, leaving."

I shake my head.

"How?"

"How? We've got a water scooter. We've got rations. We've got a head start."

"But... where are we going?"

He looks at me, as if he doesn't get why I don't understand him. His full lips purse into a grimace and I feel my heart beating in my throat. No longer from fear, but from excitement. For somehow I know what he's going to say.

"We're leaving the Five Regions. We're going into the Foreign Territory."

The Foreign Territory.

Everything happens so quickly.

I hear the sound before I see where it's coming from. The sound of a water scooter approaching rapidly. Not just one water scooter.

A group of them.

Max jumps from the sofa and runs to the window. The sound of the throbbing engines fill the air, the whole room, as if a rabid growling bear has been released in the small room. I can do nothing but hold myself in fear, hold in my breath.

"Fuck," says Max as he stares at what's happening outside.

"Fuck," he says again as the engines sputter and the sound slowly dies away.

"FUCK!" he yells as the shouts sound from the other side of the island.

I breathe out.

And jump up. Max is back with me, his hands hastily gathering our things littered everywhere. As if escape is still possible.

His gaze crosses mine. I know what he wants to say. I know and accept it, return it to him and hide it safely away. I keep it near me as I hear the footsteps. I hold on to it as I hear shoes scraping on the gravel in front of the door. I embrace it when a familiar, soft voice says: "Max, Nina, we know you're here.'

MAX

'Felix?'

Nina blinks her eyes, her hand waves indecisively in the air.

Felix? Is his name Felix? Of course I recognize him. That voice, that slippery, sweet voice. I didn't know his name, let alone that Nina knew him. How can she know that Dry?

"Felix?" I whisper to her.

"Dad's PA..."

"Nina? Are you all right, Nina?"

Again that voice. Friendly, oh so friendly. But I know what's behind it. I know it all too damned well.

"Nina." I take Nina's hand. She doesn't resist but she doesn't assist either. It's as if that man has bewitched her.

"Felix..." she sighs.

"Come!" I call louder.

Escape, says everything in my body. Desperate, useless says my mind.

"We won't hurt him, Nina. If he surrenders, we won't hurt him."

That does it.

Suddenly she's back. She's Nina. The girl I know. She squeezes her eyes together, turns away from me, and hisses more furiously than I've ever seen her: "Felix Feliks. He's got a nerve!"

She looks at me, finally she looks at me.

She nods.

It's an act of desperation, Max.

"Nina? Max?" sounds behind us. So smooth, so sickly smooth. I nod back.

"Stay where you are Max!"

I close my hand around Nina's and pull her with me to the rear, to the broken-down door that opens onto the path running through the bushes.

"Let her go, Max! *Max!*"

Feliks's voice disappears in a rage of spat out orders just as we open the back door and run as if our lives depend on it.

They do depend on it.

I run ahead.

My hand brushes away the twigs. Snow is falling for a second time and drips from my nose. Sudden fluttering and screeching. Black shapes rise up like a thunder cloud. Noise. What a noise! I wave my arms. Those damned creatures! Get off! Piss off! We've got to get away.

Oh fuck.

Nina. I've let go of her. Where's Nina? Where is she? I turn round. Those creatures. They attack me, nothing makes them stop. There! A patch of blond. Her hair. She's trying to hide. Or...no. She's doing something. She's pulling away the branches. What's she doing? Why isn't she coming?

NINA!

The sun flickers as it sinks into the water.

And I see it. I finally see it, idiot that I am. The water scooter. She'd hidden it. I sprint to her, flailing my arms, and help her drag off the last few branches. Together we push and the thing slides into the water as we jump on it. Nina starts the engine.

Hope makes its way upwards, right through my torn body and mind. How stupid could you get?

I look round.

Red. Red everywhere. Blowers. Ten. Twenty. Thirty even. Too many to count.

"Max! I will warn you one last time!"

Feliks. Bright eyes, burning like the chimneys of the industry. His head is pale and threatening, his skinny hands form fists in the air. I turn round and throw my arms around Nina. The water scooter shoots forward.

"Max!!!"

A shot sounds.

And another.

The engine sputters, grumbles and stops. I hear a sigh and a voice. "Max... Oh no, Max!"

"Nina?"

Everything is suddenly strangely quiet.

I look down. Red. Red on my shoulder. Red on my chest and on my arm. A stain that spreads rapidly, like ink on blotting paper. Suddenly the pain. The stabbing pain that penetrates everything. I hear a soft, groaning sound, want to look up and comfort her; it'll be all right, it'll all be all right... but it's me.

"Max!"

I feel groggy. I turn my head in the direction of the voice. Nina? I see spots before my eyes, blue and red and green. It's beautiful, it's so beautiful. I'm dizzy, so damned dizzy. Something touches my cheek, a cool hand, finger tips that tap and hit. I fight to stay awake.

Stay still, Max. Stay still.

"It's over, Max. Give yourself up." Smooth, slippery smooth. Who's saying that? I know who it is. I know, dammit! I try to turn round, I want to know. I want to know!" I spin and sway, as if one side has suddenly become heavier than the other. I stretch out my arms, I must be able to grab onto something.

I lose my balance and my body breaks the bobbing surface.

Ice.

Water.

Air.

Air!

My legs kick, as if by themselves. Up. I have to go up. But when I use my arms, such a bolt of pain goes through me that my body refuses to do anything. I feel paralyzed. I'm fucking paralyzed. My head begins to beat in panic and I automatically gasp for breath. The water, that has been waiting its chance, immediately takes the opportunity. Salt and iciness stream inside. I choke and cough, but no breath comes, it can't come any more. I feel the pressure increasing on my lungs. And the water streams in, streams in deeper, in me, through me, round me.

Through everything.

I stop kicking

My arms hang down my side.

I'm weightless. I'm weightless and glide through the water, like a bird through the air. Look at me! Nobody can get me! Nobody. I'm flying!

No.

No, I'm drowning.

I'm fucking drowning.

This is how it feels. My question is answered. This is how it feels to drown, Pa.

Pa?

PART THREE

MAX

"Pa?"

I see him sitting at the bottom of the dyke. The rod hangs loosely in his hands, his wellies on his feet. Next to him, a thermos flask that certainly doesn't contain tea.

"Hello, son."

Pa smiles. I walk out of the water. I'm drenched. My clothes are dripping and feel like lead.

"Cold?"

"It's winter, Pa." I'm surprised he doesn't know that.

"Then what are you doing in the water, Max?"

"I'm drowning. Or... I've already drowned." I don't even know myself.

Pa grins.

"Just like me."

I nod.

"Just like you."

"Then we're in the same boat, son."

He quietly picks up the thermos flask, unscrews the top, and takes a sip.

"Ahh! A man needs that now and again." He stretches out the hand with the flask. "Want some? You're a man now."

My hand has taken the flask, but I change my mind. I stare at him.

"What do you mean?"

"Hm?" He stares past me, across the water.

"What do you mean — I'm a man now?" I drop down onto the grass next to him.

"You've made a choice, haven't you?"

He winks as he points his finger at me like in that old commercial — "You know what you want." That's Pa: never really serious. Drove Ma mad. "Here, take a sip. Warm you up."

I look at him distrustfully but take a sip anyway. The stuff burns in my throat. I remember taking a sip from his thermos flask when I was a boy of six, and then he got angry. Li had dared me to do it.

'Make it yourself?" I ask as I wipe my mouth. It certainly warms you up.

"Nothing better, son!" Pa guffaws.

We drink together. Take turns. We stare at the float like we used to, but it never seems to go under. How long have we been sitting here? My clothes won't dry and when I look at the horizon, the sun is still in the same place.

"Pa?"

"Yes, Max?"

Our words slur. Pa only has one hand on the rod and the thing swings dangerously up and down.

"Is this heaven?"

Pa stares at me for a second, then laughs loudly. "Heaven? Ha ha, son, you're killing me! Heaven, hell, do you believe in all that?"

"No! I mean..." I say quickly.

Pa laughs and laughs. He can't control himself.

"Pa!"

He hiccups with laughter, tears stream down his cheeks. "Heaven! Hell! What a kid..."

He almost rolls from the dyke into the water. I just manage to stop him.

"Pa!"

All at once he's quiet.

He's crying.

I don't know what to do. I've never seen Pa cry. I want to run away, but it's as if I'm glued to the grass. I carefully place my arms around his heaving shoulders and pat him on his bent back. He suddenly looks so old. Not my pa, but my old father.

Suddenly he throws off my arm, roughly, andt now it's me who almost rolls from the dyke. He scrambles up and almost falls over again, but he manages to stay upright. He pulls at my hood until I scramble up and stand upright.

The rod lies at our feet.

"Get going."

"What?"

"Get going."

"Where to?"

"Son, it's about time you learned that I don't have all the answers."

Grin. And a pat on my back.

"Pa! I don't know where to go!"

"Son, how should I know where you should go? I don't even know myself!" He laughs again and picks up his rod. He skilfully takes the thing, throws the line backwards and then forwards into the water. Nobody could do it better than Pa.

"Pa!" I call, but he's forgotten all about me. He stares at the float, still bobbing uselessly on the water.

"Pa!" I scream, but I'm up to my middle in the water.

"Got one!" Pa shouts triumphantly. The line is taut and there is the familiar sound of the reel, as the water rises higher and higher, creeping over my chest, my neck, and finally only leaves my eyes uncovered for one last moment.

Pa holds up his catch: a gold locket, dripping with blood.

NINA

Any hope I had disappears when I look in her eyes. Her constantly absent eyes that don't want to see. I know enough.

"Nina, oh, Nina!"

Mum grabs me and hugs me. She murmurs incomprehensible words and strokes my hair without stopping. Tears dribble in my collar. The Dry Defenders have not managed to persuade me to take off my moth-eaten coat.

"Oh Nina, you gave us such a scare! We thought..."

"You thought I was dead." My voice sounds hollow in our house's high hall.

"Nina." He's standing behind Mum. The man who is my father. "Nina," he says again. He takes the two steps that separate us and grabs me.

I stiffen.

Does he know? He throws his arms around me and presses his face against his chest. Isa and I sometimes called him "big bear" when we were small. We always wanted him to pick us up.

"We will get all those responsible, Nina. They won't get away with it." His warm breath falls heavily on my head.

The taste of coffee is bitter on my tongue – "Quickly. Something hot for Miss Bradshaw. Hurry up!" Felix had said with his velvet voice. Sick. I feel sick.

"Nina?" says the man who is my father.

I saw Max fall. He looked so surprised.

I dived after him without giving it a moment's thought.

I saw nothing. Nothing at all. I didn't have enough air and quickly surfaced, gasping and coughing. I dived again and again until I found him. A hand, an arm, his chest, his head. His wet, lifeless head.

It all comes out.

I throw up, half on my father, half on the cold, marble floor. Brownish-black flecks of coffee splash onto the shining, pick tiles.

"Nina!" Mum pulls me away from him.

I don't know what to say. I don't want to look round. My father says something to him, to the man with the velvety voice, then walks past us; he briefly drops a hand on Mum's shoulder and a shoots a worried look at me. They disappear into the study.

Mum takes me upstairs.

I begged him to help Max.

He wasn't breathing. His face, always so warm and full of life, was as pale as a corpse. I hit him, pressed down on his rib cage. Blood bubbled from the wound in his shoulder. Dry Defenders grabbed him and tried to pull him away from me. I fought, I kicked, I didn't let go.

"Please, oh please! Do something!"

Calm bright blue eyes looking at me with some interest. "He's dying!"

A cool smile.

Then a Dry Defender took Max and started pushing down on his chest. He opened Max's mouth and blew into it. And blew again. Water and blood gushed over his black-blue lips. His chest moved. A soft whistling sound.

"Max?"

I wanted to hold him, but I couldn't compete with four Dry Defenders.

They picked him up as if he were a sack of potatoes and carted him off. His arms hung limply, like those of one of the puppets in my old toy theatre. A trail of blood was left behind.

Mum opens the door to my room and gently pushes me inside.

"Light."

A light goes on. Too bright for my tired eyes.

"Come on, darling. Let's get you cleaned up."

I pull my coat closer around me.

"Darling..."

I clasp my arms even tighter round my body. Mum sighs, lets me go, and walks to the bathroom.

A moment later, I hear running water.

He took me with him. He spoke reassuringly to me, gave me a blanket, and ordered the Dry Defenders to stay out of the way when I refused to take off my clothes. "She's in shock."

He digiphoned the Governor.

"We have them, Excellency."

He gave me a crooked look.

"No, just the boy."

He turned round but didn't do his best to talk any softer. He wanted me to hear the words.

"They've done something with her, Excellency. Brainwashed her, I suspect. She thought he'd saved her. The boy almost drowned, but his condition is stable."

He listened.

"Yes... I understand. Hm, hm. Keep him under control. Guarded at all times. Yes."

Another glance at me.

"She's calmed down."

A question.

"In fourteen hours, all being well. Yes, a helicopter would be faster, but the weather conditions, Excellency..." Silence.

"Straight to your residence. Understood, Excellency."

He closed his HC and smiled at me. Just like that time when Dad made me repeat the rules at dinner. Amused by our family drama. But I didn't look away. I wouldn't give him the satisfaction. I've long got over any shame.

And I realized: Max will be taken to one prison, me to another.

"Nina? I've run a bath for you."

I read it again in her always absent eyes.

"You can..." She hesitates, looks with barely concealed distaste at the jacket and the equally filthy jumper under it. "You could perhaps wash it. What you've got on."

She hasn't asked him.

"You can keep it, darling," she says quickly. "We won't take it away from you."

I blink at her. Mum smiles. How dare she? As if they haven't take enough from me! I walk away from her without saying a word and lock myself in my bathroom. I wait until I hear her footsteps die away, until she closes the door behind her and locks it. Until I am finally alone.

Only then do I let everything out, really everything. My anger, my fear, my sorrow, and my guilt.

Because it's my fault. My own, stupid fault. I trusted her. I trusted Mum not to go to Felix with her personal HC. I told her that Max had helped me escape, that I was safe. But she didn't believe me. And she didn't ask Dad anything.

I spoilt everything for us.

Soft, salty tears flow one by one along the sides of my nose over my multi-colored cheeks. Wet.

Not enough. Not wet enough.

I step into the bath with all my clothes on. I place my hands on the edge of the bath and slowly sink into the water, layer by layer, until I am completely submerged. I let the warm water nourish me. I'm a baby, back inside my mummy's belly. Back to the start, back to the beginning.

Salt meets fresh. Cold meet warmth.

And Dry meets Wet.

MAX

I see stars in the blackness in my head. My head is pounding as if somebody has used it as a punching bag.

Pa.

I don't believe all that bullshit about your life running past like a film when you're nearly dead. But Pa was real. I see the golden locket that he held up so triumphantly. Blood on his hands. Blood on my hands.

I'm so screwed.

"The Wet's waking up," sounds a voice.

"Send a message at once to..." begins another, but he disappears before I can hear what he says.

What? Who...? Where am I?

I try to get up but it's as if I've been hit by a bulldozer and a stab of pain goes through my shoulder, so sharp it makes me groan.

"Listen, lad, you're not going anywhere, so I'd just keep quiet if I were you."

Another voice, lower than the others. He sounds older. He talks like me. District Seven. It can't be. I open my eyes for a fraction of a second but the light is so bright that I shut them at once.

Calm down, man. Calm down.

I slowly open my eyes. Very slowly so that they can adjust. I see red.

Blowers.

Instinctively I flinch, and a second wave of pain flows over me.

"I told you to keep quiet."

I open my eyes for the third time and a man around fifty is looking at me. His weathered face gives nothing away. He's got a crew-cut like the rest of them, but it suits him. A Wader. Two young faces — one dark, one light — appear next to him and it isn't difficult to guess what they're thinking. Dries.

"Is he awake?"

A tall man in a white coat comes towards me. Before I can do anything, the man has pulled open my left eye and is shining a torch into it.

"Keep still," says the Wader again, as if he can read my mind.

Now the right eye. Then the man pumps something round my biceps and listens to my heart. All the time, he says nothing.

"What's the last thing you remember?"

The question comes so quickly that I almost answer. But the memory of Nina's voice, Nina's scream, Nina's hands on my broken body, the agonizing pain as if a herd of elephants were dancing on my chest, my own voice, hardly audible, trying to reassure her, and then the black; that's mine, for nobody but me.

I clench my fists, even though it fucking hurts.

"Can't remember?" insists the doctor. An odor of dry sweat and disinfectant creeps into my nose.

"No."

The man knows I'm lying, but I couldn't give a damn. He shakes his Dry head and without warning pulls me up to inspect the wound on my shoulder.

Fuck! That hurts!

"You were lucky," he says indifferently. He ignores my groan of pain. "The bullet grazed your chest, bounced off a rib and exited through your shoulder blade."

Lucky? I've been lucky? But I keep my mouth shut because the Wader's holding me tight, his big, warm hands around mine. He catches me when the doctor releases me and ties me up. Calmly, without hurrying. "Just lie there, lad. And keep your mouth shut." He stares at me for a fraction too long, his dark eyes sunk into deep slits. I know him. But where from?

"I'll come back tomorrow. I'll give him something to take away the worst of the pain. They'll want to interrogate him shortly."

The Dry doctor looks past me as he bends over with a needle in his hand. Panic kicks its way up when I think he's going to stick that thing in me, but his hand goes to the drip hanging next to me. At first I feel nothing. Sure, pain in my head and in my shoulder. The stuff slowly does its job. Mist hanging before my eyes and forcing its way into my body. A heavy, warm blanket that falls over me and muffles all the pain, all the thoughts.

No. Stay awake. I don't want to go back into that black hole.

"That should do it," I hear the doctor say. I can hardly keep my eyes open. His Dry head disappears, footsteps die away in a bare corridor.

Something is hanging above me. Another head. The Wader. I taste his heavy smoker breath. Where are the others?

"Max Morris."

"What?" It comes out as: "*Whaaaa*?" I sound like Pa when he's had a few too many.

"Rob, Robert Morris, was your father?" There is something about his voice. Changed. Different.

"Yes... Pa..."

"They'll be interrogating you, lad."

I stare at the Wader, don't understand what's up with him. Black patches float by like oil on the water.

"And if I were you, I'd tell them what they want to know."

"Wh-what d'you want?" My eyes, my eyes can't fight it any more.

"I'm telling you for your own good, lad. You're in deep shit. It can't get any wetter.'

Own good? My own fucking *good*?

But before I can say anything, I'm out of it. Back in the blackness of my head, where the stars have gone out.

NINA

Max is everywhere.

He stares at me from every DOS screen, his dark eyes gleaming and always with that grin, as if he was laughing inside when the photo was taken. How old would he have been there? Fifteen? Sixteen? He's pulled back his shoulder-length hair into a pony tail and his coffee skin is flawless. It takes me a little while to realize what it is about the photo that looks off to me; he hasn't got any bruises or scars.

Nobody tells me how Max is. Dad is at the Regional Hall and Mum is avoiding me. Back to how it was. Back to Isa. She knows I'm angry at her. She knows! It's exactly as it was back then, and I don't know where to go with my fear, my pain, and my anger.

There is considerable speculation by reporters. They rake up the Mainland and keep on showing pictures that by now are all too familiar to me. It is announced for the first time that one of the daughters of the Governor died because of the actions of a Wet, Robert Morris, and that now his son has struck. It's a masterly move, for who would ever think that the Governor himself had anything to do with what happened on the Mainland? Furious Dries protest and yell slogans at the entrance to the Regional Hall. They demand "immediate action" and "justice". All I can do is look past their wooden signs, past their snarling faces, at the high doors. Because that's where they're holding him: behind those high doors. Max Morris. The WEtTO. The terrorist. A seventeen-year-old boy.

What are they going to do with him?

How is he? Are they taking good care of him? Is he completely alone? Are they letting his mother see him? And... what is he thinking about? Is he thinking of me the way that I'm thinking of him?

Max.

What are they going to do with him?

My thoughts continue in the same loop. I'm back to the beginning.

Dad and Mum know that he came with me when those Wet boys were after him. They know I've been to his home. And they know he's suspended.

Mum: "Why didn't you tell us, darling?"

Dad: "That boy's been making a fool of you all this time!"

Mum: "We really want what's best for you, darling."

Dad: "Nina, tell us what he did to you!"

But what's the point? I've already told them. And all they are willing to believe is that I've been "brainwashed." It's the only answer that works for them. To their advantage.

I feel warm inside. Too warm. Hot.

Max Morris is their whipping-boy, so I have to be his victim.

And if I do say something, if I kick up too much of a stink, they'll watch me even more closely than they already do. If I want to be able to do something for Max, I'll just have to keep quiet. And wait for the right moment.

But...

What is the right moment?

Only after a week do I hear that they haven't tried him, despite all the speculations in the gossip press.

"We want to give the suspect the chance of defending himself. We judge nobody who is not capable of speaking for himself. Naturally the rule of law is not in danger. I can assure you: we do not make any hurried decisions. We are there for all people of the Five Regions, both inside and outside the Closed Communities."

Governor Bradshaw is addressing the Fifth Region, Felix, as always, is at his side. I can't listen any longer and turn off DOS news. I'm sitting in my room and Bob Dylan is singing softly. It's Christmas.

I think of Max and his rage. I'm beginning to understand how he feels.

I refuse to go downstairs when Dad knocks on the door.

He's angry. I heard them talking yesterday. I heard Dad say that it can't go on like this, that I'll have to see a psychiatrist Mum tried to smooth things over, saying that it was all still fresh and that I had probably experienced terrible things at the hands of those monsters. That he had to be patient.

Then he got really annoyed. "Patient? Patient? Eline, I have no time for patience! WEtTO has been making a fool of me for months. Their actions are becoming increasingly violent. The food supplies are shrinking every day and I have no way of replenishing them. And then there's Cavendish who's trying to turn the Council of Five against me! They want results." He fell silent. When he finally started talking again, I had to try my hardest to hear him. "And Nina was there, Eline. In the lion's den. She saw more than she's telling. She knows more than she says. I'm sure of it."

Mum didn't say anything to him. Nothing.

"Nina?"

Now it's Mum's turn.

"Nina." Softer this time. "Why don't you come downstairs? Maria has really done her best to make you some dinner."

I want to repeat that I'm not coming, but something stops me. For the first time since my return, we're alone.

Mum is silent. She's waiting. I hear her calm, regular breathing. I imagine how she looked in her long, black evening dress, the one with glitters in the satin fabric. The one Isa took from her wardrobe to wear to Johan's graduation I bury my hot face in the cable sweater Max gave me.

"Nina?"

I don't know how I manage, but I get up. My legs move automatically. My hands find the door. I only know what I'm going to say when the words leave my dry mouth.

"Why, Mum?" My voice sounds strangely twisted, as if my throat is being half strangled.

Silence. Mum is always silent. Her breathing quickens. I hear her hand sliding down the door.

"Why?" I repeat. "I know you can hear me, Mum." Still no answer.

"Why didn't you ask, like I asked you to? Dad must tell you, Mum. Don't you want to see? Don't you want to know?!" My voice breaks. "Or... or do you already know and you're hiding yourself again, just like when... Isa died?" The tears start by themselves. I sob. "Why don't you believe me, Mum?'

"Nina," she says. "Darling."

She takes a breath, moves her hand; her silver bracelets tinkle harshly, cutting through Dylan. I close my eyes and see myself telling her. I want to tell her so badly. If Dad doesn't tell her, who will?

"Nina..." She hesitates, take a breath. "You don't know what you're saying, darling."

You don't know what you're saying. Somewhere in me, a switch is thrown, just like that time with Max in the abandoned classroom at the Delta College.

I don't know what I'm saying?

My hand clenches into a fist. A fist that only has one place to go. I slam it hard against the door.

And everything pours out. One last desperate attempt.

"I know exactly what I'm saying, Mum! You still don't get it? Don't you believe your own daughter anymore? Don't you want to know what happened on the Mainland? That Dad let fifty Wets drown to save Isa? That one of them was Max's father? Why won't you see it, Mum? You won't see it, just like the rest, just like everyone! And Max... You let him take the blame. Because he's just a Wet? They're already down there in the mud and..."

"NINA!"

Her scream cuts through my torrent of words. Then it is silent.

That's all.

She says nothing more. Nothing. Although her silence says enough. She doesn't want to hear. She can't handle it and I'm blaming it all on her.

But I'm different. I'm different now.

"Nina... We're worried about you, Nina."

I walk away from the door.

"Nina, please!"

I concentrate on DOS.

"Ni–"

Dylan sings over her, drowning out everything I don't want to hear.

I'm coming, Max. I'm coming.

I just have to wait for the right moment.

MAX

Nina.

Her blond curls tickle my face. She's lying next to me, naked, and I'm fucking turned on. She turns onto her side and raises herself slightly. A cool finger plays with my ear lobe. She slowly bends forwards, closer and closer. I breathe in. I breathe her in. A girl's scent of fresh soap and something light, sunlight in the early morning perhaps. She comes closer and closer until her lips touch mine. She's trembling. I can't hold it much more. I breathe in her breath. She breathes in my breath. She giggles and places a hand on my chest where my heart is going crazy. Oh man, I can't hold it much more. She grabs me just above my buttocks and pushes herself against me. I know she can feel me. I know damned well for sure she can feel me. When her tongue finally touches mine, I explode like a supernova.

I'm awake.

"Dreaming, Max?"

I open my eyes and look straight into those of Felix Feliks.

He's sitting on a chair next to my bed, his right leg crossed over his left. His elbows are on the arms, his fingers are clasped together in front of his beaming face. Of course he's wearing a suit, with a tie and everything. Impeccable, Ma would say. When Feliks sees that he has my attention, he arches his almost invisible eyebrows.

I say nothing. I thank God on my Wet, bare knees that this Dry can't look inside my head. Fortunately I woke up just in time.

"I asked you something, Max."

He stares at me and I stare back. I won't let him frighten me again. How much older than Li can he be? And whatever he has in store for me, I can't get much deeper into the shit. He blinks, unfolds his slender fingers one by one, and slowly gets up. One step and he's hanging over me, so close that I can smell him. Expensive aftershave and a sour trace I can't quite identify. Automatically spittle collects between my tongue and teeth.

Feliks laughs out loud. "If I were you, I'd leave that where it is."

I want to get up, punch him in his filthy Dry gob. But I'm tied down and can't move. It really feels as if someone is bashing my head with a hammer.

"Max, Max..." His left hand pulls at a non-existent beard. "You've caused a lot of trouble."

I so want to punch him.

"The Governor is not very amused. Quite the opposite, in fact. He is furious."

If there is a God, dammit, let me punch that bastard!

"It doesn't look too good for you, Max."

Two cold hands grab me and lift me up. I try to turn away, but Feliks is quicker. He grabs me by my chin and forces me to look at him. His hungry eyes almost eat me up. What does the Dry want?

"You're angry, aren't you Max? You know what I'm talking about?" I say nothing. I fucking say nothing.

"You don't need to end up like your father, Max."

Knot. Calm down. Keep. Your. Cool.

"If you help us, I can put in a good word for you." If he could, he'd tap my thoughts.

"You've really got yourself into a fix by kidnapping Nina, Max."

Nina.

A warm, sweet wave passes through my tense body.

He's talking about Nina. My girl, Nina. I close my eyes and imagine that she's standing next to me, laying a cool hand on my hot head. The knot dissolves. I swallow my rage and let her take me with her, back to the hermit's house, back to...

"That's the boy?"

I recognize the voice immediately. Governor Bradshaw. Feliks's grip relaxes.

"Yes, Excellency." Feliks lets go of me with obvious reluctance. I fall back on the hospital bed with a thud.

"Get anything out of him?"

"Not much. He's still weak and knows how to keep his mouth shut."

"When can he been arraigned?"

"That's up to the doctor."

"I want to take care of this as quickly as possible, understand?"

"Yes, Excellency."

Then the governor turns towards me.

This is the man. Nina's pa. This is him. *Pa's murderer.* I've already forgotten Feliks.

He is shorter and older than he appears on DOS. Grey hair, bags under his eyes, red face. His suit is expensive and Dry. He's wearing a watch that's worth twice as many Points as Nina's locket.

He says nothing. Just stares at me. What is he doing here? Viewing me? The dangerous terrorist? The boy who was able to grab his daughter from right under his nose? A bead of perspiration glistens above his right eyebrow.

I don't look away.

"Excellency..."

"Not now, Felix. Not now."

He takes a step closer. I can count the dents on his nose. He reaches into his inside pocket, takes out a crumpled handkerchief, and wipes his gleaming forehead. He blinks as if he's got something in his eye.

I damn well don't look away.

He sucks in his bottom lip and nibbles softly at the broken skin just above his chin. What's going through his mind? If I didn't know better, I'd almost think that he, that he... No. It can't be. He can't be... scared... of me?

"I know what happened," I say.

He immediately knows what I'm talking about. I can see it in his eyes, which are not seeing me but something in the past, something he never wanted to see again.

"I know what happened on the Mainland, Governor. I know about the fifty men. I know about Isa."

Bradshaw shakes his head. The handkerchief falls from his hand, flaps to the ground.

"Excellency, perhaps it would be better..." Feliks places a hand on the Governor's arm, which he impatiently brushes away.

"You're in no position to play games, boy!" A bead of perspiration falls to the ground. "I'm warning you!"

I'm not afraid any more. I've got nothing to lose.

"Nina knows as well, Governor. Nina knows everything," I say and I grin.

He hits me across the face.

The blow makes my head explode as if he's let off a fire-cracker. His hands take my shoulders and he shakes me as if I'm a Dry piggy bank. He screams that I'm a filthy liar, that he'll string me up with his own hands. Two Blowers rush in and try to pull the Governor off me, while Feliks tries to calm him down.

"Sir!"

"Excellency!"

"You'll hang for this, you little bastard!"

Bradshaw has gone crazy. He is beside himself. The Blowers have to do their best to get him outside. Bradshaw curses and rages and swears. His red face is redder than the reddest tomato. I enjoy the rush of my victory. I don't care about the pain.. *For you, Nina,* I think. I'm fucking enjoying myself.

Until I feel Feliks's thin hands on my biceps. Hands that wring the blood out of my veins, and would love to squeeze the life out of my throat. Until I hear his voice hiss: "And now we'll see what you have to tell me, Max Morris."

NINA

Christmas is finally over. I'm sitting on the sofa in the living-room. I'm waiting. Mum is in bed and Maria is in the kitchen. Raised voices come from the hall, slowly coming closer.

"I want it done this week, Felix! This week. Do you hear? This week."

"Excellency, we have to take into account..."

"Take into account? Take into account? Who? Martial law should prevent things like..."

He abruptly stops talking.

"Nina," he says in surprise. His hand automatically goes to his gleaming forehead. No handkerchief.

"Miss Bradshaw," Felix gives me what is supposed to be a friendly nod.

"Dad, Felix." I get ready, ready to make room for them.

But Dad does not wave me away. He stares at me. His blue eyes are big and blood-shot. Felix pretends to look something up on his HC. His greedy eyes register everything. The latest performance in the Bradshaw drama.

"Nina," says Dad again. He places a hand on my arm. I look down, at the swirly pattern in the expensive carpet under my feet. What does he want?

"What Dad?" I feel his hand burning on my arm.

"How are you?"

The question is unexpected. This time no lecture or one of his demands, but an actual show of interest. I look up.

"What do you think?"

Dad still has his hand on my arm. He tries to fix my gaze, but I won't let him. He's after something. What?

"It'll be all right, Nina. Really." His eyes are agitated, constantly shifting back and forth. He hesitates, then moves his hand from my arm to my cheek. His hand is warm and large. Something in me wants to give in, wants him to offer more than a hand.

"Really?"

It comes out all wrong. I blink and a tear forms. Dad smiles and wipes it away. He looks at me as he sometimes looked at Isa.

"Really, Nini."

He uses my old pet name. He pulls me to him and holds me tight. I recognize the familiar scent of his aftershave, which Isa and I used tomade jokes about.

As always, he looks immaculate, but I can hear his heart beating and detect a light odor of sweat. He's doing his best. And again it flashes through me: what he did, he did for Isa. Immediately the hope follows: could he perhaps understand...?

Suddenly I know.

I know what I can do.

The right moment. This moment. Dad and I are not on the same side any more.

"Dad?"

"Yes, Nina?"

"May I visit Isa?"

He releases me.

"Isa?"

I realize that it's the first time in months that I've heard him say her name.

"Isa's grave," I add.

"Her grave."

He runs his hand through his grey hair. There are fewer blond streaks in it than there were before.

"I've... I've never been there," I stammer, and I sniff. I pinch my arm hard, so that tears appear again. I try not to think of Felix who is watching all this. Dad hesitates. I feel his inquisitive gaze. Finally he nods.

"If your mother goes with you. It's dangerous out there."

"Thanks, Dad."

I go to walk upstairs, but he doesn't let me go. Again he grabs me and holds me tight. Now his eyes do not release mine so easily.

"I miss her too, Nina. We all miss her." His voice sounds uncertain and soft. Is this Governor Bradshaw? Is this Dad?

He takes a deep breath. "I'll make sure nothing else can happen to us, that we can stay together, the three of us. I'll make sure of that, I promise." And he breathes out, pulling me even tighter to him.

I nod. I don't know what else to do. I nod automatically. My head moves back and forth against his shoulder. "Can I go upstairs now, Dad? I'm tired." I'm trembling. His hands are hurting me and I don't want to lose control of myself in front of Felix.

He releases me. "Okay, Nina."

His eyes, Felix's eyes, seem to follow me until I've shut the door of my room behind me. Dad *and I are not on the same side any more*. I repeat it like a mantra. I slide down to the floor, my back against the door. I let everything flood over me. I haven't any tears left.

But I've got a plan.

MAX

"A visitor for you."

I try to open my eyes but it feels as if they're stuck together with super glue. My throat feels as if I've swallowed some sand and my head is about to burst. In a flash I see him in front of me again.

The sadist.

He hammered. For hours. I didn't give him anything. Nothing. Not even that my brother's a prick and my Pa's a liar. It's nothing to fucking do with them. Keep that bastard guessing? Keep Bradshaw guessing? Whatever I say, I know what's going to happen with me. He eventually left me like a wrung-out sponge. The Dry doctor came and injected something. I've no idea how long I've been under this time.

"Wh-what?"

"A visitor."

It's the Wader's voice. The Wet who asked about my pa.

"Who?"

"Your ma."

He walks off.

Ma.

I try to sit up, but it's as if the bones have been ripped from my arms. I've no strength. What does my head look like? My fingers feel scratches on my cheeks and a deep cut in my chin. The old wound in my eyebrow is open again. I don't want Ma to be shocked by my appearance. I don't want to make her worry. I'm such a dick. Her one son is a wanted terrorist, the other is as good as condemned.

"Max. Oh, Max!"

She's in the doorway. The Wader holds up his hand — five minutes — and closes the door.

"Ma."

And I burst into tears. Just like a baby. She comes over and takes hold of me.

I bawl my head off.

"Shh, son, shh."

She rocks me softly, back and forth.

"What have they done to you, son? What have they done to you?"

I'm ashamed of my cowardly tears.

"Take it easy, son. Let it all out."

Ma's on to me at once.

When I've finished sobbing, she sits down next to me on the bed. Her hands rest on the handcuffs as if they're not there.

"Well, no need to ask you how you are." A wry smile makes her lips curl. I answer her with a weak grin.

"Is there any water around? My mouth feels like sandpaper."

She smiles, shakes her head, and picks up the glass standing on the table next to my bed.

I don't just sob like a baby, I have to be fed like a baby. Completely fucking helpless. I don't know what to say. Five minutes isn't much and the walls have ears here. I throw a short glance at the camera in the top left corner. Ma understands what I mean.

"I know, son."

"Pa..." I don't know how to say it and I throw another glance at the camera. Fuck, they already know. He already knows. It makes no fucking difference. "Ma." I swallow. "Pa was..."

"You don't need to tell me anything, Max."

What? Did she know about Pa? My jaw drops open.

Again she guesses my thoughts. "Suspicions, Max. I didn't know." A short laugh. "First I thought he had someone else. Always getting in late. Out all night, sometimes days on end. All those little lies. And that job in... Well, you know where. That wasn't his usual work."

"But... how?"

"I only worked it out later. When Liam started the same behav...." Ma falls silent, her gaze on the camera. "I wanted him to leave you out of it, Max," she continues. "But..."

"But I met Nina."

"You met Nina."

Ma places her hand on my cheek. Cool. My head feels so hot. "I'm sorry, Ma." My voice is hoarse and breaks. Not a man, a frightened little kid.

"Sorry for what?"

"That you couldn't trust me. That I lost my bloody mind."

"Did you do that?"

She's really amazing.

"I, I.. wanted her... I was so fucking angry, Ma!"

"Shh. I understand."

Her eyes go to the camera, but I have to tell her. I have to!

"Li suddenly turned up, Ma, and he told me about Nina, who she was and what her pa had done, and that bloody knot... I wanted to punish her, Ma, I wanted her to feel ex-

actly what I've been feeling all this fucking time. But then...
then Liam started about Pa and the rage in my head started
to reel and I remembered that Nina wanted to tell me something, about her sister of course, I didn't know she was on
the Mainland as well, and Li... Li completely lost it, he really
lost it, Mwhen he realized I was leaving with Nina..."

I can hardly catch my breath, I'm panting like a dog. Now
they're really got you, Max.

"Shh, Max. Shh." She places a hand on my chest, where
my heart is trying to break out, it's beating so fast. She places
her hands against my face, wipes away a few tears with her
rough thumbs, and says: "You have something Liam has
never had, Max. And Liam..." She sighs.

The door opens with a lot of noise. Two Blowers come in.
Ma looks at me.

"I love you, Max," she says.

Then she turns round and walks out of my cell, the two
Blowers on either side. She's small, but so big. My ma. "I love
you too, Ma," I whisper, but she's already gone. I'm alone.

"That was your ma?"

The Wader is there again.

I nod.

"I almost didn't recognize her."

The Wader looks at me silently. What's he want? He walks
across to the control panel in the cell, types in something and
licks his lips.

"Now we can talk freely."

Is this a trick to get me to talk? I don't trust him one tiny
bit.

"The camera's running, but the sound's off. The others
are on a break."

"What do you want?"

"I want..." He purses his lips. "I want to know whether it's true. What the Dries say about your pa, that he was a terrorist."

"Why?"

Again he hesitates. His hands reach for the button holes in his sleeve and he scratches his flaky wrists. He's clearly uncomfortable.

"Because he saved my son," he finally says.

What?

"My son Ron was on the Mainland. In your pa's team. He sent him back. Just in time."

"But there were fifty of them. They all drowned," I object.

"He'd gone there with his friend. He wanted to work. That boy always does things without thinking first."

"Pa..."

The Wader doesn't hear me.

"Your pa saw him and when the siren went, he sent him back. He tried to send more of them back, but they wouldn't let him. Too dangerous. He helped the apprentices out, until he suddenly took off. Nobody understood why."

"Ron..."

It suddenly dawns on me. Ron. I see him before me. Ron Richards. The same age as Li. A big, slightly stupid boy who was always playing football. I look at the Wader and now I recognize him.

"Jan Richards."

"Ron was in your brother's class."

"Yes."

We fall silent. What's he doing here? Why has he betrayed

366

his own neighborhood? What did they promise him? He's waiting for an answer, an answer I don't have. Pa helped people out and then took off? Had he locked Isa up somewhere? Did Pa realize she would drown if he didn't do anything? Did he go to set her free? I'll never get the answers; Pa is dead, just like all the others who could know.

"No, my Pa wasn't a terrorist."

When I say it, I am certain of it. In this mess, even Harry isn't a terrorist. A dick and a murderer, okay, but no terrorist. Whatever Pa was planning, whatever he did, he wasn't a terrorist. Those are Dry words.

Richards nods briefly and walks to the control panel to turn the sound on again. Before he disappears into the corridor he says: "Oh yes, you should keep your head down, lad. You're being arraigned the day after tomorrow."

NINA

Dad is hardly ever at home. Is he avoiding us? Is he avoiding me? When he is at home, he's in his study, generally with Felix. I don't need to hear what they're talking about. Mum hasn't shown herself either since our clash. She's been lying in bed for days. On Isa's bed, needless to say. She only lets Maria in, and then only to take her food. Once we came outside together; I came from my room, she from Isa's room. We looked at each other. I saw her, my mother, for a fraction of a second, but she immediately hid herself again behind a veil of safe memories and self-chosen ignorance.

Today, Friday, Max is being arraigned. The first day of the new year.

"I want it done this week," says Dad. The trial will take place no later than ten days after the arraignment.

The charge is loud and clear. Kidnapping, complicity in murder and intentional infringement on the safety of the citizens in the Five Regions. The prosecutor's demand: the death penalty. I swallow. The reporter states the ruling as if it has already been passed.

Everywhere in our house, DOS screens show the pictures. Not that there are many. The arraignment takes place behind closed doors. Only when Max is taken from the cells to the main entrance of the Regional Hall does the camera catch a glimpse of him. I sit glued to the screen.

They've given him Dry clothes. A beige fabric pair of

trousers and a brown checkered sweater over a light shirt. They want to make him ridiculous. My hands clench into fists. A mob is kept at a distance behind barriers, but it's still difficult to follow him and the five Dry Defenders accompanying him. There. A glimpse of his face. So pale that the coffee seems drowned in the milk. His dark eyes are black holes without the familiar bright twinkle. His arm is in a sling. A shock goes through me when I see that one of the Dry Defenders purposely pulls him up the steps to the entrance by his injured arm. Max seems to want to wrestle to free himself and opens his mouth. Is it a scream of pain? For a brief moment, he looks straight at the camera with wide, astonished eyes. Then he is roughly pulled away and they drag him into the court building.

The man they have assigned to him as his *pro bono* lawyer, a Dry who has just finished law school, shows little interest in his client. He pleads for life imprisonment, but admits to the reporters that there is little chance of that. "The evidence is, unfortunately, very clear. I have advised my client to plead guilty and hope for clemency." Everything he does and says makes it more than clear that he has been forced to take the case.

Max neither admits nor denies anything.

The reporter continues. "We are here in front of the Regional Hall of Region Five, where the suspect Max Morris has just been arraigned. It is expected that Morris will stand trial in less than two weeks' time after which any sentence handed down will be carried out within three days, as was the case recently with Ramon Campion. Campion, who has achieved the status of martyr in the outer districts was sentenced for the murder of one hundred and eleven people who lost their lives in the attack on the digiscope in CC1. WEtTo has issued a statement that they will consider his execution and that of any other WEtTo members as a direct declaration of war and shall act accordingly. An anonymous pamphlet..."

"Off."

The DOS screen turns black. The sudden silence hangs heavily in the room.

I don't want to see or hear it anymore. I close my eyes and press my face into one of the colorful cushions next to me. As if I can erase the images like that. Just a few more days, I say to myself. Just a few more days.

"Are you okay, Miss Bradshaw?"

Felix is standing in the doorway. Bright blue eyes stare at me with undisguised curiosity.

"Yes, a lot better, Felix." I force myself to smile.

"Good, good."

He stays where he is and I sit where I am.

"Haven't you anything to do, Felix?" I ask. I can hardly hide my revulsion for the man. My father's faithful servant.

"Things to do?" He raises an eyebrow. It's so light that it's hardly visible.

I say nothing.

"I certainly have something to do." He smiles again. "I have quite a lot to do."

I look away. I wait until I hear his footsteps disappear down the hall.

I fall back in the soft cushions in the enormous sofa. I stare at the plaster ceiling that perfectly matches the patterns on the floor. Everything has to be perfect in this house. Everything. But it's all nothing.

Just a little while. Just a little while. Then I can start step one of my plan.

MAX

The Dry lawyer sitting opposite me seems to have the ability to look everywhere except at me. His client.

"You know the procedure?"

What does the bastard think? That it's my habit to get picked up and tried? I shrug.

"Right. Then I'll explain."

They've put me in a cubicle with him; my lawyer, who's not yet dry behind the ears. His dark hair shines as if it's been sprayed with high gloss and his gown could easily be hanging in one of their expensive shops. I think back to the arraignment. Behind closed doors, he'd said. The whole performance didn't last as long as a Wet meal. Outside, they'd drummed up a mob and umpteen reporters who shouted the loudest. If the Blowers hadn't kept hold of me, I wouldn't have got far. They fucking enjoyed it.

My lawyer explained briefly how the trial would proceed. What I had to do, what I had to say if I wanted a chance of getting out of all of this with my life. I say nothing, I don't nod, I stare past him at the bare wall. I can play the game as well.

"Say, are you listening?"

I slowly shift my eyes to him and look at him. I repeat what he has just told me, in his expensive, Dry words. The Dry looks away. Now he's the one that's nervous.

"Any questions?" He has already put away his HC. Oh, he really wants to get out of here.

I want to shake my head no, but change my mind.

"Will the public be allowed in to watch?"

"Because of the fast-track trial, there will be a jury and public servants, Dry Defenders and, of course, the Governors."

"So no public?"

No Ma. No Nina.

"An exception is made for the immediate family," says the lawyer brusquely. "And for the other party directly involved, of course."

"Nina." I say her name out loud. It is like breathing. My oxygen.

"Nina Bradshaw, yes," he confirms. "That is the procedure."

"Procedure?" What does he mean?

"It is customary for the victim to be present at the accused's prosecution and execution, as compensation."

I stare at him. Just briefly. Until it clicks. And I lose my head.

I'm faster than the Blower in the corner who is supposed to keep an eye on me. Before he can get to me, I've punched my so-called lawyer in his filthy, hypocritical face. It takes all my strength and the pain cuts rights through my shoulder into my arm. But nothing is as satisfying as the cracking sound when my fist slams into his astonished face.

They quickly get the better of me.

One Blower holds me, and the other rams his fist into my nose so that blood spurts from my nose. They almost pull my arms from their socket and tie me up tightly as they drag me from the room. I hear my lawyer cursing and I grin, even though it fucking hurts. I can hardly walk and my feet stumble over every obstacle in our path. They throw a sack over my head when we go outside — the Regional Square again? I haven't the faintest idea — until we get back to my cell. The smell of decay and piss and fear rushes to meet me like a Wet whore meeting a Dry. The Blowers dump me on my bed and leave me lying in my own shit, in the dark.

I don't know how long I've been lying like this when the door opens. "You couldn't behave yourself, lad?"

The light goes on. Richards is standing in the doorway. I smirk. "I'm beginning to understand why they call you a hot-head. You don't attach much value to your own life." My sneer disappears.

"Here, let me wipe away that blood. You look as if they picked you up in the slaughterhouse." Richards begins wiping a damp cloth over my face. It's not the sort of work he's used to, obviously, because it bloody hurts.

"It's beginning to color nicely." He points at my left eyebrow and shakes his fat head. Have they managed to hit me there too? A hard wipe across my cheek bone. I curse. I have to distract myself so I say the first thing that comes to mind.

"How's Ron?"

"Hm?"

Richards looks up from his bloody work. The water in which he's wringing out the wet cloth is pinkish red. It looks just like the water paint they had at play school. I always made a mess with it, much to the irritation of the teacher. I can hardly believe it's from me. It's bizarre. How often have I been beaten up recently?

"Ron's doing fine." I see him glance at the camera in the corner.

"Is he still working?" I ask quickly, as Richards dabs some

biting stuff or other on the old wound in my eyebrow.

"Yeah."

"In cc1?"

"You're nosey, aren't you?"

I grab my thigh when he stuffs some cotton wool in my nose. "Everything all right in District Seven?"

Richards picks up the bag with cotton wool and stares at me. He slowly shakes his head. "Not here. Not now." He stands with his back towards the camera and whispers the words. I can hardly understand him. I know what he means; he's warning me.

So everything's not all right. I grimace. "Pleased to hear it." It's out before I realize it.

"Shut your mouth, boy, or I'll have the others come here and they're a lot less patient!" He stuffs a new wad of cotton wool in my swollen nostril.

Richards won't push it. He's careful.

Silently he finishes his work. When he wrings out the cloth for the last time and throws it across his shoulder, he just stands there. We look at each other. He nods one more time and disappears into the dark corridor.

It feels good to hear the District Seven is no longer as peaceful as it once was.

NINA

I've been to the cemetery before. Once, with friends on the Mainland. The boys climbed over the old graves while the girls giggled behind the trees. Isa and Johan were just starting to go together and they stayed behind on purpose. I was jealous.

Now it's empty. The odd person is visiting a grave to lay flowers. Few people dare to leave the ccs.

Mum sits next to me, as quiet as a mouse. She says nothing. She doesn't make any movement to go with me. She has never dared visit Isa's grave. I'm counting on that.

I get out and climb the artificial mound that has been created for the Dry dead. I'm not planning to visit Isa's grave, but my route takes me past it and involuntarily my eyes remain on it. An angel stares into the grey sky. She sits on a marble stone with her wings spread and her hands folded. I walk round the monument and am shocked when I see it's her face. Isa. Ice-cold and lifelike. This must be Dad's doing. It's typical Dad.

I quickly move on. It's late afternoon and the sun will be setting in an hour. Max said his mother worked in the clinic. She can't leave earlier than three o'clock.

"She visits Pa's grave every Tuesday," he said.

The air is heavy and dark. I hope the rain will hold off for a while. The low sun peeps out from under the clouds, turning everything orange. It gives the cemetery an unearthly glow. As if anything can happen.

I walk farther down the hill and arrive at the old section of the cemetery. Here are the stones from before the Great Floods. Old and weathered, eroded by the salt water, names hardly legible. People who lived in a different world. But who perhaps knew Bob Dylan, just like me, just like Max. I smile.

I soon reach the mass graves of the Great Floods. Row upon row, stone upon stone, name upon name. Innumerable dead. I quickly move on.

I give a sigh of relief when I see her there. I recognize her immediately. The same posture as her son, only shorter. She has tied her dark hair into a practical pony-tail and her grey scarf hangs loosely round her neck. She has a rake with which she is clearing the leaves from a small stone. She bends down and places her naked hand on it.

"Mrs. Morris?"

She's startled. Her dark eyes narrow and she adopts the pose of a predator that can spring at any moment.

"Please, stay. I'm alone. I swear it."

She stands still. She studies me with the fiery look that I know so well that it is strange to see it in another.

"Nina Bradshaw." She says my name as if tasting it with the tip of her tongue, as if testing its freshness. I remember that inquisitive look she gave me the first time she saw me. "The Dry girl who managed to tame one of my boys," she says finally and pulls the familiar grimace. "And it's Yvonne, not Mrs. Bradshaw."

I grin back.

We move towards each other at the same time and hug. It doesn't feel strange or unnatural. It happens all by itself. She even smells a bit like him. For the first time since Felix found us, I dare to be myself.

"Max...?" I ask as soon as we let each other go. She keeps hold of my arm. She is so completely different than my own mother, and yet so much the same.

"I've seen him. He feels better than he did."

"What have they done to him?"

"The first week, nothing. Then they questioned him. They give him just enough painkillers to get him through. They want..."

"... to keep him fit for the execution."

"Yes."

"Can you go and visit him again?"

She shrugs her shoulders. "I don't know. And if I can, then never alone. There are cameras. They can hear everything." Of course.

"If they let you see him, can you... can you tell him that I..." I stutter. I don't know how to say it, but Yvonne places a hand on my am and nods.

"Thanks."

We fall silent and I look at the stone. It is dark and overgrown, but in some way or other, it feels better than at Isa's enormous tombstone. I bend down and trace the names with my finger until I reach Max's father.

"Do you know what happened?"

I don't have to ask anything more. She nods and says: "I told Max that I suspected Rob."

"Oh."

"I wasn't certain about Bradshaw, I mean your father. I didn't know he had another daughter."

"Isa."

"Isa was your sister."

"Yes."

"We have all lost someone."

We fall silent. I know we're both thinking the same thing. "Nina, you didn't come here just to visit a grave?" Yvette raises an eyebrow.

"No."

"What do you think you can do?"

It's now or never.

"I want to contact Liam."

"What?"

She throws the rake to the ground and places her hands on her hips. Her dark eyes are stern, but I've been with Max long enough not to allow that to scare me off.

"I've got a proposal for WEtTO. Something they can't say no to."

"Nina, you don't know what you're getting yourself into."

I laugh bitterly.

"I know precisely what I'm getting into. But I want... I must do everything..." I don't finish my sentence, for she knows exactly what I mean.

"For Max."

"For Max," I say.

"I can get into Dad's hc, into his personal dos page. I can get information WEtTO could never get its hands on, not in a hundred years. They can't hurt me as long as I don't give them anything. They need me. They can hack the whole system if they do what I ask." I rattle on, talking far too quickly, but I know I absolutely must convince her. Everything depends on it. "They've got the means, Yvonne!" My voice echoes over the silent stones. "Only with their help do we have a chance of freeing him, before, before..." I can't say it. I refuse to say it. I beg her.

"Nina..."

"Yes?"

"I don't know where Liam is."

My courage drops.

"But...I can send him a message. He left something behind for me. Just in case I got into difficulties."

"They'll intercept it. They're watching you via DOS."

"If you give me a different code? And if you use a different HC?" suggests Yvonne. A vague smile plays across her lips. "Then they won't know where the message came from."

"Yes!"

"It's still risky."

"Everything has been risky since I met Max."

Yvonne shakes her head and laughs briefly.

"I'm beginning to understand how you managed to tame my Max,"

"And I'm beginning to understand how you managed to stick it out with the three of them."

We hug each other.

"Go, Nina," says Yvonne. "I'll be here again the day after tomorrow. Can you come?"

I nod and hurry back to the waiting car, where Mum is still sitting in silence.

Two days later I give Yvonne the new code. The day after, I get a message from Liam. On Isa's old HC.

MAX

He's sitting on the dyke again.

I've been running. My body is on an adrenaline high, the feeling I thought was the best ever — until I met Nina.

Pa is sitting on his old stool. I climb up the dyke, still panting from the effort. It's warm, a summer day. One of those days when the light shimmers between the concrete blocks of flats. Inside it's as if somebody is building up the pressure until the glass in the windows shatter and the heat can finally escape.

I've escaped.

"Hey, son. Good run?"

I flop down beside him.

"Not bad."

We stare at the float. I pick up the thermos flask and take a sip of weak tea. No booze this time.

"Is Li after you again?" He keeps staring at the float.

"Li's only after himself."

Pa laughs. I throw a stone into the water.

"A stone makes the same circles in the water as a body." I don't realize I've said it out loud until Pa says: "I know, son."

He's piled his catch next to him. A CD sleeve, an old shoe, a broken HC version 1.0, and next to it the golden locket where the blood has now dried. What a catch.

"Do you remember Jan Richards?"

Pa picks up the Thermos flask and takes a sip before he answers.

"Richards? The name sounds familiar."

"His son apparently worked in your team. The boy was a bit nuts."

"Ah, Jan."

"He says that you saved his son."

"He says that?"

"Yes."

"Then it must be true."

I want to say something, but Pa's got a bite. He jumps up and starts to reel in the line. It takes ages and Pa's arm trembles from the effort. I want to help him, but he pushes me away and I stare at the water, where something slowly emerges.

It is a skull.

"Yes!" says Pa triumphantly. His eyes gleam and he waves the rod around until the dead thing is safely on the dyke. He immediately walks over to it and picks it up. He admires it as if it's the best catch ever.

"Pa, it's a fucking skull!" I shout. What is going on in that stupid old mind of his? Had he gone mad?

"I've found it. I've finally found it!" I don't understand. What? What has he found?

"Pa?"

He turns round and holds up the skull next to his weather-beaten face.

He grins.

"We look like each other, don't we Max?"

"What?"

"It's my head, son! The one I lost in the water!"

"Your head?"

"My head," confirms Pa.

I stare at him, my old Pa, and suddenly I see it. It's his head.

NINA

"We want to see first. Tomorrow, 09:00, same place. L."

I stare at the message.

I'm in Isa's room. Mum has already gone to bed. The message came in on Isa's PP; her bright purple Personal Page with flickering greenish yellow letters and in the background a drawing of the two of us together, one I made for her.

Liam's got some nerve.

But what choice do I have?

I wait until they've both gone to bed. I wait until I hear Dad's familiar snoring and Mum's restless turning. Then I rush downstairs, to Dad's study, my bare feet cold on the marble floor. My hands reach for the panel next to the door and my fingers tap in the code. I wait for the signal to appear.

"Access refused."

I draw a sharp breath. Confused, I type in the code again. Perhaps I missed a number?

"Access refused."

I know: the third time sets off the alarm.

No! This can't be. This can't happen! Dad never changes his code! This must have been Felix's idea. Max... o, Max! What can I say to Liam? And to Yvonne?

I force myself to get up and walk back upstairs, down the hall, into my room. Softly, carefully, I close the door behind me and only then do I breathe out.

I can't get into Dad's study. I haven't got anything to show Liam tomorrow.

I know what that means. The stitch in my stomach, which I grab with both hands, knows it, so does my trembling heart. Oh Max! What should I do?

I'm sitting in the car next to Mum.

I tried it again this morning. Without any success. I try to buck myself up. I have to play for time. I must be able to find out Dad's new password. It can't be that difficult. There's still time.

There's still time, isn't there?

Outside the world passes by. Now that WEtTO is lying low, there are people on the streets again, in the parks and in the shop amusement centers. The number of Dry Defenders is just as large. No risks are taken. The wrought-iron entrance gates to the cemetery loom up behind the grey Regional Offices and the car stops. This is the end. It's all been for nothing.

I'm so sorry, Max.

I've just opened the door when I feel a hand on my shoulder.

I turn round and open my mouth, but Mum puts a finger to her lips and shakes her head. What? Again she shakes her head and nods towards the driver. He mustn't hear anything. I look at her in surprise, but keep quiet as her hands search through her bag, find what she's looking for, and place it in my hands. I look. It's a datacard.

What is it? What does it mean?

Mum says nothing. She gives me a push. Go.

I give her a hopeful smile, push the door open further,

and step outside. I take the first steps slowly, but once I'm through the gate, I can't stop myself. I run over the hill, past Isa's grave until I see him. I clutch the datacard tightly in my hand.

I recognize him immediately, even though he's wearing a hood and standing with his back to me. From a distance he looks so like Max that I feel a stab. My breath screeches and the stitch in my side is so bad that I almost fall over. I know he's seen me, although he doesn't make any move to come closer. I have to go to him.

Only now do I realize that I'm meeting my kidnapper.

I slowly walk down the hill. I breathe in and out. Deeply. Memories of the kidnapping surface. How I wet myself, how dirty I was, the hate in their eyes. His eyes. The fear.

Keep going.

Keep going, Nina.

I stop ten feet away. Liam slowly turns round. What is he looking at? At his father's grave? His hands are in his pockets. He's armed.

I cough.

He slowly turns round.

His eyes...

"First let me see the goods, then we can negotiate."

I'm so scared. My whole body shakes as I stretch out my arm and open my hand.

He walks towards me and takes the card. He plugs it into his HC, which just like Felix is integrated in his arm. So WEtTO has access to the newest technology. The tension is unbearable, the time passes agonizingly slowly. Liam's eyes jump impatiently back and forth, from me to the screen to somebody or something in the shadow of the trees.

He looks up and grins. Exactly like Max.

"Smart. So smart," he murmurs.

"What?" I manage to say.

"We can certainly use this."

"There's more," I say quickly, although I haven't the faintest idea what he's talking about. "If you help me."

He fixes me with his dark look. "This is a good start."

I don't look away. I will not look away. Never again.

"You know what I want. If you help me, there's more."

"You've got some nerve, Dry."

"I don't have a choice."

Liam purses his lips. His dark eyes narrow and he takes another step towards me. "No choice?" he says. I can almost smell him. "A Dry who doesn't have a choice?" He throws his hands in the air and laughs loudly. "Am I suddenly living in fucking Heaven?"

I blink, but force myself to stand still. It would be so easy to turn around and run. But I've got to try.

"All I want is for Max to be free! He hasn't done anything, Liam. You know that. And your mother, she.."

"Leave Ma out of this."

I stop at once. I see how he keeps his hands in his coat pocket to hide his trembling. He can't control himself. He's just like Max. But without anybody to stop him, to hold him and tell him it's all right.

"How can I leave your mother out of this, Liam?" I swallow and look straight at him. "How? Tell me. I'd like to know. Max is her son. And so are you!"

"I said: Leave Ma out of this!"

But I can't stop the words.

"You're not the only one who's lost somebody!" I take a

step forward. "My sister drowned, your father drowned and fifty others drowned. Yvonne's got everything to do with it, I've got everything to do with this, all those others have everything to do with it! It's not just about you, Liam. It's about everything, about this whole damned world!"

I'm shouting now, I feel tears welling up and I suddenly so angry. Angry at myself, at the stupid tears, angry at Liam, who is just as blind as Dad and angry at the world, which always gives you hope only to take it away at the last moment.

Liam stares at me. He stares at me as if the words haven't yet got through to him. Then the coin drops. And I've no time to get away. His face is inches from me when he roughly grabs my chin. His breath mixes with mine and oddly enough I think: he even smells a bit like Max. The gun's barrel presses threateningly against my temple.

"Shut. Your. Fucking. Dry. Mouth."

He spits out the words and in his anger almost lifts me off my feet. It's an absurd situation.

I know what I have to say, even if he doesn't want to hear it.

"He's your brother, Liam." I whisper the words, but he hears them. Oh yes, he hears them. I feel the heat of his body, so close to mine, the force of his rage and his breath in my neck as he bends over me and whispers in my ear.

"I have no brother."

He releases me. I fall and trip over my own feet. Tanja appears from behind the tree. Liam raises a hand before she can get near.

"Agreed," he says. He is in control of himself again. "After the trial, we'll contact you. If your material's any good, then..." He waits, gathers some saliva in his mouth, and spits it with force onto the ground. "Then we'll free the turncoat."

With these words he turns round and leaves.

Only now do I start trembling. I look at my hands that I can't keep still anymore and then notice the flowers on the grave. Fresh flowers. Liam? I have to get back.

I turn round and am about to start waking when I see her on top of the hill. Mum. She is holding herself and waits for me to reach the top. I want to ask her why she helped me, but she beats me to it.

"I don't want to know, Nina. I don't want to know anything,"

"What don't you want to know? Did you see him?" She knows I mean Liam.

"No." Is she lying? I couldn't say. Does it make any difference? "But why did you give me...?"

"Losing someone you love once is enough." She says the words in a flat tone, as if she has learned them by heart. But from her trembling hands, from her sickly pale skin and from her eyes that look right through me into a vacant emptiness, I know that the words hurt her.

I don't know what to say.

Her hand rummages in her bag and she fishes something out.

"Here." She gives me a second datacard. "This one has the new codes."

I take the card.

"Thanks."

Mum doesn't answer me and walks off, her head turned away from me. I follow. We walk down the hill, past Isa's grave and go through the gate. The car's engine is already running.

Then I think of something. How did Mum get into Dad's study, when the code was changed?

"Mum?"

She slowly turns round. Her eyes are distant. "Yes, darling?"

"How did you get into Dad's room? He's changed the code." For a moment she returns to the here and now.

"But darling, it's so easy."

"Easy?"

"You father is so transparent. An open book. The new code was your birthday, darling. You are his one and only daughter."

MAX

'Today's the day, lad."

Richards places a hand on my shoulder and slowly shakes me awake.

They give me sleeping pills. I try to resist, but there's no point. Since the day of my arraignment, they've kept me drugged. I feel like a machine that they can turn on and off when they like.

I dreamed. Of Nina lying next to me, of Li shooting at me, and of Ma weeping next to my freshly dug grave. I dreamed of Erik's dead face and of the scent of Nina's piss, and of the dark starry nights in the Submerged Territories. I dreamed of Pa again.

"Today's the day, lad."

"What?"

"The trial."

The trial.

The old man is concerned about me. He's got two sons. He's a father. Why do they keep letting him in? Because they think that'll make me cooperate?

"I've come to help you dress."

"I can bloody well do that myself."

"Oh yes?"

I support myself with my good arm when I'm half standing, then feel a wave of nausea and I throw up everything that I have in me. Not that that's much. An acid mix from the very depths of my stomach drips down my chin into my neck.

"I can see that."

Richards takes a rag and wipes the mess away. It's humiliating. I think of Nina, when she asked me to wash her. Now I know how she felt. I feel so damned guilty.

The nausea disappears when Richards gives me something to drink. Side effects of the painkillers, he says. He's got clothes for me. Not Dry, but my own Wet clothes.

"Your Ma brought them."

"Did she say anything?"

Richards doesn't say anything, but strips off my hospital clothes until I'm not wearing anything, not even underpants.

"Can I see myself?" I ask when he has dressed me.

I feel better now that the nausea has passed. My shoulder hurts less than it did and my head is no longer throbbing as if Liam has used me as a punch bag.

Richards purses his lips as if he has to think about it. "Okay," he says at last and leaves my cell. When the Wader comes back, he's carrying a mirror.

"Don't be shocked."

"I've never been shocked by myself."

He holds up the mirror.

Fuck. Is that me? My head looks twice as big, it's so swollen. My nose is like an overripe strawberry and my eyes are buried so deep in the bluish purple that I have difficulty recognizing myself. I should be glad I still have all my teeth. Only my hair is the same. Short black stubble covers my hard skull.

"The color will go away," says Richards.

Before I hang? goes through my mind. But I keep my trap shut. I give Richards the mirror.

"I'm ready."

Richards gives a signal and two Blowers appear in the opening. They say nothing as they secure my hands and feet with a chain. Richards helps me up.

We walk through endless grey corridors. I try to see where they're taking me, where I am, but it's a maze. Windows look out onto bare, concrete yards and the only thing I see of any size is the dark sky which seems to be brewing for a storm. How appropriate.

The Blowers walk quickly and if Richards hadn't have been there, I would have stumbled over my own feet. It doesn't surprise me when my wound starts to bleed again. How much of that stuff does a person have?

This time we don't go outside. No chance for eager reporters or angry citizens to make any protest. After what seems like an endless maze of corridors, we finally reach a double door.

"Okay, lad. I can't go any further."

Richards places his hands on my shoulders. The two Blowers exchange a glance that I recognize all too well. I say nothing. What should I say? My so-called lawyer has made it very clear what I can expect of my trial.

"Keep your head, lad. Keep your head," says Richards as he softly squeezes my good shoulder. Then the Wader turns and walks away.

When Richards has gone, one of the two reds grabs me roughly by the arm and pushes me forward, through the double door. Gone the grey corridors, the concrete and the cold. And like the first time, my mouth gapes at the sight of so much Dry wealth. The floor is covered with a dark red carpet that — I swear on my pa's grave — feels like a cushion under my feet. Elaborate wooden panels cover the walls and Dry judges look at me with contempt from their portraits. I expect the Blowers to take me to the same place as my arraignment, but we walk on, into an enormous hall with a glass dome high above us, through which the first flash of lightning can be seen racing towards earth as a warning. All corridors meet here. Double doors, much larger and more impressive than those we just passed, are the entrance to what must be the court.

Somebody else comes hurrying along another corridor. When he is close enough, I see it is my lawyer. I look at his bruised jaw with a sense of satisfaction. He gives a quick nod, but doesn't shake my hand. He doesn't want to burn himself on a Wet for a second time.

"How long?" asks one of the Blowers.

"Five minutes," answers my lawyer as he glances at me nervously.

Another five minutes. Five minutes before I see her again.

For that is all I can think about. Nina. The rest... I don't dare think about the rest. I hide the rest and push it far, far away.

NINA

The doors to the court open.

I'm sitting between Dad and Mum, right at the front. Beads of perspiration are running down my back. I have to suppress the urge to stand up and search for his face.

The pro bono lawyer is walking at the front, the man I saw on DOS news. He walks quickly, as if he has a more important appointment waiting and this is an irritating delay. He approaches the judge, shakes his hand, and takes his place to his left, next to the summary jury. A Dry jury.

Then comes the accused.

A sharp, rattling sound cuts through the deathly silence. All eyes are focused on Max. I swallow when I realize that the sound is coming from his restraints. What do they think a wounded boy of seventeen can do? He is flanked on either side by two Blowers who lead him to the dock, between the prosecutor and the judge. I catch a glimpse of a leg in his old, frayed jeans, an arm in a grey sweater and his short stubbly hair. My heart beats faster. Then, as if a red curtain is pulled aside, the Blowers disappear and I can see him at last.

Our gazes immediately meet, hold each other, and say everything that our mouths cannot say.

I now see his whole face.

Oh Max.

What have they done to him? He sees how shocked I am

and leans forward, an instinctive, protective reaction. Immediately he is roughly pulled back. He clenches his teeth in pain, but I keep looking at him until he is there again, until he has himself under control again and I smile. Everything'll be all right.

A Blower has Max take the Oath of the Five Regions. They stand him up and ask him to raise his right hand. My gaze holds on to him as he recites the words as quickly as possible: "I believe in the Five Regions. I believe in the struggle against the water. I believe we shall ultimately defeat the water. I believe that in the end we shall all find dry land."

The trial begins.

The prosecutor, a tall, thin man with dark blond hair and a pair of blue reading glasses on the tip of his nose, reads the charges. In the summary trial, only the accused will be questioned, he says, and the trial will not last longer than one day. The charges are read: kidnapping, complicity in murder and intentional infringement on the safety of the citizens in the Five Regions. The prosecutor gets up and walks to Max.

"Are you Max Morris, son of Robert and Yvonne Morris?"

Max nods.

"Yes or no is sufficient," says the prosecutor calmly. Max's mouth twitches. He answers reluctantly.

"Yes."

"Your brother is Liam Morris?"

"Yes."

"Who just like you was expelled from the Delta College Combined School for violence?"

My gaze turns to Max's lawyer. The man says nothing. After a brief hesitation, Max answers. "Yes."

"You know that one of the boys you hit on the day of your, eh... suspension has lasting injuries?"

Max frowns.

"No."

"Are you familiar with WEtTO?"

"You mean the World Entente for terminating Terror and Oppression?"

Well done, Max.

"Yes."

"Then I am familiar with it."

"And did you know that your father, Robert Morris, belonged to this organization?"

"No."

Max shifts uneasily on his chair.

"Thus... you were not at the time aware of the plan to kidnap Isa Bradshaw?"

Max's face hardens. Calm down. Just answer.

"No." He forces it out.

Oh Max.

The questions continue for a while and Max answers each of them with a short, clear answer. It is not difficult to guess what the prosecutor is driving at. He wants to show that Max cannot be trusted, that he is a violent terrorist, just like his father and brother, and that he had thought up everything in advance. The jury will believe it because it is what they want to believe and Max knows that. He knows it doesn't make any difference what he says.

"So you did assignments for school together with Nina Bradshaw?"

"Yes."

"And your family knew about this?"

A slight hesitation. "Yes."

"Whose idea was it, Max?" The man immediately pounces. Behind me, I hear Yvonne take a sharp breath.

Take it easy, Max.

"There *was* no idea."

Yvonne breathes out. The prosecutor won't drop it.

"You deny that you helped kidnap Nina Bradshaw?"

Max remains silent He tries to shift in his seat. The clatter of his chains breaks the pregnant silence.

"Your answer, Mr. Morris?" insists the judge.

Max's eyes find mine. I know what he's going to say. He will not lie. In any case, not to me.

"No..." begins Max. The prosecutor is ready to pounce again. "But..."

The man taps his fingers again his cheek and finishes the sentence for him. "But you deny knowing who Nina was?"

"Yes."

"You discovered it on the day of your suspension?"

"Yes."

"And after you had kidnapped her, you changed your mind?"

Max waits He knows he will be as good as declaring himself guilty if he gives an honest answer. The prosecutor is trying to bate him.

"I remembered something she had said to me," he says carefully. "And... then my brother told me what really happened on the Mainland."

I feel Dad stiffen next to me. There is an immediate murmur from the public.

"Yes or no, Mr. Morris," orders the judge.

Max looks at his cuffed hands. There is no place for the truth here Max.

"For the last time, what is your answer?"

Max trembles. Even now, wounded and drugged by the painkillers, he still has too much energy. He opens his mouth and then immediately shuts it again. A thought line suddenly makes him appear older. Does he still think that it matters what he says? Does he still think that this is about him, about me, about us?

"Yes, I helped kidnap Nina and yes, I changed my mind."

A collective sigh sounds through the court.

Max lowers his eyes, hardly aware of the murmuring people and the judge who is calling for order. I know that he feels guilty, so terribly guilty.

Oh Max.

"So when you discovered the truth about your father and Isa Bradshaw, you went to Nina?" continued the prosecutor.

"Yes." His voice cracks.

"To kidnap her yourself?"

"What...? No! I wanted to get her away from there, away from my brother... from WEtTO!"

His eyes are large and gleaming, sweat glistens on his forehead.

"You wanted her all to yourself?" insists the prosecutor eagerly.

Max is silent. Too silent. And in his eyes I read: yes. Yes, he wanted me and it is absurd, but I blush. I blush because a boy wanted me for himself.

"Your answer?"

"I wanted to set her free." He tries to sit up straight. "I wanted to set her free," he repeats. His eyes do not wander from mine.

"You wanted to set her free from the situation in which you yourself had placed her?"

The prosecutor smiles.

Max answers without thinking. I see it coming. "Yes."

I shake my head. No, Max. No! Please, stay calm.

The prosecutor takes a step forward. He folds his hands and tilts his head to one side. He looks at Max, turns to the public, and finally addresses the jury. His words can be clearly heard by everybody. "How romantic. The Wet kidnapper falls in love with his Dry victim."

Max!

But he doesn't see me. His eyes are burning and he charges forward, his fists clenched, spit on his lips. Two Blowers violently push him back into his chair. People mutter and point. Max's lawyer seems not to have heard the remark. Only when a civil servant points it out to him, does he object to the insinuation. But what has been said, cannot be unsaid.

"I have no further questions," says the public prosecutor as he straightens his tie and sits down.

The pro bono lawyer coughs and clears his throat, quickly looks at his HC. Nobody seems to notice that the man is not in the least prepared. His argument is over almost before it begins.

An uneasy silence falls when he finishes.

"You do not want to ask the accused any questions?" says the judge finally to the lawyer.

"No, your honor. The accused has confessed his complicity. The only thing I would request on behalf of the family is a sentence suitable for a minor."

The whole trial is a farce!

The judge nods.

"Then I hereby declare the court in recess for the extent of the deliberations."

The judge stands and with him the jury. Together they leave the court. They have long decided their verdict.

MAX

They leave me where I am. Why should they take the trouble to move me? They won't be long with their so-called deliberations. This trial is one big fucking lie.

I couldn't care less. I see Nina.

I look, I stare, I completely suck her up. Perhaps this is the last time. No. Fuck. I don't want to think that. I don't want to think about what comes next. I'm here now and Nina is here. My girl. I imagine I'm sitting next to her and place my hand on her chin, pull her to me and kiss her, just like then, just like that first time. She was shocked when she saw me but she didn't look away, just as she's not looking away now.

I know that Ma is here too. I saw her when I came in. They didn't let her see me after that one time. She's on her own. The only Wet in a room full of Dries. Straight-backed and proud.

Bradshaw is sitting with his red face in his hands. The man is nervous. He is nervous, even though he can do whatever he likes with me. Occasionally he looks to one side, at Nina. Once he stretched out a trembling hand, but he pulled it back at the very last moment. Feliks, who's sitting behind him, smiles. I don't want to see him again. At least that's one wish that will come true.

Nina doesn't notice.

Her blue eyes are glued on me and I smile. I look like a

fucking serial killer with my beaten up face, but she still looks at me. At me. The Wet terrorist. Let her think it perverse. I couldn't care less. It's damned perfect. Because it's possible. Me and her. Her and me. I don't feel sorry about Nina. Why should I? I only feel sorry about myself.

When they come back into the court, the bustle abruptly stops. The judge sits down, orders silence and asks the jury whether it has reached its verdict. A small, grey woman stands up. She answers yes and hands over the HC with the vote to the judge. She looks briefly in my direction but doesn't dare look me in the eye. The judge studies the result as if it could surprise him, coughs, and asks everybody to stand. Chairs move, people nudge each other.

Nina smiles and I smile back.

I can take on the whole fucking world.

"Max Morris," begins the judge. "The jury has found you guilty on all charges."

Nina doesn't let me go. We don't let each other go. I don't let her go.

"Since we are unconvinced of the possibility of rehabilitation..."

I hardly hear him, because I'm with her, with Nina, with my girl... "... we have decided, under these exceptional circumstances..." Nina, my Nina.

"... and with the authority invested in the court during the imposition of martial law..."

I swallow, but don't release her eyes, her blue, blue eyes. "... to sentence you to..."

Nina smiles. She smiles and she lights up my whole world with her smile. My girl. My fucking girl. She smiles and nods. She points to me and to herself, and clasps her hands together.

"… be hanged by the neck until you are dead."
Nina!
Immediately pandemonium breaks out.

The few reporters who have been let in to report on this sham trial turn to me, waiting for my reaction. I don't see them. I see nobody except Nina. I laugh, I grin, I'm high in the treetops, in the clouds, in the sun. Nina and I look at each other, we look and we look, and we drown in each other just as our bodies drowned in each other. And when the Blowers unfasten me from the bench, force me to stand and drag me out of the court, we still look. I twist my neck as far as I can to see as much of her as the reds will allow me, I plunge into her blue, blue eyes, I sniff the air for a whiff of her sweet girl scent, I search in the air with my fingers for her soft curls, a hand, a tingling of her skin against my skin, and my eyes, my Wet, Wet eyes throw out a net and catch her final look. When I am almost out of the court, I open my mouth and shout as loudly as I can: "Nina Bradshaw, I love you!" I grin, even though a hand is clamped over my mouth and I feel a needle in my throbbing neck. I grin, even as it starts to go black and I fade away for the umpteenth time into the darkness in my head.

Man, how beautiful the world can be when you've got a girl.

NINA

His words resonate. They're mine. I suck them up and hold
them tight and when the door closes behind him and I feel
dozens of eyes on me, I am not scared, I do not feel alone
because I have his words.

I have them and I will never let them go.

I feel what it does to my heartbeat (it quickens), to my
stomach (it burns) and to my head (I can't stop grinning). I
close my eyes and think of how we were together. Which
pieces of each other we know, and which we have still to dis-
cover. I remember the hairs on his stomach, soft and curly,
his knobbly knees with that bit of gristle that moved under
my finger, and I feel his soft, short hair, his almost perfectly
round skull in my hands.

I want more. I want so much more. I want everything.

I didn't know that love could be so demanding.

If WEtTO doesn't cooperate, this is the last time I will
ever see him. Dad would never let me be at the execution.
Never.

Yvonne walks past. Our gaze meets and she smiles. I smile
back. We hope. We can smile because we have hope. How
dangerous is that?

Slowly the court empties. People talk. Voices I cannot distinguish from each other. They stare at me. They think I'm
mad. Dad gets up and walks out with the Vice Governor,
their heads together. Felix is waiting for me on the other side

of the court. He has folded his arms and his eyes are pinned on me. Quickly I shift my gaze.

"Are you coming, Nina?" Mum places a hand on my arm and the sudden touch makes me jump.

I look around. The court is empty, with the exception of a few civil servants. A Wet cleaner is working in one corner.

"Hm?"

"Home?"

"Home," I repeat. What is that?

She leads me outside, where a car is waiting for us. Dad is staying in Regional Hall. Emergency meeting with the other Governors. Mum says he probably won't be home until tomorrow morning. I won't miss him.

I stare outside, at the familiar streets, the familiar people, and the familiar houses. That's where Isa's best friend lived. Blowers are at the gate, rifles in their hands. What was her name? Tamara? I don't know anymore. It's all so long ago. And isn't that Mrs. Heston with her dachshund, who babysat for us when Maria wasn't working? The park is actually quite close, but Isa and I always thought of it as a day out when we went to visit it. It was, after all, outside our gate, outside out home. What is my home? CC1? Our house? My room? The summer house?

Maria has dinner ready when we get home. The kitchen is filled with comforting smells. "Ma'am." She greets Mum as she puts the finishing touch for her casserole. "Nina," she says softer, when I come in after Mum.

"Maria."

I now understand why I think the kitchen is the nicest place in the house. It is not a Bradshaw place, it is Maria's domain. She rules here and decides who may come in.

I sit down opposite Mum. Maria places the casserole on a stand, takes a spoon from one of the drawers and starts dishing up. When I ask for more than usual, she smiles.

"Hungry?"

I nod. She puts the casserole back on the stove and is about to leave us alone when Mum calls her back. "Join us, Maria."

Maria stops. She says nothing. When was the last time Maria joined us for dinner? In our previous house perhaps? I echo Mum. "Yes, join us."

She protests. "But... I haven't made enough."

I've not often seen Maria embarrassed and it's rather comical. Her hand goes to her pinned up hair, to her flower, a red one today. Warm, vibrating red.

"We always have some left over," I say.

"We'd really like you to stay," adds Mum.

"I'll get another plate." I get up and open a few cupboard doors at random. I have no idea where Maria keeps the plates. Maria watches for a moment, shakes her head, and opens a cabinet directly next to the refrigerator. She takes a plate and some cutlery, puts them on the table, and sits down.

"Just this once then," she says.

"Fine, Maria." Mum smiles.

I'll miss this, I think, as I look from Maria to Mum and back again.

MAX

The stuff they inject in me doesn't keep me out for long.

When I open my eyes, I'm not back in my cell. This room is smaller, much smaller, and bloody dark. They've thrown me on a bed with a dirty, old mattress. No blanket. After a while, I realize that the smell of sewage that's penetrating my nose is coming from the corner opposite me. The can. I can just see the pot in the semi-darkness. My mouth is dry and when I open it, my lips split. For the umpteenth time, I taste blood. They've removed the cuffs and I try to move. I can't manage it. I try to stand up, but immediately fall back on the mattress. It fucking hurts.

Is this the cell for the people they're going to hang? Hang. My throat seems strangely raw, as if a noose has been round it.

Nina.

I try to see her in front of me, but there's something that makes it difficult. That damned absurd feeling of happiness in the court, the high of the moment, is gone. Did I really shout? Yes, that was me. Fuck, that was me and I meant it and I still mean it. I smile when I think how Pa would have looked.

Oh man, I want to see her. I can't conjure up her face properly. It's like the stars. When you gaze at a star, it disappears, but if you look next to it, you can see it perfectly. But you're looking next to it. You don't really see it. And even if you could see it, then you wouldn't see the star as it is now but from goodness knows how many light years ago.

I only see pieces of Nina. Not the complete Nina. Not Nina. It makes me scared.

They'll hang you in three days.

Three days. Seventy-two hours.

Li once challenged me. How long I could go without sleep. I was twelve, he was fourteen. Pa and Ma had to work. We drank that filthy coffee surrogate and made up all sorts of tricks to keep awake. It had already turned light when I fell asleep, and I swear that I stuck it out longer than Li. He always slept for a long time, the lazy bastard. But of course he claimed high and low that I was the one who fell asleep first. He really had the gift of the gab and I almost believed him.

I feel so alone.

I'm certain they've given me something. I'm certain of that. They're playing with my head, they want to know what I think. They've taken her away from me.

My eyes snap open. I didn't even know I'd closed them. Nothing has changed. Semi-darkness, sewer smell, and myself. Take. Deep. Breaths. Max.

I rock myself. Back and forth. Back and forth. I can't close my eyes. I'm scared of what I see. Thoughts race through my head, pictures of the day of Pa's death, his cold, dead body, Ma's pale face, her empty eyes, the pain. Dead. Dead as a doornail.

I tap my fingers on the steel bed-frame. Tick, ticky tick. Tick, tick, tick, ticky ticky tick. Yes, that feels better. That feels almost good. If I concentrate on that, there's no need to think, and maybe I'll see Nina again. See her completely. Tick, tick. Tick. Ticky ticky tick.

Ticky ticky ticky ticky ticky ticky ticky.

Tick.

Tick.

Tick.

Nina, where are you?

Tick. Ticky tick. Tick.

Why can't I see you?

Tick.

Please.

Tick.

"Will you stop making that damn noise!"

A Blower storms into my cell. Tick goes my finger. "Stop the racket!"

Tick. Ticky tick.

"Wet thug."

And he throws a punch — his fist landing right on my nose. I hear and feel it break. Blood gushes from both my nostrils and the metallic taste and stabbing pain bring me straight back to the here and now.

"Get it?"

I nod stupidly.

"Good."

He leaves the cell.

I carefully feel my nose. The thing is completely crooked. I've got nothing to stop the bleeding, can do nothing but wait for it to stop. I pull up my legs and allow myself to be numbed by the throbbing pain. No Nina, but it keeps the other shit at a distance.

"Max?"

Richards comes into the cell. He's carrying a bucket and a cloth. It's getting to be a habit.

"Come to clean me up again? Not much point." My words are slurred. Something inside has worked loose and now mixes with the blood and saliva in my mouth. I spit it out.

"You simply can't keep your head down, can you lad?" Richards shakes his head. He soaks the cloth in the water and begins wiping the blood from my face.

"My nose..."

"Want me to straighten it?"

"What?"

"Want me to straighten it? I can do it, but it'll hurt."

"Is there any point?"

"That's up to you."

He's not easily worked up.

"Why are you doing this, Richards?"

He blinks.

"Why are you doing this for me even though I'll be a rotting corpse in three days?"

He holds the cloth in his large hands, red dripping to the floor. A patch of pinkish light reflects in the bloody water, like the sun going down and lighting up the clouds one last time.

"Why?"

Richards looks at his hands. Bloody hands. My blood. His blood. Everybody's fucking blood. He drops the cloth in the water. Rain falls like a red curtain, the sun has gone down. He takes the two steps to the door, pokes his head outside, comes back in, and slams the door.

He stands in front of me.

"Listen."

He bends over and holds my head straight into front of his.

"Listen. They're going to take you away this evening."

Something in my body shrivels up.

"They don't want to take any risks. They want to be rid of you before WEtTO can do anything."

There is hope.

"Now you know, lad."

"Now I know."

"You'll keep your mouth shut? You're not supposed to know anything."

I nod.

"But you have the right to know."

Right. Wrong. What's the difference?

"Do it." I don't know why, but I want him to straighten it. "Straighten it, Richards."

"You're sure, lad?"

"Yes."

My voice quivers. I'm scared. And not just for the pain I feel when Richards grabs my head, holds me still, and straightens the bone with a firm tug. Tears spring into my eyes and I can't suppress a scream. I clench my fists and try to breathe through the pain.

"At least I'll look my best when I go."

Richards places his hands on my shoulder.

I let my head rest against his arm. It happens all by itself. Safe. I feel safe. With a Wader! I look up.

"Why?"

"Why what?"

"Why do you do this work?"

Richards sighs. "It was this or Region Four. The mines. Alone." I read fear in his eyes. The mines; that's dangerous work. How often do you hear about accidents on DOS news? But coal is one of the few fossil fuels that can still be mined.

I fall silent. He falls silent. What a fucking mess.

"Richards?"

"Yes?"

"Can you do something for me?"

"Depends on what it is." He's on his guard against me.

"Ma... Can you also tell my ma?"

"What?"

"The truth."

He squeezes his eyes together and rubs a hand along his creased forehead. He nods.

"I'll tell her."

But I'm not finished.

"What? You want more?"

"I mean today. Can you tell her today?" I don't know why, but I have to say it. Richards flinches. He clenches his fists and curses. I've never heard him swear before. He holds up a hand and shakes his sweaty head. "No, lad, no! I've done everything I can for you. I can't do any more. Honest. I'll tell your Ma when... After... I swear it, but I can't do anything more for you!"

I don't know what it is, his scared, cowardly Wader's look, his weather-beaten fists hanging helplessly down his side or the idea that I believed him, that I was sorry for him, for a turncoat, but I feel the knot and gather the saliva still left in my mouth and spit it on the ground in front of him. We both know what that means.

"Sorry, lad. Sorry."

"I'm sorry too."

"I've done my best. Your father understood how..."

"Leave my pa out of it!" I shout louder than I realize, for I immediately hear footsteps in the hall.

Richards looks at me one last time in confusion. Then he turns round and leaves the cell. The lock clicks and I hear him calming the approaching guard.

I've never been so scared in all my life.

NINA

After the trial, Liam said. I should have asked him when. I should have demanded it, but he was gone before I could say anything. *You've still got time, Nina.*

Three days. In three days.

Isa's HC is on her desk. I'm sitting on the bed. The pink bedspread is soft and smells of lavender, her favorite scent. I keep on getting the urge to get up, to check for messages. But that's nonsense. I'll hear it the minute it arrives.

Suddenly I know where I want to be. I get up and walk to the desk. My hand hovers above the HC. I won't take it with me. I won't be gone long.

"Nina?"

Mum is standing in the doorway.

"Yes?"

"Are you okay?"

I stare at her, but do not answer.

"I'm going to the summer house."

"The summer house," she repeats, absently.

"I won't be gone long."

My eyes wander automatically to the HC on the desk. *Three days.*

"Okay, darling."

It's cool outside. The temperature must have dropped below freezing again, for the grass crackles under my shoes. It is clear, and spite of the bright light from the lampposts, I can see a few stars. When I near the edge of the wood, I see the dark shape changing into individual trunks, branches and leaves, flashing silver in the pale light of the moon. I hear rustling in the woods. I'm disturbing the peace and quiet. I stop on the wooden veranda of the summer house and look back at the main house. The light in Isa's room is still on. Mum must have stayed. I even believe I can see her laying on the bed. Maria will take her to her own room. I enter the summer house.

I immediately feel it again, the tension, the expectation, the desire. The idea that things can happen here that can't happen anywhere else. And which happened.

It was here that Isa and I told each other secrets.

It was here that I showed Isa for the first time what I had drawn on my HC. It was here that Isa told me she was in love with Johan.

It was here that I was kissed by a Wet boy.

I'm probably deceiving myself, but I think I can still smell him.

I drop down onto the old sofa and lie down, my legs stretched out. I stare at the ceiling covered in cobwebs. Maria never cleans here. Where dust gathers, together with secrets and other things that shouldn't get out.

I relax and think of him.

MAX

Fear eats at you. It eats at your body, at your head, at your soul.

Richards has left and won't be coming back. I hear voices in the hall. Laughter and clinking of bottles. They're drinking and playing.

Tonight, said Richards.

When is it tonight? When will they come for me? It's too dark to know what the time is, how much more time I have to breath, to think, to be.

I keep my head down. I don't want to be banged around anymore. I've pulled up my legs and hug them tight, even though my hands are trembling. My whole damned body hurts. I feel the throbbing pain in my shoulder and my head is bursting. I don't want to be unconscious for the last hours of my life. I want to keep my eyes wide open.

I know for certain that Pa did that. I believe what I said to Richards. Pa may have lost his head, but he wasn't a terrorist. I damn well won't believe those Dry words.

I don't want to die.

Fuck. I don't want to die!

I must have dropped off, for I jump when the door to my cell opens. Two reds come in, cuff me, and pick me up without saying a word. For a change, I don't do anything. I don't ask where they're taking me. I don't kick. I do nothing. When you're beaten, there's nothing to gain from desperate resistance.

We walk through poorly lit corridors, go up some stairs, and arrive at a door that leads to a courtyard. A single lamp is lit and is shining on a dark Blowers' van. A door opens and a man gets out. He remains in the shadow of the car Cold air wraps round my head. My eyes search the sky. New moon. Not a cloud in the sky. I can even see the stars. Perhaps Nina is seeing them as well, is seeing the same past as me. One of the Blowers grabs my head and roughly pushes it down. The other opens the van's rear door. A dark hole yawns in front of me.

Oh fuck.

Approaching footsteps echo against the four walls and dissolve into the night. Who? Heavy, panting breath, as if he's just run a marathon.

I see him before he sees me.

Bradshaw wants to make sure personally that I disappear from his daughter's life. He stops a few feet away, his hands on his knees. When he's regained his breath, he pulls himself up.

Our gazes cross.

What does he see? What's going through him? Does he think he's got rid of the problem? That if I disappear from his life, everything will be blissful. The Mainland is pursuing him just as it pursues me. It will never go away. Whatever he does. Bradshaw chews his lower lip and dabs his forehead. He slowly breaths in and out. Then he raises his hand and nods. I can't see who he's nodding at, because the Blowers pick me up and dump me in the van. They jump in and close the door. Bradshaw disappears behind the tinted windows. Doors are slammed. The engine starts. The van jolts. For a moment, I'm back in that other van, with those other people.

"So, Max. Ready for the last ride of your life?" says a familiar voice.

NINA

I must have fallen asleep, for I'm woken up by banging on the window.

"Nina!"

I jump from the sofa. Too quickly. I have to grab at one of the folded deckchairs to keep upright. "Nina!"

I turn round and see Maria. I'm startled, because I've never seen her like this before. She's beside herself. So scared. She has something in her hand. She holds it up and presses against the glass. It's Isa's HC. The screen is flashing.

There is a message.

I'm suddenly wide awake. I reach in my pocket and find the key. My hands are shaking as I try to put it into the key-hole. Something's wrong. After three attempts, I finally manage to open the door.

Maria tumbles in and presses the HC in my hands. "Oh, Nina!" She's panting and sweat drips from her forehead onto the dusty wooden floor.

I hardly dare to look.

There is something seriously wrong.

The message is from Yvonne.

"Max is being transported tonight. I don't know where they're taking him. But they're going to hang him at sunrise. That's certain."

"Max ... "

I completely lose it. I scream and hit and kick and I try to push back the tears into my eyes. I don't want to cry, I don't want this to happen, I don't want this to be true.

Maria grabs me with a strength I would never have expected from her.

"Nina. Listen." Her voice sounds at the same time broken and strong.

"Max..." I feel myself go limp.

"Listen," says Maria louder.

"He's dead!"

She shakes me hard. I look up in astonishment.

"What...?"

"Max isn't dead. Not yet," she says.

"But what can I do? I don't know where they're taking him! Liam doesn't know anything and I can't get away!"

"You can get into your father's room, can't you?" Her black eyes glisten.

"Yes..."

"Then you can find out where they're taking him and how."

I nod. I'm still not completely following her. "But how do I get out of here?"

"You can get out," says Maria. "With outside help."

"How?" I really don't get what she means.

"Come on." She takes my arm. "First get inside. First you've got to know where they're taking him."

"Maria..."

She takes both my hands.

"Trust me, Nina, sweetheart."

I swallow.

I nod.

"Come on."

I follow Maria.

MAX

Feliks gives me a friendly smile. He's on the seat behind the driver, his legs lightly crossed. Light shines behind him and that makes him look bigger than he is.

Knot. That damned knot again.

"You."

"Yes, me. How very clever of you, Max. Very clever."

This man is going to murder me and I don't know anything better to say than "*you*". Dammit, man. Is he really going to do it? Is Feliks really going to dirty his hands? For Bradshaw?

"Bradshaw wants to make sure I'm out of the way?"

One of the Blowers wants to hit me, but Feliks holds up a hand. "Max."

His thin lips try to curl, but they can't.

"Max." He shakes his Dry head. "Haven't you learned anything? And you were the smartest of the lot."

I may be Wet, but I'm not an idiot. He's pretending.

Knot. I close my eyes. Keep cool, man. If I can't see his Dry mug, I can keep myself in hand.

The van jolts and bounces. It's fucking surreal. After they've hanged me, will they bury me? Give me back to Ma? It wouldn't surprise me if they dumped me in the water. That's where a Wet belongs, isn't it? You go back to where you came from.

Where are they taking me?

Where is he taking me?

For I suddenly know what he means. What he wants to say. What I've "learned." Because I'm the "smartest of the lot."

"You," I say again. I open my eyes and look at him as if seeing him for the first time.

"Well done, Max. I thought you'd never guess."

NINA

It's exactly what Mum said. The new code is my birthday.

For a moment my hands hang above the screen, but thoughts of Max make me put Mum and Dad out of my head, and I type in the code and slip inside. Once I'm inside Dad's room, it doesn't take long to find the information I need.

I put the info on a datacard: the transport, the route, the place, and the time. Dad is always very precise. The Dry Defenders who collect Max from the Regional Hall don't know where he is being taken and will be relieved by a new group of guards who in turn are unaware of what they are transporting This extra security measure is my only chance. I gulp when I see the time. Not much longer. Quickly I put the datacard in my HC and transfer the info. The next step is contact with WEtTO. Only WEtTO has the resources to replace the new group of guards.

Mum's sleeping. Pills. Maria has taken care of that. She gave her an extra one, just to be sure she doesn't wake up. I hope Maria knows what she's doing. I couldn't handle Mum waking up.

Maria takes me to the kitchen and sits me down on a chair. She takes a pair of scissors from a drawer and begins, without a word, to cut my hair. My curls fall like skeins of gold onto the cold, marble floor. When I'm surrounded by my own golden wreath, she helps me from the chair to the sink and starts washing my hair. She rubs in the dye, massages my light head until my hair is as black as water in the night. After a while, she rinses out the dye and blow-dries my short curls.

She holds up a mirror.

A pair of bright blue eyes look at me from a thin, pale face. Wild black curls frame a strong jaw, high cheekbones, and a small nose.

"I look like a boy."

"All the better."

Now I have to wait. For an answer. For WEtTO.

If they don't reply, it's all over.

Would they do it? Would they take so much risk for what I have to offer them? There's no time. There's almost no time left.

Oh, let them reply.

Please.

Please.

Please.

A pink envelope appears on the screen. My eyes suck up the words.

"Always thought you'd ask for it. Be ready. L."

They're coming. They're coming. Oh God, they're coming.

Let them be on time.

MAX

I stare into his quiet, blue eyes. The knot begins to tighten and squeeze. I feel it stab in my stomach.

Was it Feliks who...?

I'm not given any time to think, because he grabs my head as the two Blowers hold my arms. As if this is the damned arrangement.

"Max Morris." He says my name as if I'm some sort of vermin, a flea in his coat. His sharp nails dig into my cheeks. "Your father was also a pain."

"What do you know about my pa..."

A blow hits my head and it spins with pain. A bump in the road and I fall over onto my knees. Tears well in my eyes.

"Listen, Max. Listen. Your father wasn't good at that either." I'm about to tell the Dry dick to go to hell, but stop myself. Feliks raises one of his thin eyebrows. "Good. You're learning."

My eyes ask the question. Of course he knows what I'm asking. He's bloody enjoying himself by keeping me waiting as long as possible.

"Your father was just as evil as you, Max."

I say nothing, but I shake, I sweat, I sniff. The Blowers drag me to my feet.

"Oh, don't think I don't know rage. But I know how to control myself. I think ahead to get what I want. As a Dry should."

He places his filthy Dry hand on my shoulder. I feel him fucking burning. I spit on the ground. It's all I can think of to let out some of this damned rage. Without warning, without taking his other hand from my shoulder, he gives me a clout. It makes me dizzy and I taste blood. The metallic taste has become all too familiar.

"Stay polite. Always stay polite, Max."

"What do you want?" I swallow my own blood, I retch. "You've got me. You had my pa. What the fuck do you want?"

"What do I want?"

Feliks's eyes suddenly look larger and when I look at him, I'm shocked by what I see, just like the time he sat in our kitchen. Feliks fucking enjoying this. *Because he believes in what he's doing.*

"I want you to listen, Max. I'll have to make do with you alone, for I cannot permit myself to appear in public. Look, Max, what I do, I do for the Five Regions. I give everything I have in me, even if sacrifices have to be made. I want you to realize that sacrifices are necessary, Max. *Loyalty* is necessary."

What's he going on about? *Sacrifices?* Was Pa a sacrifice? Am I a sacrifice?

For I'm pretty sure that Feliks tricked Pa. But I had never expected what he says next.

It is much, much worse.

NINA

I'm in the living room when they arrive.

I've already replaced Isa's HC and asked Maria to leave; I don't want anyone to know she's had anything to do with all this. Once she left, I went upstairs. Mum was sleeping with her legs stretched out, her light curls spread out over the white pillows. Her breathing reassured me that she won't wake up anytime soon.

I start when I feel a hand on my shoulder and catch a glimpse of something red.

"You had so much fun the first time, you want join up with us again?"

Liam. In the uniform of a Dry Defender and with close-cut hair, just like Max.

"That red suits you, Liam. Matches your personality," I snap.

His eyes burn, but he controls himself.

I see why. Behind him there are more so-called Dry Defenders. Harry and Tanja and three others. One woman is vaguely familiar, but I wouldn't know where I've seen her before. The men are older than Liam, younger than Harry. One is tall and dark, the other light and short.

"You got past the gates without any trouble?"

My voice quivers. I'm scared.

"You do indeed have excellent information, Nina Bradshaw." Harry gives me a friendly nod.

I lower my gaze.

"Not that this reunion isn't charming, but might I suggest that we get going?" says Tanja, taking a step forward. She has rope and tape in her hands.

You asked for this, Nina.

"Assuming all plans are proceeding on schedule, they've just left. I've got the route here." She holds up her HC and points it at me. "You realize that we aren't wearing these monkey suits for enjoyment. So..." She holds out the rope.

"Liam," gestures Harry. Liam nods, grins for a moment and starts tossing the house. The woman helps him. Mum's vases crash, then Dad's golfing trophies. A sharp knife cuts through the creamy leather upholstery on the sofa, allowing the fluffy, white filling to spill out.

"I'm sorry, Nina. It has to look real."

Harry doesn't mean a word he says.

"You'll keep me conscious," I say. "No drugs."

"Whatever you like, Nina Bradshaw."

"And I go with you when we've got him."

"You'll have to." Harry laughs brusquely, without humor. Tanja walks towards me.

I'm amazed at what I read in her eyes. I can't put my finger on it, but whatever it is, it isn't the Wet aversion. Routinely she ties me up. She is more careful than the first time and leaves enough slack so that I can move my wrists and ankles.

"Let's go."

Liam grins, picks me up in one go and carries me out of the house.

He has no intention of being careful.

MAX

"Isa was such a sacrifice."

Max's mouth drops open.

"No, of course you don't understand, Max. Just as Bradshaw wouldn't understand." Feliks gives an exaggerated sigh. "Bradshaw is a fool. He's weak. But if we want to beat the water, sacrifices will have to be made. I want you to know I will make sure of that, Max."

"But Bradshaw..."

"We'd been following your father for a long time. We knew what he was up to. The flood was not, of course, planned, but sometimes... sometimes, well..." He drops his hands to his sides. "Sometimes everything comes together beautifully."

Beautifully? I swallow. I begin to understand where he's going.

'Your father was wild, Max. Anger makes you rash. He didn't think. He was easy to follow. He had locked Isa up and we knew that he went to get her when the water came. We followed him and grabbed him before he reached her."

He smiles and I feel a shiver down my spine. Pa. Oh, Pa.

"And then I had a flash of inspiration."

He looks upwards and folds his hands as if even God is his audience.

"It was easy to convince Bradshaw. He signed the order without thinking: everything for his daughter. The water did the rest."

He shakes his head as if Bradshaw is deranged and not him. "It all worked out so well, Max!"

Feliks is absolutely, fucking delighted.

"After that, Bradshaw was like putty in my hands. And WEtTO — WEtTO had been given a stern warning. No mercy, Max. There's no mercy in war."

He grabs my T-shirt and pulls me close. His bitter breath prickles against my skin.

"And it is war."

He releases me. I fall. The van turns right and I am thrown to the left. I scream with pain as questions shoot through my mind. *He just left them there? He conned Bradshaw for... for what? He left Pa and Isa and the others, even though they could all have been saved.*

Fuck!

No.

NO!

Feliks looks at me. He knows exactly what effect his words are having on me. *Feliks wanted you to know, before he finished you off. Just like he wanted Pa to know.*

I can't stop him. The rage. That damned rage that eats me up from the inside. The knot that as usual pulls and pushes and unravels. That damned overpowering rage that has destroyed everything. Pa and Isa. The forty-nine others. Erik.

And Nina. My Nina.

When Feliks sees that I understand, he nods at me. He laughs softly, in himself, and in the silence of the night the sound has nowhere to go except inside. It creeps into my head and overturns everything.

I can't control myself.

I can't.

I am Wet.

The knot takes total possession of me. Total. From my trembling fists to my throbbing head, from my convulsing stomach to my weeping eyes and from my bitter mouth to my hammering heart.

And I've never felt so fucking awful in all my bloody life.

NINA

My codes got them in, but getting out will be more difficult.

Will the clothes work?

Liam stays with me in the van when the others get out at the gate.

"We've got one of them from WEtTO here," I hear Harry say. "Our orders are to take her to Regional Hall. At once." Voices consult with each other.

"Come on, man! We've got orders!" warns Tanja.

"And we've got orders to check every incoming and outgoing van," replies a woman's voice.

Harry sighs and walks over to the car. "Liam, hide yourself," he hisses. Liam drops me with a thud. I groan. Light shines in, straight into my shocked face.

"That her?"

"That's her."

"Doesn't look all that dangerous."

Harry laughs and points inside.

"Why don't you find out for yourself?"

I don't even have time to think about Harry's invitation, for one of the Dry Defenders springs in and grabs me roughly. I do the first thing that occurs to me: I kick the man in his balls and spit in his face. The man doubles over and curses loudly.

"I told you." Harry laughs.

Now we're in for it, I think.

The man punches me hard on the chin. The pain isn't less because I am expecting it.

"Filthy Wet bitch!" He gives me a final kick and jumps out of the van. "Go."

More words aren't necessary.

When Harry has closed the doors, Liam reappears. He studies me in the weak light from the torch in his hand. He gives me a brief nod.

Was that actually a compliment?

Harry starts the van. Tanja takes my hands and unties me. I rub my cheek. It's stinging painfully.

"You'll only make it worse."

I look at Tanja and drop my hand. She fiddles around in one of the crates.

"Here, hold this against it."

She gives me something in an old face flannel which feels pleasantly cold. The pain is still there, but it's soothed.

"Thanks."

Tanja pulls up one corner of her mouth into something like a smile, crawls into a corner, and shuts her eyes.

The van begins to pick up speed.

Liam keeps his eyes on me. They bore into my head. He wants me to feel ill at ease, but forgets that I already know another Morris.

"If you want to say something, say it." I look straight at him.

He grins and says: "That color suits you."

It takes a while before I realize what he's talking about. My black eye.

"Ha ha, very funny."

"Humor is a Wet specialty." He shrugs.

434

"You probably don't have any Dry humor."

"Is that an insult?"

"Take it as you like."

"Touché." Tanja laughs. I thought she was sleeping.

"Shut up, Tan." Liam scowls at her.

Tanja laughs again, that half smile of hers.

"Come on. Admit it. What she just did with that Blower... That was Wet. Really Wet."

"One action by a Dry doesn't make a Wet," retorts Liam.

"You're so arrogant, Li."

"And you let your mouth run away with you."

"You always have to have the last word."

"Better the last fucking word than no words at all."

"Cool it, Liam." The dark man places a hand on Liam's shoulder.

"Drop it, Raf. I'm cool."

Tanja is still grinning.

Liam sniffs. "We'll see how you get on, Dry. We'll see."

A shock nearly makes the four of us fall over.

I jump. The van is standing still.

Harry looks at me indifferently through the mirror.

"We're there."

MAX

The van suddenly stops. My cuffs bite into my skin. Feliks
turns round one last time.

"So, Max." He smiles. "This is where we say farewell."

NINA

"Are we there?" My voice sounds strangely hollow.

Nobody answers. Tanja takes guns from the crates and throws one to me, as Liam opens the doors.

"Do you know how that thing works?" she asks.

I stare at the gun in my hands. I went to a shooting range once.

"You stay near the van. This is only if something goes wrong."

I hear an engine and see a second van approaching in the distance.

Max.

Max is in that van.

It stops about ten yards from us.

So close. Max is so close.

"Okay. Go!" hisses Harry.

Stars, water, and grey-green grass. Doors open. Footsteps approach. A gull croaks, the wind picks up. I smell the salty smell of the water.

Voices.

I crawl to the rear door and carefully look out. Harry is talking to someone. They are standing just too far to understand them. The wind plays with their voices, picks them up, brings them close, only to snatch them away at the very last moment, out of my reach.

I know that voice. So soft, so deceptively soft.

I'm sure of it. Where do I know it from? I stretch but something is standing in front of me. The dark man. Raf.

I count one, two, three... four Dry Defenders. At least. Where is Max?

Where is Max?

But...!

I don't believe my eyes.

Who's walking there towards the Dry Defender's van? Is that... is that Liam?

Has he gone mad?

MAX!

MAX

I don't have any time to do or say anything. The two Blowers carry me out as Feliks leaves the van through his own door.

Once again, the cold hits me round the head. A salty smell penetrates my nose and I suddenly know where we are. The dyke.

Feliks is talking with somebody. I can't see who it is; the Blowers are holding me so damned tight. The wind makes it impossible to hear anything.

I take a chance to look that way and see red.

A lot of red.

Could I run? They haven't bound my legs. Perhaps I could get away. If it's true that we're on the dyke, I know places nobody could find.

I don't want to die.

"Move, Wet."

The Blower behind me slams the butt of his gun into me and I stumble forwards. A strong hand stops me and I look up.

"Hello, little brother," he says softly.

What the f...!

"Keep moving, Wet," says Li louder and gives me a firm push on the shoulder. I groan with the pain.

But, but... How can Li be here? Nobody knows except... Richards.

Richards told my Ma after all.

But that means that she and Nina... that Nina...
NINA!

NINA

He's seen me.

Max has seen me.

Now everything will be fine. I'm sure of it.

Then I know where I know that voice from. That velvety soft voice.

MAX

She's in the van. She came. She's going to get me out.

Next thing I know, Li is dragging me across the ground. Blowers laugh at me and one gives me a kick, right in the middle of the stomach. I double over and groan. Another red pulls me upright. Is he with Li? Li grabs hold of me and drags me to the van, identical to the one I came in.

How did she get them to do it?

Li walks behind me, holding my arms firmly. He is tense, his whole body is wound up for action. The other reds walk ahead. I see a dark man and a woman in the shadow, waiting at the new van.

I don't know why, but I look round.

And see Feliks.

Feliks supervising my exit from his Dry little life. He thinks he's got me and that Dry mug of his is plastered with that repulsive little smile. And I smile back. I automatically smile back. When Feliks sees that grin, he holds up his hand.

Fuck.

"What's the matter?"

Only then do I recognize Harry in front of me.

Feliks says nothing and walks over to me. He stands still right in front of me and looks at me inquisitively. "Have you some reason to smile, Morris?"

I keep my mouth shut.

"You know, Max? Your father did precisely the same thing." Oh fuck.

Fuck. Fuck. Fuck.

"He really thought he was something, your father. He really thought he could do something..."

Feliks allows a silence to fall. "... do something good. But he wasn't good, Max. He was a terrorist who murdered people. He had no reason whatsoever to make fun of me. None whatsoever."

I feel Li stiffen behind me.

"And do you know what I did then, Max?"

If only he can keep control.

"Well?"

I have to say something. I have to do something.

Let him get me. Not Nina. Not the others.

I spit at Feliks, straight in his naked, Dry gob.

"You only get to do that once, Wet bastard," hisses Feliks. He reaches in his inside pocket and pulls out a revolver. My arm is almost pulled off. Li ... !

"We have our orders, sir. It's getting late." Harry wipes the sweat from his forehead.

Li takes a step backwards. I stumble along. Almost at the van. Almost.

Feliks ignores them both.

"Don't you know it's not polite if you don't let people finish what they're saying, Max? No, I'm sure you don't, a Wet like you." He pushes the gun's barrel against my head, straight at my sweating temple. I close my eyes and think of Nina. Of Ma. I think of Pa.

Li's breathing gets heavier.

"I let him beg for his sorry Wet life, Max. For your sorry

Wet lives. Your father thought he could keep you out of it. And then..."

He squeezes the trigger a little. Shut up, shut up!

"... and then I let him choose. You or Bradshaw's daughter. And he believed me, with his stupid Wet head. He believed me, Max."

"FILTHY BASTARD!"

My fucking big brother.

I hear a curse and a crash and fall to the ground.

Everybody starts shouting at once.

"It's an ambush!"

"Shit!"

"MAX! No, Max!"

I struggle upright. My head is spinning and my legs are like jelly. Feliks is a fraction faster than Li and when I see the pistol pointing at me again, I know this is it.

I swallow.

Feliks's fingers begin to squeeze oh-so-slowly.

It's over.

Finished.

CLICK.

NINA

A shot is fired.

And another.

I drop the gun.

"MAX!"

I'm with him before anyone can stop me and pull him away before a second shot can hit him. He seems confused, smiles when he sees me.

"Nina."

"Ambush in section D4. Immediately assistance requested," screams a Blower into his HC before a bullet takes him down. Everybody spreads out, taking cover against the metal rain. Felix curses as he holds his thin hand against his shoulder. Blood seeps through his bony fingers. He's as white as chalk and turns round, searching for the protection of his van, the pistol hanging loosely in his hand.

Max tries to get up, but I hold him tight and push him down onto the wet grass.

He can't see this.

"Li?" Max tries to look around me.

I was just too late.

I lost my nerve. My hands trembled and I had already withdrawn the safety catch. All my fingers had to do was squeeze.

I lost my nerve and was too late.

"Li!"

"Max, we've got to..." I say.

"Fuck. NO! Li!!"

And he pushes me away.

The pool of blood spreads quicker and quicker.

Blood is like water. It gives life and it takes life. It streams through a body that is just as weak as the dyke we're standing on, the dyke that must protect us all.

Water is like blood and blood is like water.

MAX

"Li!!!"

I crawl, run, stumble on hands and knees to him, bend over the convulsing body of a red, wind and salt and wet. He's lying in the grass on the slope of the duke, one leg folded strangely under him. Even in the dark of the night, I can see the spreading patch under his body.

"Li ... "

I grab him.

"Prick!" I scream right into his face. "What have you done?" He stares at me, but I know he can't see me. His eyes, usually so fierce, look odd and glazed.

"Li, look at me. Stay awake! I'll get you out of here."

I start pulling at him, but he gives a blood-curdling scream and grabs my arm with one hand.

"I don't want to die, Max! I don't want to die!"

I've never seen him so scared, my big fucking brother. "You're not going to die, Li. Do you hear? Let me..."

"It hurts so badly! My chest!"

He removes his bloody hand from the place the bullet entered and he starts sobbing. Sobbing like a small kid.

"Shh, take it easy, Li, easy."

"Max!"

Nina is calling me. She can't get to me. Too many bullets between me and her. I gesture for her to stay where she is. From the corner of my eye I see Harry, but I ignore him.

"Max..."

Li grabs me again, but his bloodied fingers slip away. "Li, keep quiet!"

"Max..."

Blood trickles from his mouth and I know he wants to say something. I hold my head against his lips and listen.

Nothing.

He says nothing.

He's gone. His eyes are empty. The fire is quenched.

My brother is dead.

My big brother is dead.

NINA

"Max!!!"

I scream and scream, but he doesn't come, he's clutching the body of his brother, pulls him to him, beats his fist into his bloody chest, even tries to blow breath into his dead mouth. If the slope of the dyke and the body of the dead Dry Defender hadn't largely protected him from the rain of bullets, he would have been shot by now.

"Do something!"

Harry nods at me. Raf may have shot the Blower who called for back-up, but they're almost certainly on their way. We have to get out of here.

Now.

It's strange, but I'm not scared. I act mechanically. It mustn't fail, not now that I'm so close. I pick up the gun I've dropped. The gun with which I shot someone for the first time in my life.

"Max!"

Finally he looks up and I see the tortured look in his eyes. He doesn't let go of Liam, but he lies still, flat on the ground, against Liam's body.

I feel a hand on my arm and turn round.

It's Tanja.

"I'll cover you. If you go over to that dead Blower and wait for my sign, you can drag him away. I'll make sure Harry and the rest of them know when to come and get you to the van."

I nod.

"At my sign..."

I keep my finger on the gun's trigger. I feel so strangely detached from everything. I only have one purpose.

"Go!"

There's a new round of shots and I run as fast as I can to the dead Dry Defender. One bullet barely misses me, and immediately after I hear a bang and a loud scream. I don't look, I fire wildly all round, try to keep the force of the gun under control but fall over twice and scramble up until I reach the body with a wildly beating heart and labored breath. I try not to think what it is, who it is, I'm hiding behind. Max is lying in front of me, his hands still on the body of his brother. He's shaking so badly, his whole body convulses.

Has he been hit? Is he in shock? I have to get to him.

Tanja puts up her hand. Wait. I gesture that there's no time.

But she resolutely shakes her head and points. Felix.

He's running, flanked by the last two Dry Defenders, in the direction of Max and Liam. One of them gives him a new gun. Harry and the others can't hit him from where they are. I know what he wants to do. He wants to finish what he started. He's coming for Max.

Max has to let go of Liam.

He has to let go of him.

"Max!"

He looks up.

"There! Felix!"

I see his doubt. In the stuttering movement of his hands, in his fingers that continue grasping the bullet-riddled body of his brother, in his dark eyes that look from Liam to me and back again.

"Max! Please!" I look round at Tanja who nods at me. I don't wait any longer and start crawling.

And as I start crawling, so does Max. He strokes his hand over Liam's open eyes and turns round towards me. It costs him so much, so much more than effort; blood drips onto the grass and mixes with the mud. I thank God that he doesn't see what is happening to Liam. Felix shoots, but he is not fast enough. He hits Liam, in his head, his chest, his arms, and his legs. Blood sprays up. Tiny fountains of red water, ghastly but beautiful in their random choreography. I try to concentrate on Max, only on Max, until I have him, until I grab him and pull me to me and never let go. When we are close enough, the others come to our aid.

"In the van!" hisses Harry and Raf throws Max over his shoulder in one swift motion, yanking our hands apart.

I climb into the back of the van. When I pick myself up and turn round, I am staring across the battleground, straight into the eyes of Felix.

Shots make dents in the metal of the car, a strange horizontal hail storm. Somebody closes the doors and starts the engine.

I still see him through the grimy window.

While our gazes are locked together, fear creeps over me like a thief in the night. Felix knows that I'm the one who shot him when Liam threw himself at him. I see that he knows, for he nods at me and smiles. Felix is not somebody who forgets.

Suddenly the hail storm ceases. Shots fade into the distance, until they have finally died away. What remains is the sound of seven people breathing heavily, a churning engine and the gently lapping water outside.

I get up, walk shakily to the trembling Max, and lie down next to him. He is covered with blood and seems only half conscious. "Li," he says. And: "Pa." His gaze has turned inwards.

I talk to him.

I tell him it's over, that he's safe. That he can sleep.

I stroke his hair which is no longer as short as it was. I kiss his swollen eyelids, his bruised cheeks, and his grazed mouth. He is in shock, but slowly his body begins to react to my touch. I gently unclench his fists.

I wrap my arms around him and hold him tight.

That is what I do.

I hold him tight.

EPILOGUE

MAX

The dyke. Warm and cloudless. Grass smells of spring. Li is standing next to me.

We look at Pa who is standing up to his hips in the water, gazing at the float.

"Fishing?" says Li.

I nod. "Pa and his fucking hobbies."

He lights a cigarette, inhales, and blows out the smoke in a straight line.

"At least he knows where he is." I point at the skull lying next to the box of bait.

Li follows my finger and laughs. He punches me in the shoulder, as always just a bit too hard. I want to say something to him, but Li walks into the water and stands next to Pa.

Pa smiles in surprise.

"Hello, son."

"Hi there, Pa."

I want to go to them, but I can't move. My bare feet have sunk into the mud. I call, but they don't hear me. Or they pretend not to hear me.

Li takes the rod from Pa, Pa takes a drag on Li's cigarette.

I look at my pa and my brother.

Tears stream down my cheeks. A delta of rubbed in salt.

"Max?"

I turn round. She's standing on the dyke.

"Coming?"

Sun shines like gold on her curls. She stretches out a hand.

I turn round one last time.

Nobody. Only water as far as the eye can see. "I'm coming."

I run up the dyke.

AFTERWORD

The book in the assignment undertaken by Max and Nina for Collingwood, Zeitoun, actually exists. It was written by the American author Dave Eggers and tells the true story of Abdulrahman Zeitoun, a Syrian Muslim who was married to an American and lived in New Orleans when the city was devastated in 2005 by the hurricane Katrina.

Zeitoun decides, as building contractor and house owner, to remain behind, despite warnings about the hurricane's rapidly gaining strength. When the city flooded – because the waterworks that were supposed to protect the city had not been maintained properly – he paddled around in his canoe and assisted wherever he could. Then, without warning, he was arrested because it was said that he was plundering. Zeitoun was then taken to a makeshift prison, a sort of Guantanamo Bay, where hundreds of people like him were locked up. Zeitoun is subjected to very humiliating treatment, is not allowed to phone anybody and is not taken for trial. Only after searching for twenty-three days can his wife take him in her arms again.

Bob Dylan's "A hard rain's a gonna fall', to which Max and Nina listen together, is more than just a protest song. Dylan wrote it in the summer of 1962, when the US was in the middle of the Cold War and the Cuba crisis held the whole world in suspense. The record sleeve in which the album appeared, Freewheelin' with Bob Dylan, states: "Every line in it is actually the start of a whole new song. But when I wrote it, I thought I wouldn't have enough time alive to write all those songs so I put all I could into this one." "A hard rain's a gonna fall" is perhaps his ultimate protest song.

When Dylan was asked whether the number was perhaps about nuclear rain, he answered that that was not the case; it was "some sort of end that's just gotta happen..."

Even more applicable to *Flooded* is his explanation of the last verse: "In the last verse, when I say, "the pellets of poison are flooding their waters," that means all the lies that people get told on their radios and in their newspapers." (From: Cott (ed.), Dylan on Dylan: The Essential Interviews, 2006)

CPSIA information can be obtained
at www.ICGtesting.com
Printed in the USA
BVOW03s1453081116
467233BV00002B/62/P